I0584908

Lewis Adelbert Norton

Life and Adventures of Col. L. A. Norton

Lewis Adelbert Norton

Life and Adventures of Col. L. A. Norton

ISBN/EAN: 9783337341602

Printed in Europe, USA, Canada, Australia, Japan

Cover: Foto ©Andreas Hilbeck / pixelio.de

More available books at **www.hansebooks.com**

LIFE

AND

ADVENTURES

OF

COL. L. A. NORTON.

WRITTEN BY HIMSELF.

OAKLAND, CAL.,
PACIFIC PRESS PUBLISHING HOUSE.
1887.

AUTHOR'S PREFACE.

———·⟨⟨❖⟩⟩·———

IN unveiling my life to the public gaze, I am not actuated by any eulogistic or mercenary motives. Nor do I think that the life of any man in the ordinary walks of life is going to electrify the world, or even be extensively circulated or generally read, in this day and age when so many are rushing into print. And as evidence that this sentiment is honest, the small edition of one thousand copies is sufficient.

Notwithstanding this declaration, I imagine I have a history, and in many respects a remarkable one; and that it is fraught with interest which will repay the reader for his labor, and more especially the young American who is so unfortunate as to be turned out on the world without a penny or influential friends to aid him. It will at least show him what one waif, cast out upon the stormy billows of life, has accomplished; or, in other words, what a determined spirit, possessed of energy and perseverance, may accomplish. But my principal object in writing these sketches is to leave my record with my children and friends. And I will further say that I have long hesitated before publishing, and it is now with a feeling of great diffidence that I permit the work to go to press. Not that I fear that it does not possess interest sufficient to warrant its reading, but from the extent and strangeness of many incidents that it contains.

But facts are stranger than fiction, and there are so many living witnesses to the most remarkable scenes and events here narrated that I take courage, although I have omitted many things that have occurred, and sights which I have seen, because I felt that they would not be credited. For instance, in writing up my memoirs, in one place I had stated that, at the ancient city of Pueblo Viejo, Lieutenant Conkling and myself lay beneath the shade of a castor-bean tree which was more than thirty feet in height, and more than eighteen inches at the butt, and which was undoubtedly more than thirty years old. A friend at my elbow said, "Norton, strike it out; I know that your statement is true, but you cannot make the Northern world believe it." I struck it out, and yet when any of my readers go to Los Angeles, if they will go down in the old Spanish portion of the town they will find a castor-bean root with four branches coming from it, either of which is over six inches through; and any one who will go to Anaheim, Los Angeles County, and travel a mile northeast from that place, can credit my cactus story.

But enough of this; no man should apologize for telling the truth; for "he who most investigates will most believe." Read my whole volume, skeptic, then reply. I have often heard it remarked that the preface to a book is seldom read, hence I refer the reader to the contents of the work.

L. A. NORTON.

CONTENTS.

——◦✦◦——

vi CONTENTS.

CONTENTS. vii

POEMS.

THE LIFE AND ADVENTURES OF

COL. L. A. NORTON.

CHAPTER I.

HISTORY OF THE NORTON FAMILY.

THE history of the Nortons, of which I am about to write, antedates the Revolutionary War, how long, I do not know, but the traditions of our branch of the family commence with a sea captain, an Englishman, who owned and sailed his ship. This man had two sons, both of whom he settled in America, one in what is now the State of Connecticut, and one in Virginia. As to the Virginia stock, I know nothing about it; as to the Connecticut settler, tradition follows back six generations, commencing with Eleazer, and passing down successively with John, Mirum, Daniel, Lewis, and Lewis Adelbert—the subject of this sketch.

Daniel Norton, my grandfather, at an early day moved from some of the Eastern States back into Lower Canada, near the line of New York State, in the town shire of Hemmingford, upon a stream called Norton Creek, named after him. The country was very heavily timbered and sparsely settled. At the time of which I write, he had made considerable improvements in clearing, fenc-

2

ing land, etc. The American Revolutionary War was
then raging. My grandfather's neighbors were principally Tories, while his sympathies were with the Whigs,
although up to this time he had taken no part in the
struggle. He was building a barn, and was on the roof
shingling when a lot of men passed (eight in number, I
believe) who had been to a logging bee, and some of them
were a little the worse for liquor. One of them said,
" Let us drive that old Whig off from the barn," and
they ordered him to come down. He paid no attention
to them, whereupon they commenced throwing stones at
him. Presently one of the stones struck him, hurting him
pretty badly. Being a very passionate man, he rushed
down from the barn roof, with his hammer in his hand,
when he was met by the crowd. Their leader attempted
to strike my grandfather, who dodged the blow and
struck his antagonist on the head with his hammer, and,
unfortunately, killed him, having by chance hit him on
the temple. Of course he was then compelled to surrender himself to the authorities, who, after an examination,
discharged him from custody. But he could not continue
to reside among the Tories after that, so he removed
across the line and settled in New Hampshire, and afterward to Connecticut, where my father was born.

After the close of the War of the Revolution, however, he removed back to Lower Canada, and again settled on his old farm in Hemmingford, and remained there
until 1808 or 1809, when he emigrated to Upper Canada
and located, with the younger portion of his family, in
London, a district town of Westminster. At this place
he remained up to his death.

In the meantime my father, Lewis Norton, had married

Elizabeth Burhart, who was of German extraction, having been born and raised in Pennsylvania. On their
marriage they settled in the State of New York, near
Chautauqua, close to the Canada line, where they remained until the war of 1812. When the British had
massacred the inhabitants of Black Rock and Buffalo, the
New York militia was called out, my father among others.
At this time he removed his wife and three children to
the village of Batavia, Genesee County, New York.
He was engaged in the affair of the destruction of Black
Rock, and also at the burning of Buffalo. When the
enemy's forces were at last driven out, they were concentrated against the garrison of Fort Erie, which was on
the Canadian side of the Niagara River and occupied by
the Americans. A call was now issued to the New
York militia for recruits to join the regular force for the
defense of Fort Erie. My father volunteered, and in
the three days' fight before Fort Erie, at a *sortie*,
he, and about three hundred others were made prisoners, having been cut off from the main force. My father,
when taken, had Thos. C. Love on his back, wounded.
Love at this time was a young lawyer. Being wounded,
he was exchanged. He afterwards rose to eminence,
and was for many years on the bench as judge. He
died some years since, at or near Williamsville, New
York. My father was sent to Halifax, where he was
kept a prisoner till the close of the war.

Soon after the war, my grandfather gave my father
the old homestead in Hemmingford, the buildings and
other improvements having been destroyed during the
war. My father returned to Chautauqua, Franklin
County, New York, in 1818, where he resided at my

birth, in 1819, after which he returned to Canada, and settled again on Norton Creek, about twelve miles below the old homestead, on what was called the Domain, where he resided till I was eight years old. I was the fifth child of a family of nine. This being a cold, rocky, and barren region, my parents moved back to Franklin County, New York, where I remained till I was eleven years old.

As my parents were poor and had a large family, I was determined to look out for myself. Early on the second day of May, 1829, I tied my worldly possessions in a pocket handkerchief, strung it over my shoulder, and, like a young quail with a shell on its back, I left the nest with twenty-five cents in my pocket, and "dug out" on foot. The second day I arrived at the Read Mill, St. Lawrence County, New York, where I hired to a man by the name of Tibbits, at four dollars per month, and I worked four months. At the end of that time I again shouldered my pack, with my sixteen dollars, and went to Ogdensburg, where I crossed the St. Lawrence River and took a Canadian steamer to Queenstown, *en route* to Upper Canada, now known as Canada West, where I had uncles residing. I then walked to Niagara Falls, and, after visiting the Falls, went up the Niagara River and crossed to Black Rock, thence to Buffalo, and, after a couple of days at Buffalo, I found a schooner going up Lake Erie and soon made arrangements to work my passage on board of it up the lake.

It was claimed that the vessel was loaded with brick; I have since been of the opinion that it was a smuggler. On our way up we encountered a heavy gale, but at length we landed in the woods at an anchorage they called Nanticoke. I went on shore in the schooner's boat, and again, with my pack on my back, I threaded the Canada shore of Lake Erie for several miles through the woods before I came to any settlement; but at length, after a day's hard traveling, I reached Long Point, where the farmers were not yet through their harvest. Hands were scarce, and I soon contracted for fifty cents per day (half a man's wages). I worked twenty days and got ten dollars, and again pursued my journey.

I had been told that I would have to go by the way of Cettle Creek, and when I had journeyed about half a day, I commenced making inquiries for Pot Creek; but I was made all right on that point by a party informing me that it was Cettle, not Pot, Creek that I wanted. In due time I reached my uncles in Westminster, and found them to be close-fisted, thriving farmers. I was well received and went to work for one of my uncles; no wages was named. I worked for him four months, for which he gave me a pair of sheep's-gray pants and made all square by so doing.

I will here take occasion to say that, during all my perambulations, I never lost an opportunity to learn to read and write. On leaving my uncle's I went to London Gove, where I made arrangements with an old Dutchman to do chores night and morning and go to school. Here I got three months' schooling, and, being quick to learn and having a retentive memory, I advanced with my reading, writing, and spelling very fast. As spring approached I hired to a man by the name of Perkins, for six months at six dollars per month. From him I got only a small portion of my wages, and that in store pay. I continued to work that summer and the

winter following. Having clothed myself and having
some money in my pocket to pay expenses, I went to
Oxford Center, where I expected to meet my brother;
but not finding him, I hired out to one John Falin, a
h)tel keeper, for ten dollars for a month's work, when I
fully resolved to return to Chautauqua and try to induce
the family to move to Upper Canada.

CHAPTER II.

LIFE AFFECTED BY CIRCUMSTANCES IN YOUTH.

I HAVE come to the conclusion that there are circumstances in early life which color our future existence
and stick to us like the shirt of Nessus until the day of
our death. About the year 1832, when a mere youth, I
found myself, after eighteen months' rambling over the
wilds of Canada, some seven or eight hundred miles from
home. The country, at that time, was sparsely settled.
Travel was almost entirely local, farmers traversing the
country with ox-carts or wagons, from their homes to
the small market towns. Mails, in most instances, were
carried on horseback, with once in awhile, on the mor :
frequented thoroughfares, a stage-coach. But if a man
wished to make a journey of any distance, it was generally performed on foot.

For the year past I had been working by the month,
at eight dollars per month, and at the end of that time
found myself in possession of what then seemed to me
to be all the wealth I needed. I accordingly resolved
to visit my home in Lower Canada, near Montreal. I
therefore invested about twenty dollars in a nice suit of

moleskin, pocketed my wealth, and about the eighth day of June, 1834, with my little bundle (change of clothes), left John Falin's hotel, town of Oxford, London District, Canada West, for Hamilton, where I expected to take water conveyance, going down the lakes and St. Lawrence River. Of course I was on foot. At nightfall I arrived at the town of Paris, on the Grand River.

Paris was then a small town, on the west bank of that stream. The town was mostly composed of wooden buildings, but as I entered the place, somewhat remote from other buildings, I noticed quite a large stone structure, upon one side of which I saw a large bonnet pictured. In fact it was the picture of the bonnet that particularly attracted my attention to the house. I passed it and continued my tramp down a slope to near the river, where I found a hotel, the "Travelers' Home." I entered the house, and deposited the bundle with the landlady, who seemed to be the "man of the house." She was, I should suppose from her appearance, about forty years old, short and florid, with a light complexion, and an immense amount of carrot-colored hair, that looked as though it and a comb had been strangers for months. I judged her complexion more from the color of her hair than from the color of her face, as that was extremely streaked.

In receiving my pay from Falin, I had got a London one-pound note, and, boy like, rather to make a show than through fear that the bank would break before morning, I called for a glass of beer and got my note changed into silver, when I soon noticed that this action caused the garrulous woman to commence plying me with questions regarding my trip, and where I was going.

Lower Canada was a long distance—over seven hundred miles. "You must," said she, "have plenty of money to take you that distance; where do you get your money to travel with?" etc. To all of which I replied that I· supposed I had sufficient money for my journey; that I worked for some of it, and some my father gave me to travel with. During supper-time and all the evening the burden of her theme was on my money, which made me feel rather uncomfortable. I gave her but little further satisfaction on that point, but finally told her that I was tired and would like to go to bed.

She called on a couple of men, I think she called them James and John, and told them to "take that boy to bed." It struck me as strange. I took a glance at the two worthies and found them, in appearance, a couple of as well-defined cut-throats as it was ever my misfortune to have seen (in fact they were all foreigners, Irish or Scotch, I should think). The men lit a lantern and told me to come with them. I began to be frightened and rather hesitated; but one of them casually observed that they had lately moved there and their beds were not yet removed to that house, when I reluctantly followed them· We proceeded along the road by which I had entered the town, to the large stone structure with the big bonnet p ointed on the outer wall, heretofore mentioned, which we entered.

The first room seemed to have been used as a barroom, although at the time it was wholly divested of furniture. We crossed the room to a landing. A door opened to the left of the landing, which revealed a large room which seemed to have been used as a dining-room; that was also unfurnished. We stepped upon the landing and commenced ascending spiral stairs, passed two landings, and ascended to the third story of the building; all the lower part of the house seemed unoccupied. After making our final landing we passed through a hall, at the end of which they showed me my room. A half dozen times I was on the point of turning back, telling them I would go no farther, but diffidence and shame prevented me. Well, I entered my bedroom, which was on the south side of the building. They gave me a piece of candle which they made stand up by melting some tallow on the window-sill, and sticking the unlit end of the candle into it; then left me alone in my glory.

The two worthies retired to an adjoining room, which had a board partition between them and myself. I pulled off my boots, took up the candle, and first examined the door to see if it could be fastened, but found nothing but a common latch on it. Having heard of dead-falls and trap-doors, I next commenced an examination of the room, but found nothing unusual in the floor. I next investigated my bed, to see if it stood on a trap, but nothing suspicious presented itself. I then took a peep from my lofty roost out of the window, but it was far down to the hard street, and a leap from there would be attended with sure death. I then returned to my bed and examined it to see if the bedstead contained a cord. I found it did. Then my next thought was to take it out and place the bedstead by the window, and tie the cord to it to aid my flight, if necessary; but pride and shame again carried the sway, and I resolved to go to bed and await results.

I had not so much as a penknife in case of necessity;

so I placed my boots at the head of the bed as my only
weapons. My bed consisted of a straw tick, two blankets, and two pillows. I divested myself of coat and
vest and turned in with pants and socks on. I put both
pillows under my head, so I should be able to carefully
watch every movement. There was a full moon shining
obliquely through my window, so when the candle was
extinguished it was not dark in the room; and there was
a small crack in the board partition separating me from
the room where the two roughs were sleeping, and through
that I could discover that their light had not been extinguished. This continued to burn until eleven or
twelve o'clock, when it was extinguished. That circum-
stance allayed my fears a little, but yet I dared not go to
sleep. I had a vague feeling of danger, for everything
to me seemed suspicious. Many times I started, thinking that I heard light footfalls in different directions.
Knowing that all my senses were wrought to the highest pitch, I would attribute it to imagination, which was
probably correct.

So time passed on until nearly two o'clock, when I
heard some person ascending the stairs. The step came
up—up—up. I lay intently listening, most devoutly
hoping that it would stop short of my room; but such
was not the case. On came the light tread, until my
door was quietly pushed open and a man entered the
room with a bull's-eye lantern in his hand. He was a
man of about thirty years of age, well dressed in a business suit, and had nothing of the villainous appearance of the other two He stopped at the door and
turned his lantern until he threw the light full upon me.
He stood and looked steadily at me for a time that

seemed to me ten minutes, but it was probably not more than two, during which time I had laid perfectly still, with my eyes apparently closed in sleep; but, in fact, the lids were sufficiently open to allow me to watch him closely. I came to the conclusion that it would not do to feign sleep; consequently, all of a sudden, I arose to a sitting position, thrust my right hand beneath the pillows, and, with all the firmness that I could command, by voice, look, and gesture, I demanded: "What do you want, sir?" The party replied: "Oh, nothing. I did not know how you were resting, and I thought I would step in and see. Shall I not come and fix your pillows under your head?" I replied that my head was all right; that I was very tired and wished not to be disturbed. He replied: "I shall not disturb you," and turned and left my room.

But I could tell, first by the step and then by the light that penetrated to my room through the crevices heretofore mentioned, that he had entered the room of my two first-named companions. He remained there some little time, when I heard him descending the stairs, but could see that a light had been left burning in their room, which to me, in my affrighted state, was no g od omen. While I lay considering what to do, the downward step seemed to stop at the second landing, and apparently entered a room; and presently, from the same direction, I heard a kind of ticking sound which I could not describe until many years after, when I heard it repeated by water dropping on an uncarpeted floor from a table.

I now formed a resolution to attempt my escape from the den. I think the light left burning in the room where the two men were had much to do with my de-

termination. I stepped quietly out of bed, put on my
coat, vest, and hat, took my boots in my hand and moved
towards the door, the room being quite light, as the full
moon shone straight into the window. And here was
something that I have never been able to account for.
As I approached the door I noticed it was ajar, in fact,
open about four inches. I carefully pushed it open and
saw something black beyond, coming clear unto the
threshold. I put out my foot and found it was a hole in
the floor! The thought flashed across me that I assuredly came through a hall before coming into the room.
But I seated myself on the door-sill and felt around with
my feet for the stairs; but there were none, and this fact
further increased my terror. I thought I was fastened
in; but, to my relief, on further examination, I found the
door through which I had entered, shutting on the same
jamb, and swinging the other way, closed, but not fastened. I left the room, passed noiselessly through the
hall and down the stairs through the old bar-room. I
found the outer door locked, but the key was in the door.
I soon passed out, slamming the door behind me. Then
I did some good, lively running for about a block, when
I sat down, pulled on my boots, and made for the hotel.
No one can tell the joy I felt at my escape. I went and
rapped at the hotel door. The landlord, whom I had
not seen before, got up, let me in, and asked me what I
wanted. I told him I wanted to pay my bill and be going; that I heard the blacksmiths at work and thought
it was time for me to be traveling. He remarked that it
was only between two and three o'clock, and that the
ferryman would not be out for some time, and that I had
better take a rug and lie down by the fire, and he would

call me when it was time to go. I did so, and was soon asleep. He aroused me all too soon, and informed me that I would find my bundle in the store, or baggage-room.

I found my bundle, as per directions, apparently all right, excepting that a woman's stocking was protruding from it. I pulled it out, threw it on the floor, and bade good-by to the "Travelers' Home." I asked the ferry-man what kind of a house they kept at the "Travelers' Home," and he said it had a bad reputation. I then told him my story. He simply remarked that he thought me in luck to get away as well as I did. I gave him the facts just as they occurred, without comment. Whether any reasonable explanation could be given to the appearance of things and the conduct of the parties, I do not know; but there is one thing I do know, and that is, that from the effects of that night's scare, no person can enter my room, even in his stocking feet, without awaking me.

CHAPTER III.

A PERILOUS VOYAGE AND ARRIVAL HOME.

ON leaving the ferry, I trudged along until I arrived at Hamilton, where I soon made arrangements with the captain of a schooner to work my passage (as cook) down to Prescott. I went down in the forecastle, where the mate was shaking with the ague, and pulling off my coat (which contained my money in a side pocket) some change rolled out as I threw it upon a coil of ropes. I replaced it and went to work, helping about loading the vessel, when in the course of two or three hours the mate asked the captain's permission to go up town and get some medicine for his ague. The captain remarked that he had better send the little cook, as he could not be of so much use on the vessel. I saw that he seemed loth to let me go, but after a little hesitation he handed me my directions, with the money. I at once recognized the stamped fifty-cent piece as being of my money, and as soon as I got away from the vessel I looked for the remainder, but not one cent was left. I got the medicine and returned with it, and in the presence of the mate went to the coil of rope and commenced looking for my money (knowing well that it was not there), when the mate, in a savage manner wanted to know what I was doing there. I told him that I was looking for my money. He cursed me, and told me that if I went ransacking around there he would break my little neck. I picked up ten cents that had escaped the fate of the rest, and went to the captain with my complaint. He said he could do nothing, and asked me good-naturedly if I did not know that all sailors would steal. We left the little bay at Hamilton on May 12, 1832. The wind was blowing very hard and the captain was advised not to venture from the harbor, but he was an old "salty," very headstrong, and sometimes reckless withal, and when we got fairly out on Lake Ontario it was blowing a terrific gale, which constantly increased. As soon as we got fairly out they began to shorten sail; but the wind continued to blow at a fearful rate. Some of the halyards got foul (I think that was what they called it), and before they could relieve the foremast she went by the board, and that smashed the bulwark. Cutting the lines and shrouds, they let the mast go.

There were two "fresh water" sailors on board, who soon gave up and went below, and no threats or persuasions could get them upon deck. Night came on and we were running under the bare poles without a rag of canvas. Every man ha l a line around his middle and fastened to the mainmast. The sea was constantly breaking over. We had a deck load of flour, but the waves had carried away our bulwark 'midship, together with the deck loading; also my galley and stove. At about ten o'clock at night I went to my berth, my hands having been all blistered and the blisters worn off to the bare meat. I could not sleep, and it was with difficulty that I could keep myself in the berth; the wind had not abated its fury in the least. The captain was swearing because he had not sea-room. He and the mate and one sailor did all that men could dare and suffer; but about noon the second day the wind howled so that we could neither hear nor see anything save snow and sleet everywhere. Ropes and shrouds were covered with ice, and the captain exclaimed, " D—n her, she will go to the bottom."

I had attempted to set the table once, but it was no go; the cloth would slide from the table, and about this time the blind light in the stern was burst in, and the lockers were all drenched, the water being knee deep in the cabin. They got planks and spikes and temporarily stopped the water from coming in behind; but there was one thing that they protected, that was one jug of spirits. They had that lashed to a berth and made frequent visits to it. When the captain said the vessel would go to the bottom, they put her square before the wind and let her take her chances. They dare not attempt to make any port, but just at dark that night we reached the St. Lawrence River and got protection of the Thousand Islands. That storm the 12th, 13th, and 14th of May, 1832, will long be remembered. The corn was well up and some of the grain was headed out. The extreme cold froze the corn, injured the oats and barley, killed the leaves on the beech trees, and in some portions of the State of New York the snow fell to the depth of eight inches, which must still be remembered by the old men of that day.

We dropped down the St. Lawrence, and the next morning we lay off Prescott. They hitched lines to the anchor, and we were compelled to pull the schooner ashore by the line (they called it working it in). When we had landed I got my breakfast—some "hard-tack"— on board, and invested my ten cents in a passage to Ogdensburg, and from there I soon made my way down to Tibbits' place, six miles. They were delighted to see me, and at once gave me work. I worked there until I had earned sufficient money to take me home, when I continued my journey on foot to Norton Creek, where the family had removed. When I joined them, and as soon as we could make preparations so to do, we all returned to Upper Canada. For the next three years I worked by the month for the most of the time, doing a man's work and receiving from thirteen to fifteen dollars per month, after which I engaged with my oldest brother in a fishery business. On what is known as Catfish Creek, or rather its mouth where it empties into Lake Erie, we ran one season and made several hundred dollars each.

CHAPTER IV.

A TERRIBLE STORM, AND A NIGHT IN A FOREST.

I HAD one brother who had left home at an early age, and from whom we had not heard for six or seven years. At length we received a letter from a lady in Buffalo, stating that my brother was seriously afflicted with the hip complaint and in indigent circumstances; that she had interested herself on his behalf until she could hear from his friends. The next day after receiving the letter, I was on my way to find my brother. That was in the latter part of October, 1837. I went to Buffalo, where I soon found him, and after compensating the lady for her trouble, I had him removed to a hotel until I could find some way of transporting him up the lake. Finding a schooner that was going part way, and would land near the mouth of the Grand River, I determined to get my brother on board and take chances of getting him from there by land. His condition was such that he could only be moved on a 'bed or stretcher. Well, I got him on board in the forenoon, and we were to sail the next day. The schooner lay at the wharf in Buffalo Creek; the weather for the time of year was calm and pleasant, a breeze being scarcely perceptible. The sky was clear, the sun shone brightly, and everything looked fair for a prosperous trip. But about two o'clock P. M. the water commenced rising in the creek, and a mighty tide seemed pouring in from Lake Erie; it soon crept up on Lighthouse Point, nearly covering the sea-wall, which at that time was but partially constructed, and the water in the creek raised until it was nearly up

3

to the top of the wharf. From the northwest the fleecy clouds could be seen coming up and skurrying along high in the heavens with the speed of a war-horse, accompanied by a low, roaring, or moaning sound in the air.

We had an experienced captain on our little craft, who seemed to comprehend what the signs of the times predicted. He ordered the moorings to be made more secure by stanchions, and as the water continued to rise he had several spars run down perpendicularly between the schooner and the wharf, and firmly lashed to the vessel above, so as, in case of emergency, to prevent its passing over the wharf; and this foresight saved us. Presently the wind came on in fitful gusts, constantly increasing in frequency and violence; and ere the sun was below the horizon a thick gloom and darkness pervaded everything, while a regular tornado was raging with such force that it was almost impossible for one to keep his feet even when supported by the stays of the vessel. The waves seemed to be lifted by the fury of the wind from the surface of the boiling flood and dashed in spray upon surrounding objects, while on the land, church towers and building roofs were whirled through the air like feathers. Ere darkness had closed in upon the scene, Buffalo Point had entirely disappeared beneath the flood, and the waves of Lake Erie rushed in upon the city. The storm increased until midnight, carrying a general wreck and ruin with it, a perfect devastation marking its track. From Buffalo Point there were eleven residences washed out, and as the water commenced receding, floated out of Buffalo Creek and down the Niagara Falls. In these houses alone it was estimated that over sixty persons perished. Eight or ten canal boats broke from their moorings and went out into the Niagara River, and thence over the falls. The next morning almost the entire shipping that lay in the creek at the commencement of the storm lay high and dry in the lower part of the city. One brig lay with its bowsprit sticking through an upper window of a two-story house—the bow resting against the house while the stern was on the ground. The entire lower part of the city was strewn with boxes, barrels, bales of goods, and furniture of every description; nuts and fruits were spread out in abundance, the water during the night having been from twelve to fifteen feet above its ordinary level. Thanks to the foresight of our captain, the spars that were placed on our boat kept us on the right side of the wharf, and the next morning found us in deep water and all right.

The storm began to lull about midnight and by morning had entirely abated, and at noon the lake had rocked itself to sleep. There was just sufficient breeze to leave a smile on its silver lips. Nor would you have supposed that such a passion as had raged in its breast during the night could ever have so distorted its placid brow. But 'tis ever thus. Deception is found everywhere, in nature as well as in art. And frequently that which we most admire is the first to wound. We loosed from our moorings, and, with a light breeze, made the best of our way for Port Dover, on the Canada shore, which place we reached the second day in the evening. .

I tried to hire a conveyance to take my brother home, a distance of about fifty miles by the lake shore, but over seventy-five miles by the main road. The roads were next to impassable for a team; the mud had frozen

but not sufficien ly hard to form a firm crust. The
horses would break through and cut their legs, and in
places the wagon wheels would also break through.
No one could be induced to turn out, for love or money.
The consequence was I was compelled to go home,
where friendship would insure what money could not
buy. To follow the wagon road I would be compelled
to go north to Talbot Street, which would be at least
twenty-five miles farther than to follow up the lake shore.
Consequently I resolved to take it on foot up the lake
shore, and, getting my brother settled, I "struck out."

I got started about ten o'clock in the forenoon, traveling some of the way by trail and sometimes by wagon
road, through a new and sparsely settled country of dense
forests and small clearings. Along in the afternoon I
fell in with an old pioneer of the country, who told me
that I would arrive about night-fall at a certain small log-
house, and that I must stay all night there, as that would
be the last house and clearing for fourteen miles, and
that there was no road but a very faint trail, as during
the summer there was a beach upon which all the travel
was turned, but which, during the fall, was washed away.
" But," I said, "perhaps he will not keep me." His
reply was, " He must keep you, for you could not make
it in the night. You would break your neck over a precipice, if nothing else." I parted with the old man and
continued my tramp, arriving at the log-hut, in a small
clearing, just as the sun was setting.

It was clear, cold, and frosty. I stepped to the door
and asked the man for lodging for the night. He replied that he could not keep me. At that age I was
very diffident. I was about turning from the door when

my situation rushed vividly upon me, and I asked,
" Could you not allow me to sleep on your floor?"
He replied, " No, I have potatoes on the floor." I said,
" I am told that it is fourteen miles through the forest,
and no road, and such a cold night as this I may perish
in the woods." He replied that he could not be accountable for that, but that he thought I could get
through. I then asked him if he could not let me have
a few matches. His reply was that he had no matches.
So I turned into the woods on a dim trail; but as soon
as I had got into the thick forest, and darkness set in, I
lost the trail, and could only keep my direction by skirting the lake shore when I could see openings through
the trees. However, I soon found myself in windfalls,
brush, and briers, the small brush constantly coming in
contact with my face and eyes. My flesh and clothes
were torn by brambles while clambering over logs, or
feeling my way up and down precipitous gulches, aiding
myself by clinging to brush and roots.

As I had no means of making a fire, I dared not lie
down to wait for morning, but pursued my toilsome
march. Exhausted by fatigue and chilled by frost, I
still traveled on until I came upon a stream about a
hundred feet wide. This brought me to a stand. It was
now, as near as I could judge, about midnight. I crept
along up the stream in hopes of finding it narrow, and
perchance a log upon which I could cross. But I could
find nothing of the kind, and discovered that I must
either wade or swim across. I got hold of a strong
pole, and feeling the bottom with it, waded in. Fort-
unately I did not have to swim, but found it in the deepest place a little more than waist deep.

After reaching the opposite shore I climbed a precipitous bank and continued my journey. I found the
woods a little more open, and consequently fewer obstructions. But now the wolves set up such a howl, as
though ten thousand devils had broken loose. They
seemed to be but a little distance from me. (These
wolves are of the large gray kind, but they seldom
attack a man, unless in depth of winter, when the snow
is deep and they are nearly starved.) I continued to
make my way as fast as the rough condition of the country and my exhausted strength would permit, for about
two hours, when I came to another stream similar to the
one already described. I crossed it as before. There
was a small open flat on the west side of the stream,
and looking down towards the lake I saw a light. Oh,
blessed sight!

I made my way down to the lake, where I found that
there was a narrow beach and some men fishing. They
stared at me at first as though I were some apparition
or goblin from the forest. Their conduct was so strange
that I was really afraid of them. I merely asked them
about what time of the night it was, and how far before
I would come to a house. They informed me that it
was about two miles to a house, and about two o'clock
at night. I asked them if they would let me have a
brand of fire, which they did. I went on about half a
mile, kindled a fire, upon which I piled a lot of drift-
wood, and stretched myself alongside of it in the sand,
and was soon asleep. I awoke about sunrise. My fire
had burned down, and I found myself very cold. My
clothes next to the fire were dry, but on the opposite
side were frozen stiff. I replenished my fire, thawed

myself out, and pursued my journey; called at a farm-house, where I got some breakfast, and reached home before I slept. We started a team out the next morning, and within four days my brother arrived home. For the first few weeks he seemed to improve, but his disease was of such a character that there was no chance for a recovery, and he lived but a few weeks.

CHAPTER V.

THE CANADIAN REBELLION OF 1837.

BEFORE leaving home in search of my brother Clark, I had enrolled myself as a minute-man, to turn out with the Patriot forces; or, in other words, in the rebellion against the British Government. The arrest of Lount and Mathews at Toronto had forced the rebellion, and on the twelfth day of November, 1837, we were called out to form a company under Joshua Done, to be known as the " Spartan Rangers." We assembled at the village of Sparta, in the town of Yarmouth, where we organized, choosing Joshua Done as our captain, and at once commenced our march for Otter Creek (a village of Richmond). Here we encamped for the night, and stationed our sentinels. Of course we were but crudely armed, our arms consisting of rifles, shot guns, old muskets and pistols, knives, swords, and dirks. We had no drill or discipline. We were perfectly raw, and I do not believe that there was a man in the entire company who even understood the manual of arms. Yet we were informed that we were marching out to meet an enemy drilled

and disciplined. And I never shall forget what I suffered in mind, for twenty-four hours after my enlistment,
for fear that I would be a coward, and would not be able
to keep my legs from running away with me at the first
fire.

News came in during the night that the enemy had
rallied quite a force and were tearing up the bridge on
Otter Creek, and intended to meet us there in the morning. We sent out some scouts, however, and a guard to
protect the bridge. The next morning we commenced
our march, crossing the bridge without opposition, and
had marched a couple of miles beyond it when we were
fired upon from ambush. A ball pretty well spent
struck me in the muscles of the back, just grazing the
spine. The enemy had waited until we had passed, before firing. I forgot my wound, and, with the others,
rushed into the woods pell-mell, firing at the twenty-five
or thirty fellows who had ambushed us.

When the skirmish was over I was the most delighted
fellow you ever saw—my legs had not run away with
me. My wound proved not to be serious, and I continued my march the entire day. At night we arrived
at Norwich, where we met Doctor Duncombe and his
forces, who informed us that they were retreating before
a superior enemy, led by Sir Allen McNabe; that we
would move on to Dorchester Pines, and would there
make a stand, where the enemy could not play upon us
with their artillery. We got some food, rested for an
hour, and again took up our line of march. We went
through the pines, and encamped for the balance of the
night at a little place called Sodom.

The next morning, when I awoke, our command had

disappeared, and I found myself comparatively alone. I saw some notices posted, which were to the effect that a superior force was upon us, too formidable for us to attempt to cope with, and advising every man to look out for himself. There was a young man by the name of Benjamin T. Smith who was a great comrade of mine. We met and consulted as to what was best to do. My wound had become swollen and quite painful, as nothing had been done by way of extracting the bullet from my back. But after moving around for a time the pain became somewhat allayed. At length Smith and I made up our minds to retain our arms and boldly make for home. After Duncombe's cowardly act of disbanding his forces the Tories of the country took heart and were making arrests right and left.

The snow was about eight inches deep, hence it was desirable to take the road, and we accordingly took up our line of march for Durham Forge. We had advanced but about three miles, when I saw the glitter of arms in advance of us, moving in our direction. Evidently we had not been discovered, so we stepped outside of the road into the brush, and presently an armed squad passed by. When they had passed out of sight, we again pursued our journey, and had made some ten or twelve miles when we arrived at Squire Dobie's. The house stood close to the road, and as we passed the door out sprang three men, all with arms in hand, and exclaimed, "We know you, you are some of Duncombe's rebels. Surrender or we will blow the tops of your heads off!" In an instant both our rifles covered them. I said, "But raise a muzzle and you are dead men." They replied, "We will have you before you go a mile!"

We pushed on and had advanced through alternate woods and fields for about three miles, when I heard a great clatter of hoofs behind us. I turned and saw a squad of horsemen rapidly advancing upon us. We immediately left the road, and as we were mounting the fence to take to the woods, they fired a volley at us, one of the bullets coming in very close contact with my skull, having just grazed my head and passed through my cap. We discharged our pieces at them and took to the woods, I minus my cap, which had fallen on the wrong side of the fence. Ben loaned me his handker-chief, which answered the double purpose of staunching the blood and making a covering for my head. We found it would no longer answer to keep the road, so we steered through the forest for Otter Creek.

In the middle of the day the snow had thawed on the top, but when the sun went down, it had frozen such a crust that at each step it would break under foot and crack like the report of a pistol. We took our course by the stars and continued our tramp until late in the night, when we came to a house which we entered, weapons in hand. We aroused the family, whom we discovered to be loyalists, and demanded something to eat. We got a cold lunch and warmed ourselves by a log fire. The man exhibited the Queen's proclamation offering a free pardon to all who had been engaged in this "unnatural rebellion," and had not been guilty of arson or murder, if they would lay down their arms and return peaceably to their homes. I took the proclamation, and we continued our journey, following a road which they said led to Richmond.

But we soon discovered that the road was patrolled,

and we once more took to the woods, and after a time we came to another clearing. The moon was shining brightly, and, on a distant rise of ground, we could see a village, and men moving about very actively. There was a stream before us, a saw-mill and a mill-pond, with saw-logs frozen in the ice. We managed to cross the stream on the logs, and on the side to which we crossed there was a band of colts. In order to shield ourselves from observation we drove them ahead of us until we reached a little grove of small pines, which we entered for consultation.

Now we were satisfied that the place we saw above was on Talbot Street (a Government road running through the province), but what was the town? If Richmond, we wanted to cross above it; if it was Troy or Almer, we wanted to cross below it. At any rate we wanted to cross Talbot Street, as it runs east and west, and we were making south; and if we could get across the road and into the Quaker settlement, we would be safe. Ben and I disagreed as to where we were. While thus consulting, there was a general rush and clattering through the snow's crust and in a minute's time our grove was surrounded by a band of armed men far too numerous for us to cope with. We saw at once that we would of necessity be compelled to surrender, so we immediately hid our arms and walked out.

CHAPTER VI.

A PRISONER OF WAR.

I FOUND that I was acquainted with the militia captain who was in command, and on arriving at the hotel I found old John Burwell, a cowardly, pompous old Tory magistrate. He raved, ranted, and charged, declaring that he never would lay down his sword until every radical was exterminated. I was suffering very much, and succeeded in getting a bed, when I went to sleep and lay until about 9 o'clock in the morning. I now found my wounds very much inflamed, and I was also tired out and hardly able to get up. But Smith got some hot water and soap and to the best of his ability dressed my wounds. That upon my head was a mere scratch, the bullet little more than cutting through the skin.

When my wounds were dressed I came down-stairs, where I found almost our entire command prisoners, having been picked up in attempting to make their way to their homes; and in fact many were arrested who had not turned out at all. Among others were David Sturges, a merchant, and William Herrington, a tailor. One had kicked old John Burwell, and the other had cowhided him. But now it was Burwell's turn, for, as a cruel magistrate, and captain of the militia, he almost held the power of life and death in his hands so far as these men were concerned.

I got myself somewhat strengthened up, had procured a hat, and had improved my personal appearance by a wash. When thus refreshed I took the Queen's proclamation from my pocket, read its provisions, and demanded my liberty. But after much shuffling, backing, and pulling in the matter, they came out and boldly declared the proclamation to be a forgery, as they said, to catch rebels with. The upshot of the matter was, that at two o'clock in the afternoon of that day, we were all marched off as prisoners to Simcoe jail. The next day, after we were all lodged in jail, orders were received to not allow any bail in the case of Sturges or Herrington. Of course, to them, it was a warning blast.

Simcoe jail was a new building, in fact the scaffolding was still up, and guards were stationed on the inside. They gave me the name of Davey Crockett, and insisted that Tory bullets would not penetrate my hide. Although a prisoner, and very young (having just entered my seventeenth year), from some cause, I know not what, these proscribed men seemed inclined to place confidence in me. They came to me and explained everything; said their lives were worth nothing unless they could escape, and that they could not escape without assistance. In return, I told them that they could depend upon me; that I would look around and see if any opportunity offered for their escape.

Now the room in which we were quartered was the court room, and from that, in the shape of an L, was a small room to be used as a jury room. There was a low trestle-work, covered with boards, where we slept— some sleeping below on the floor, while others slept up on the boards, stretched out like a long table. In looking out of the window I noticed that the scaffolding poles were still standing, with the planks forming the scaffold all intact. But I found that the windows were solidly fastened in, and that the sashes were immovable. ·I also noticed that the window-panes were about 10x16, and the idea struck me of passing the two men through the sash out onto the scaffolding. I communicated my plan to Sturges and Herrington, but told them that I would be compelled to take old man Blake into our confidence. Blake was a character. Notwithstanding the fact that he must have been about seventy years of age, he seemed active as a boy. He would sing songs, dance, and create a world of amusement. I approached him, and found that he was ready to aid me.

I now notified Herrington and Sturges of my plan, which was as follows: Blake was to get up a regular entertainment to attract the attention of the prisoners and guard while I went into the jury room to break the window, and prepare for their exit. All worked like a charm, with one exception; there was a young fellow a little older than myself lying in the jury room, and I could not get rid of him; hence I had to make a confident of him. Sturges was a large man and I was compelled to cut the munnion of the window to let him have the space of two lights. So I got the young man to pound with his heels on the boards, while I broke the glass and cut the munnion. When all was accomplished, in the midst of old man Blake's dancing, I gave them the wink, and in ten minutes they were safe out on the staging and slipping down the staging poles.

They went to the stable and stole their own horses and saddles, and rode them until they could go no farther, and then pressed others, on the plea that they were riding Queen's Express. All that was necessary to prove their loyalty was to tie some red ribbon or red

flannel around their arms and hats. There was no telegraph in those days, and they rode Queen's Express
triumphantly out of the country.

When the fugitives left the jail, and while yet on the
scaffolding, they advised " Davey Crockett " to accompany them. I declined, thinking that as I was but a
boy they would turn me out in a few days. Delusive
hope ! the Tory magistrates called all the boys before
them for examination in regard to the escape of their
leaders. I was examined among the others, and the
most important query among the many was, Who aided
Herrington and Sturges to escape? It was evident from
all the circumstances that they must have had inside
aid, and unfortunately for little " Davey Crockett," the
young man who pounded with his heels while " Davey "
broke the glass, peached.

My friends had been mourning me as dead, as my
cap had been shown to persons who knew it well, the
parties who exhibited the bullet hole in the cap stating
that a company had attempted to arrest me, but I had
resisted to the last, and was shot through the head. So
when my friends received a letter from me, and learned
that I was still alive, they came immediately and tendered
bail for my release. But it was no use; bail in my case
was refused. The charges stood thus: I had, by force
of arms, resisted arrest at Squire Dobie's; had again
resisted in the pine woods; had fired upon the squad sent
out to arrest me, and had aided and abetted the escape
of David Sturges and William Herrington. While all
under the age of twenty-one years were to be discharged,
the boy of sixteen was held a prisoner without bail.

This made a kind of hero of me in the eyes of my

fellow-prisoners, and one week from that time it gave
me sufficient influence among them, when we were about
being removed from Simcoe jail to London prison, to resist the attempt to shackle us. We insisted that every
man was deemed innocent until proved guilty, and that
we would go anywhere with them without resisting if
our limbs were left free, but not one step otherwise; that
we would die with our limbs free, but would not live
with them shackled. This resolve of ours created a discussion between the guards and officers, but at last it
was settled by their taking our parole, and we went un-
bound. Erelong I discovered by their maneuvering that
they wanted nothing better than for us to make an
attempt to escape, that they might have an excuse for
a wholesale slaughter. This was evident by their apparent carelessness in guard duty, and, in some instances
insinuating that we were fools in not making a general
rush for our freedom. But no attempt was made to
escape, and at last we reached our destination.

My condition was not different from evil-doers generally. My reputation followed me and I was sent to the
cells; and now a word regarding our treatment. While
cooped up in Simcoe jail we had a large-sized sheet-iron
stove (a common heater) in our apartment for our sixty
prisoners to cook their own rations upon, and one thin
blanket at night, and this in the midst of a Canadian
winter. But this was comfortable when compared with
our condition in the cells of London prison. When I
say the cells, of course I don't mean the cells proper.
Each cell was filled, but that was scarcely a beginning,
as there were over six hundred prisoners in the castle.
Every hall was crowded full, and there were no blankets

or other covering save what the prisoners had on. As to the floors, they were filled with large-headed spikes, the heads sticking up about three-fourths of an inch above the floor. And to augment our misery, there was an aperture about four feet wide and longitudinally the length of the building, and extending to and through the top of the structure, as an air passage to ventilate the building. In this condition we were kept for more than a month, when we received a supply of blankets; that is to say, each man received a blanket, and our condition was further improved by many of the men in the cells being removed. Some were released on bail, while others were removed to upper and more comfortable rooms. This so reduced our number that we who remained in the cells were enabled to crowd into the cells proper, where we could enjoy bunks and yet have the privilege of the hall.

About this time occurred a circumstance that much added to my comfort. One year before I had resided a short time in London, where I made the acquaintance of three ladies, sisters, one single and two married. I made the acquaintance of the two elder sisters through the younger, as she and I had become acquainted and were on terms of mutual friendship. They were all estimable ladies. The eldest married a merchant named O'Brien, and the next one also married a merchant, by the name of Olvero Ladd, and my little friend had in the meantime married Samuel Parks, the jailer. The Tories had also imprisoned Olvero Ladd, on suspicion of treason, and thus Mrs. Parks' attention was drawn to me. She still proved to be a good and true friend, and as long as I could get the privilege of the hall I was all right, as

4

there was a diamond hole through to the kitchen, through which Mrs. Parks was in the habit of slipping provisions and delicacies, as also candles, matches, and Yankee newspapers, with many a caution not to let the turnkeys catch me. This went on until my friends at home came to visit me, when they made such strong appeals in my behalf that I was removed to the room above, which, however, did not agree with my taste.

CHAPTER VII.

THRILLING INCIDENTS OF PRISON LIFE.

THE authorities had now organized a Board of Examiners (we called it the "pecking machine"), which consisted of four magistrates and the lawyers, who sat every day and had prisoners brought before them for examination. For nearly two weeks I was brought before the Board daily. At first I attempted to play the fool, and would answer their questions just as it happened, or as thoughts would strike me, without rhyme or reason. I continued this course for three or four days, when at last one of the commissioners spoke up and said, "Look here, young man, we have your history, and it is useless for you to assume to be a fool. Your former operations give that the lie."

They continued to recall and dismiss me from day to day, but at length they changed their tactics, and patronizingly said to me: "You are very young, and have doubtless been led into this by men that are now enjoying their liberty, while you are here lying in prison. Now all we ask of you is to disclose the names of your

leaders and you will be released. Do you not know
Jake Beamer, or Finly Malcolm?" and many others that
they named.

At last I got out of patience, and turned upon them
and said: "Yes, I am very young, perhaps too young; for
I have not lived long enough to learn to turn traitor to
my friends. And what I know, will never benefit you,
for before I would betray one of my unfortunate companions, to use the language of another, "I would lie
here until the vermin should carry me through the key-
hole." Upon this retort, one of the Board exclaimed,
"Let that fellow go back where he came from." I said,
"Thank you, gentlemen; then I shall soon be in the
State of New York." "No," he exclaimed, "we mean
to your room, and give us no more of your insolence,
sir, or you will go to the cells." I quietly asked, "Can
you get me any lower than the cells?" The reply was,
"Remember this, your life depends upon your future
conduct." I said, "I have one consolation, however:
you are mean understrappers, and can neither take my
life nor save it!" They little knew what a boon they
were conferring when they sent me to the cells, where I
could get something fit to eat, from Mrs. Park's kitchen.

But the next time my friends came there was another
tearful petition went before the commissioners to release
me from the cells. Their petition prevailed and I was
again sent to my room. By this time my wound had
healed, and I was as lively and active as a cat—a tall,
slender boy, height nearly six feet, and weight one
hundred and thirty pounds.

We used to indulge in all kinds of athletic sports for
exercise. We had a regular caravan; each had the name

of some animal. I was the great anaconda, because,
they said, I could tie myself in a knot. At this time I
had been a prisoner about three months, and prison life
had no terrors for me. And here I would say, by way
of parenthesis, that after one month a man will be as
content in jail as anywhere, and jail life has no further
terrors for him. After becoming thoroughly accustomed
to it myself,· it used to amuse me hugely to see new
prisoners come in. They would rant and tear around,
kick the door, curse the turnkeys, and raise a general
rump is for the first two weeks of their prison life, when
they would invariably have a sick spell. Recovering
from that, they would strengthen up and lapse into a
passive state.

Thus things ran along. The prison became less
crowded, many having been tried, and either convicted
and banished to the penal colonies, hung, or acquitted.
Our food was so meager that had it not been for aid from
friends, and the privilege of purchasing what we got by
way of notions, it would scarcely have sustained life.
Each man was entitled to eight ounces of meat per day,
and one pound of bread. But contractors were as rascally
then as now, and the meat was saved up for outsiders,
while enormous bones were weighed out to the prisoners.
And as for bread, the stuff furnished us was a burlesque
upon the name of bread. All the wheat in Upper Canada in the fall of 1836, owing to the long-continued rains
about harvest-time, had sprouted in the fields, not only
that which was in stack, but also wheat standing in the
fields. Some of the sprouts were from one to two inches
long. After the rains were over, this grain was dried
and threshed, generally for feed; but it was deemed

good enough to grind and make bread of for rebels.
We could break a loaf of our bread in two, and one man
take one-half of it and another take the other half and
walk apart, and it would make a rope twenty feet in
length.

I remember on one occasion that we took a loaf of
bread, broke it open and elongated it for about ten feet;
then we tied a lot of bones together, decked them out
with red flannel strings as evidence of their loyalty, and
hung them from the window fronting a public square,
where all might see them.   Among the more humane
citizens, even of the Tory party, they created quite a
sensation.   We claimed that it was unhealthful, and it
was submitted to a Board of Physicians, who decided
that the bread was perfectly healthful, but not fit to eat;
that it might do for hogs to masticate, but not for men.
The effect was that we were served with a little better
quality of bread.   Those who were able to purchase
supplies did so, and those who had neither money nor
friends were helped to a more bountiful supply by taking the rations of those who could purchase food.

And food was not the only thing that was purchased;
they were in the habit of paying the turnkeys to smug-
gle in liquor, the effect of which finally resulted in a disastrous row.   One afternoon some of the prisoners sent out
and had a twelve-quart pail full of whisky brought in instead of water, and before night some of them got pretty
"mellow."   We had a violin in the room, and a very good
violinist.   The music was started up, and dancing commenced, and everything was jubilant.   The dancing was
continued until after nine o'clock at night, when they
were notified to stop, but this they declined doing.   The

musician refused to play longer for fear they would take his violin from him. Stephen Bronger, a young English-man, who felt pretty merry, handed the violinist his watch to indemnify him in case his fiddle should be taken from him. Then "the ball" went on again.

In a short time the janitor came up with a ser-geant's guard, with guns and bayonets. The prisoners instantly formed in front of the music, each man seizing a billet of wood. The guns and bayonets were unwieldy in the room, so they were ordered out and in a few min-utes the guards returned with their bayonets in their hands, in charge of a captain. The prisoners again took their position, and the soldiers also formed in line, and the skirmish began. Alexander Nealy, one of the pris-oners, happened to be fronting the little English captain; he had an iron fire poker, which the captain ordered him to lay down. Nealy refused and placed himself in an attitude of defense, when the captain made a pass with his sword and gave Nealy a very severe scalp wound. Before the captain could recover his guard, Nealy dealt him a terrific blow on the head with the poker, which felled him like a beef. Nealy sprang upon the captain like a tiger, and would have dispatched him had I not sprang in and interfered. I had not drank any liquor, hence I was sober and did not take any hand in the row until my interference was necessary to save life. The boys had driven the soldiers back to the prison entrance, but Sam Parks, the jailer, had got through the ranks and was making for the violin, when Bronger discovered his object. They were both tall, powerful men; Parks prided himself on being the best man in the country, but he found his full match in

Bronger. They both seized the fiddle about the same time, and a more lively rough-and-tumble I have seldom witnessed. They finally broke the fiddle in two; Sam had the drum, and Bronger had the neck, strings, and bow.

Hostilities ceased as by common consent. They picked up the captain and helped him out, and when all was settled down they returned and arrested Bronger with his half of the fiddle (which he still retained), and a few others whom they recognized, including myself, although I was only acting to stop the row, as before stated; yet in the excitement I was mistaken for one of the active participants. We were all shoved down into the cells, the most of us, in our shirt sleeves, left in the hall without bed or bedding, or clothes to keep us warm. So the only thing we could do was to make night hideous, which we did to perfection, by hoots, yells, and howls. Bronger fastened the fiddle strings to the finger-board, stuck a jack-knife under them for a bridge, and with the bow made such a horrid noise that no one could sleep in the lower part of the prison.

In this situation we spent the night; but the next morning we were marched back to our room, without any attempt at further punishment. I am of the opinion that they had come to the conclusion that they had exceeded their duty in thus assaulting the prisoners when there was no attempt to escape, and were therefore quite willing to let the matter rest.

When the prisoners were first incarcerated at London, the guards were all raw militia and were not at all acquainted with fire-arms, and through their awkwardness several guns had been discharged in the prison.

One gun had been discharged in the room in which I was confined, and the ball had passed directly up through the ceiling, or floor of the room above; and the contents of another piece had passed through a partition connecting two rooms occupied by prisoners. While we had nothing better to do, with our knives we had, from time to time, cut and bored the door to our entrance until we got a little peek-hole through, from one-half to three-quarters of an inch in diameter. The turnkeys grumbled about it, but that was all the good it did them.

Every little while there would be new prisoners brought in, and we were always very anxious to hear from the outside world. One day the turnkey of our room had informed us that several wounded prisoners were brought in from " Point O'Play," where there had been a severe battle on the ice (in which the British got the worst of the fight). We were all anxious to communicate with them, but how? At last some one suggested the bullet-hole through the plaster and floor. I think our room was about twelve feet from floor to ceiling. We had several pieces of four-foot lath brought from the upper part or garret of the building. We sharpened one end of a lath, split the small end, and inserted a paper on which was written the words, "Ream out the hole;" then, by means of a high bench, we were enabled to stick the point of lath containing the paper through the jagged hole in the ceiling and upper floor.

The prisoners above readily took the hint, and with a knife enlarged the hole to the size of an ounce ball, which enabled us to roll a half sheet of paper around the stick and slip it up to them, which they could answer by running a dispatch back in the same manner. This

easy communication was established between the rooms,
and once having the idea of communication suggested,
a reaming out of holes became the order of the day.
The bullet-hole in the room east of us was also reamed
out, so that dispatches were sent back and forth.   Then
up-stairs, in the "House of Lords," as we called it, there
was a hall or large passage between that and a room
east of them, with doors opposite, which did not swing
close down to the sills.   Two laths would reach from
one room to the other, and by attaching them together,
and a paper to one end, communication between the
rooms was effected by sliding the laths back and
forth.   So we soon had a perfect postal system established between all the rooms.   We were taken out about
once a week, on top of the castle, for exercise, and on
our return to our rooms we would occasionally pick up
a lath and walk off with it without comment.   In this
way we had no lack of laths.

But that was not the full extent of our communication.   I suppose it will be understood that the turnkeys
were stationed outside of our rooms, and when our
friends would come to see us we would be called for by
name (that is when a permit was granted, which was
not always the case), and an officer would stand by to
hear all that was said and see all that was done.   So it
was but very seldom that anything could be slipped
from one to the other.   But one time when my sister
visited me, on bidding her adieu on her departure, I got
her back turned towards the officer in charge, gave her
a knowing look, and, as I took her hand, I slipped a little paper into it telling her that she could come and talk
at any time through the little hole that we had drilled

through the door; and by standing close to the hole her body would ·cover it, and papers rolled up small could be easily and softly exchanged. This she communicated to the friends of various prisoners, and one can hardly imagine the fidelity with which all these secrets were kept.

After that we would hear much that was occurring outside, and our friends could know all from the inside. A dispatch received at the door would be immediately forwarded to the proper room and address, and an answer returned to the messenger. For instance, John Doe, "House of Lords," East Room; Richard Roe, "House of Lords," or "House of Commons." Ours, being below, was called the "House of Commons;" that above, the "House of Lords."

Where I was located, in the "House of Commons," the room was about eighty feet long and about sixteen feet wide, with several windows about eighteen inches wide, with one single two-inch bar running up and down through the center. In hours of idleness men must be thinking, and seeking some employment or amusement. So, among other things, our boys made investigations in regard to moving the caps from off the window-sills. We soon discovered that the lower ends of the bars were split in the center about six inches and then turned at right angles, forming a T reversed, the upper end being passed through the caps above and spiked down in the brickwork below with six-inch spikes, holes having been punched into the split ends of the irons for that purpose. Then a notch having been sawed out of the window caps the size of the bolt, the cap was slipped back and nailed down, holding the lower end of the bar. This had been temporary work; and hurriedly done for the accommodation of the rebel prisoners. Having discovered how they were arranged, we went to work and cut around the nail heads (the cap being of soft white pine), which was but a small task, when we could take the caps right up. Then to hide our work we chewed up some of our sticky bread and put it about the nail heads, forming a kind of putty that matched very well the dirty white paint.

In the room where I was quartered, there were two small fire-places, in which were wrought-iron fire-dogs, the ends of which had been burned off. One day when we had one of the bars exposed by having the cap off, I took an andiron, placed the end of it in the notch of the bar, and getting a lever purchase, without difficulty raised the bar, the spike being quite easily drawn down from the brickwork. When I moved the bar up a little they swung it into the room and it came right out. Then we put it back just as it was before, and concealed our work; and in less than a week every bar in the room was loosened and left for some future occasion, but with very little prospect of ever being available to us for any purpose. We were some twenty-five feet from the ground, and the walls being white would show every object that came in contact with them; besides, there was a sentinel at every angle of the building, and there being fifty angles, we were very well guarded.

But I must not forget to notice a little incident which occurred during my stay in the "House of Lords." The British officers were in the habit of punishing the soldiers very severely for drunkenness, and of course when they found themselves the worse.for liquor they would hide away and sleep it off. One of them, on getting pretty full, attempted to hide himself in the garret, or rather under the roof of the castle. Now the "House of Lords" was the upper rooms of the castle, above which was the garret, and this fellow was attempting to creep under the roof immediately above one of the rooms, when he made a misstep and came down on the lathing instead of the joist, and one leg protruded through the ceiling. A regular shower of plaster came down into our room, and as we saw the leg hanging there, some of the boys caught hold of it and pulled the man down. The fellow was terribly frightened, and could not for a moment conceive what had happened to him. When informed that we had taken him into a rebel camp, he seemed to have the impression that he was to be dispatched at once; but he was soon disabused of that idea, and finding us inclined to be friendly, he was soon very much at home with us. I took him under my wing, and in an hour we were fast friends. We played cards a great deal, and my new protége taught me a trick with cards which he assured me no man in America could solve, at the same time pledging me not to reveal it. And I never have found a man who understood the trick. In the course of the afternoon I made an arrangement with the turnkey to let the fellow out and say nothing about the affair, he having become perfectly sober.

CHAPTER VIII.

FRUITLESS EFFORTS TO ESCAPE.

AS time passed on the number of prisoners became so reduced by bail, death, trial, transportation, and removals to other prisons, that at last there were but nine left in our room. We were known as the "old stock." We had a guard who had been attending on us for a long time, and with some of its members we had struck up quite an acquaintance. As on petition we were now permitted to have our outside door chained open nine inches for fresh air, we had an opportunity to converse freely. I had become quite familiar with one of the guards, and in the course of conversation, on his inquiry, I told him my story. He said it was a shame, and had he lived in the country he doubtless would be where I then was. He was an Irishman and a Catholic, and the most of that class sympathized with us. He remarked that if he could he would willingly leave the door open and let us walk out. I caught at it.

It was a dark, cloudy day, with a drizzling rain falling. I said, "You will be outside to-night on guard; it doubtless will be rainy and the sentries will be in their boxes; now, sir, here is a new English lever watch worth at least sixty dollars; you say you come on at midnight under our northeast window. If you will be snugly stowed away in your sentry-box at one o'clock in the morning, and not discover us nor make an outcry, the watch is yours." He readily acceded to the proposition. I gave him the watch; we agreed upon everything, and I informed him that we would tear up blankets to make a rope, and descend from the window. We were occupied all the afternoon making arrangements for our flight. We were not disappointed regarding the character of the night. It was intensely dark and our arrangements were made to cross the south branch of the Thames River, enter a narrow neck of woods, follow by a path well known to me to Westminster Street, and then south to near the second concession, where there was a wood-chopper's hut in a bushy by-place on my uncle's land; here we would be safe until the search was over.

At length the hour came. I mounted on a jury table and stuck the blanket rope out of the window and commenced letting the end run down the white wall, when bang! went an old musket from below, the ball passing my breast and striking the face of the window-jamb, knocking off a lot of brick and mortar, which fell to the ground with a thud. The cry then came, "Is he dead?" The reply was, "Yes, the poor fellow is dead;" but they soon discovered that the falling body was but brick and mortar. The whole command, apparently, came rushing up-stairs like a band of sheep, but after a little the excitement subsided, and the authorities entered our room to find us all lying under the jury tables "fast asleep." But the tell-tale bar and blanket-rope lay on the top of the table.

The officers began cursing us for rebels and ordered us out. We crept forth, rubbing our eyes. They hastily counted us, but could make out but eight. Where was the other? The officer in command ordered the men to fire up the chimney, but the mouth of the chimney was so low, and the throat so small, that it was impossible to insert a gun at the required angle; but they unfixed bayonets and ran them up the chimneys. In fact, the throats of the chimneys were but four inches wide, and would not have admitted a baby, much less a man. I remarked that I thought if they would count us more carefully they would find us all there. We were immediately marched to the cells, the officers saying that they had a mind to " skiver " us.

They kept us a few days in the cells, when we were taken out and promoted to the " House of Lords," which by this time was almost deserted, and the few tenants already there, with our force, did not at all crowd the room.

There had been several attempts to rescue the prisoners, on the part of a lot of braggarts that ranged up and down the St. Clair River, boasting what they were going to do. The Tories were really frightened, and were resolved that we should not be released. So they excavated below the building in which we were confined, and deposited many barrels of powder, I do not know how many, but enough to send us to glory anyhow. They covered a train to the barracks and gave public notice that if an attempt should be made to rescue us, they would fire the train and blow us all up.

I must say for a few days after this I was not anxious to be released; but as time rolled on, the news reached us that a large force had crossed into Canada and was advancing on London. Scouts were sent out, but were afraid to go out of sight of the city. They would retire to some secluded place and ride their horses until they would get them in a perfect foam; then come rushing in and report the rebels surrounding all sides of the town. Another would come in and report them nearer. At

last they got them within three miles of the town, when
Hughey, the turnkey, came rushing into our room and
exclaimed, " I would give a hundred dollars for an ax
to cut down the bridge ! " The rebels, he said, had
taken all the axes and hid them. People were hastily
packing up and leaving the city. The Tory magistrates
had left, and the report had gone out that the invaders
had proclaimed that if the prisoners were blown up that
no quarter would be shown to man, woman, or child;
and a deputation of citizens was appointed to call on
the commanding officer to revoke any order for blowing
up the castle.

During the excitement, Mrs. O'Brien came rushing
into our room, and the moment the door was closed behind her, she commenced jumping up and down, clapped
her hands and exclaimed, " They are coming! They are
coming ! They are coming ! and they dare not blow you
up; I've heard them say so." The truth of the matter
was, that an unusual number of Indians had collected
at Maldon, and the word went out that they were rebels,
and as the report traveled, the number increased until it
swelled to a prodigious army. Mrs. O'Brien said to me,
" I had a terrible time to reach you; I went to Sam Parks
[he was her brother-in-law and the jailer], and he said
that he dare not let me in, that I must go to the sheriff,
Colonel Hamilton. He said that times were so troublesome that I must go to the commanding officer, Colonel
Maitland; and he would not give his consent. I then
went back to Sam Parks, and told him that unless he
let me in to see those poor prisoners I would make
O'Brien commence a foreclosure suit against him in less
time than twenty-four hours. I did not like to do this,"

she said, " but I found that nothing less than the thumb-screws would do any good, and he knows very well that I have kept O'Brien from suing him for the last year." " Well," I said, "what then?" " O, he hustled me up the back way and through the east room, and here I am."

Well, the imaginary army did not appear, and as there were no signs of the approach of the enemy, and a teamster having arrived with his team direct from Maldon, everybody commenced plying him with questions as to the position, number, and equipment of the rebel army. The poor fellow was taken aback, and could not for a moment imagine what the people were after. The "rebel army!" he had seen none. There was no unusual excitement more than that a large number of Indians and squaws were holding one of their annual festivals near Maldon.

Thus the bubble had bursted, and an investigation proved that the whole story had originated in the gathering of the Indians for the green-corn festival, and some shrewd, patriotic parties had spread the story of the invasion, until the people had been so scared that a handful of brave spirits, properly led, could have taken London.

About this time there was a great deal of nervousness and unrest in the country, owing to the excitement and rumors of invasion from the Patriot sympathizers on the American side of the line; and the Patriots were ready to make another move whenever a rallying point should be indicated. The Scotch were all rebels, as we were called. I had two uncles living on Westminster Street, six miles from London, and there were many staunch Patriots in the neighborhood; and, besides, my

5

uncles were at the head of the Scotch, of whom there were over two hundred, all well armed with rifles, who could at any time be called together by the blast of an enormous tin horn.   In fact, my uncle David had a large, dry cellar beneath one of his barns, filled with arms and munitions of war; and the organization was so perfect that in two hours' time a force of from three to four hundred men could be called together.

In this connection I will introduce a very remarkable character, Mrs. Anna Burch.   She was my father's sister, and was, of course, my aunt.   At the time of the rebellion she was between thirty-five and forty years of age, but would not have been taken for more than thirty. She was of a very fair complexion, with auburn hair, and coal-black eyes, and I thought her the prettiest woman I ever saw.   Her weight was probably about one hundred and twenty pounds; she was as agile as a cat, brave as a lion, and one of the finest female equestrians that I ever met.   She was, to all intents and purposes, a rebel spy.   She assumed the character of a doctress, rode from one end of Upper Canada to the other, had a very good idea of the use of herbs and simple medicines, and with an unusual amount of shrewdness and daring she mingled with all classes and complexions of political creeds.   Thus she managed to be in possession of much valuable information from both sides.   And what was more singular than all, she managed for several months to avoid suspicion.   She notified many a Patriot who was to be arrested, in time to allow him to escape, and in her labors in the cause she seemed to be almost ubiquitous, and always to be found when most needed.

One day, just before our attempt to escape, my aunt

visited me, and while talking with me, when the guard's attention was drawn for a moment, she turned her back to the door where it was chained open nine inches, and I grasped a letter. To account for her back being turned to the door and her face to the sentinel, she addressed him and said, " Did you speak to me ? " At last they began to suspect her, but were unable to fasten anything upon her, and at the close of the rebellion she lapsed into a state of quiet, and finally spent her days and died at a ripe old age.

On reading the letter which she had passed to me at the door, it notified me that on a certain day (I do not now remember the exact time), at three o'clock in the afternoon, Colonel Maitland, commanding the Thirty-second Regiment, who was then guarding London, would start on a march down the river to Delaware, and another command, with a large supply of military stores for London, would, by a night's forced march, reach London about six o'clock the next morning. When Colonel Maitland should evacuate the town there would be but thirty raw recruits to guard the town from three o'clock in the afternoon until six o'clock the next morning; and if my uncle could be encouraged to sound his trumpet, assemble the Scotch and the little band of Patriots on Westminster Street, they could make a night attack, capture London, and release the prisoners.

It was a bold conception for the woman, but another plan struck me. Oh! how I wished for my liberty, if but for twelve hours. At this time the road leading from the east to London ran through what was known as Dorchester, or Buckwheat Pines. The road the soldiers would have to travel passed through this pinery for

seven miles, and they would enter the forest about twelve
o'clock at night, and get through about two o'clock in
the morning. At about three in the afternoon of the
day that the troops were to leave, I asked permission to
go out. There were guards stationed all around, and
being so well acquainted with Parks and the turnkeys, I
was permitted to wander about at will, sometimes for
an hour or two. Consequently I walked boldly out, and
sauntered up-stairs and out on the top of the building,
where I could see all over the city.

I noticed when I went up that the guards were
changed, and that the militia had taken the place of the
regulars. It was not long until I saw the baggage
wagons drive in. The command was formed with the
artillery in advance and marched out of town. Oh, could
I only escape, what might I not do for my adopted
country! I knew that in one hour or thereabouts the
guard would be relieved. The last sentinel was close to
the trap that admitted us to the roof, and in my soft
listing slippers I could walk close to the hole undiscovered, and might catch the countersign. I resolved to
make the attempt, and waited until I heard the relief
coming long the hall, when I crept close to the hole
and caught the countersign without the least trouble. It
was quite loudly and distinctly given.

One point was gained. I had the countersign; now no
time was to be lost in trying to use it to my advantage.
I waited till it was dark, when I walked boldly down the
corridor and down the stairs until within twenty feet of the
front door. I could not see any sentinel. I watched
for about fifteen minutes, when I advanced towards the
door, and when within six or eight feet of the door the

sentinel stepped out from behind a column, and walking up to me said, "Well, boy, is it not about time you were in your room?" I was taken all aback, but in a moment after he spoke I recognized him as one of our old turn-keys. I laughingly remarked, "Well, you would not lose much if you were to let me go." He said it would be poor policy, when they had got me fast enough to hang, to turn me loose. After a short time in light con-versation of that nature, I turned around and walked up-stairs. But, boy as I was, if he had had no assistance at hand, I would not have stopped; I felt that I could disarm him in a minute, but in that case I should risk having the whole pack onto me before I could get any further. I went into my den, but there was no sleep for me that night.

Had I succeeded in my efforts to escape, I would to-day have been able to tell a more brilliant story, or else I would not be in existence at all. And this was my plan: As before stated, my uncles were at the head of some four hundred brave men. All that was necessary to call them forth was a leader and a reasonable hope of success. I should have made my way to my uncles' as fast as my legs could carry me; aroused the Scotch, took about fifty ax-men to the Buckwheat Pines and felled trees across the road, to make a barrier in front of the soldiers. The road was cut out four rods wide, and the trees were very thick. Then I would have cut trees on both sides of the road ready to fall, with drivers back to force them across the road. Then I should have cut a barrier ready to fall in the rear to hem in the whole command; and when they should have been hemmed in by the barricades, the ax-men could have hurled the

trees onto them.   Thus massed as they would have been,
there could be no escape, and the riflemen could pour
their volleys into them.

We must have inevitably won an easy victory.   We
could have marched into London the next morning,
and taken it without firing a gun.   And such a victory as we could have won there, with the ammunition and supplies, would have given us the principal
city, with vast military stores, and would have enabled
us, with the forces we could command, to follow up
Maitland and capture him and his army before they
could reach Delaware, and before they would be aware
of any force in their rear.   And I could not bring myself to believe but what some bold spirit would see and
take advantage of the opportunity, until the next morning when I saw the troops come gallantly marching
into London.   Poor aunt Anna had exerted her ener-
gies in vain, and I could not escape to reward her efforts.

CHAPTER IX.

FROM PRISON TO HOSPITAL.—FINAL RELEASE.

ABOUT this time I was taken down with a fever that
prevailed in the city, and which had at last reached
the prison.   The physicians pronounced it bilious, inclined to typhus.   The last thing I remembered, for
some time, was holding onto a broom handle, and the
physician bleeding me; and the next thing I remembered
was seeing my fellow-prisoners, with my mother and
sister, around me crying.   I thought to myself, I must
be very sick, and will probably die, but I will be out of

the hands of the Tories; and again I recollected that I was being moved from the prison on a mattress. Coming in contact with the fresh air temporarily restored me to consciousness.

Being acquainted in London, I tried to make out what part of town they were taking me to. Then all was again a blank, until one day I saw Doctor Moor by my side, with a snuff-box in his hand, as usual. He said, "Well, young man, you have cheated the devil this time." I had previously been acquainted with him. A year or more before this, while he was courting Prie t' Cronin's daughter, and they were engaged to be married, on one of his calls she attempted to talk French to him, and made a terrible blunder, which caus d an estrangement between them for some months. The matter was finally explained to his satisfaction, a reconciliation ensued, and they were married. I had heard the joke, and when he told me that I had "cheated the devil this time," I thrust his wife's French at him. He appeared startled, stepped back, and exclaimed, "Who the devil are you?" My mother and sister seemed frightened at the recognition, but the joke passed off, and after the doctor had left his directions and departed, I again sank away. My sister told me that an hour after the doctor had gone, I commenced shaking so violently that she could hardly hold me on the bed.

I have neglected to mention that on removal from the prison I was taken to the hospital, where I was confined. The doctor, on leaving, promised to return in an hour, and when he did so, he found me in the condition referred to. He said that was the turning point in my disease. When the shaking had subsided, I recovered, and retained my senses, yet I had no more mind than a child; as an instance of this, I was constantly importuning my mother and sister to let me get up and go a-fishing. I remembered a trout stream where I used to fish, and I was determined to go and catch a mess of trout. They told me I was too weak to go, and soothed me as best they could, but I was resolved to get the doctor's consent and go. Consequently when the doctor came in I said, "Doctor, can I go fishing?" He replied, "Yes, of course you can, and it will do you good." I exultingly whispered to my attendants, "I knew the doctor would let me go;" and I was going to get right up, but as I tried to raise my arm I found that I could not do so any more than if it had weighed a ton. Then I understood why the doctor so readily gave his consent. Still I could not give up the notion of fishing, and commenced teasing my friends to get Mr. Comstock to make me a pair of crutches so that I could go.

I was improving very fast, and had a good appetite. I would cry for food, and my sister would cry because she dare not let me have it. I drew my rations of beef, and as I could not eat it, it was hung up near the fire-place to dry; and while my attendants were in another room, I raised myself up, took hold of the bedstead, and tried to pull myself up so I could reach the beef. But as I got partially straightened up, I lost my balance and down I came, measuring my length on the hard, uncarpeted floor. As I was but a mere skeleton, the skin was peeled from my bones in several places. My mother and sister rushed out, gathered me up, and put me to bed again, where I lay for several days pretty quietly, until I got over my bruises, and had from time to time been helped up to a chair by the fire.

But one morning they left me sitting in a chair while they ate breakfast in another room. The meat that still hung above my head was too tempting for me, and I stuck my fingers through a knot-hole in the lath where the plaster was off and pulled myself up. But not yet being strong enough to steady myself, I lost my balance and away I went. There were no banisters around the well-hole of the stairway, and in my efforts to recover my lost balance I got so near the opening that when I fell, I went thumping and bumping to the bottom. The Irish sentinel exclaimed, "And what are ye doin' there?" I answered, "Trying to break jail!" By that time my attendants were at the head of the stairs nearly frightened out of their wits. The sentinel helped them carry me to bed, and I was not trusted alone again for a long time.

When I had sufficiently recovered to walk about and begin to think, I discovered that my mind was almost a blank, and things came back to me quite tardily. I was also left with a severe cough. In fact, the doctor told my sister, who was still with me, that though I had weathered that attack, I could not live a year—that I would die of consumption. But I got so much better that the authorities began talking of sending me back to prison. I did not want to go back, and commenced thinking once more of escape, this time, by dressing up in my mother's clothes and passing out before the sentry in the evening. Now my mother was called a tall woman, but when I got on one of her dresses my long spindle-shanks stuck through a foot, and I soon discovered that the plan would not work, and I was forced to abandon it. I had been indicted for high

treason several months before, but could not be convicted, as I owed no allegiance to Great Britain, and as
yet they had not determined what to do with me. As
soon as I was able to do without a nurse, I was sent
back to prison. But it was no longer the immortal nine;
there were but eight left. James Watson had died of
the fever that had prostrated me for so long a time.

It was not more than a month, however, after my return from the hospital until we received our sentence.
It was rather a peculiar sentence, too, being a decree of
voluntary banishment. This was judgment and sentence
without a trial; but it was a kind of sentence by agreement, as each prisoner was asked the question, "Do you
accept the sentence?" When it came to me, and the
question was asked with all solemnity, I answered,
"Would a man refuse to be banished from hell to
heaven?" Our final sentence was that if caught in Her
Majesty's dominion after the expiration of three days
we were to be taken as felons and suffer death. The doors
were then opened, and we were permitted to pass out
without a guard.

I had about two dollars in my pocket, and my friends
lived in the opposite direction from which to go to get
out of the country. Mrs. Parks was present, and I bade
her good-by. Mrs. O'Brien insisted that I should go
home with her, which was but a short distance, and get a
good meal before starting on my journey, and I readily
complied. She gave me a good dinner, with all the
port wine I dared drink, and offered to give me money, but
I was too proud to take it. I thanked her kindly, and
in taking leave of her she said, "Lewis, something tells
me that you will one day return in triumph; and if you

do, remember your friends." I joined my companions, who were ready for a start, and as I headed for my native country, I found from my extreme weakness that a common road was scarcely wide enough for me to walk in, but I was naturally a good walker.

We had ninety miles to make on foot to get out of the country, and I think that the Tories devoutly hoped we would fail. I fell behind, and at dusk of evening I could just discern my companions in the dim distance. They had found a hotel, and I came up, dragging my limbs after me. I got some refreshment and stretched myself on the soft side of a long bench, where I spent the night. I awoke the next morning a little sore, but on the whole much refreshed. We got some breakfast and about seven o'clock we again started on our journey. That day I kept up with my companions, walking over thirty miles. We passed the second night at a kind of wayside hotel, having about thirty miles to go the next day to reach the St. Clair River. The exercise, bracing air, and good food, had temporarily revived me, and the third day I was one of the leaders in the march, and when we reached the river bank our companions were just coming in sight, trudging along, almost tired out. The last day we had suffered terribly for want of water, and at one time I was nearly blind from thirst. But near the road, in a swale where a tree had been uprooted, there was a muddy pool filled with midges, tadpoles, and lots of little red bugs; from this pool I took a refreshing drink, and was thankful for my good fortune in finding it. As soon as all the company had arrived on the bank of the river, a boat was secured, we exhibited our passes, and in an hour we were at Black River in Michigan, I having borrowed eight cents to pay my passage.

CHAPTER X.

EXPERIENCES IN MICHIGAN AND ILLINOIS.

THERE was a good deal of sympathy expressed for the poor Patriots, who had been released from a Canadian prison, and who had been banished from the Canadas, and their property confiscated. There were constant arrivals, from Black River to Grand Rapids, of persons seeking employment on the railroad, but there was an offer of work to our boys in preference to all others. As for me, I looked like the wandering "ghost of Colitus," and a single glance would have convinced the most casual observer that I could not go into the forest and wield the ax or the pick and shovel. But the contractor was very kind, and gave me employment as boss of a job of grubbing and clearing for the laying of the track through the Black River Swamp. My condition at this time was such that I could not sleep lying down, but had to assume a half-reclining and half-sitting position, coughing all night. The people where my washing was done remarked that the poor fellow would not come for his washing many times more.

There was a garrison of United States troops close by, and there was considerable talk of war with England on account of the burning of the steamer *Caroline;* and I thought if I could only enlist, and live until we could attack the British forces, I would sell my life as dearly as possible, and die content. I tried to enlist, but the examining physician told me that I had better seek a hospital rather than the barracks. As they would not receive me, I returned to our camp and resumed my duties, hoping against hope for a continuance of my life.

One day shortly after this occurrence, the men cut a large pine tree, at the heart of which there appeared a kind of acid. It bubbled up out of the center of the stump as clear as spring water, and as sharp as the strongest vinegar. Among others, I tasted it, and it seemed to go right to the affected part, throwing me into the most violent paroxysms of coughing. With me it was anything that would kill or cure, and I had the boys scallop out the stump so as to hold the liquid, which I continued to use as a constant drink. And about the same time I commenced chewing spikenard root, which grew there in abundance. I also collected hemlock gum and made plasters, which I applied externally to the region of the pains.

I continued this treatment about two weeks, and felt the beneficial effects very sensibly. When we struck another pine producing a like acid, I continued to drink it, still using the spikenard root, and applying the hemlock plasters. At the end of a month I was, so to speak, a new man. I had had a little property at Jamestown, in Canada, which was confiscated, and I was solely dependent on my wages for a living. But as soon as my family heard of my whereabouts, they disposed of their property and left the country, emigrating to Illinois. My brother called for me where I was at work, and I joined them, and we all reached Chicago, Illinois, late in the fall of 1838.

The Michigan canal was then in course of construction from Chicago to La Salle, where we all found employment; but as my health improved, my military ardor increased, and I commenced planning an expedition to invade the Canadas. There was plenty of material around me—daring, reckless spirits, who were filled with enthusiasm. Many impromptu meetings were held, and in thirty days after the thing was started, I had over six hundred men enlisted for the expedition. But it was impossible to conduct the proceedings with that degree of secrecy that would insure success. They would hoot and cheer, and carry me around on their shoulders, with boastings and demonstrations that I could not control. Consequently I hurried my arrangements.

Chicago at that time did not contain over fifteen hundred inhabitants; in fact, it was but a village. There was an arsenal with a few hundred small arms and two six-pound brass cannons, with some fixed ammunition, but not enough to carry out my plans, which were as follows: I would first arm and equip the men comprising the expedition, and also provide a supply with which to arm others after landing in Canada. I intended to lease a good large steamer, ship my command, and land them at Maldon, on the Canada shore; then commence a rapid march to the interior, sweeping through the settled parts of the country, compel every able-bodied man to join our standard, forage on the country·for supplies, and leave nothing in our rear to oppose us. My march was to be so rapid as to give no time for plotting treason in the ranks, and but little time to array forces in front. Expecting by the time I reached London, Canada West, that I would have at least ten thousand men, I intended to garrison all captured towns with them and men loyal to our cause; for I was confident that at least two-thirds of the inhabitants of the entire country would be in sympathy with the move.

But it is useless to give the plans of an exploded expedition in detail; suffice it to say it was my intention to sweep the Canadas, manufacturing my broom from their own timber. But while corresponding with parties at Detroit regarding arms and munitions of war at that place, the United States Marshal, one morning, tapped me on the shoulder and said, "Young man, several of the contractors on the canal have been making complaints against you, charging you with the intention of invading Canada. These men are acting from interested motives, as in case you carried out your scheme it would leave their jobs without hands. I am frank to admit that I sympathize with your cause, but unless you disband and abandon the expedition I shall be compelled to arrest you; so you had better take warning in time to avoid trouble." I remonstrated with him, and asked him if he could not take a journey, or volunteer and go with us; but he declined all overtures, saying, "I will do better than that, I will keep you all from getting your throats cut."

Through the vigilance of the contractors and the marshal, our expedition came to an end. I worked that fall and winter on the canal, and the next spring drifted up to Warrenville, Du Page County, Illinois, where I remained some time with Harvey T. Wilson, who was very kind to me, and put me on track of some vacant Government land, of which I located one hundred and sixty acres. I gave my brother-in-law an equal interest in the land, and, being a good sawyer, my services were soon called into requisition at Garey's sawmill, at thirty dollars a month.

I worked there several months, during which time I

learned that one of my old _Patriot friends, Caleb Kip,
was residing on the west side of Fox River. We were
very intimate friends, and I made up my mind to visit
him. So one day I set out, mounted on a favorite mare,
which I prized very highly, on my contemplated visit.
On coming to the river, I found it so swollen by the
spring freshet as to carry off all the bridges, and there
was no crossing short of Elgin. I was informed, however, of a ford that could be crossed in ordinary stages
of water, and I resolved to try the ford. Arriving at
the designated crossing, I found the stream running
high and wild, and in the middle the current was very
swift. But, nothing daunted, I plunged in.

At first my mare found good footing, the water only
coming half way up her sides, and I was congratulating
myself that it was not much of a feat, notwithstanding
all the cautions I had received. But suddenly the
noble animal dropped into the boiling current and went
under, head and ears; however, she soon came to the surface, and gallantly stemmed the flood with her ears and
eyes out of water. The rushing current carried us rapidly
down stream, but she continued to swim for the opposite
shore; yet I could see that she was beginning to fail,
that the effort was too much for her, and I was seriously
thinking of throwing myself off from her back when
she struck bottom. About this time I saw an old gentleman by the name of Hill running down to the river
for his boat. The mare continued to wade toward the
shore, which was yet at a considerable distance; but having gone some forty or fifty yards, down she went
again and had to swim for dear life. I now saw that
there was but one show for her or me, so I slid off

behind, seizing her by the tail, and thus relieved she brought me to shore. The old gentleman met us at the point of landing and assisted me to the house, for I was so chilled and benumbed that I could scarcely stand. He built a big fire, and while I was warming myself and drying my clothes, he took care of my horse. He gave me a big horn of whisky, and presently some dinner, and in an hour and a half I was on my way again, arriving safely at my friend's house without further adventure.

The next afternoon I went back home, but not by the same road; I went by way of Elgin. I resumed my work at Garey's; the thaw continued, the ice was broken, and we expected, with the force of the ice and the immense flood of water rushing upon the mill-dam, that the dam must give way, although we were making almost superhuman efforts to save it. Several of the hands, myself among them, had been all day on the lookout, and wherever a hole was discovered we would stuff in straw and dirt.

Night came on and I remained with a lantern to watch for breaks in the dam. Next to the mill there was a large bulkhead, and fifty feet from that, out near the middle of the dam, was a second bulkhead, and between the two there was a low place, about four feet lower than the rest of the dam, which was called the "roll-way." Over this roll-way, where the surplus water escaped over the dam, was extended a small log, about eighteen inches at the butt, running to about six inches at the top. We used to walk this timber to get from the mill to the middle of the dam, which was the highest part and was above water, making a little island; and as

6

the water kept washing it away, it became very small.
Time had passed, the water was rushing and moaning on
every side of me; it had become evident that the mill
and dam and everything must soon go before the force
of the flood.   I must escape from there or be drowned.
Still I remained on the little island in the middle of
the dam.   On one side was a swinging pole or timber
that swayed to and fro with my weight, and passing over
the roll-way was a boiling, seething flood, resistless in its
force, and terrible in its fury.   It is true that in daylight, and when the water was at its normal stage, I had
often walked the log; but now, over the raging flood,
with a roaring cataract all around me, by the uncertain
light of a lantern, and the log slippery with water, could
I succeed in the undertaking? and would it not be
courting death to make the attempt?   To fall and go
over the dam would be just as fatal as to go over Niagara Falls; but what was to be done?   I would have
to take to the water like a spaniel—no, not like a
spaniel, for he could not have survived two minutes.
The dam on that side was made by spiking two-inch
plank onto a timber foundation at an angle of about
forty degrees, leaving nothing but the edge of the plank
as a footing or top of the dam; and over this the water
was pouring waist deep for a distance of three hundred
feet.

All on shore had been aware of my danger for hours.
I could not hear anything that was said on the shore,
but they were gesticulating violently and beckoning with
lights for me to cross the log.   But I felt that it was impossible for me to accomplish the feat.   But I must do
something, and that seeming to be the only chance, I

must try. I took the lantern and made the effort. The small end was next to me, and I started out, the water running below my feet with lightning speed, as seen by the dim, uncertain light of the lantern. My head began to swim and I was losing my balance; I was falling, but I could not turn. I was about twelve feet out on the log. As a last hope I threw myself backwards, making a desperate leap. My feet, legs, and lower part of my body struck in the water, but one arm had struck over the timbers of the waste-gate. I was at least temporarily saved and dripping. Again I took the position but a minute before abandoned.

My little island in the middle of the dam was constantly growing less as the flood arose. But there was one hope still left, and I lost no time in trying to take advantage of it. The water was waist deep where it was pouring over the dam on the west side. I took a long pole and ran it down in the water on the upper side of the dam, and commenced wading and feeling with my feet for the edge of the plank, steadying myself with the pole, and in this way I waded some fifteen rods to the west shore, where I arrived without a dry thread on me, and chilling from the icy coldness of the water. I was safe from the perils of the flood, but there was no house or habitation on that side of the stream within two miles.

What was to be done? I dare not attempt to reach a house on that side, and I concluded to try to cross the stream. There was a bridge below the mill, but covered at this time with three or four feet of water. I took my pole and wading in to the approach of the bridge, found that the planking had been all floated off, but the abutments being yet firm in the earth, the stringers had not gone. So I felt my way over, steadying myself with the pole, and safely reached the other shore, where I was soon made comfortable.

The next spring, that of 1839, I went over to St. Charles, on Fox River, on a fishing excursion, and there met an old gentleman by the name of Calvin Ward. He wanted to hire a man to work as a common laborer, offering fair wages. I soon struck up a bargain and went to work for him, continuing about three months, when the old gentleman wanted me to cut prairie hay for him and in payment he would sell me town lots. I made another agreement with him and commenced cutting hay. At this I made about five dollars a day, and soon found myself the owner of thirteen town lots in St. Charles. It was a growing little town, and in one year my lots had quadrupled in value.

In the meantime I had made the acquaintance of a young lady by the name of Fisk, and married her in the fall of 1840. Fisk was a native of Massachusetts, and had come out to the West for the purpose of locating in the country, and Christianizing the heathen, as well as improving his worldly condition; and, to use his own language, he thought he "would find the people poor, ignorant, and honest." He said he "found them poor enough, and ignorant enough, but could not boast of their honesty." He brought five thousand dollars out with him, and the poor, ignorant, and honest inhabitants of the West had got it all from him, and all that he had to show for it was a settler's claim to a beautiful piece of prairie land about two miles east of St. Charles. However, his father was a wealthy man and he was heir expectant.

We soon arranged matters; I was to go onto the farm, extinguish a small lien upon it, and, when the land came into market, pay the Government and then we would own the place in equal sh res. I took possession of the farm, and Deacon Fisk went back East to visit his parents. I cleared the indebtedness from the farm and deeded it, and at the end of a year the deacon returned, but not wishing to farm it he settled in Geneva, selling me his interest in the place.

At this time money was very scarce in Illinois, and nearly all business transaction was in trade. 'It happened that I turned out to be a pretty good trader, and at the end of the year I owned my prairie farm and about eighty acres of timber land situated on a small creek, when I took it into my head to erect a saw-mill on the creek, to the infinite mirth of my neighbors generally. And many of my sympathizing friends remonstrated against my folly, telling me that it was a pity that I should squander my property, for which I had struggled so hard, on so foolish a project. Notwithstanding the many cautions, I struggled on, completed my mill, and made it a paying institution; and instead of its ruining me, I paid for it in the first four months run.

My wife was a little, fragile woman, and sick much of the time. She was an only child, and her mother insisted on her remaining with her most of the time, which broke me up very much—so much that in fact I was in a worse condition than I would have been if I had had no wife at all. I was leading a miserable existence, when circumstances occurred which for a time changed my whole course of life.

CHAPTER XI.

MEMOIRS OF THE MEXICAN WAR.

ALL will remember, on the declaration of war by the United States against Mexico, how nobly the State of Illinois responded to that call. Thousands of her citizens left their various occupations and offered their services to maintain the honor of their country; and this outburst of patriotism was not confined to class or creed; the artisan, mechanic, laborer, and professional man alike, rushed to the field to swell the ranks of our citizen soldiery; and at very short notice six regiments marched to the seat of war, from that State. Kane County soon furnished her company, which was fortunate enough to be received as Company I, Twenty-second Illinois Volunteers; term of enlistment, during the war. I say fortunate, for many companies were too late to be permitted to join in that struggle. I raised the company referred to, and having been promised the position of quartermaster, I refused to be elected captain, from which a suspicion arose among my men that I did not intend to accompany them to Mexico. I assured them that I would go if they had to carry me on a litter.

We took steamer at St. Louis for New Orleans, and *en route* I was taken down with the measles. A person could not well imagine a more uncomfortable spot to encounter such an enemy, crowded as we were between the decks of a Mississippi steamer, in the month of July, in that climate; and when we reached Carlton, seven miles above New Orleans, where we were to await a ship for our transportation, the measles had broken out and I was in a burning fever. I took a carriage for the hotel, leaving my servant to take charge of my baggage. On reaching the hotel the landlord remarked to me: "Young man, you seem to be ill?" I answered in the affirmative, and told him that I wanted the best accommodations he could give. To my surprise and mortification, he informed me that he was very sorry, but he could not take me into his house, as by so doing his boarders and customers would all leave him; that the yellow fever had broken out in New Orleans, and that every sick person would be suspected of having that disease.

I remonstrated, but in vain; he was inexorable, and I ordered the driver to take me to the next, and only other hotel in the place. There, after informing the landlord of my true condition, I was taken in, and after being seated in my room I rang for a pitcher of ice water, when, not the ice water, but the landlord put in an appearance and informed me that it would be impossible for him to keep me in his house, for if he should do so his guests would all leave him; this information, sick as I was, very much irritated me. I asked the landlord if there was any military hospital in the place. He replied in the negative. I then asked him if there was any officer of the quartermaster department there. He informed me that he believed there was a quartermaster-sergeant there. I requested that he be sent to me. He soon called. I related to him the condition of things, and asked if there were any arrangements made by the quartermaster department for the accommodation of the sick. He told me that a building had been rented for that purpose, and a few cots provided—nothing more. I informed him that I was acting quartermaster of our command, and ordered him to place furniture in the building, and make it as comfortable as possible; then directing my servant to have my baggage brought to the hospital, I took my satchel in my hand and accompanied the sergeant to the place, traveling more than a mile in my condition, through the broiling sun at midday.

When we arrived at the place I threw myself down on a cot, and that was the last I remembered for about eight days. On my returning to consciousness I was informed that a lady living near the place had been my nurse, and gave me all the attention that could have been bestowed on me at my own home. With careful nursing and the attention of our surgeon, Wm. B. Whitesides, and aided by youth and an excellent constitution, I was enabled to weather the blast. When very weak and scarcely able to stand alone, I was informed that a ship had arrived to transport us to the seat of war, and that our place of destination was Tampico; but to my chagrin, I learned that the doctor had declared that it would be wholly impossible for me to stand the sea voyage, and that the colonel had ordered me to remain in the hospital until I had recovered my health sufficiently to stand the trip.

When I was informed of that fact I was very much disheartened, and resolved to go at all risk. I accordingly sent for my colonel and the surgeon, and begged of the colonel to countermand his order. He said he had acted with a view to my good, but if I insisted on going he had no objections. The doctor (I suppose for my consolation) informed me that if I made the attempt they would have to bury me at sea. I could not see it in that light, but told the doctor that

I was going, and if I died on the passage I wanted them to bury me on the Mexican shore, and not at sea, for I had started for Mexico, and to Mexico I was going! I gave my servant twenty dollars for the woman who had nursed me, and told the boys to prepare the litter, for I intended to keep my promise with them; but instead of the litter they mounted me on the colonel's horse, with a man walking each side to steady me, and in that way transported me to the ship.

We had a pleasant voyage, in due time arriving at Tampico, which lies on the north side of the Tampico River, about six miles from its mouth, in the State of Tamaulipas. This has the reputation of being the most sickly place in the world. Yellow fever and black vomito sweep off its hundreds yearly. The place is almost surrounded by stagnant pools and lagunas. On our arrival I was not only alive, but was able to walk the decks of the vessel. We had no fighting at this place. Captain Chase was the American consul, and on the first arrival of the American ships of war, Mrs. Chase hoisted the stars and stripes at their residence, and Tampico surrendered at discretion. I was soon domiciled at the St. Charles Hotel, kept by Mexicans, of course. They spoke no English, and I could not speak a word of Spanish; the consequence was that I would call for one thing and they would bring me another; but we managed to get along for three or four days, while my quartermaster-sergeant, under the supervision of Dr. Whitesides, was perfecting our hospital arrangements.

About this time the doctor called in to see me, and announced the fact that they had so far progressed as to get a building; had supplied the more urgent necessities of the sick, and had made a couple of rooms ready for myself and attendants. All that was now lacking to make me comfortable was a supply of water, which, by the way, was hard to be obtained there, as I afterwards learned; all that was used, except what was saved from the winter rains in cisterns, had to be brought down the river from above tide water, in casks. I was much elated with the idea of again getting among my command, for they all looked upon me as their captain. As Lieut. W. G. Conkling used to say, Captain Harvey never drilled his company in his life, which was literally true, and when I was engaged in my staff duties Conkling generally commanded the company.

The morning after my interview, Mr. Chase, hospital steward, came down to the hotel to see me; I requested him to allow me to lean on his arm and I would attempt to go with him to the hospital. He consented, and when arriving there I did not feel exhausted, and asked him to walk along with me and we would try and procure a glass of strong beer or ale, as I felt somewhat thirsty. We had not advanced far before I noticed, sitting in well-furnished apartments, an elderly man of rather light complexion, who, as I thought from his appearance, was not a Mexican, and perhaps could speak our language. Being on the sick list I was attired in citizen clothes, and looking in sharply at the old gentleman, he arose and in good English asked what I wanted. At that I turned in towards his door and informed him that I would prefer a glass of strong beer or ale to anything else at that time. He remarked, " Pretty well, that a British consul should be called on so early Sunday morning for beer." I quietly informed him that if he had not got it, I should propose getting it in Tampico, as the English were all lovers of good ale. It being a national joke, the old man burst into a hoarse laugh. I turned on my heel and informed him that I probably enjoyed the joke as well as himself.

Time rolled on; I had recovered my health, and as my quartermaster duties were light and many of our officers were then sick, I volunteered to do duty in the lines; and as I was riding my rounds as officer of the day near the western defense of Tampico, one evening, I fell in with the British consul. He seemed very affable, and among other things asked to what command I belonged. I informed him that I belonged to the Illinois regiment, when he observed, "I have a good joke to tell you of one of those green 'suckers.'" He then proceeded to narrate the beer story, stating that he thought to awe the man by informing him who he was, but observed that the cool answer of the fellow amused him. I asked him if he would know that green 'sucker' were he to meet him again. He said, "No; how should I know him when there are so many calling on me every day for something?" I raised my cap and said, "Behold in your humble servant the green 'sucker' that called on you for the beer." He seemed somewhat surprised, and then added, "Why didn't you tell me who you were? I had no beer, but I possessed some very nice wine and good old brandy;" and at his earnest solicitation I was induced to accompany him home to take the proof of his assertion, when we made a night of it.

I thought no more of the matter until the next Saturday, when a paragraph appeared in the Tampico *Sentinel* giving the anecdote of the green "sucker" calling on the British consul for beer, and hinting that the green "sucker" turned out to be an officer in the army. The story was copied in most of the Eastern papers, and again made its appearance in Tampico, when it became a question as to who was the green "sucker." Major Jerolt had come down from Altamira with most of his command, and we were having a good time at the office saloon in Tampico, when the question was again asked, "Who was the green 'sucker'?" I called the crowd to the bar, and after filling, I told them that I could not keep a good joke, although it might be at my own expense. I "acknowledged the corn," and was ever after known as the veritable "green sucker."

Colonel Gates, with brevet rank of brigadier-general, was military governor at Tampico, and commander of the forces stationed at that place, being about two thousand five hundred in all; and by his orders our regiment, or rather battalion (as one battalion of our regiment was ordered to join General Scott), was stationed on the north side of the city, when we first began to enjoy the beauties of camp life. We were quartered in our tents, and compelled by orders of the commander to maintain a guard around our encampment, making a regular detail of about thirty men. Owing to the great number sick, and the small numerical force, together with the extreme heat, the duties were very exhausting and laborious, and our colonel had made several efforts to obtain an order reducing or entirely abolishing the guard, but without success. After things had continued in this state from four to six weeks, an occurrence took place which entirely relieved us of this guard duty; it happened thus: We had enlisted a man by the name of Tubs, who was of fine intellect, and had been the recipient of a liberal education; but spirituous liquors were his curse, and Tubs was but little more than a common drunkard, and in fact would never be sober when he could get liquor on which to get drunk. This man was on guard one night, and happened to be stationed on our line where it commanded the Altamira road, and it appears that Gates, the commander, had in the evening gone out in the western portion of the town, purposes unknown, and about eleven o'clock at night came riding in and advanced on Tubs, the sentinel. Tubs challenged him.

The general replied, "A friend." Tubs said, "Advance and give the countersign!" The general replied, "I am General Gates, commander of this post." Tubs again ordered him to stand. The general was furious, and made a move as though he would force the guard, and again reiterated, "I tell you, I am General Gates, commander of this post!" When click, click, went the old musket, and Tubs said, "Advance a step, and I will blow your head off! I don't know General Gates, commander of this post, but I know I am commander here." The general was compelled to stand; trembling with rage, he said, "Call the sergeant of the guard!" Tubs replied, "I don't want the sergeant of the guard, and do you remain where you are until the relief comes; and if you make any attempt at escape I will shoot you!" He then kept the old general frothing and swearing an hour and a half until the relief came, when Tubs remarked to the sergeant, "I have a prisoner there who could not give the countersign; he says he is General Gates, commander of this post, but any man could say that." The sergeant advanced to the general, saluting him. The

general demanded : " Where is your colonel ? call him ! "
The sergeant went to the colonel's marquee, called him
up, and told him who awaited him.   On the colonel's
approach, the general bellowed out, " What fool have you
got there for sentinel ?   He has kept me standing here
a prisoner for two hours ! "

The colonel apologized and said it was impossible for
the sentry to know him.   The general swore vengeance
against poor Tubs, and declared he would have him severely punished.   He then turned to Colonel Hicks and
said, " Remove this guard; it is of no earthly benefit, and
is becoming a nuisance."   The order was promptly
obeyed; Tubs was never punished, but was drunk as a
lord the next three days, the boys furnishing all the
liquor he could drink.   His dissolute course at last proved
too much for his organization, and in about two months
after the occurrence referred to, the boys fired a farewell
shot over his grave, and we left him to take his final
sleep in the lowlands of Mexico.

Things began to assume shape; we had strengthened
the western defenses of the city by erecting strong field
batteries commanding the Altamira road on the north
and the Panuco River, above Tampico, on the south side,
the two principal points from which an attack could be
made from the interior.   On the north side of the river
and to protect us from attack from Pueblo Viejo or
Tampico el Alto, we had erected heavy batteries below or
east of the city in such a manner as to protect the east
and south.   This measure was deemed highly essential
as we were informed that there was a heavy force of
Mexicans and Indians stationed at Tampico el Alto meditating a descent upon Tampico.   This information pro-

duced such an effect upon our commanding general that
he had a strong guard placed all around the city, as well
as patrols in different directions; and this was a very
necessary precaution, for at the time we had not penetrated the enemy's country more than fifteen miles in
any one direction, and consequently were ignorant of
their resources or forces, or at what time or point we
might be attacked, by superior numbers, hence all was
under vigorous military discipline, and our volunteers,
as a general thing, had assumed the appearance of
veterans.

But all commands have their exceptions; we had our
awkward squad, and some had been sick ever since landing in the country, having had no opportunity to improve as soldiers. I found a laughable case in our command; he was an Irishman belonging to Company A.
Pat had been in the hospital most of the time since our
arrival in Mexico, but had recovered and was reported
for duty. The first time he mounted guard, being
wholly ignorant of the duties or responsibilities of his
position, or the penalties attached thereto, he comfort-
ably seated himself beneath a shade and went to sleep.
The relief, it appears, found him in that condition, stole
his gun, awakened him, and placed him under arrest;
but finding him so wholly ignorant of the consequences
of his act, the officers of our command concluded not to
prefer charges against him. His captain gave him a
severe reprimand, and assured him that if he was ever
again found asleep at his post, or even allowed any one
to get possession of his gun, he would certainly be shot.

One night, not long after Pat received his reprimand,
I was on duty as officer of the day, and Lieutenant

Poleon was officer of the guard; as we were riding our
grand rounds and came up to old Fort Ann, at the
western defenses of the city, I saw a sentinel walking
his post as large as life, without a gun. .I said to him,
"Where is your gun, sir?" Pat replied, "And that's
what yed be findin' out now!" I said peremptorily,
"Where is your gun?" Said Pat with a knowing grin,
"'Tis not the likes o' ye I'd be tellin' that same now."
I called the sergeant of the guard, and ordered the fellow under arrest, when Pat exclaimed: "Ah! bad luck
to the day I iver intered the army; and shure the captain
tould me if iver I lit them get me gun again they'd shute
me like a dog, and now here I'm bein' arristed for not
lettin' him get it." He turned his head and seeing Poleon, exclaimed: "Shure and this is me own leftenant;
tell me, mon, fwhat shall I do?" Poleon rode up to the
fellow and quietly asked him what he had done with his
gun. Pat said, "Will they not shute me if I let the
spalpeens git me gun?" Poleon explained to the Irishman the nature of his duty, and after a while he began
to understand the condition of things. At Poleon's request I had him released, when Pat beckoned us to
follow; he marched to the other end of his beat to a
heavy piece of ordnance in battery, and running his
arm down the bore of the cannon, drew forth his musket;
he had it safely hid there to keep the "spalpeens" from
finding it. Pat was an odd stick, but turned out to be
a good soldier, and a brave man, and evinced much daring at Agua Cotta.

While speaking of different characters, perhaps it
would not be out of place to give a passing notice to our
New Orleans recruit. At Carlton, a quite boyish and

good-looking fellow made application to enlist; was examined by the mustering officer, received and mustered into service. When we had been in Tampico about two months, one morning a good-looking young woman stepped into Colonel Hicks' quarters and said, "Good morning, Colonel Hicks, I have become tired of soldiering, and would like my discharge." The colonel looked at her with surprise, and remarked, "You have the advantage of me; I fail to recognize you." She laughingly answered, "Don't you know your New Orleans recruit?" The colonel seemed rather taken aback at first, but, rallying, said, "You have your discharge, but whether it is honorable or not, depends on yourself." Though she had her election, I fear it was not a very honorable one; as I ofttimes thereafter saw her at fandangoes and other public places, sometimes in male and sometimes in female attire. She followed the army to the city of Mexico, where I lost track of her.

CHAPTER XII.

MEMOIRS OF THE MEXICAN WAR—CONTINUED.

IN writing this memoir it is not my intention to reproduce the written history of the war between the United States and the Republic of Mexico, nor any part of it; but merely to refer to scenes in which I was the principal actor, or which came under my immediate notice. Being so intimately connected with self, it presents an appearance of egotism that I most keenly feel, but cannot avoid; hence I hope those who may think it worth their while to trace me through our campaign

7

will discard the idea of any intent on my part to lionize myself. With this half apology I shall dismiss that part of the subject.

In a previous chapter I referred to Tampico as being the most sickly place in the world; but that is not all I have to complain of. There is scarcely anything that can afflict humanity but what is found there. In the first place there are alligators of enormous size; they line the banks of every stream and bayou; land crabs are on every side and around you; lizards and swifts run before you in armies of thousands, and when you are seated they are running over you in all directions. They run over your food, your bed, and every other place; in fact, they are literally your bosom companions; while the mosquitoes and gnats are inhaled at every respiration; wood-ticks of several different kinds will attach themselves to your person, and serve you very badly; the jigger is a perfect bore, of which I ofttimes had the most painful evidence; and centipedes were our frequent bed-fellows, but they were small and their bite not fatal, though very painful; the tarantulas are there, not numerous, but very deadly in their sting; these and the scorpions are, of all the poisonous insects, the most dreaded by the natives. To protect us against the mosquitoes, Government issued single mosquito-bars to the men; each was furnished with four pins, one at each corner; the pins were stuck into the ground and sufficiently raised to allow a man to lie under it, and the flaps on both sides would lie on the ground; this did very well for mosquitoes, land crabs, and lizards, but it was no protection against gnats.

After we had been stationed at Tampico about two months, I became very bilious, and was attacked with

yellow jaundice. My doctor advised me to ride on
horseback, and in compliance with these directions, I
had been riding all around the outskirts of the city; but
this was too limited, and it would not do to take the
Altamira road, as several men had already been picked
off by venturing too far from camp. On the north and
east side of the city there was a dense chaparral; indeed,
it was so thick that a bird or rabbit could scarcely penetrate it, and ranged in height from three to fifty feet.
Every bush was provided with sharp thorns; in fact,
all the rank grass of that country has thorns on the end.
In riding along the edge of the chaparral one day, I
noticed a roadway or tunnel penetrating it. I ventured
in, and rode for some time in a regular straight tunnel,
cleared through the jungle; the work had the appearance
of having been completed for a long time, as there were
no stumps or roots below, nor any dry and withered
branches above; once in a while I could see where a
bush had lopped down sufficiently to obstruct the passage, and had been cut away, but no other evidence of
recent work was visible; but riding along, once in about
every quarter of a mile I could see where there had been
a narrow trail cleared out, which looked like a rabbit or
coon trail, leading from the main artery.

The first day I rode along the avenue in a most lovely
soft twilight, entirely shut out from the sun, in one
unbroken mass of chaparral or jungle, I should suppose
about five miles; then I returned to camp and related
my adventures, and we all speculated over the strange
tunnel through the dense vegetable mass; but I had as
yet formed no conception of its use, and my curiosity
was at flood tide. I was resolved to further prospect

my haunt the next day, for as yet I had met with no adventure, not having seen a living being on the route. Accordingly the next morning I started out; it was about five or six miles from the city to where I entered the chaparral, having to make a circuitous route around a small lake, or laguna, and wind my way through patches of chaparral and open ground, before I came to the dense mass. Thus the entrance to the hollow pass was concealed from the lake shore, and only discovered by chance in the first place; but having a good horse under me, I was soon at the entrance of the passage. I was not afraid of wild animals, although jaguars and American tigers, very formidable animals, abounded in that region, especially the latter; but the brush was too thick to have any serious apprehensions of that, and my only fear was warlike men. I was satisfied that the slight trails that I had seen the day before were made by men, as the beasts could never have cleared them out. I cautiously continued my ride that day, I should think about eight miles, when I came to where a similar road crossed the one I was in, at right angles.

Not having seen anything larger than a lizard in all my ride, I turned my horse's head once more towards the camp. I had retraced my steps about four or five miles, when I came to one of those little paths closed by a dry bush, which nearly concealed it. I made up my mind to venture on an exploration of its mystery. Accordingly I hitched my horse and removed the obstacle. Following the little trail, I had advanced about one hundred yards, when all of a sudden I emerged into an open space or clearing, and was surprised to see before me an adobe house, out-sheds, etc., and a field of about two acres under a high state of cultivation. There were nice corn, sweet potatoes, beans, melons, etc. A large blood-hound was in sight, but he was chained; he barked, growled, and made a desperate effort to get at me; his noisy demonstrations brought a man out of the house, who was, as near as I could guess, about fifty years of age, and to all appearances much more intellectual and fairer than the general race of Mexicans. He was unarmed and seemed friendly; I asked him by motions and imperfect Spanish for a drink of water; he got a gourd, and, stepping to a well, drew the water with an earthen bucket, having a hole on each side, in which a rope was fixed as a bail. I noticed that the well was about twelve feet deep, and the water seemed purer than that which we generally got at Tampico. He maintained a gentlemanly but dignified demeanor, and I could see that his astonishment was equal to my own. I returned to my horse and made my way home to camp, and again reported.

After this I daily prosecuted my chaparral rides alone, as before, as none seemed to care for such adventures. I not only went over my old grounds, but followed up the newly discovered tunnel in an easterly direction until I came out into open ground at Altamira, fourteen miles from Tampico, and afterwards followed the other branch in an easterly direction until I came out at the pilot station at the mouth of the Tampico River, on the Gulf of Mexico; but it was much farther than to reach the same point by the regular Tampico road; however, it was so much cooler and pleasanter than riding in the hot sun that it became almost my daily resort while riding for my health. I now began to prospect my foot-paths more thoroughly, and I found quite a numerous settlement a short distance back in the chaparral from the main tunnel or road; but after prosecuting this source of amusement for some time, I had occasion to cut it short. I had from time to time penetrated the small foot-paths, and visited the strange people who seemed buried from the outer world. They seldom went beyond their small domains; this idea was strengthened by the fact that I never met one in the main tunnel, or hollow pass; each place had its rocks and fixtures for grinding up corn for *tortillas*, and all that a Mexican in his simple mode of life would covet, including oranges, bananas, and plantains.

But, as I said, I had occasion to cut short my visits to these strange hermitages; it happened that one day I followed one of the little paths to an inclosure, and found the occupant with a long cane knife, the blade of which was about the length of an ordinary sword blade. He seemed to be hacking away at some chaparral that was invading his domain; and he had two ferocious blood-hounds with him. As he saw me approaching, he seemed much excited, and at a word from him the two dogs came bounding at me with their big red mouths open. I dared not retreat further than where the trail opened into the clearing, as they were too near upon me to allow of escape to my horse; I accordingly placed myself in the entrance of the trail, facing the enemy. I drew my revolver, and as the foremost one advanced to within about fifteen feet of me, I shot him. He fell and began yelping, turning round and round upon the ground; at this the other retreated a few paces. When the Mexican saw that I had fired, seeming to think that my piece was empty, he rushed at me with the big-cane knife; and, encouraged by the manner of his master, the other dog came to the attack. I again fired, but missed. I cocked and fired the third shot, and wounded the second dog. The Mexican seemed surprised to see me keep shooting, apparently having no idea of my weapon. He halted, and I leveled my revolver on him, motioning him back with the other hand. He evidently had come to the conclusion that I could shoot as often as I pleased, and he beat a retreat, leaving his two com-rades slaughtered on the field of battle.

Very willing to leave him master of the field, I mounted my horse at the main alley, and soon reached quarters at Tampico. I related my adventure of the day, and curiosity regarding these strange people ran so high that we made inquiries of the people of Tampico as to who or what they were, but they seemed ignorant of their very existence. About this time Capt. C. L. Wight, of Company A, concluded to accompany me on my chaparral ride; he said he would go out with me in the morning, as he had an appointment at the pilot sta-tion at two o'clock P. M. of that day, and that he must return in time to keep it. We started out and he pene-trated the chaparral with me for about six miles, when he drew rein and said, " Norton, this is wonderful, but for God's sake let us return! I don't believe that white man's horse's hoofs ever pressed this soil before; and you recollect my appointment at the pilot station." I begged him to give me just one-half hour more of his company, assuring him that he should be at the station in time, as the day was yet young. He consented, and before the half hour had elapsed I brought him out to the pilot station on one branch of my tunnel. You may imagine his surprise at this, as he expected that we would have to return to Tampico, where he would take the road to the station. The captain told the officers at the station of all the explorations I had made on my chaparral rides, with his own peculiar embellishments, until he quite lionized me and made me ashamed of myself. I am not unmindful of the fact that this recital savors strongly of fiction; but I have given the simple facts as they occurred, and am satisfied that this will meet the eyes of some who can vouch for its correctness.

Information reached Tampico one evening that a noted guerrilla chief with his band had made a descent upon Tankesneca, a small trading-post some sixty or seventy miles in the interior, and were robbing the inhabitants of that place. .Our commander was resolved to send out a detachment to quell them, and Company I was so fortunate as to be selected for that duty. All was hurry and bustle in our camp, as we were preparing to leave in the morning. The expedition was a leap in the dark, for all we knew. We had to ascend the Panuco River in large dug-outs, to the mouth of the Tamosee (by our geography called the River Lemon), and then follow up that stream. A lofty butte stood far in the west—a spire-like peak. I had often looked upon it in the blue distance as it reflected the last rays of the setting sun. It was pointed out as the terminus of our trip; we were, however, provided with a guide. I say *we*, for I left my quartermaster duties with my quartermaster-sergeant, and on a four-day leave of absence, as a volunteer, made one of the number.

The officers consisted of Capt. A. Harvey, Lieut.

S. G. Conkling (now Major Conkling), Lieut. Hugh
Fullerton, and myself; although two or three other
officers accompanied us, they took no command.
Though Capt. A. Harvey was nominally in command,
I don't believe he was much counted on, as I received
instructions to closely observe the route, and to make
careful measurement of depth of water, calculation of
distance, topography of country, and report on my return.
Captain Harvey and Fullerton constituted one officers'
mess, and Conkling and myself constituted another. We
took rations for four days; believing we could make the
trip in that time, and my leave of absence extended no
longer. Conkling and myself took along one bottle of
brandy, and Harvey and Fullerton supplied themselves
with twelve bottles; and I may as well admit here that
from some misunderstanding there wasn't the very best
of feeling between the parties; we went in pairs. All
was ready, and we were soon on board and sailing up
the Panuco River, our propelling force being awkward
Mexican paddles and setting poles.

We ran up the Panuco to the mouth of the Tamosee
in about three hours. The country on both sides of the
river for two or three miles was low valley land, and
extremely fertile, occupied by a mixed race of Mexicans and Indians. A great portion of the land was
cultivated in sugar-cane. I was told they planted about
once in seven years, and as fast as the cane was cut it
sprouted up from the root and produced another crop.
But, like Tampico and neighboring towns, it was very
sickly. The alligators were lying all along the shores,
basking in the sun, looking like so many old gray logs;
rolling into the water with a splash at our approach, they

would disappear, leaving but a whirling, bubbling eddy behind. The shores seemed to be entirely composed of vast deposits of mussel shells. On reaching the Tamosec we found a bar of these shells across the mouth of the river, having but about two and a half feet of water over it.

The stream was running like a mill-race; it ran with such rapidity that we consumed the balance of the day in getting our canoes over the bar and into the deep water above. The shells were so yielding that we displaced many tons of them with our paddles in propelling the canoes up the swift current over the bar. I saw that the wheels of a steamboat constantly worked would soon, together with the action of the water, remove the obstruction to navigation, and so reported on my return; upon which report the authorities at Tampico acted, and the *Red Wing*, one of our steamboats, proved the correctness of my views, and in about three weeks afterward ran to Tankesneca.

After all were safely over the bar, we made preparations for camping, Conkling and myself occupying a small wall tent. While Captain Harvey and Fullerton, and their convivial crowd, camped at a short distance above us. They had a regular spree, and made the night hideous by their jubilant hurrahs and laughter. Next morning Captain Harvey's orderly came to our tent and wanted to know if we had any liquor; that the captain was very sick and wanted some. Conkling replied, " Tell Captain Harvey that he cannot get a drop here."

Our hasty meal over, we were soon aboard and underway. The stream was smooth, deep, and sluggish, although the water was sweet and generally pretty clear. There was on either side of the stream a wide and fertile valley, as on the Panuco. Back of the bottom-land the country became undulating; and with a gradual rise became hilly, and finally in the distance rose into lofty mountains. This is the Sierra Madrè country, and close to the water it makes a picture that would baffle all description. No pen or pencil could portray its native beauty—one must see it to appreciate it.

But I must attempt to give the reader some faint idea of what I saw. Along each shore there was a species of reed, the stocks from one to four inches through, some of them perhaps more, and growing to the height of seventy or eighty feet. Up these reeds ran flowering vines of all kinds and descriptions, to their very tops; and over these hung long festoons, the heft of which bent the tops of the reeds toward the stream. These vines were perennial, were clad in flowers of every color and hue, and appeared as though planted by art; once in every sixteen or twenty feet a squash vine could be seen running to the top, mingling with the other vines, and forming the festoons spoken of; about a foot apart were hanging little yellow squashes, some four inches in diameter, looking like so many golden bells, and wherever there happened to be a small space in the reeds, there would be a most lovely and picturesque bower, the recess being completely covered with vines. This canopy wholly sheltered us from the sun, and continued for many miles.

Emerging from the scene just described, the face of the country considerably changed; the inhabitants were very few, the valley was narrow, and the wooded country came clear down to the stream. On the right bank was a dense forest of banyan trees, with trunks tied together; a limb would project twenty or thirty feet from the trunk, from the under side of which were pendants reaching down, all the way of a size until they reached the ground, when they would catch the earth, take root, and in their turn form trunks, throw out limbs, and then their pendants as before. And thus the forest was so completely tied together that the ax-men could only fell a tree by cutting it off at the base and, then climbing up and cutting ligatures until it was severed from its surroundings.

The forest on both sides of the river seemed alive with game; the armadillos swarmed upon the shore, looking like pigs with shells on their backs; parrots of several kinds, and paroquets without number made the woods' resound with their incessant chattering. Monkeys of three or four species could be seen capering in the trees and cutting all the antics peculiar to their nature; wild turkeys were in great abundance, to which our boys helped themselves without stint; wild hogs abounded, and were next in ferocity to the jaguar or tiger.

There being no current along that portion of the river, the boys made a good run until about two o'clock in the afternoon, when we were informed that it was much farther by water than by land—the river making a large bend. It was therefore concluded that we would march across the country, and leave a sufficient guard to protect the canoes. On the trip around by water, Lieutenant Conkling took charge of the canoes, while I marched across the country with the men. Harvey got a horse and found himself able to ride. . I took charge of the men, and commanded the march across the arid plain, with the sun pouring down its scorching rays upon us. I had been led to believe that a three hours' march would bring us to Tankesneca; but our men had not had any exercise on foot for four or five months, and some of them having been in the hospital and not having fully recovered their strength, this, with the intense heat, before an hour's march caused many of them to lag, the weaker falling to the rear. I then changed the order and marched the rear in front, keeping the stronger back; but their canteens began to give out, and then came suffering from thirst, and no water on the plains. Finally, I found it impossible to push the men, and the last hour before sunset we did not make to exceed one mile; all the weaker men were exhausted to that degree that I was compelled to camp on the open plain without food or water.

The next morning at day-break we renewed the march, and arrived at Tankesneca about seven o'clock, taking the people by surprise, and the guerrilla chief prisoner, together with some of his men; but I soon let the men go and held on to their leader. The canoes ran most of the night, and arrived soon after us. Captain Keneday, who was also of the quartermaster department, and a volunteer in the expedition, walked with me to the river, and while looking across at a great distance I saw an animal; I called his attention to it, and remarked that it was a deer. He laughed at me and said it was a calf. I knew better; I could see that wild motion of the head, differing from all tame animals. He had his carbine in his hand, and I asked him to take a shot at it any way, but he declined to do so. I then

asked the loan of his gun, and cocking, drew a sight
about two feet above the animal's shoulders, and fired; it
disappeared, and I declared that I had killed it. Calling a couple of the men, I got a canoe, crossed the
river, and made as straight to the place as I could.
After a short search, we found the animal—a fine, large
buck—lying dead. I had made a chance shot, shooting
him through the heart; and he had dropped in his tracks.
We brought the deer in, dressed and cooked it, and the
fresh meat was very acceptable.

While the men were resting I had an opportunity of
looking about me, and formed some idea of the place.
My first discovery was that the Tamosee had entirely
changed its character at that place. From a deep, sluggish stream it was transformed into a rapid mountain
torrent; a ledge of rocks was entirely across it, making
a natural dam about six feet high, forming a splendid
water-power. Around us was a large and fertile valley,
and about two miles distant, like a vast tower, stood the
butte, the famous landmark toward which we had been
traveling for so long a time. There was a green, grassy
slope all around it for about half a mile from the pin-
nacle of rock. The slope where it joined the base of
the column was probably five hundred feet above the
level of the plain. Then the mighty giant rose so perpendicularly that no one could ascend it; in fact, it was
the most remarkable formation of the kind that I ever
saw—similar in form to the granite columns at Slippery
Ford, in the Sierra Nevada, only much higher and with
greater uniformity of shape.

Tankesneca was a collection of rude huts, occupied
by a half-civilized mixed breed of Mexicans and In-

dians, surrounding the trading-post of Darky & Co., of
Tampico. The Indians were engaged in bringing down
logwood, black ebony, and other valuable timber from
the mountains. They would clear the sap from the
sticks, and pack them on their backs to the river at this
point, and from here they were transported in large
dug-outs down the river to Tampico, the market. I also
learned that the mountains abounded in Mexican cedar,
and also contained some silver mines. The climate
seemed delightful; it was just sufficiently elevated to be
above the sand-flies, mosquitoes, and all other vermin
that infested the low country. Neither yellow fever nor
black vomito ever reached there, and all in all I think,
by nature, it was the most delightful place I have ever
visited. In fact I was so taken with the place, that I
fully intended that in case I lived to see the war ended
Tankesneca should be my home. I learned that Darky &
Co. had a grant of seven leagues, including the best and
greater portion of the valley, and the site of Tankesneca.
I was further informed that the grant could be purchased
for ten thousand dollars. I attempted, on my return to
Illinois, at the close of the war, to get up a colony to
settle at Tankesneca. But from the sparse settlements
of the West and the great inducements there offered to
settlers, I found my project a failure; and I dared not
return alone. As near as I can remember the points of
the compass now, it lies a little north of west of Tampico, and the butte referred to can always be seen from
the latter place in fair weather. It is in the State of
Tamaulipas, and near the Potosi line.

CHAPTER XIII.

MEMOIRS OF THE MEXICAN WAR—CONTINUED.

AFTER having straightened matters at Tankesneca as well as was possible in the time we were permitted to remain there, we took to our dug-out at about two o'clock P. M. of the fourth day from Tampico, and commenced our descent of the river. A severe catastrophe now befell us: we had run out of rations, and the country was so sparsely settled along the river in that part that it was difficult foraging; but at night-fall we tied up at the bank of the river where there were a couple of small ranches, made friends with the inhabitants, and set the women to work making *tortillas;* with the scanty supply they furnished by working all night, the next morning we were enabled to advance on our homeward trip. No incident of note occurred the next day, and about an hour before sundown we again tied up for the night at a small ranch. This was the fifth day out from Tampico, and the next day at two o'clock P. M. Captain Keneday and myself were to receive five hundred wild mules, at Tampico, for the United States Government, and receipt for the same. No one there was authorized to do it. What was to be done? We did not expect to be absent more than four days, and that was the extent of our leave of absence; it was impossible to reach Tampico in less than two days by the river. General Gates was of the regular army, a harsh, strict disciplinarian, and did not like the volunteers. On our part there was no love lost; we had asked no odds and expected no favors, and if we had we would have been disappointed,

as it seemed to give him infinite pleasure to make us
toe the mark.   A failure to comply with the duties
before us would subject us to court-martial, and I had
come to the conclusion to be in Tampico at two o'clock
P. M. the next day or die in the attempt.   I made this
determination known to Captain Keneday; and told him
I intended to procure a guide and horse and attempt to
make the trip cross the country.   Learning from the
Mexicans where we landed that it was eighty miles by
land to Tampico, Keneday remarked that I shouldn't go
alone; that our liabilities were equal, and our dangers
should be shared.   I remonstrated against his risking
his life on my wild venture, but he was firm in his purpose to go with me, and our arrangements were soon
made.   We provided ourselves with two revolvers each,
with a carbine and a heavy service saber, and thus
loaded with iron we jumped into a small Indian canoe,
with a half-breed in each end, who in consideration of a
fee agreed to land us at the next point, where we could
procure horses and a guide.

The canoe was a little toppling thing, and didn't seem
capable of carrying over two persons, but our guides
kept the balance, and a little after dark we arrived at
what they called the Point.   But we were doomed to a
disappointment here, for there was nothing at the Point
but squalid young ones and cross dogs.   The children
informed us that the folks had gone to the Rancho
Ratonus, to a fandango.   We inquired of our guides
how large a place Ratonus was; they informed us that it
was but small.   We then directed them to lead on
to Rancho Ratonus, which they said was two leagues.
We told them that any attempt to betray us would cost

8

them their lives, and they set forward on a dog-trot, through an open wood at first, then merging into a chaparral route, similar to that discovered at Tampico. We continued our double-quick for nearly two hours over a level country, uninhabited and interspersed with open wood and chaparral alternately. We made a sudden turn to the right, and the Rancho Ratonus lay before us, with a fandango in full blast. There were from eighty to a hundred Mexicans and as many women whirling in the maze of the waltz.

Our guides suddenly disappeared in the crowd, and without their pay. A great confusion ensued—a hurrying and screaming of the women, and men going and coming; the music ceased and in fifteen minutes there was not a woman there. It was "presto change;" instead of the jolly dance and music that greeted our first appearance on the scene, there was now only armed men, with dark brows and glaring eyes, and gestures that would indicate that our dooms were sealed, at least in the estimation of that crowd; and I began most seriously to concur in that opinion myself, for in every face I could read that of my executioner. We were now completely surrounded by nearly a hundred of as well-appointed, dark-visaged cut-throats as I ever saw, and all armed; some with escopets, some with swords, and others with long cane knives. Their declaration of war on us was so unequivocal that we made no secret of our intentions, each drawing and cocking a revolver and facing in opposite directions—we were determined to sell our lives for the greatest possible number of dead Mexicans. The most superficial glance at the faces of the demons that surrounded us showed that no quarter could be looked for. The crowd was so thick around us that they could not shoot without killing some of their own men. Should a rush be made upon us of course we would be overpowered. To prevent this we told them to keep back, and each with a cocked revolver in one hand and a carbine in the other, · admonished them that the first who advanced would be likely to get hurt, let the issue be what it might.

We remained in this unenviable position for fifteen or twenty minutes, when an idea crossed my brain which I must ever believe saved our lives. I said, Have you an alcalde here? They replied in the affirmative. I told them I wanted to speak with him. A little fat, greasy old Mexican came forward and announced himself that functionary. I informed him that we were American officers; that our command had encamped at that river, and were to be at that place at ten o'clock in the morning, and that he would be held responsible for our safety; if any harm befell us there, that the entire place would be massacred; that we wanted horses and saddles and a guide to conduct us to Tampico, for which we would liberally pay. He retired into the crowd, and after a few moments I noticed that those human devils increased the distance between us by falling back a little, which seemed to be a favorable omen.

In a little time the alcalde again made his appearance (and no doubt he had been consulting our treacherous guides as to the truth of my statements about the troops); he said they had the horses, but he did not think he could get the saddles. I replied that it was rather singular as large a place as Ratonus could not furnish three saddles. He said he would try and procure them,

and again left us.   In something more than an hour the
guide appeared with the alcalde.   They brought a
mustang for Keneday, an active, spirited, nervous beast;
and for me, a very fine-appearing mule, large for a
Mexican and very sleek and fat.   As soon as I mounted,
I saw that he was a slow, lazy animal, and I remarked
to Keneday that we must look out, that there was more
treachery to be feared.   "They intend to separate us,
and this last hour that they have kept us waiting is not
for nothing."   I then drew my saber, encased in the old
steel-ringed scabbard, brought the flat of my weapon a
few times across the rump of my mule and waked him
up.   We rode from Ratonus, and I kept repeating the
operation with the mule until he was fairly aroused.
Every time the scabbard would ring, the mule would
jump for dear life.

After we were fairly out of Ratonus we came to a
halt and examined our guide; he was a young fellow,
not more than twenty years of age, and, like many others
of the inhabitants of those parts, a mixture of Mexican
and Indian.   We told him that any movement on his
part engendering a suspicion that he intended to betray
us, or any attempt to desert us, would most assuredly
cost him his life; but if he took us through to Altamira
all safe, we would give him five dollars extra.   Through
fear of punishment on the one hand and hope of gain
on the other, the fellow seemed to identify himself with
our cause.   He then told us that the mule on which I
was riding was very old, and he did not think it could
stand it to go to Altamira in the way that we expected
to ride.   We now understood our situation so far as our
guide was concerned, but I could not divest my mind of

the suspicion that there was some treachery to be appre-
hended; and I had the thing put up in my own mind
in this way: that the story of the men coming there in
the morning was fully believed by them, as they had
undoubtedly consulted with our treacherous guide, who
knew that the force of which I spoke was on the river
bank encamped, and as to their further intentions of
course these fellows were ignorant; hence they expected
them there at ten o'clock the next morning, and it would
not do to murder us in the little town, for fear of the
punishment threatened. And to avoid this, and still
accomplish their purposes, I believed that the last hour
they kept us waiting for our horses was employed in
preparing an ambuscade somewhere on our road. We
hurried on, these thoughts occupying my mind, when
the report of a gun was heard far in the rear; of course
it was too far off to have been fired at us, and I at once
made up my mind that it was fired as a signal, and
remarked so to Keneday. We must then have been
four or five miles on our journey from Ratonus, and we
had advanced about a quarter of a mile after the report
of the gun when Keneday remarked to me:—

" Do you see that fellow ? "

I replied that I saw something. Keneday said he had
just rode behind a clump of brush to the left of the road.
The old scabbard rang, and sword in hand I charged
around the brush, and sure enough there was a man.
As I came up to him he took off his hat, and in the
cringing manner peculiar to his race, said, " Señor." I
asked him in *my best* Mexican (which, no doubt, was
bad enough) what he was doing there. He said he was
hunting his horses. I remarked that twelve o'clock at

night was a singular time to be hunting horses, and directed him to dismount, which he did. On examining him I found no arms excepting his sheath knife, and a very long lariat on his horse. I then examined his animal as well as I could and came to the conclusion that it was a very good one, consequently I made a trade, and got the long lariat to boot. I mounted the horse and directed the prisoner to mount the mule; marched him out in the road, and directed the guide to ride ahead. Keneday rode next the guide, my prisoner next, and I brought up the rear.

We rode in this order about half a mile, where a grove of small trees appeared on our left, when all of a sudden there was a general rush, rattling of arms, and excitement, close to where we were passing. The old scabbard rang, and my horse sprang forward; I gave the old mule a whack, as I came up to him; he sprang aside, and away we went, but we presently got a volley by way of salute from the rear, followed by the clatter of horses' hoofs. We put our horses to the top of their speed for the next hour, having discharged our carbines in the rear at the first sound of hoofs behind us. We now reached a deep, sluggish stream, the ferryman, house, and boat all on the opposite bank. We hallooed and awoke the ferryman, who soon took us across in a dug-out, swimming our horses. When once across, we seized the canoe and, making the ferryman and guide assist, drew it out of the water, and up the bank so far from the water that a single man could not get it back in an hour. We then thought of tying the ferryman, but time was precious with us, and we concluded on the whole that it would do very well as it was.

We continued our trip for about two hours unmolested, when we came to another stream (or perhaps the same) with a ferry like the first. As in the first instance, we got across and secured the boat. We now rode on feeling very safe. There were no towns and but few inhabitants along the route we were pursuing, and presently the wolves began to howl as though they would howl a man off his horse. I knew then there were no Mexicans around, and those brindle devils, for once, made music to my ears.

It was now about three o'clock in the morning, and at eight we reached Altamira without further incident worthy of note. We met our friend Major Jerolt just in time to take a nice breakfast with him. The major wanted to know where we had dropped from. We told him we had come from Rancho Ratonus, relating the whole adventure. The major exclaimed, " The Rancho Ratonus! Well, the devil surely protects his own! Why, that Rancho Ratonus is the worst guerrilla hole in all Mexico! It is not two weeks since I was forced to send out two companies of cavalry to quiet that same Rancho Ratonus. They were robbing and murdering their own inhabitants, and how you ever escaped with your lives is a miracle." Refreshed with a good breakfast and a cigar, we were again prepared for action. We discharged our guide, and paid him off with the five dollar bonus promised him. Major Jerolt furnished us a couple of fresh horses and we arrived at Tampico at one o'clock P. M., received and receipted for the mules, and thus ended one of the most dangerous adventures ever undertaken by me in Mexico.

On my return from the exciting expedition narrated

previously, I found that there were extensive preparations going on for the great annual festival, or fandango,
which was to be held at Tampico Viejo (or Pueblo Viejo).
Crowds gathered from all parts of the States of Tamaulipas and Vera Cruz at that once famous but now
ruined city.   Accordingly when the day came for the cele-
bration, some forty or fifty of the officers of our command
stationed at Tampico visited the scene of the festivities.
This ancient town is situated about eight miles from
Tampico, at the foot of Lake. Tampico, and is reached
from Tampico by boats or small crafts, up the outlet
of the lake into the Tamaulipas (or Tampico) River.   It
is said, but I don't know with how much truth, that
when Pueblo Viejo was a flourishing city large crafts
could easily reach its docks.   The story is at least probable, for the only obstruction at the present day is a vast
bar of the mussel shells which abound in that country.
But at the present day there is a swift current running
from the lake into the river, a distance of about four
miles.   The lake must lie ten or fifteen feet higher
than the river, and the same distance above the Gulf of
Mexico.

The town of Pueblo Viejo is situated upon a narrow
neck of land running between the gulf and Tampico
Lake, with a large level country lying to the north,
interspersed with lakes, rivers, and chaparral; while to
the south and east it is protected from the coast by a
point of land, rising several hundred feet above the level
of the sea.   The site of the town is from ten to fifty feet
above the lake, commencing near the water and sloping
back to the hills; but the acclivity is so gentle that it
would hardly be noticed, and the whole town is situated in

a cove resembling that of Cincinnati, only on a much
larger scale; for everything there indicates that some
day far back in the dim past, Pueblo Viejo was the great
emporium of an intelligent and highly civilized people
On every side lie the evidences of that civilization;
ancient ruins of what at some day had been noble edi-
fices, but the only evidence of the time when they
flourished was the mass of trees and shrubbery that
covered the ground where they once stood. I remember
in one place a large oak stood with its massive trunk on
one side of a wall that was its only rest; its roots ran
through and descended on the other side some four or
five feet to meet the ground—the tree was two and a
half to three feet through. Next to the hill lies a
massive pile, with heavy stone columns lying in every
direction; I had no means of ascertaining the extent of
the superstructure, but it was immense. I cannot pretend to describe the magnitude of this ruined city, as I
never had sufficient time for investigation; and I do not
presume to say that, like Pompeii, it was either swallowed
up by an earthquake or entirely covered by the hand
of time. Out of the ruins of that once famous city the
present inhabitants have erected themselves dwellings;
and Pueblo Viejo now contains about three thousand
inhabitants, who wander over its evidences of former
magnificence with about as much thought or inquiry as
that other portion of the animal race which, with long ears
and docile mien, crops the grass that springs up between
the disjointed rocks strewn over the ground.

There is one relic of the ancient greatness of Pueblo
Viejo that seems to bid defiance to decay—that is the
extensive baths; a stream of pure water is brought from

the hills and emptied into a series of stone vats, twelve
to fifteen feet wide and about thirty long. They number about forty, and each is situated a little lower than
the other, say six inches, and as the water fills the upper
one, the masonry being a little the lowest next to the
adjoining reservoir, or vat, with the two outer walls
higher, it flows to the next, and so on till they are all
filled, being six or seven feet deep. There is a rock
terrace, or pavement, about twenty feet wide, running the
whole length of these reservoirs and below the top of
the water wall about three feet. Standing on this terrace, or pavement, were frequently hundreds of Mexican
women and girls, some washing their linen, but the
major portion engaged with large brown earthenware
vessels, holding from five to seven gallons, smaller at the
base than at the center, bulging outward, then contract-
ing to about eight inches across the top. These contained
corn, soaked in alkali to start the hulls. They fill the
vessel with water, set it on the pavement, and, putting
both feet into the small opening, perform a regular tread-
mill operation; they stamp away until the hulls are
loosed from the corn, then set the vessel on the massive
stone wall, about two and a half feet thick, making a
solid base of operations, where they wash the corn; it is
rubbed and put through a great number of washings,
until it is cleansed and all hulls removed; then it is deemed
ready to be manufactured into *tortillas*. This practice
has continued upon the wall for such a length of time that
there are holes worn into the solid granite rocks several
inches deep, presenting the appearance of mortars. But
I have indulged in describing the mouldering ruins of
what was once a great city beyond my first intention,
and I will now abandon them and come back to life.

I started in to tell of the great fandango, or festival, to come off at Pueblo Viejo. First, imagine a very large and smooth plaza, with two rows of booths around the outer edges, presenting everything in the shape of edibles and drinkables in the Mexican market, and the balance of the plaza covered by awnings of palmetto leaves, so as to shelter it from the sun by day and shield the lamps from the wind at night. Next, the music-stands were arranged at suitable distances, so to accommodate the whole grounds, with the gambling tables. The music generally consisted of violins, guitars, and some other stringed instruments, but what they lacked in variety they made up in quantity. On this occasion I suppose there were not less than seven or eight thousand and perhaps more, men, women and children of all ages mingling together, seeming to have but one object in view, and that enjoyment. It was a pleasing spectacle to see thousands at once in the giddy whirl of the waltz, and such waltzing I never saw before. The Mexicans, both men and women, excel in the grace of that art. Some were dancing, some eating, some drinking, and some gaming; in the latter amusement, the padres took a prominent part. Monte cards and dice were the principal agents used; but there were dozens of different games that I never observed before nor since. Little boys, five, six, and seven years old, would be seated on mats with the regular games of monte, playing where the stakes were stubs of cigars or some trifling trinket, while among the more aristocratic the old don would be risking several ounces on the turn of a card. But I have noticed that in all the playing that I ever saw at monte, the "cabala" is the favorite card with the Mexican, and he seems to risk his money with more confidence on it than on any other card.

The police regulations are conducted with a great deal of propriety and vigor. During this fandango, a noted robber chief found his way into the crowd, but was recognized by the police. I saw quite a rush and excitement of parties running to a certain point. Curiosity prompted me to follow, as well as several other officers. On arriving at the place I discovered a regular sword combat between two expert swordsmen; they seemed to be about equal in strength and skill, and each evidently meant death to his antagonist. There did not seem to be any one inclined to interfere, and the contest was long and desperate; both had received several slight wounds; finally one made a desperate lunge at his opponent, which was skillfully parried by the other, and before the thrusting party could fairly recover, the other ran him through the body, and in fact shoved the hilt of his sword nearly to the breast of his foe, who fell, the blood spurting from his mouth and nostrils, and expired without uttering a word or even a moan. I then for the first time got an opportunity to take a fair look at the successful gladiator, and to my astonishment there stood before us as fine a native of Erin's green isle as ever crossed the briny ocean. Light blue eyes, a rather florid complexion, light chestnut hair, sandy whiskers, with full red lips, and a certain undefiable air that is impossible to mistake in a regular Irish countenance. Some of our officers addressed him in English, of which he did not seem to understand a single word; but through an interpreter we learned that he claimed to be a Mexican, was born in the country, and looked upon his ancestors as

Mexicans, without any knowledge of their ever having emigrated from any other country. He stood very high in the police force, and seemed to be very proud of his last achievement; from what we could gather from the alcalde and other leading men of the place, they had long been trying to capture the slain man, he being one of the most desperate characters that had for a long time visited the neighborhood. The fandango closed in eight days, and with it I will close my description of Pueblo Viejo; notwithstanding I know friend Conkling, could he see me, would ask why I neglected to tell about the castor-bean stalk, or rather tree, beneath whose shade we lay; but my answer is, that we then agreed that it would not do to tell, and hence I leave it out among many other things that would be treated as absurdities by those unacquainted with that climate.

CHAPTER XIV.

MEMOIRS OF THE MEXICAN WAR—CONTINUED.

WE had all returned from Pueblo Viejo, each one having his private adventures of the fandango treasured up to communicate to some of his favorite companions-in-arms, which was calculated to swell the budget of camp news, when it was announced that a great cock-fight was to come off the next evening, and that Colonel Derusa of the Louisiana regiment, and Lieutenant-Colonel Marks, who were both sporting men, had each procured a very fine fowl, and that the birds were to be pitted against each other on that occasion. I walked into the cockpit in company with Captain

Harvey, and saw that the two cocks referred to had been fitted out with sharp steel gafts, and were already far advanced in their deadly combat when we entered. I noticed that Colonel Derusa's bird was the larger, and to all appearance fresh compared with the other, and would undoubtedly be the victor in the fight; every time they came together and made a pass at each other, Colonel Marks' bird would drop to the earth as though he were dead, and would come to time badly and drop again as though entirely exhausted. Captain Harvey, who had been indulging pretty freely, insisted on betting me a dollar on the result of the fight. I thought it would be almost like stealing his money to bet, as I looked upon Marks' bird as being "a dead cock in the pit;" yet he insisted, and as I had never won a bet in my life, I just thought I would win one, so I told him I would bet on Colonel Derusa's rooster. The fight went on for about fifteen minutes, Marks' bird falling and lying apparently exhausted, waiting for the men having charge of him to set him on his pins before he was ruled out of time. After many passes of this kind they came together, and Marks' bird drove both his gafts through the head of his opponent, killing him on the spot. So I lost my small bet, and learned the lesson that it will not always do to bet against dead things.

As I have commenced this chapter with an anecdote, I believe I will continue it by relating one or two that I have heretofore not noticed. When we had been in Tampico about six weeks, an Irishman, a private in Company A, got into a row with a Mexican; an altercation ensued, and the Irishman killed the Mexican; was arrested, and imprisoned to await trial. Our judiciary was organized by adopting the laws of Louisiana; and it was farther determined that neither Mexican nor private soldier could sit on the jury for the trial of the Irishman, who had been indicted for murder; hence commissioned officers of the army were the only eligible jurors. The jury was impaneled and sworn, and the case proceeded, the judge-advocate for the people, and Col. S. G. Hicks for the defendant. Witnesses were produced for the people, proving the killing, and among other testimony, a Mexican swore that the prisoner spoke good Spanish. The defense offered evidence tending to show that the killing was in self-defense.

After the testimony was in, the attorneys made their arguments; and when Colonel Hicks came to the part of the Mexican's testimony where he testified that the prisoner spoke good Spanish, Hick's remarked: "And they swear that he spoke good Spanish; I suppose that he talked Spanish about as well as one of my cavalrymen did who was out with me last year; the fellow's horse had escaped; seeing a Mexican sawing wood on the side of the street, he exclaimed: 'Halloo! *hombre*, did you see a bobtailed *cabello vamosing* down the street, without any saddle on him?' 'No intende' (I do not understand), was the response. The soldier indignantly replied: 'Confound you, can't you understand your own language?'—forgetting that he had used but three words of Spanish in the whole lingo." He then went on to show that the soldier came from Ireland about three years before, and had worked in the Galena lead mines until he volunteered to come to Mexico; that he was an uneducated man, and probably never saw a Mexican in his life before landing in Tampico, and at the date of the killing had been in Mexico about six weeks. After deliberation, we came to the conclusion that the Mexican got killed in a drunken row, and as the United States Government was paying the soldier seven dollars a month to kill Mexicans, it would not be quite the right thing to hang the fellow for killing one of them, even in a drunken row, hence we returned a verdict of "not guilty." On the jury I made the acquaintance of a gentleman named Tracy; he was adjutant-general, attached to General Gates' staff; in fact we became very intimate, and of him I shall have more to say presently.

I have heretofore remarked that General Gates was of the regular army, a great stickler for military discipline, and most cordially hated the volunteer service; consequently we did not entertain a great amount of love for him. As for myself, I procured a copy of the Regulations of the United States Army, and made myself thoroughly acquainted with my rights and obligations under them, fully intending to discharge every duty enjoined by them, and as fully determined to submit to no impositions on the part of others. While these feelings were yet being nursed by me, a favorable opportunity occurred to beard the old lion and show him that I wasn't the tamest of beasts myself. I was sitting in my quarters one day, when a detail was served on me; I did not read it, supposing it was to act as officer of the day. I dressed myself to obey the detail, and walked down to meet the relief. On my arrival I found Lieutenant Sampson—a second lieutenant—there to take his position as officer of the day. I turned to the adjutant, and asked him what it meant; he replied, "You are detailed as officer of the guard!" I consigned both him and his detail to the shades, turned upon my heel and returned to my quarters and wrote a note to Colonel Hicks that I had disobeyed his orders, but would be found at my quarters. They did not keep me long in suspense, for in about an hour an order was brought me by an orderly to appear before General Gates at four o'clock P. M., to answer a charge of disobedience to a superior officer, and to consider myself under arrest until the matter was disposed of. I immediately divested myself of my sword, and attired in a common soldier's uniform, without any insignia of rank, promptly at four o'clock was at the general's quarters; but none too prompt, as I found the general and my accusers all present and ready to proceed. The old general called out, "Where is the prisoner?" I stepped forward and saluted. He said, "Why do you appear in that garb? Where are your uniform and insignia of rank?" I replied that I was under arrest on charges which, if sustained, would reduce me to this uniform and rank.

GATES—"What is your present rank, sir?"

"First lieutenant in the line, captain by virtue of quartermaster's appointment."

GATES—"Now, sir, what were your reasons for disobeying the orders of your colonel?"

"If permitted I will give my reasons, sir."

GATES (peremptorily)—"I want your reason, sir."

I again replied that I would give my reasons if permitted. I had noticed that my friend Tracy seemed very nervous and affrighted on my account, fidgeting in his seat and giving other demonstrations of uneasiness, and seeing the old general getting in a passion, remarked to him that perhaps I might have more than one reason.

9

Thereupon the old general growled, "Then give me your reasons, sir."

I replied I was acting quartermaster of the command, and could not be compelled to do field duty.

GENERAL—"How is this, Colonel Hicks?" The colonel replied that it was true, but that during the sickly season I had volunteered to do duty in the line.

GENERAL (turning to me)—"That is no excuse, sir; so long as you volunteered to do line duty, you cannot escape it by throwing yourself behind the shield of a disbursing officer."

At this point Tracy looked so badly scared that I really felt worse on his account than for my own fate, for I knew my defense and he did not.

The general again growled out, "Have you any other defense?" "Yes, sir. I am in command of a company, and on no occasion has a company commander been called on to act as officer of the guard, and this detail is without precedent."

Again he turned to Colonel Hicks and asked him as to the fact claimed by me. The colonel admitted that the present case was the only one, and that it was inadvertently done. The old general was like an enraged tiger, and exclaimed, "Young man, this is no excuse; don't talk of precedents; your colonel has the right to make precedents."

Tracy was more uneasy than ever, and absolutely looked like a condemned criminal awaiting execution.

The old general roared out again, "Have you anything further to offer in defense?"

I quietly replied that I had, but had hoped the two reasons already given would have been satisfactory; that

I had a perfect and complete defense for my conduct, and for the credit 'of our command I hoped that Colonel Hicks would withdraw the charge and let the matter drop where it was.

At this the old general was more furious than ever, and said that it was not for Colonel Hicks to withdraw the charges; that he sat as a court of inquiry, that the whole matter was in his hands, and unless I clearly purged myself of the charge, I would be cashiered and reduced to the ranks.

By this time I had become perfectly aroused, and retorted by saying I was aware that I was standing before a tribunal that would only be too willing to convict, but I thanked God that there was some things that that court could not do with impunity; and I therefore offered as my last and perfect defense, that "I was detailed to act as officer of the guard while an officer inferior in rank was detailed to act as officer of the day."

The old general turned full around upon Colonel Hicks, and exclaimed, "How is this, Colonel Hicks?"

The colonel admitted the truth of the statement.

"Oh, tut-tut! Colonel Hicks, that will never do, that will never do!"

At the last defense I saw Tracy brighten up, and when the old general turned to me again, it was with a very different air. He said, "Young man, you are discharged; but you have run a fearful risk; it is very unsafe, sir, to take the law into your own hands. You had far better suffered the indignity than to have taken the chances that you have taken;" and then turning to Colonel Hicks, he said, "I hope, colonel, that neither you nor I will ever be subjected to a like temptation." And I have reason to believe that I lost nothing in the estimation of the general on account of the course I pursued.

The forces stationed at Tampico were the only ones on the part of the United States to hold in check the Mexicans in the Sierra Madrè country. And now rumors began to be circulated that the Mexicans were beginning to organize at or near the ancient city of Panuco. Accordingly it was determined to send a scouting party through the country, up the Panuco River, to that point, and Company A, of our regiment, was selected for that service. The company was commanded by Capt. C. L. Wight, who, though young, was a brave and discreet officer. I volunteered as quartermaster and assistant commissary of the command, and we commenced our march without any camp or garrison equipage or commissary stores further than what the knapsacks and haversacks of the men furnished, trusting to the country to furnish rations; when the people were friendly we would pay for them, of course; when they were hostile, we would borrow from them, or pay in powder and bullets, as the necessity of the case demanded. Twelve miles from Tampico, up the Panuco River, was what is known as the Lafler place. I think Lafler was an American; he had a very fine tract of land, large in dimensions and extraordinarily fertile. Upon this he had a very large coffee plantation. I think he had from six hundred to seven hundred acres in coffee—the first that I ever saw growing; it grows upon a shrub or bush ranging from eight to fifteen feet high; the leaves are dark green and the coffee grains grow two together, and are covered with a hull or skin that is red, presenting the appearance of red berries.

We encamped at Lafler's that night. During the night a tiger attacked and killed an ox on the opposite side of the river, and his deep growls seemed to jar the earth where we were; it was unlike anything I ever heard before; the next day we continued our march, passing for several miles through an unbroken forest of lime trees, the yellow limes lying so thick all over the ground that you could scrape them up by the bushel, and the forest extending in every direction as far as you could see. There were but very few inhabitants on this route, although there were plenty of evidences that at some former day the whole country had been well populated, for mouldering ruins and broken potteryware were to be seen on all sides. The water was very bad, being strongly impregnated with alkali, and was only rendered drinkable by squeezing lime juice into it.

About an hour before sunset we arrived at the old city of Panuco. I was somewhat disappointed with the appearance of the place, as I had heard and read of it as presenting so many evidences of former greatness. A brief examination showed me that the ruins in and about Panuco could not be compared with those of Pueblo Viejo, notwithstanding I had not heard any comment in regard to the latter. The ruins of Panuco seemed to be of more recent date than those of Pueblo Viejo; less extensive, and less architectural beauty displayed in the construction of the buildings, less of heavy masonry and more of the adobe buildings. On our approach we saw a few armed Mexicans, who kept at a respectful distance. We crossed the river to the main portion of the town, where we took possession of a public building that furnished us with ample and complete quarters. The alcalde was not long in putting in an appearance, and after demand, formally surrendered the town; which to the best of my recollection contained about three thousand inhabitants.

We had now been long enough in Mexico to learn that we had to watch the treacherous Mexicans, as several of our men had been poisoned by provisions obtained from the markets in Tampico (though none of them fatally). So I bargained for a live beef and had it slaughtered by our own men; then set a lot of Mexican women to manufacturing *tortillas y frijoles colorado negro*, all of which was very acceptable and satisfactory to the command. Finding that there was no concentrated force, and nothing but roaming bands of robbers, as much to be dreaded by the Mexicans as by the Americans, we began to think of our return. But many of the men, and some of the officers, indeed, complaining that their feet were so sore that they could not march, we finally concluded to press into service a sufficient number of dug-outs to transport the force down the river. There was no lack of these at Panuco; accordingly we were soon floating down the river, all pleased at the change.

As soldiers are not overly scrupulous, especially when in an enemy's country, there was no lack of provisions. About one o'clock in the afternoon we tied up under the bank and sought a shade to take a lunch, but I soon saw that the boys were hunting wood, building fires, etc., and in about one hour there were added to the *tortillas y frijoles* several roast fowls, in the disposition of which the officers were cordially invited to participate. When interrogated as to how they came into possession of them, they insinuated that the fowls made a night attack upon them, and it was not until after a long and deadly struggle that the enemy surrendered; and to the victors belonged the spoils. Of course the explanation was satisfactory, notwithstanding I could not help thinking there had been some "fowl" play. But all seemed inclined to punish the enemy, and the consequence was, we left their bones to bleach on the shore of the Panuco. When the repast was over, we took to our boats and pulled leisurely down the river.

Rounding a bend, below us something over a mile, in the center of the stream, like a dolphin resting upon the water, lay a beautiful schooner. Captain Wight had a small field-glass, and readily discovered that the vessel was an armed craft, as the glass showed the brass pieces on the side. This was something for which we had not bargained, but we kept steadily pulling towards her. Presently we could, with the naked eye, see great activity on board of her, and before we had fully made up our minds what to do, we saw a puff of smoke, and a round shot came skipping over the water some distance on one side of us. At that moment up went the flag; a glance was sufficient to show us that it was our own stars and stripes. As it happened we had a little company flag with us, which we waved in return, and pulled to the schooner. We all went aboard and received a hearty welcome. Everything about her was as neat as a pin. Her decks were as clean as a good housewife's table, and her guns shone like mirrors.

After we were on board, and had exchanged greetings with the officers, came the explanation. We having been sent across the country, and not knowing what we might encounter, it was thought advisable to send this vessel up to be on the lookout for us. We knew nothing of the vessel being sent out, and the captain of the craft was not expecting to see us on the river; hence the mutual surprise. We soon bade good-by to the schooner and pursued our way down the river; the vessel was wholly becalmed, as there was not a breath of wind to fill or flap a sail. The sun slowly sank behind the Sierra Madrè Mountains, that rose in the background to the height of from 3,000 to 4,000 feet, not abruptly, but with a long slope of fine agricultural and grazing land between their summits and the river; in fact, the whole range of the Sierra Madrè on its eastern slope is well timbered, and upon its gradual incline one may find almost any variety of climate that he chooses; and did that territory belong to the United States, it would soon develop into one of the most delightful countries in the world, for nature has done a good part by it.

We continued to descend the river, notwithstanding night was upon us; but it became necessary that we should reach some place that could feed us, as our dinner had exhausted our supplies. Thus we continued our voyage until about ten o'clock at night, when we reached the little town of Agua Cotta.

This was a small town on the south bank of the Panuco River, I think about twenty-five miles from Tampico. There had not been the least caution used in landing. and no danger anticipated; the canoes were run into the bank just as it happened, and the men, excepting a very few who were left in charge of the boats, had straggled up town in pursuit of supper—doubtless something to drink, also. However, I had made arrange-

ments for supper, and the parties had gone to work in
good earnest to accommodate the command. It was
progressing finely, when all at once I heard a shot, then
another and another; then a yell, and pretty rapid firing
in different parts of the town.

There were fifteen or twenty of the boys near me
awaiting supper, and several of the officers. Captain
Wight cried out: "Boys, defend the boats!" We made
a grand rush for the boats; and none too soon, for we
were in rear of about fifty Mexicans, rushing on to the
guards; the latter instantly formed and delivered a fire
upon the advancing enemy. The volley was returned
by them, with considerable spirit, although with little
apparent effect on either side. It was night, though not
very dark, and we could recognize their relative positions.
As the foe was between us and our guard at the boats
we could not fire without endangering our own men.
We were compelled to make a rapid oblique march to
the right, and then we delivered a volley in their flank,
for which they were not prepared. We then rushed on
them with fixed bayonets and compelled them to retreat
in disorder. Our boats now being safe we turned our
attention to the desultory firing up town. We left the
guard strengthened, and with about twenty men rushed
back to relieve the stragglers, who seemed to have
rather a hot time of it.

As we advanced, the men continued to fall into position and we soon had our little command reduced to
something like order, and in possession of the eastern
portion of the village. The Mexicans continued a brisk
fire, secreted behind buildings and fences, but their
weapons were the old clumsy escopets, from which there

was but little danger unless by a chance shot. But they must be dislodged; there was no alternative but to sweep the streets; accordingly with fixed bayonets, we rushed up the streets, running them from their hiding-places, which compelled them to mass before us. On the west side of the town there was a considerable stream emptying into the Panuco. We charged them to the edge of this stream, where many of them threw down their arms, jumped into the water, and made for the opposite shore. We did not venture to follow them, but returned to our boats, abandoning our supper, and began to make preparations to leave.

Our men were drawn up on the bank for roll-call, to ascertain the amount of damage and loss to our command, when two men came scuffling down to the bank, or rather one of them was dragging the other after him. We were soon enlightened as to the cause. It was our green Irishman; the one who stuck his gun down the bore of the field-piece, in Tampico, to "keep the spalpeens from getting it." He had captured a prisoner, and was bringing him along to the boats. He explained that as he was trying to get a drink, the Mexican rushed on him with a big knife; and as he was about running the fellow through with his bayonet, he was interfered with by the priest; and to use Pat's own language, as nearly as possible, " his riverence rushed up and sthuck the crosh in my viry face; when instead of killing him, I took the spalpeen by the neck, and jist brought him wid me." He was directed to let the fellow go.

On examination we found that we had not lost a man. Two were seriously wounded, and several slightly; we had captured thirty or forty stands of arms, several swords and other weapons.   The arms, excepting the swords, were useless, hence we threw the guns into the river, put the swords on board, re-embarked our men, and were soon silently floating down the river.   We dropped down some three or four miles, and seeing a small rancho of some half a dozen houses, tied up for the night, it then being about one o'clock.   The men were exhausted, and after placing out a guard to prevent surprise, the camp was soon silent, save the deep breathing of the tired soldiers.   The excitement of the evening had been such with me that, even at that late (or rather early) hour, I had no inclination to sleep.   I fell in with a Mexican, who seemed to be a good-natured fellow, and was keeping his watch on the part of his countrymen, and who also seemed to possess more than the ordinary intelligence of his class.   He informed me that there was a man living there who spoke my language, and that he owned a rancho close by the place.   After determining in my own mind to see and converse with the individual referred to, I laid down and was soon in dreamland, far from the banks of the Panuco and its wild surroundings.

I was awakened the next morning by Capt. C. L. Wight.   I found the morning sun shining full in my face.   The captain informed me that he had taken the liberty of interfering with my duties as A. C. S., and had made such arrangements as best he could for breakfast for the men; for which I returned him my thanks, and as that duty was off my mind, I had resolved to visit the man who could speak our language; not so much for the gratification of meeting the man, as to obtain some information regarding ancient ruins that, from "Norman's

Travels," I knew must be in that immediate vicinity.   I
strolled across the fields, and soon made the acquaintance
of the owner of the rancho, whose name I learned to be
Kier.   He was a German; had a nice place, and though
he informed me that he was a poor sailor boy when he
came there, he was now quite wealthy.   It was about
breakfast time, and he cordially invited me to breakfast
with him, which was quite to my notion, as the last time
I had broken my fast was the day before at noon.

After breakfast I returned to the command, and obtained permission from Captain Wight to retain a canoe
and four men, and lay over at this point until the next
day, as I had learned the ruins I was so anxious to visit
were but a short distance down the river from us.   Kier
had agreed to accompany us as a guide.

In the meantime the command had got under way
for Tampico, and about ten o'clock in the forenoon we
embarked in the canoe, and being provided with edibles
by our kind host and guide, we descended the river for
about two miles, to where there was another considerable
river emptying its clear waters into the Panuco; here
we landed.   Mine host had brought with him two Mexican servants, and an immensely large amount of provisions for a single day.   On my expressing surprise, he
informed me that a day's sport there would give me but
a faint idea of the place; and that he, presuming that
my stay was only limited by my inclination, had provided for our immediate necessities by bringing along
such things as he thought we might need during our
stay among the ruins.

On my way down to the landing I gained something
of my companion's early history.   He was a German by

birth; came to New York when very young; at sixteen commenced life before the mast, as a common sailor. Left his ship at Vera Cruz; worked around the docks for some time, learned to speak Mexican, and at twenty years of age he landed at Tampico. He finally became acquainted with an old don, went up the Panuco, where I found him, and in due course of time married the old don's daughter, by whose *death* he got a *living*. He further informed me that upon commencing business for himself he had a great disgust for the Mexican mode of farming; he said they used a wooden shovel plow, which would merely root up the earth, without any pretense of turning a furrow; and the rest of the labor was performed with heavy, awkward, Mexican hoes. But he went East, procured steel plows and the most improved implements for working the soil; such as harrows, cultivators, etc., and was determined to show the "greasers" how to farm it. His plows did excellent work, turning up the virgin soil from depths that no Mexican system had ever reached, and his improved harrows were a source of amazement to the Mexicans. His cultivators had superseded the clumsy hoe, and he could show such a cornfield as had never before been seen on the shores of the Panuco. " But," said he, " what do you think; my corn became like young trees, from twenty to twenty-five feet high, and without any ears whatever, and my experiment cost me my entire crop." " Well," I said, " what · did you do? did you throw away your late improvements and return to the Mexican system?" "Oh, no!" he said, " the next season I did not plow the ground at all. I planted, after harrowing the field, using the cultivator to keep the weeds down, and took off a good

crop; and I have continued to use the imported implements ever since, using the precaution not to produce
an overgrowth by turning the ground too deep. And
in fact," said he, "I have now used the ground so long
by constant cropping that there is but little danger of
too heavy growth, and even manuring has been beneficial in some places."

As stated, we had landed and were at the base of our
operations. It was a pleasant day, and along the immediate shore, at the upper portion of the grounds we
were to explore, there were a few acres of open ground
studded with large mesquite trees, which made a very
nice shade; and the water of the nameless river was pure,
sweet, and fitted for ordinary domestic uses. Hence
we determined to make our camp at this point, and my
four men in connection with the two Mexicans soon
constructed a temporary encampment. Really, it was
an attractive spot; the ground raised gently from the
shore of the Panuco and sloped back to the south, where
far in the background, terrace mounting upon terrace,
rose the Sierra Madrè Mountains to the probable height
of two thousand feet; while to the north lay the flat and
fertile valley between the Panuco and Tamosee Rivers.
We took a hasty meal in our new quarters, as it was now
past midday, and commenced our march inland and up
the nameless stream.

We had landed right among the mouldering ruins,
which approached the very bank of the river. Here were
piles of adobe walls yet maintaining their identity, and
there broken columns of granite rock giving unmistakable
evidence of the labors of men upon their surface, by the
yet visible marks of the artisan's chisel, undefaced by

the ravages of time, distinct outlines of what, at some distant day, had been magnificent statues, that might even command the admiration of the present period.

We proceeded about four miles up the stream, covered here by a heavy mesquite forest and there by patches of chaparral, interspersed with open ground, carpeted with a heavy and uncropped growth of grass. This place seemed to be a favorite retreat for the feather tribes; parrots and paroquets swarmed in the trees. Several black pheasants sprang up before us, one of which Kier brought down with his fowling-piece; while snipe and beautiful plumaged cranes lined the shore and pools along the stream. There were a few monkeys chattering in the trees, but they had ceased to be a novelty. We found the stream to be the outlet to a lake that lay between the Panuco River and the mountains. It was a lovely sheet of water, with a pebbly shore, shallow at the edge and gradually deepening until its blue waves entirely hid the bottom of the immense depth. The ruins extended all the way from the Panuco to the lake. The width of the lake at this point, as I observed, was about six miles, but I could not see its eastern extremity; and the question arose in my mind whether or not this was not an arm of Lake Tampico—which problem I never had an opportunity of solving.

Everywhere covering the ground and mingling with the ruins were large masses of broken potteryware; statuary of men, quadrupeds, and fowls, all broken and ruined, yet giving evidences of the skill and taste of the race who had some day peopled that lovely place. The statuary and figures seemed to have been attached to the buildings, standing out in bold relief, sustaining cornices and projections; although this is not universal, as in some instances the rock has been chiseled away, leaving human and other forms in bass-relief upon columns that some day had undoubtedly sustained magnificent structures. But what was more remarkable, the countenances of the faces on the columns and statuary were wholly unlike the present race inhabiting Mexico, or the Indian tribes of that country, but were rather of a Grecian type.

It was difficult to say whether the ruined city was confined to the river as a port, or whether its commercial advantages also connected it with the lake; there was one thing very evident, that there had been many massive and elegant buildings on the lake shore, and I think they compared favorably with the ruins on the river.

Night was now closing in on us, and we returned to the river, where we had established our base of operations. After supper, I seated myself on a fallen column of granite and sank into profound meditation. It was hard to realize that, where I sat at the time, more than a thousand years ago a mighty city, which now lay in ruins at my feet, had teemed with commerce, life, and action; its busy streets had one day swarmed with thousands of human beings, whose impulses and feelings probably differed but little from our own. There, had mingled the man of business, the devotee, the pleasure-seeker, the layman and the clergy; men of wealth and station, with rank and power; and vice and squalid misery had alike swarmed in the thoroughfares of this once mighty emporium. But who were they? where did they come from, and whither did they go? What great devastating power or destructive calamity had overtaken them? Were these the works of the Toltecas nation, who invaded Mexico, coming from the Rocky Mountains in 648 ? or were they the conquerors of this city, and in their turn exterminated by the Chickemecas, four hundred years afterwards. I would have given much could I, that night, have called forth the ghost of one of those unknown departed, that I might have interviewed him upon the character and fate of the now dead city. How singular is the human disposition! We Americans, with the nations of Europe, flock to the old world, and there exhaust the brightest intellects and spend untold millions of dollars in hunting for the last records and hidden treasures of a Tyre and a Troy; to relocate the lost site of a Babylon; to hunt for hidden manuscripts in the catacombs, and excavate the lava-covered plains for a buried Pompeii or Herculaneum, or hunt hieroglyphics among the pyramids of Egypt; when upon our own continent lies, unexplored and unnoticed, the richest fields in the world for the antiquarian. But I must not dwell longer upon my reflections or midnight speculations. I turned in and was soon lost to all external objects.

The next morning we took a trail through a patch of chaparral ; all the way the path was rendered uneven and rough by leading over mounds, formed by fallen walls, and blocks of stone of various shapes and sizes, until we reached that part of the ruins particularly referred to by " Norman's Travels and Explorations in Mexico," where we found the large tortoise mentioned by him. It rests upon a pedestal, and is about four feet across the base. It is still perfect, excepting the nose, which is partly broken off. It is a well-wrought piece of sculpture, and is a perfect tortoise, shell, legs, and tail, but the head that protrudes from the shell is that of a man.   10

My attention was called to a place where there had been an excavation; and about two feet below the surface of the ground there was, beyond any doubt, a paved street, as regularly flagged as the streets are at the present day. With the short time that I had to spend, and the limited means for prosecuting my researches, I, of course, formed but a vague idea of the interests that labor must develop to the scientific world. But what struck me with more force than all the rest was the extent of territory covered with buildings, and the architectural skill used in beautifying them. It was here Captain Chase, American Minister to Tampico, procured the statue of a man about which there was so much speculation and comment by the press in 1847. It was the statue of a man, apparently cut from solid rock, as no evidence whatever appeared indicating that it was composite. It was so ingeniously finished and arranged that water poured into the mouth would escape at the extremities.

After spending a couple of days among the ruins, I bade farewell to my friend and guide, and in a few hours after reported myself safe and sound in Tampico.

CHAPTER XV.

MEMOIRS OF THE MEXICAN WAR—CONTINUED.

IT had long been reported that there was a ravenous tiger which had his lair on the peninsula between Lake Tampico and the Gulf of Mexico, ending on the Tampico River, and that he was in the habit of making nocturnal descents upon the stock of the ranchers located

on the borders of the lake. He had become a terror to
the inhabitants of that community, and for want of something better to do I concluded that a tiger hunt would
be a pleasant adventure. I got six adventurous spirits
to join me in the expedition, and we asked and obtained
leave of Colonel Hicks to make a descent upon this
renowned denizen of the chaparral. I was the only
officer, and was dressed like the rest, in the uniform of
a private. We provided ourselves with canteens, haversacks, short Roman swords, muskets, and bayonets.
Each took a lunch in his haversack, and water in his
canteen. All were ready for a start at about eight
o'clock in the morning, and we crossed the river and
traveled on to where the land commenced to rise abruptly
to a plateau, say two hundred feet above the level of the
plain. At the base of this rise we found a nice cold
spring, from which we replenished our canteens. Then
ascending the plateau, we proceeded in an easterly
direction, across an open country, and soon came to a
ruined *hacienda*, an orange orchard long neglected, and
a forest of cactus. The latter was the most extraordinary
I ever saw, covering an area of some ten acres; the trees
were some thirty to forty feet in height, and as dense as
a hay-stack. (I would not dare tell this in a cold climate!)
We made our way around it (an army of ten thousand
men would have had to do the same), and passed through
alternate patches of open ground and chaparral, with
here and there a few mesquite trees, making our way
towards the coast. But the further we went, the more
chaparral and less open ground, until in many places we
had to pass over the tops of large masses of chaparral,
it being so dense that we could sustain ourselves, though

with difficulty, upon the top; the loftiest branches we
would lop with our swords. But our progress was very
slow, the heat becoming intense, and there was considerable grumbling by some of the men, although I took the
lead; and consequently the brunt of the battle. We had
now got so far that we could not suppose it would be so
bad to go through to the gulf as to return. But it proved
to be a great misfortune to us that we could not comprehend the future as well as the past.

As I could see the tops of some mesquite trees in
advance of us, I called out, to encourage the boys, that
there was open ground ahead. We continued our toilsome march, ever and anon losing our footing and falling down among the thorny mass eight or ten feet, the
thorns tearing our flesh and clothes; but we would again
scramble up and push ahead for the timber. At last we
reached it, and finding open ground, congratulated ourselves on having at last overcome the principal obstacles
in the way, and hoped to soon reach the coast, as we
could hear the surf beating on the shore very distinctly.
We were all perfectly exhausted and suffering with thirst,
and sat for a few minutes in the shade while we ate a
little lunch; it was but little, as we were all too thirsty
to eat much. At three o'clock in the afternoon we
again commenced our march for the gulf; but we had
not proceeded more than half a mile before we discovered that the open ground was but an island in a dense
sea of chaparral, and nothing but death or the most desperate exertion was before us, as we must reach water
or die.

My feelings were anything but pleasant. Not so
much for myself did I care, as for the poor fellows that

I had induced to engage in this hair-brained adventure;
nothing was left for me but to clamber to the top of the
chaparral that surrounded us, and encourage the men as
best I could, although probably suffering more than any
of them, as I had taken the lead and lopped the brush
all day. We again commenced our novel tramp, and
traveled and continued to travel, the men begging to be
allowed to throw away their muskets and bayonets; to
this I positively objected on two grounds: first, that we
could not tell what use we might have for them before
again reaching camp; and secondly, when we slipped
and fell into the chaparral, the muskets, by holding them
in a horizontal position, would catch and hold us up.
When my remonstrances were about to fail, and the last
hope seemed to vanish, we struck waves of sand beneath
us, where the shore of the gulf some day had been, but
had . receded. From this all took courage, and we
persevered. Although we were marching on the top of
the chaparral, so many of the branches ran above our
heads that we could not see more than fourteen or fifteen
rods ahead of us, unless the object was higher than we
were; hence we could only judge by the sound of swells
breaking upon the shore how near we were to the water.
Thus we toiled until the sun was down, and until twilight
was fast fading.

At last the shore burst upon our view. More dead
than alive, we threw ourselves down upon the beach, and
dug holes in the sand, hoping to get water that would to
some extent alleviate the thirst that was consuming us.
But this was to no purpose; the briny wave of the Gulf
of Mexico was a poor substitute for water. In that condition we lay for about one hour. The damp atmos-

phere and cool of night had by that time somewhat
revived us, and we started down to the beach to reach
the pilot station at the mouth of Tampico River. We
came to a little hamlet of Mexicans on the opposite
side of the Tampico River between ten and eleven
o'clock at night, and at once called for water. The
scoundrels asserted at first that they had none, and secondly, that they did not have the keys of the house
where it was kept. I just seized upon the person of
their principal liar, and told him to show us the door
that led to the water or I would cut his lying tongue
from his head. He then soon found his way to the
place; it was locked, but the boys soon made the door
ring with repeated blows with the breeches of their
muskets, which induced the waterman to put in his appearance with the keys, and we all drank without stint.
Then we wanted them to take us over to the pilot station; this they absolutely refused to do, not even for
money. I told them that we would then take their
boats forcibly, there being two canoes, when they rushed
to defend them. I ordered the men to fix bayonets;
I threw them in line, and charging upon the largest
canoe, took possession and was preparing to break the
lock or chain, when they signified a willingness to take
us over for one dollar each. I paid the seven dollars,
and we were all safely landed at the pilot station.

I noticed on arriving at the station that our coming
was an enigma to the parties occupying it, and that
there was something wrong generally at that place.
There were four Americans at the station, while all their
assistants, servants, etc., were Mexicans. This was at a
time when many rumors were afloat, and it was generally

believed that the Mexicans had made some successful fights, and claimed important victories over the Americans. The consequence was that it emboldened the Mexican guerrillas and robbers in that section to make some few attacks for purposes of plunder, and I soon discovered from the quiet conversation at the station, and preparations for defense, that they were expecting an attack that night. I further came to the conclusion that while the men were glad to see us come into the station at that opportune moment, they thought that there was no head to the affair; that we were but a straggling squad, unofficered, and, consequently, did not confide the condition of things for fear we might leave them to their fate. In a few moments I comprehended all this, and more; they had several blood-hounds that kept rushing towards the edge of the chaparral, and growling and barking in such a way that it left no question in my mind but that our arrival for the protection of the station was very opportune. I maintained all the reticence on my part that was evinced by those in charge of the station; but I ordered our men to stack arms in the center of the floor, and placed a guard over them, while the men lay all around in such a manner that they could seize them at a moment's notice. Those in charge of the station sat up all night. I laid down, but could sleep very little.

The next morning I remarked to Captain —— (I forget his name), who was in charge, that they had had quite a night of suspense. He remarked that they had, and a night of danger, too; but for our timely arrival they might all have had their throats cut; but as there was no officer with us they did not tell us of the danger, for fear we might leave them to fight their own battle. I then disclosed my rank, and told our adventure; they blamed me for not letting them know I was an officer, but I assured them that by my comprehending the difficulty as I did, and the arrangements made, they would have had all the assistance that they could have expected from seven men. In due time they got us up a good breakfast, and as this was but seven miles from Tampico, with a good road, we were in camp before noon, not once having thought of the tiger, from the time we commenced scaling the chaparral until after we had reached camp.

CHAPTER XVI.

MEMOIRS OF THE MEXICAN WAR—CONTINUED.

IT was now advancing toward the rainy season, and it became necessary, for the protection of the troops, that we should furnish better shelter than our canvas tents, from the storms that were likely to ensue. Accordingly it devolved upon me, as quartermaster of the command, to provide quarters suitable for the rainy season. After consultation and advice, I erected sheds covered with palm leaves, under which we could pitch our tents, and be dry and comparatively comfortable. This kept me employed for some time, but rumors began to reach us that there was a large force organizing at Tampico el Alto, numbering five thousand or more, and meditating a descent on Tampico. Our effective force being now reduced to less than two thousand men, an express messenger was dispatched to Washington to report the condition of affairs at Tampico, and to solicit reinforcements for that place. Every day brought fresh rumors of the forces gathering at Tampico el Alto, until it was determined by the commanding officer at Tampico, as a precaution against danger and surprise, to send out a detachment in the direction of Tampico el Alto to watch the movements of the enemy. For the purpose of carrying out this plan Company I, of our regiment, was detailed, and ordered to repair to Pueblo Viejo, to watch the movements of the Mexicans. We were ordered to make our headquarters at Pueblo Viejo, and send out a scout in the direction of Tampico el Alto to prevent our being surprised and captured.

This was in the fall of 1847; the murky clouds were gathering, and for the first time since landing in Tampico, in July, the sun was obscured. Company I broke camp, and we all embarked on board of such small boats and crafts as were at our command, and commenced our expedition. In three or four hours we landed at Pueblo Viejo, found quarters for the men, and made such necessary arrangements for the comfort of the command as was thought advisable for the short sojourn we were to make at that place. Captain Harvey was nominally in command of the company, but as soon as we had landed he called upon the alcalde, was a willing recipient of his bounties, and engaged in imbibing copious libations of *muscal* and *aguardienta;* owing to his immense capacity, he was carrying the load of two ordinary men, and the command devolved first upon myself and second upon Lieutenant Conkling.

Night was approaching; there had been a smart shower of rain in the afternoon, making the ground

quite wet and the streets slippery. Conkling and myself had made our arrangements thus: We were to
establish a local guard in the town, I was to take command of a small scouting party, and under cover of
night, advance on the road to Tampico el Alto, while
Conkling held command of the balance of the company.   The local guard was stationed; among them was
a boy by the name of Spalding Lewis; he was a tall lad
of sixteen, and was determined to go to Mexico with
us from St. Charles.   His mother was a widow, and I
think Conkling, as well as myself, promised the mother
that we would, as far as possible, protect and guard her
son from all harm.   Well, when Spalding was placed
on guard, I directed him to challenge all who approached
him, and stop them.   But, said he, if they will not stop,
what then?   I replied, you know your duty, *stop them.*

The guard had been stationed half an hour.   I had
my scouting party all in line, when I heard the report of
a musket.   I ordered the scouting party on a double-
quick, and we soon reached the spot from whence the
report proceeded.   There I saw Lewis deliberately ram-
ming home his cartridge.   I said, " Spal., what are you
shooting at?"   He quietly pointed down the .street,
remarking, " That fellow came up; I challenged twice,
when he started to run, and I slapped it to him."   I
looked in the direction, and saw a Mexican lying on his
face, making some feeble attempts to raise himself.   I
approached him, and found that he was shot through
the heart, and in less than two minutes he was quite
dead.   I handed him over to the alcalde, assuring him
that unless he took more pains and kept his men within
their proper limits, more of them would share a like

fate. The victim was soon recognized by the police, and the alcalde said it was no loss, as the fellow was a notorious thief and cut-throat.

On our return to camp, I found Captain Harvey, who immediately assumed command of the company, and wanted to know what I was going to do with so many men. I informed him that I was about complying with the orders of General Gates, by throwing a scouting party out on the road to Tampico el Alto. I had intended to take thirty men, but he blustered around, and said he could not spare so many men from the command, as it would endanger its safety. But the gallant captain had forgotten that I was placing myself between him and all danger. After considerable wrangling, it was agreed that I might take twenty, and I was to select my men. (But my young blood was up, and I cursed him, and called him a drunken coward.)

I selected Sergeant Efner to take charge of the men, and took Lesser Lebenstein, my interpreter; the alcalde furnished me with what he claimed to be a trusty guide. The information we had received regarding the enemy was that they numbered about five thousand, and were comprised of Mexicans and Indians. But whether the force was reduced to anything like discipline or not we had no means of knowing. I had supposed them to be a kind of wild and roving band, assembled for marauding purposes, rather than an organized force to be dreaded by a well drilled and disciplined command.

Night had set in, and it was intensely dark, owing to the cloudy and misty weather; and about half-past eight we took up our line of march, following the main road, leading up the mountains toward Tampico el Alto. Not a sound was to be heard, save the tramp of the men and an occasional low curse or growl at the steep and slippery condition of the roads. In this way we had continued an unbroken march for about an hour and a half, when I called a halt to allow the men a short rest. They had scarcely come to a stand, when I heard an unusually heavy peal of a bell in the distance, that told the hour of ten. It then, for the first time, crossed my brain that Tampico el Alto might be something more than a collection of huts. I called the guide, and through my interpreter, interrogated him as to the size of the town of Tampico el Alto. He informed me that it was a large place; and when asked how many inhabitants it contained, he replied, over four thousand. The thought flashed through my mind that there was a chance for me either to distinguish or extinguish myself and the twenty brave companions that were with me. But I hesitated. My life was my own, and if I saw fit to barter it for that bubble called fame, the trade was mine, and none could complain. But the other twenty; had I a right to hazard them on a desperate venture? that was the question. My order was to throw out a scout in the direction of Tampico el Alto, to prevent our little command being surprised. Surely my orders would not justify the rash scheme that I was contemplating, to wit, the assault upon, and capture of Tampico el Alto, under cover of this dense darkness, with my little force of twenty men. I gave my orders for a forward march and began maturing a mode of attack on the place, and calculating my chances of success. It ran something like this: The soldiers are probably camped out of the town, and are controlled by the civil authorities of the place. Now, could I succeed in catching the principal officers of the place, or get possession of the stronghold, during any temporary panic that would be created by a sudden dash upon the town, I might hold the place until reinforced, or hold their leading men as hostages for our safe return, and if successful we could solve the great mystery, Had the Sierra Madrè country anything to fear from the long-talked-of force gathering at Tampico el Alto? While these plans were being revolved in my mind, we reach the apex of the hill, and Tampico el Alto, with a long string of lights, burst upon our vision.

On the southern slope of the mountains, and within one mile of us, lay the information wanted; and for one, I thought the bait too tempting to be denied. I ordered a halt, called the command around me, and told them there was a great mystery hanging over the command at Tampico as to whether or not there was an organized enemy at Tampico el Alto, and if so, as to their real numbers and probability of an attack upon our forces; what should we do? Before us lay the long lines of light, showing to a certain extent the size of the town. I asked the men what their feelings were on the subject; should we make the attempt to dispel the mystery? when with one accord they said, " Lead on, and we will follow wherever you think best to go!" I then called my guide, and from him I learned that there were two alcaldes and many priests in town. I directed him to lead me to the principal alcalde, and we commenced a rapid march for the city. As we entered the suburbs, I ordered a double-quick, and we went thundering down the rough-paved streets like a command of cavalry.

After marching for some distance down the street,

the guide pointed out a large building as the residence
of the principal alcalde. As we were rapidly approaching it, I saw something white flit across the street
before us, and, on approaching the house, we were
informed, on inquiring, that his highness had just
stepped out. Thinking he had slipped through our fingers, I directed the guide to lead us to the principal
priest. He at first resisted, but I admonished him of
danger more near than priest's curses, when he led off.
We caught his holiness just as he was retiring, and
informed him that he was wanted—that we were Americans. He seemed to be very much affrighted at the
name *Americanos*. I informed him that we wanted
quarters for the night, and must have possession of the
strongest buildings at his command. If he hesitated or
declined, we would worship with him at his own church
altar. In his terror he was ready to do anything; he
seized a large bundle of keys, and I directed Efner to
bring up the men. (He had drawn them up alongside
of a high wall, and in the darkness of the night it was
impossible to judge of their numbers.)

I trudged along with the priest up to the public square,
or plaza, where there was a large building, inclosed by
double walls. We entered the gates, and in a short time
his holiness had opened rooms sufficient to quarter at
least five hundred soldiers. When I informed him that
the room already at our command was sufficient for our
troops, and seeing that we had a position where we could,
for a time, resist Santa Anna and all his forces, I
released the padre, and threw myself down to attempt
to get a little rest. Before retiring, however, sentinels
had been placed at both outer and inner gates, thus

guarding ourselves from danger by assault; and knowing that they could not have the least idea of my numbers, they would naturally wish for a parley, and that would enable me to ascertain what I wished to find out, to wit, the amount of the enemy's force, if any, stationed there; for as yet we had not seen even a sentinel.

In less than an hour there was a challenge at the outer gate; I hastened to ascertain the cause, and found a delegation from the alcaldes, saying that they wished to see the commandant. I well knew that it was no time to show the white feather. I thrust a revolver in my pocket, buckled on my sword, and taking Lebenstien, my interpreter, followed the delegation across the plaza to what seemed to be a large council hall. Here I found assembled the two alcaldes, the priest we recently had under arrest, and about twenty of the principal officers of the town. On our entrance, the ordinary salutations being over, some remark was made by the principal alcalde to Lebenstien, to which he replied, evidently in not the purest Spanish. The alcalde, then, in good King's English, asked him if he spoke English. I then advanced and told him if he spoke that language, I could answer for myself; if not as fluently as Paul did before Festus and Agrippa, at least sufficiently so to make myself understood. Upon this, he remarked that I must be aware that the entering of their town by an armed force required some explanation. I promptly answered that my mission was, if they offered no resistance, to protect; but if hostile, to reduce their city. He said, "By what authority?" I answered, "By the authority of the American Republic, and a force of one hundred men, sufficient to reduce any city in Mexico." A smile crossed his face, and he turned and addressed something to those around him. I added, " I learn that there is a large force assembled at this place, meditating a hostile descent upon Tampico." He turned to me and said: " You have the positive assurance of our pacific intention, by permitting you to take possession of the stronghold of our town; and so far as the force is concerned, of which you speak, there were about five thousand assembled, but not for the purpose you suppose. It was a land difficulty, and the descent meditated was not against the American forces, but upon Pueblo Viejo, to redress aggrievances; but they have given up the expedition, and disbanded eight days since, not having received the assistance calculated on by our citizens. If a formal surrender of the town is demanded, as your language would imply, the proper authority is present for that purpose." I informed him that while we demanded the surrender of the town, it was not my intention in the least to interfere with their local government, or police regulations, and that he would continue to conduct them the same as usual; but they must from henceforth consider themselves an American town, under the conquest of General Gates, of Tampico.

The principal priest then filled a large foot glass, the largest I had ever seen, with wine (and as I thought, resembling the " cup of Hercules "), and presented it to me to drink. I gave them to understand they must first try their own poison, which the alcalde readily understood; and after drinking to our commander, passed it, in which I pledged the alcalde and officers of Tampico el Alto. The alcalde then asked if they could be of any service to our command; I told him if he would furnish a couple of buckets, and allow two of his men to accompany two of mine to fill them with water, I would trespass no farther. This he readily assented to, after which the alcalde gave me a cordial invitation to accompany him home; to this I consented, spending a couple of hours very agreeably with him. I learned from him that he had been educated in New York, and had traveled much in the United States.

I took my leave of him about one o'clock, and assured him that I should return with my force early the next morning as quietly as I had entered the place. This I did, and at eight o'clock in the morning was with Company I at Pueblo Viejo. The same afternoon I reported myself to General Gates, together with the facts heretofore stated. I was severely reprimanded, and threatened to be cashiered, for disobedience of orders.

Perhaps it served me right for bursting the bubble, as General Gates' report showed that Tampico el Alto had fallen into the hands of the Americans, and there being now nothing to threaten Tampico, so large a force was no longer needed; consequently we soon received orders to join General Scott before Vera Cruz.

CHAPTER XVII.

MEMOIRS OF THE MEXICAN WAR—CONTINUED.

AMONG the troops concentrated and designed to march upon the Mexican capital, was the regiment under Walker. The command was known as the Texas Rangers. I had often heard Walker spoken of as a daring officer, and one who had long been imprisoned by

11

the Mexicans, having been captured by them in the
struggle between Mexico and Texas. I had imagined
the appearance of my youthful hero, and I had pictured
him as a large, stalwart, dark man, whose very look
would cause an enemy to quail before him; but, on meeting him for the first time, my idol was shattered and
fell to the ground; for in the real Walker I found a man,
to the best of my judgment about five feet ten inches
high, thin and wiry, of light complexion, with pale blue
eyes, and of a fine nervous temperament. Out of a thousand men, he would be the last that you would take for
a fighter.

I find that history has said but little in regard to him,
and I cannot throw much light on the subject further than
this: I know that he led the advance in the line, captured
San Juan, routed a small band of guerrillas at the Robber's Bridge, sacked and partly demolished Santa Anna's
hacienda at that place, met and dispersed a lot of lanceros at Agua Cotta, made a brilliant dash and took the
castle of Perote and put the most of the garrison to the
sword, remembering the fate of his brother at that place;
and thereby hangs a tale.

During the war between Texas and Mexico, Walker
and his brother were attached to a command who were
captured and made prisoners by the Mexicans, and after
a long and harassing march and untold privations,
reached the castle of Perote, where they suffered a long
and solitary imprisonment, until at length the prisoners
became a burden to the powers that were, and they
finally came to the determination to rid themselves of
the burden. There being no exchanges to be made of
prisoners, with that wanton cruelty and hatred at that

time towards everything that was American, they resolved to dispose of the prisoners there confined, about three hundred in number. They prepared a sack and placed therein a number of beans, corresponding to the number of prisoners. Two-thirds of these beans were black, while the other third was white. The prisoners were then each blindfolded, as they were led out, and compelled to draw a bean from the sack. He who drew a black bean was posted at the side of a wall and shot immediately. Colonel Walker drew a white bean and was liberated, while his brother drew a black bean, and with other unfortunates was immediately shot. I afterwards saw the place and took several of the battered bullets from the wall in front of which they were placed and shot.

Walker, before leaving the castle at the dead hour of night, deposited a ten-cent piece beneath the foot of the main flag-staff of the castle, and, with uncovered head, upon his bended knees, in the presence of his God and the stars that twinkled above him as solemn, silent witnesses, there he registered his vow that, should his life be spared, at some future day he would come in triumph or die in the attempt. The war between the United States and Mexico had offered him the opportunity to make an attempt to carry out his pledge, an opportunity he was not slow to embrace. After the castle was taken and after blood and carnage were stayed, our hero again, with reverential awe and uncovered head, devotedly knelt at the foot of that flag-staff and removed his talisman of evil (to the Mexicans) amid the congratulations and cheers of his companions-in-arms, as the stars and stripes, the emblem of America's great nation, com-

menced slowly creeping up the same staff, meeting the
Mexican flag descending. As it went aloft, its folds
unfurling to the gentle breeze, it created surprise and
consternation among the gaping throng of Mexicans
who had hastened from the city of Perote. All was done
with such celerity that it seemed rather as some feverish
dream than a reality to the denizens of the place. I am
devoting the most of this chapter to one heroic man,
who evidently did not have influential friends at home
to give one blast on their horn to sound his praise, or to
record the deeds of the brave heart and strong hand
whose remains lie mouldering near Huamantla; but I
will follow him to the end, and return to our march.

To the right of the road leading to Puebla, about
twelve miles distant, lies the important town of Huamantla, where was garrisoned quite a force of Mexicans,
and it was thought proper to reduce the place. Colonel
Walker, with his rangers, was ordered to advance upon
the town, throw out a skirmish line and contrive to
occupy the Mexican force until the infantry and artillery
should arrive; but contrary to orders and caution against
recklessness, Walker, in approaching the city, charged,
sword in hand, when a sharp conflict ensued. The
Mexicans were routed, and Walker took possession of
the place. But at this juncture Santa Anna, with eighteen hundred black horse cavalry, made his appearance
over the hill from the north side of the town and made
a desperate attack upon Walker's command. But
Walker was not found napping. He met the charges
in battle shock, and in a few minutes a large number of
the Mexicans was placed *hors du combat*, while the
balance left the field in the utmost confusion and with

more expedition than they had entered it. Walker, undoubtedly supposing that they would rally and return to the charge, had directed and was superintending the erection of a barricade across a prominent street, with his right resting upon a church, and placing a piece of ordnance to sweep the street (at this time the place had entirely surrendered and white flags were flying from most of the windows), when a shot was fired from one of the windows of a house from which floated a white flag. Walker was shot dead, and fell into the arms of his black body servant; and thus in glory ended the brilliant career of one of our most devoted, brave-hearted, and distinguished officers. Of this man I know nothing more than that I do not find his name inscribed high on the escutcheon of fame, and hence I presume, as I before remarked, that he left none behind him that had the ability or disposition to pay to the dead hero the tribute that his valor demanded.

Now, having gone forward to dispose of poor Walker, I will return to the main thread of my story. The little town of San Juan was situated on a small creek twenty-one miles from Vera Cruz, on the road leading by the way of the National Bridge. On our arrival at San Juan we found nothing but blackened embers where the town had once stood. Walker was in advance. It was a very good camping-place and we were camped there for several days. It was at this place that our regiment lost its first man after landing at Vera Cruz. Up the creek about a mile and a half, in a beautiful wooded country, was situated one of Santa Anna's many *haciendas*, with gardens, fruits, and flowers, and an extensive orange grove.

The buildings had become the head-quarters of a band of guerrillas, numbering about one hundred and fifty, who came down and made a sudden descent upon us at break of day. The pickets were driven in, the camp was astir, and the long roll was sounded; soon all were under arms and ready for fight, but no enemy was to be found. The menace was harmless, as no one was hurt. One company of our regiment was camped a little below us, towards the creek. There was a grove just out of musket range of this company. This company had been recruited in the southern part of the State of Illinois. The captain was sixty-five years of age (I have forgotten his name), and his company looked upon him as a kind of father to them, rather than as a commanding officer. About four o'clock the next afternoon this band of lanceros filed out from the grove and made a sudden dash on the old man's company, and, forming a line, by a skillful maneuver, nearly half the command poured a shower of escopet balls into the camp. The casualty was small, one man being shot through the head, while some three or four were slightly wounded. The company was not, as you might suppose, thrown into confusion, but delivered into the ranks of the running enemy a well-directed fire, which sent some five or six horses away riderless, while one horse did not get off the ground.

As soon as the enemy had made good their retreat, the old captain came rushing into the main camp, his eyes almost starting from their sockets, his nostrils expanded, his face flushed, and great drops of perspiration rolling down his cheeks, exclaiming, " Now something must be done; they have killed John; they have shot him through the head, and the varlets must be extinguished." The captain claimed the right to take his company and go out, like the Israelites of old, and chastise the enemy, but he was at last convinced that it would be very imprudent for a single company or, in fact, any other force at that time, to go in pursuit, as the enemy was well acquainted with the country, and, being mounted, they could ambush or avoid us as they thought proper.

On consultation it was thought most advisable to send out spies, and, if possible, find their rendezvous, which was accordingly done, when we ascertained that they had possessed themselves of the *hacienda* before referred to. Accordingly two companies were detailed for a night expedition. Companies I and G were detailed for the service, and as soon as night had fairly set in, the command was on the march. We had procured a plan of the grounds and the situation of the stables, as well as their relation to the *hacienda*. The command was to be divided. One company was to go on the east side of the mansion and slip in between the shrubbery and the house, and the other company was to come up on the south side and make a bold attack, the force on the east side to prevent them from reaching their horses. But, by some mistake, the company that was to attack from the south side, got clear around on the west side, and from some cause, I know not whether from a sentinel or by accident, the alarm was given. The guerrillas, as might have been supposed, rushed for their horses, while our men, on the east, attempted to cut them off from their stables. The affair was of short duration. The party which was to have kept them from their horses was a little slow, and the most of them had reached the stables, but not before the company on the west had fired into their ranks. The party on the east side mistaking the fire of our own men upon the lanceros, returned it, which, had it not been for one of those club cactus fences, would have been disastrous to our own men; as it was, but two men were wounded, and those not dangerously.

The building was then entered and proved to be well filled with beautiful and very valuable furniture, containing French mirrors, glass more than a half inch in thickness, inclosed in beautiful mahogany and black ebony frames, fine rosewood and mahogany chairs, sofas, ottomans, etc. The building was a rather rumbling structure and apparently fitted up in haste, and seemed to be a favorite resort of the one-legged veteran. But we made short work of things there. We gathered together the most combustible portion of the furniture, piled it in a large room and then applied a match to it. We also burned the barn and out-houses, leaving no shelter for guerrillas. From the light made by the burning, we picked up six dead and dying Mexicans. We returned to camp well satisfied with the first lesson of our guerrilla hunting on the route to Mexico.

In a few days we broke up camp and moved on to the Robber's Bridge, when the Mexicans showed themselves in considerable force. But a few shot and shell completely dislodged them. We continued our march until within a short distance of the National Bridge, when we were opened upon by a strong fort just above the bridge, on the river and on the opposite side from us. Their position was a very strong one, and com-

manded the road for a great distance. We also opened
upon the fortifications with shot and shell, but to little
purpose, as their position seemed impregnable. But
Yankee ingenuity and the consummate skill of our Scott
was not long in finding a solution to the problem. A
force of cavalry was thrown across the stream at a
remote point, undiscovered by the Mexicans, gaining the
rear and coming up behind on a sloping hog's back, and
ere the Mexicans were aware of it, plunged into their
works, sword in hand, cutting the gunners down at their
posts and making prisoners of the remaining officers and
men, and, ere the day closed, the batteries commanding
the bridge were silenced, and the National Bridge, protected by a well-equipped Mexican force, with all its
natural strength, which heretofore had been thought to
be impregnable, fell into our hands. I have hardly ever
seen a point better calculated for defensive operations or
better entitled to be deemed impregnable than the National Bridge. In fact, it seemed the master-key to lock
us out from the Mexican capital. Having full possession
of the National Bridge, the next door that we were to
force was the strong natural defense of Plano del Rio,
or "river of the plains," and the pass of Cerro Gordo.

As we advanced on the Plano del Rio, the Mexicans
blew up the bridge and we were compelled to dig a road
down a steep hill, or rather mountain, in order to cross
the stream. However, General Hardy made the Mexicans perform the principal labor. We crossed the stream
and encamped on the opposite side, in a small valley
that extended up and down the river at the base of the
Cerro Gordo Mountains. The country hereabout is
very rough and rugged, interspersed with deep and dark

ravines, fantastic caves, rolling hills, and lofty mountains, and through this picturesque country runs the Plano del Rio, a rapíd mountain torrent of cold and pure water. The bridge, which was blown up at our approach, was of solid masonry, built long ago, of water-washed cobble-stones and cement, and the rock and cement had become so inseparably united that when the bridge was blown to pieces the rifts were straight, breaking the cobble-stones and cement alike.

Our principal forces were concentrated at this point, meditating a descent on Santa Anna in his favorite stronghold. In speaking of our operations here, it is not my intention to reproduce a history of the many hard-fought fields or glorious victories achieved by our soldiery in the war with Mexico; but these are portions of the history of that war that have never been written. And perhaps I might go much further, and with a great degree of justice, and say that the history of the Mexican war never was written. Though the historian has dwelt upon the achievements of our forces on many a bloody field; has eulogized the acts of those whom fame has proclaimed immortal, other important events of that history are wholly omitted. The deeds of daring of those who had influential friends at home to raise their standards for them, have had their colors flying to the breeze and their names emblazoned upon the pages of history; but who shall chronicle the record of the friendless captain, lieutenant, non-commissioned officer or private, who there offered up his life as a sacrifice upon the altar of his country? Nor is this the only unwritten history.

I presume there are many who will remember our

encampment at Plano del Rio, near the foot of the Cerro Gordo, as heretofore stated; that Scott's head-quarters were still at the National Bridge, and that General Patterson, being next in rank, was in command at Plano del Rio, and that Patterson was confined to his tent by sickness, and among the general officers present were Generals Twiggs, Worth, and Pillow. Worth being temporarily in command, and very ambitious (and what officer of rank is not?) ordered an attack on Cerro Gordo. The attack was to be made at four o'clock the next morning, when we were to charge upon the Mexican works at the base of the hill, and march directly up the road to Jalapa. Men who carry the knapsack frequently have as good an idea of the practicability of an attack as their officers in command. That night you might have traversed the encampment and heard men making their non-cupative wills on every side. John would say to Jim, " Now, Jim, if I am killed to-morrow, and you escape, I have five dollars in my pocket and Dan Jones owes me two and a half; collect that and send my blankets and knapsack to Sally, etc." But the attack was not destined to be made. General Patterson arose from his sick bed, resumed his position and countermanded the order for an attack and sent a courier to inform General Scott of his condition, begging him to hasten forward and take command of the army, as he was too sick to hold it, and if he surrendered it to Worth, that officer would sacrifice it to his ambition.

Scott hastened on and assumed command and continued the countermand until he matured his plans of attack, and with the consummate skill for which he is so justly renowned, he soon discovered that the mountain

peak about half a mile south of Cerro Gordo commanded the summit of the latter mountain.   Upon the
top of Cerro Gordo Santa Anna had his head-quarters,
at the point known as Telegraph Station.   With infinite
labor Scott secretly got several heavy pieces of field ordnance placed in battery, then sent out sappers and
miners to clear out the hollow pass at the right of Cerro
Gordo Mountain, and gave each command its position
and signal for attack.   It will be well remembered,
doubtless, that charges were preferred against General
Scott, and the subsequent court of inquiry, and that he
was ordered home for trial.   The countermand of the
order for attack on Cerro Gordo, sustained by Scott's
order continuing the countermand, I believe to have
been the foundation of those ridiculous charges, of
which Worth and Pillow were the active agents.   In
saying this much, I am giving you but a faint hint of
some portions of the unwritten history of the Mexican
War.

But before passing entirely from Cerro Gordo, I cannot help mentioning one fact connected with Scott's order
for the battle fought at that place, and the way it was
carried out.   Of course it was published and reached
the House of Lords in England.   When the Duke of
Wellington read it, he uncovered his head and arose in
his place in the House and said: "England in her more
prosperous days has achieved victories; France, under
Napoleon, was the pride of the world; but Winfield
Scott, of the United States Army, is the first man who
has ever reduced war to a science."

That general order was not the only thing that should
have called forth the admiration of the whole civilized

world.   Here was a spectacle heretofore unheard of:
A mere handful of men, entering with hostile intentions
a nation of the magnitude of the Mexican Republic;
they, a nation trained to arms from their infancy, boasting of their military prowess and achievements in by-
gone days; we, leaving a Congress behind us debating
whether they would furnish us the means of subsistence
or whether we should be left to our fate, and some of
that Congress wishing that we might be "welcomed by
bloody hands to inhospitable graves;" yet we pushed on,
with a force never exceeding eleven or twelve thousand
men, first capturing their metropolis, then penetrating to
the heart of their country.

They not only placed obstructions to prevent our advance, but literally blocked up the roads behind us; in
fact, this practice was carried on to such a state of perfection by the Mexicans, that when we compelled them
to open the road to admit our trains, it was easier in
many places to construct a new road than to clear out
the old one.   It was the uniform boast that not one of
us should live to tell the story; yet still we pressed on
until victory, on many a hard-contested field, at last
enabled us to make ourselves masters of their capital,
where our flag proudly waved over the halls of the Montezumas, and "these northern barbarians," as they
termed us, dictated terms of peace, and settled our
troubles with the erring sister republic with honor to our
nation and a laudable pride to the actors in the scene.

Under General Scott's general order, Cerro Gordo was
fought, and one of the most brilliant victories obtained
over a largely superior force, over one-half of the army of
the enemy on the field being captured.   It was Scott's

intention to gain their rear and cut off their retreat to
Jalapa. This plan failed in part, but the Mexican army
was cut in two, and Santa Anna only escaped capture by
cutting his lead mule out of the harness, mounting upon
his back, and beating a hasty retreat,—leaving his carriage and wooden leg as trophies to our Illinois volunteers, while his money-bags and treasures were left.
Our boys as they passed would take their knives and
cut the money-bags without breaking ranks, pocket a
handful of Mexican dollars, and continue the charge
upon the flying foe. Santa Anna's wooden leg was
brought home to Springfield, and deposited in our State
capitol, as a relic of the great victory.

At Cerro Gordo and near the telegraph station,
for more than a month after the great battle, the
boys might be seen exploring the dust in quest of
Mexican dollars, with which they replenished their
purses. Santa Anna fell back upon Jalapa with a rem-
nant of his defeated and demoralized army, reporting a
great victory over the enemy, and making a forced loan
of the Mexican merchants at that place, to entirely an-
nihilate the Yankee army. But he was not permitted to
remain long with his shattered forces at that point, but
was compelled to make a hasty retreat along the road
leading to the city of Mexico, while the victorious Scott
occupied Jalapa. Here our regiment was left to guard
and hold the post for some time, while the main army
was encamped outside the town.

In this connection, I would remark that there is a
most lovely mountain stream flowing to the west of the
city, upon which an English company had erected a
large woolen factory, employing a great number of

hands. I do not know the altitude of Jalapa, but it must be some 8,000 or 9,000 feet above the level of the sea; in fact, it might be considered a mountain town. And, while lying there, we experienced several quite heavy frosts; yet in the rear of the city, in the month of November, I picked some very fine blackberries, found coffee maturing and oranges in all conditions, from the blossom up to the ripe fruit, the frost seeming not to affect vegetation. I have many a time stood on the hills back of the city and seen the clouds rolling far below me over the valley.

After leaving this point, we pursued our march *en route* for the city of Mexico. Through a deep gorge at first, then descending quite a high range of mountains, we at length reached the famous pass of Tahoya, or Black Pass. Here the Mexicans rallied and attempted to make a stand. That point is well calculated to oppose any advancing enemy, as the pass seems to be through the exhausted crater of a volcano, and the whole country for miles around is covered by a sharp *pedregal*, while the road was blockaded by immense walls of the same material, over which it was almost as difficult to travel as over broken glass. But Yankee ingenuity soon overcame all obstacles, and the road was opened and the Mexicans flying before a salute of grape and canister. After crossing this mountain, we reached an elevated plain, with the Perote Mountain to our left, and upon this same plain, at the foot of the mountain, is situated the city and castle of Perote.

The Perote Mountain exhibits one of the most peculiar freaks of nature that I ever saw. At one point it forms a cone-like peak, upon the top of which is an immense rock crown which projects on every side like the top of a center-table over the pedestal. It resembles a large box or chest, and hence it is called the Cofre de Perote. Upon its lofty summit stands the coffer, with its huge proportions resting upon a much smaller base containing its immense imaginary treasure. To that lofty summit each morning, the eyes of the don, the señora, and peon are alike turned up, with an inquiring look, to note whether their treasures are still safe in the strong rock-box on the summit of old Perote. There has been some gold discovered at the foot of the mountain, and from that fact, undoubtedly, arose the name and also the legend that the coffer contains untold treasures of gold, and at some time the coffer will, with its immense treasure, come rolling down the mountain.

This place is remarkable for sudden changes of weather and is consequently very sickly. The sun may be shining brightly and in fifteen minutes afterwards the rain may be pouring in torrents, and again clearing up as if by magic. These changes frequently occur a dozen times daily. The city of Perote contains several thousand inhabitants, yet it presents but a squalid appearance, being built principally of adobe, and the houses generally but one story, rough and hovel-like in their structure. The castle is about a quarter of a mile from the city and upon a level with it. The whole works are situated upon a level plain. Around the castle is a deep moat, which in times of peace is dry, but which is so arranged as to be filled with water at very short notice. in case of necessity. All around inside of the outer wall are immense lions' heads, with their huge mouths open, and at a given signal they vomit forth immense volumes of water to fill the moat.

The country around, as before stated, being one vast level plain, up to the base of the mountain, and the mountain being beyond range of artillery, there is nothing to command it, and, therefore, in the hands of a careful garrison, it would be a place of great strength, but of no possible strategic value. The town is of no importance, and both town and castle, from the nature of the country, are easily turned, and there are passes in advance that would be easily fortified, avoiding the danger of guerrilla access or leaving an enemy in your rear; in fact, I could not see what was to support so large a town in that place. It is too much elevated to produce tropical fruits, and I saw but little cultivation of the soil. In fact, the plain looked to me to be rather sterile and to be adapted to grazing purposes only. For aught I know, it may be supported, in part, by mines in the Perote Mountains, but I had no evidence of this.

From Perote, many miles west of us, to the right of our road, lay Mount Santa Cruz, or Mount of the Sacred Cross. This landmark, as it rises from the level of the plain to a height of some three thousand feet, may be seen for many leagues around, and we tramped a long and tiresome day's march to reach it, finally encamping about three miles to the south of its base, which seemed to be scarcely half a mile distant. Upon its lofty peak which shot up into the heavens like a spire, had been erected a cross, when the country was invaded by Cortez. It looked from the plain like two straws placed at right angles, and as we were marching along during the day, a discussion arose among the officers as to how long it would take a man to ascend to the top and bring down a piece of the holy cross. Some thought two weeks to

12

go and come, while I became the butt of ridicule for the
crowd by asserting that I could go to the summit and
bring down a piece of the cross in twenty-four hours.

We closed our day's march and camped at a Mexican
village of about two thousand inhabitants, called Tepeaca.
When I had finished my supper the sun was almost an
hour high.   I went to one Henry Stickler, a member and
private of my company, and asked him if he would
like a little adventure, stating to him at the same
time that I proposed that night to climb the Santa
Cruz, and to bring down a piece of the holy cross before
morning.   Henry was a well-knit, daring man of about
twenty-three years of age, and always ready for an adventure; consequently our arrangements were soon made
and we took up our line of march for the base of the
mountain, which we expected to reach in about twenty
minutes; but as we proceeded the mountain seemed to
recede, and night had fairly set in before we really commenced our ascent.   But while there was the least
streaking of twilight in the west we shot up the steep
ascent like two young eagles.   The full moon was up,
but it gave us little light, and as we were on the west
side of the mountain, the moon being in the east, it
brought the mountain between us and the light.

Still we held our course for the lofty summit, clambering over the immense rocks and bowlders which time
had reft from the mountain-side, not knowing but we
might start them from their long-used bed and precipi-
tate them and ourselves from their airy station to the
plain below.   About two hours' labor brought us to a
shoulder of the mountain where we stopped to take a
rest, and, with that rest, a general view of our position.
Before us lay the shadows of the mountain stretching

for more than a mile west of us along the level plain, like the picture of Cleopatra's Needle, with its sharp point pictured on the bosom of the valley. The mountain seemed almost split asunder by an immense crater, whose escape was to the west. Consequently we kept around to the east side. Now, being aided by the moon's rays, we again commenced our tortuous ascent, and about two o'clock in the morning, we reached the extreme summit, where had been planted the Cross of Vera Cruz, by the early Spanish invaders. It was composed of Mexican cedar. The timber was about twenty inches square, the upright being about twenty feet high, the cross-piece about ten feet long and about fifteen feet from the ground. With the aid of some rocks, and some boosting on the part of Henry, I was enabled to reach the cross-piece, and as I sat upon it, I chopped off two good-sized pieces, one for each of us.

But that was not all that we did. Our command was escorting what was known as the big train, and the Mexicans swore in their wrath that it should never go through. They had made several raids, but were always defeated, and we knew that guerrillas were hanging on each flank. As I stood on the summit of Mount Vera Cruz, apparently right at my feet burned our camp-fires. To the left and over low ranges of hills, burned the enemy's camp-fires; and yet, from appearances, their camps were larger than ours. We commenced our descent from the mountain, and at half-past four o'clock in the morning we passed through our lines and reported ourselves in camp, bringing the evidence that the cross could be reached in less than twenty-four hours, as well as the important discovery that the Mexican forces were hovering on either flank of our command.

CHAPTER XVIII.

MEMOIRS OF THE MEXICAN WAR—CONTINUED.

AS I am writing my own memoirs, and not the history of the Mexican War, I pass on in our advance march by Agua Caliente Huamantla, to the right twelve miles (this is where Walker was killed), and taking Puebla, San Martine, and other villages on the west, from Puebla to the City of Mexico, and at length arrive at a stream high up in the mountains called Rio Frio, or Cold River. I have seen snow on its banks in the summer. There is quite a valley in the gorge of the mountains, and, in fact, from the immense height of the Popocatepetl Range, it is comparatively a very low pass that we cross to reach the City of Mexico. The altitude from the summit to the base I never knew; but it is about that of perpetual snow in that climate. There is quite a village at Rio Frio, and we stationed our troops there during the war. The aspect of the place is cold and rather forbidding. Among other troops stationed there were the Texas Rangers under Col. Jack Hays. After Walker's death they were of but little importance to the service. They were not uniformed and but little drilled, but they were rather dreaded by non-combatants of all classes. Colonel Irwin's right and Captain Little's company of cavalry were also stationed at this place for a long time after the fall of Mexico.

When we had crossed the mountains at this point, we descended into the valley in which is situated the City of Mexico. I cannot recollect the distance from the base of the mountain to the City of Mexico; but I remember distinctly that there was no town of any note on the

main road to the city, between the base of the mountains
and the city; but, in order to reach the city, we had to
cross a morass, or what in by-gone ages and what in
winter is still a shallow lake, upon a causeway about
eight miles in length. At the eastern end of the causeway on the south side of the road, arises a small but
abrupt mountain, called Piñon. This point Santa Anna
had made impregnable by three tiers of fortifications, one
above the other, which commanded the plain along which
the road approached it, and the entire causeway to the city.

Scott's keen perceptions convinced him that it was
useless to attempt to enter the city in that way; hence
he kept up a feint before Piñon, and marched the command around to the south, at the base of the mountains,
a distance of sixty miles, when Santa Anna awoke to a
realizing sense that he and the fortifications at Piñon
were "left out in the cold," and that the "northern barbarians" had whipped their forces at Contreras, and were
likely to enter the capital on the west, instead of on the
east side. And after taking San Angelo and whipping
them at Churubusco, Molino del Rey, and Chapultepec,
we did absolutely enter the city from the west, in the
face of a large square battery, hastily erected to give us
a suitable reception. And they did make it so warm
for us that we were compelled to order up sharp-shooters
to run from the pier of the aqueduct until they had the
parties within easy range and picked them down from
their guns. As the Mexicans marched out on one side
of the city, we marched in from the other, and from the
evidence of joy at meeting us, I could not help thinking
that they thought we must have been there before.
White flags were waving from every window, and every

balcony was crowded with ladies, all welcoming us and waving their white handkerchiefs at us.

After quiet was restored in the city, I quartered my regiment in the convent of San Domingo, with many others, establishing my office as acting quartermaster and acting assistant commissary at the custom house. True, the women were all lovely and kind, but many of the men were jealous and hostile, though it was soon discovered that there were a great many Mexican men who got badly pricked with the side-arms of officers, and that called forth an order forbidding officers off duty to wear their swords, which order was strictly enforced; yet there was a fine lot of 5x8 steel bars in the city, and when polished and pointed and ingeniously fixed into a hilt, they made a very fair defense against toads, and each of us soon had a toad-stabber.

The city is built on a square, with streets generally of a respectable width, and also contains several public squares or plazas, which is one of the prettiest features of Mexican towns of any note. The drainage of the city is below and along the center of each street, and discharges the contents into the moat that surrounds the city. The present State house, or palace, is a very imposing structure, and is situated on the east side of the main plaza, and almost adjoining this is the museum, in which is deposited many robes of fine texture and furs of every description, bows, arrows, javelins, and other weapons, they being arms and clothing claimed to have been preserved from the days of the Aztec race; but what struck me as the most curious of all the relics, was an immense copper man and horse, standing on a pedestal of colossal size, the whole weight of which must be from thirty to forty tons, judging from appearances. This marvel of art I was informed was a present from some king of Austria, or some one of the German States, and had been transported by the way of Vera Cruz over the mountains to the City of Mexico. Opposite the hall or palace, across the plaza and on the west side thereof, stands the famous Bella Union, a hotel and the principal gambling hall in the City of Mexico, where it is said a million of dollars changes hands in a single night. It is a building of immense proportions, four stories in height. You enter through a hall into a covered court inside, which is lighted from above by a glass dome. The lower or ground floor of this vast court is circular in form, and the entire walls are covered with large mirrors. The floor is composed of marble blocks, each about twelve inches square, alternately black and white.

There is a series of galleries from the bottom to the top, the rooms all fronting inwards on this immense court, around which verandas are built, as before stated. The rooms run through to the outer walls, through which many of them are lighted by windows. The inner porches or verandas, as well as many of the rear rooms, are filled with gaming tables, which as a general thing are filled each night with players. I have often witnessed the old don marching ahead of his servant, who followed with his small iron trunk loaded with its golden freight of doubloons. On one occasion I watched the betting of one who came in thus provided for, at a monte table, and remained a quiet observer from nine o'clock in the evening till two in the morning. The old fellow was out of luck, and I saw his sack of doubloons gradually melt away. I saw him stake seventy-two doubloons on the turn of a single card, and lose. He took the thing with the utmost composure, smoking his cigarette all the while. They were still playing when I left, but I learned the next day that the bank had broken him.

The south side of the plaza was principally occupied by stores, while on the north side was situated the famous cathedral of Mexico. I never made myself thoroughly acquainted with the outside of the city. There were three things which prevented it: First, though the city was in the hands of the Americans, it was all that a man's life was worth to ramble off in the outskirts alone; secondly, I was very busy while there; and thirdly, my right arm was in a sling, and I was not very well able to defend myself in case of trouble. And hereby hangs a tale which I thought I would leave untold, or rather leave it for others to tell; but as I am writing of my own personal adventures, perhaps it would not be right for me to omit it.

There was no one better acquainted with the fact than the Mexicans, that commissary and quartermaster stores were hard to get by an American army invading Mexico, and, consequently, they were ever on the alert to cut them off. I was acting quartermaster, and, following up our brilliant successes with our supply train, with a mounted guard of two hundred men *en route* from Contreras to Churubusco, when at a short distance from San Angelo, I saw a command of from five hundred to six hundred lancers coming up on a brisk trot and their leader bravely riding in advance of the column. In fact, he was so far in advance that I thought he wanted a parley. I rode out towards him, when he immediately drew and charged out to meet me. I drew my saber and we met about midway between our commands, and, as we advanced, I suppose that we were each measuring our man. At least I was measuring mine. He was a compactly built man of less length of limb, but rather higher than myself. He was mounted on a splendid (and speaking comparatively) large mustang. I was mounted on an active American horse. We met. I at once discovered that our horses were about equally trained, but, with all my boasted skill (having been trained in cavalry saber exercise by Lesser Lebenstein, the Pole), my antagonist was the better swordsman of the two.

His first attempt was to cut my rein. Finding that I was no novice in the art, and I, about the same time, discovering that I had more in my man than I had bargained for, business commenced in earnest. We both held ourselves close on our guard, while we rapidly plied our cuts and parried with all our skill. I pinked him a little in the right side by an interpoint that he had not fully parried, when he rose in his stirrups, dealt me an over-hand cut, which I had not found laid down in our tactics (hence I claimed it out). I tried to parry, but his blade followed mine down to the hilt, severing my guards like straws, and buried his blade deep in my wrist and palm, severing the cords and pulsating arteries of the palm, and being heated by my exertions in the fight the blood spurted for many feet, and full in the face of my adversary; but, unfortunately for him, he had buried his blade so deep in my guards that he could not immediately withdraw it, and by suddenly turning my arm and by a rapid motion of my left hand, retaining my rein, I seized my revolver and opened fire. When

I had discharged four shots in rapid succession, such had been his exertions that he had withdrawn his blade to within six inches of the point. During this contest, there had been no advance, nor was one shot fired by either command; but when they saw his saddle empty a most deafening shout went up from my men. I wheeled my horse, ordered an advance, and rode through the lines to the rear. The first volley from our carbineers was at point blank range. Still advancing and drawing their holster pistols, they literally fired into the enemies' faces, while they were blazing away with their old escopets with but slight damage to my command, and by the time we came to the saber, the foe was in rapid but demoralized retreat. My boys would have pursued their advantage further but I did not allow them to do so, as my duty only extended to the protection of my train. As it was, I never saw as many men *hors du combat* for the length of time and numbers engaged, the whole affair after their leader fell, not occupying more than ten minutes; but I could no longer keep my saddle, and was borne to the rear, when it was discovered, from the great loss of blood, that they could not take up the arteries, and the surgeon was compelled to give me alcohol to raise a pulse so as to enable him to take them up. It was found on examination that twenty-seven of the enemy were dead on the field, beside fifty-two wounded prisoners. And thus ended the hottest little time I ever experienced in Mexico. And though I never have been able to boast of much good luck, I congratulated myself here as having made a very lucky escape with the comparative loss of the use of my right hand. It is true that it was unfortunate for me, and equally so for those who have to decipher the hieroglyphics made by the same hand. From this digression, I will return again to the city.

Our command was stationed in the convent of San Domingo, near the custom house. This is one of the most perfect labyrinths that I ever saw. A regiment of men could be lost in it. I made it a point never to occupy more space than was needed to quarter my men; and this fact was always appreciated by the padres. Consequently; they and myself were on the best of terms. I always guarded as much as possible against that spirit of vandalism that pervaded the army. The building covers two blocks, having been arched over a street which runs under a portion of the vast structure. In discussing the magnitude of the building, I heard a wager offered and refused that a man could not step into and write his name in each room, in twelve hours.

One of my friends, a principal among the padres, kindly offered to take me through and show me the chapels. The day was appointed, and we commenced our tour of inspection. I went through nine different chapels in the building, but I was so much indisposed that I was forced to quit my promenade for that day, and I never afterwards had an opportunity to finish up the exploration. The chapels which I visited were ornamented with great taste and the appointments without regard to cost. There were many of the most beautiful chandeliers that I ever saw, with many other cut-glass ornaments, which I was assured were all the handiwork of the padres. There was also a great number of exquisite paintings adorning the walls, which were also the work of the padres and the nuns. While passing through these gorgeous apartments, I felt as though I were treading the halls of Monte Cristo palace, rather than a place for the worship of God. The priests and nuns only know the extent of this edifice, and I presume there are many who have been immured within its walls for years who know less of its extent than myself.

CHAPTER XIX.

MEMOIRS OF THE MEXICAN WAR—CONTINUED.

IN the City of Mexico I was filling three important offices, to wit, acting quartermaster, acting assistant commissary of subsistence, and ordnance officer, yet I had much of my time to myself while in camp or garrison. The condition upon which I accepted the appointments was that I should have the privilege of going into the command and selecting therefrom just such assistance as I needed; accordingly I had selected three clerks, one for the quartermaster department, one for the commissary, and one for the ordnance department, and they were all men much more competent in a practical business sense than myself. Consequently I had but little more to do than to sign vouchers and make my reports to Washington. We had not been in the city more than a month, when, during my leisure, I had visited the cathedral, the halls of the Montezumas, Chapultepec, the aqueduct, and other prominent places in and about the city, with various other adventures unimportant to my narrative. But at last I stumbled upon one which I think is worthy of relating, and consequently I give it a place.

Near the center of the city is a magnificent plaza, or

public square, ornamented with low shrubbery, water fountains, flagged walks, low palms, and rustic seats; and outside of these is a nice flagged walk for pedestrians; then, outside of that, a small border of grass, about four feet wide, with low curbing, some four to six inches above the level; and again, outside of all, is a lovely carriage drive, where myriads of fine carriages are, through the day and until late in the evening, constantly driving. One pleasant afternoon I was strolling leisurely around this plaza, when I noticed a magnificent carriage drive past quite close to where I was walking, and I also noticed that, as it approached me, the horses (two beautiful blacks) slackened their pace and kept along on a walk for some time. But as I was lounging and stopping every few steps, admiring shrubbery, etc., I paid but little attention further than to notice that the carriage mended its pace as soon as it passed me. I thought no more of it, and had commenced retracing my steps, when again I was attracted by the splendid equipage, and, as before, when it approached the spot where I was, again the pace was slackened. I then noticed that there were but two persons connected with the vehicle—the driver outside, and a female dressed in black, and shrouded in a thick black veil. As before, after they passed me, the carriage increased its pace. By this time my curiosity was thoroughly aroused. I continued for some time in the place where they passed me, when I slowly continued my walk, and, for the third time, I noticed the carriage approaching, and again slackening its pace. This time, when it came opposite to me, the lady passed her white handkerchief before her face, and quite naturally dropped it out of the carriage.   I sprang forward, picked up the handkerchief, and presented it to the lady, who acknowledged the compliment by an inclination of the head, at the same time passing me a card, and away went lady, carriage, and driver.   The card contained some writing in a lady's hand, but in Spanish, which I could not read.

I made my way to head-quarters, called my man Lebenstein, my interpreter, and the card proved to be a request to call at a certain street and number that evening.   Lebenstein insisted that I must not go, as there was treachery at the bottom of the matter.   I pretended to coincide with his views, although secretly determining to investigate the matter.   Accordingly, the first thing I did was to find the street and number, and discovered that it was in the most fashionable part of the town, and but a short distance from my quarters.   My next move was to confide the matter to two trusty friends, Sergeant Efner and Henry Stickler, and, after some deliberation, it was arranged that they were to patrol in front of the building, ready to catch the first alarm in case of treachery.

At nine o'clock sharp, we all went on the ground; I rang the bell at the outer gate, and was promptly admitted by a female servant, who conducted me through an arched passage to an inner court.   I was not long in discovering that I was entering the premises of wealth and luxury.   The court was large and commodious, with a beautiful jetting fountain in the center, statuary stationed at intervals, and two or three orange trees, which are quite common in that country.   All around this court were projecting balconies, covered over by the upper roof, with hanging lamps that lighted up the whole place.

I followed the servant up a flight of stairs to the first floor, where I was ushered into a most magnificent drawing-room, when the girl informed me that her mistress would be in presently. She withdrew, and in less than a minute the object of my adventure made her appearance, and, O ye gods! what an appearance! I had seen women in dreams, in story, and in reality; but nothing in point of beauty and loveline ss equal to the being that now stood before me. Remember that I was young and impressible, and internally exclaimed, "A goddess!" She moved toward me with all the grace of a sylph, with embarrassment upon her countenance offering an apology for her seeming boldness in inviting a stranger to call on her at that hour, and assured me that secresy in the matter could only secure her protection. I stammered out something, I know not what, in reply. But she soon made me understand that business also had dictated her course, and when seated, she attempted to enter upon a more elaborate explanation, stating that her business was of such a nature that, in those troublesome times, she could not entrust it to the Mexican authorities, and that she had no friend among the Mexicans to whom she could confide her troubles; that being near my quarters she had often seen me, and had made up her mind that if I would befriend her, she would confide in me.

I assured her of my willingness to do all in my power to aid and protect her against wrong and intrigues; but as she spoke no English, and I but little Spanish, it was impossible for me to learn the true condition of things, except through an interpreter. She had already informed me that she had been a wife; that her husband had been a general in the Mexican army, and had fallen at Cerro Gordo; that he was wealthy; that she was his sole heir, but that some of his relatives were attempting to cheat her out of her property. After considerable conversation on her part, I not understanding a quarter she said, I asked her if she had any person about her estate who could talk English. She informed me that she had not; that she kept but three trusty servants,— a man and wife, and coachman, none of whom could talk English. It was at length arranged that I was to entrust Lebenstein, my interpreter, as I thought him safe, and I was to renew my visit the next night, at the same hour, and bring my interpreter, when the subject was dropped for the evening. She rang and ordered refreshments, among which were champagne and Madeira wines, nuts, candies, bananas, oranges, etc.

At eleven o'clock I took leave of my goddess, with many kind assurances, and met my companions at the street gate, who scolded me for keeping them on guard so long. To satisfy the boys, we repaired to an oyster saloon, took a stew, and then went to quarters, where an adjutant from General Butler bore marching orders for our regiment, the next morning at five o'clock. I shall not attempt here to analyze my feelings. I first rushed to Colonel Hick's headquarters and begged him to let me remain on leave for two days, when I would follow. But, as I expected, my efforts were unavailing; for as acting quartermaster the regiment could not move until I had put it in motion. I then flew back to the house of my angelic one, rang the bell several times, but could get no response, and was compelled to give the matter up at least for that time, trusting to the chapter of accidents to make it right.

Our destination was the city of Puebla, where we arrived on the sixth day, and it took me about one week to get the regiment fairly quartered. At the end of that time I applied to Colonel Childs, military governor at Puebla at that time, for permission to return to the City of Mexico on an eight-day furlough. He refused to let me return to the city, saying that I could have my business done through the department at the city. I then forwarded a like request to General Scott (who had always been my friend). He gave me leave of absence for eight days. I joined a party of officers, and in three days thereafter I was in the City of Mexico. I waited until nightfall and then repaired to the residence of my lovely unknown. I rang the bell, but to no purpose; and after a long investigation and thorough exploration of the surroundings, I became fully satisfied that I was the only person about the premises, and that the house was closed. The three weeks that I had been unavoidably detained, I found had separated me from my fair one forever. Of her fate and fortune I have never learned a word; but such beauty as hers, her pleasing manner and address, would be sure to command friends everywhere.

I was determined, while on this trip, to revisit the battle-field of Contreras. In accordance with that notion, I tried to raise a small party of officers to accompany me from the city. The distance, as well as I can now remember, was about nine miles. After considerable effort I failed to get any one to venture out; consequently, I thought I would venture as far as San Angelo, that being our outpost, and trust to luck to get company from there. I therefore mounted my horse

13

and rode to that point, where I again tried to get a
party to go out with me to the battle-field, which was
three miles distant from that place.   But I was assured
that it would be unsafe for me to go out there with a
small party, as the whole country thereabouts was
swarming with guerrillas.

But I had made up my mind to go, and go I did,
against the remonstrances of all.   I rode out there without adventure, and when I reached the field, I dismounted and unbuckled my sword and fastened my
sword-belt around the horn of my saddle, and was leading my horse over the field on the east side of the sod
embankments, looking for some memorial to take from
the battle-field.   As I stooped to pick up some brooches
from a Mexican cap, two shots were fired in rapid succession.   My horse sprang, reared, and pulled away from
me, and ran like a frightened deer towards San Angelo,
which, by the way I passed in coming to Contreras,
caused him to perform quite a circuit in following the
road around the hill, while I ran straight down the hill
and attempted to intercept him.   When about half-way
to San Angelo, I met a non-commissioned officer with
twelve men, who had been sent out to look for my body.
They were leading my horse, but expected that if they
found me, they would find me dead.   The sh ts were
fired from quite a distance, and I thought no more of
the matter.   The horse in running had thrown out one
of my holster pistols, which, of course, was lost.   With
that exception, all was right.

When I reached San Angelo I treated the boys at the
post and took my departure for the city by the way of
Tacuba, which place I had passed about one mile,

when I met two infantry officers—a major and captain.
They were going towards Tacuba, and soon afterward
I discovered six lanceros, who came riding at a break-
neck speed. I at once drew my revolver in one hand, and
my remaining holster pistol in the other. I put my
horse at the top of his speed and charged through.
They opened to the right and left to let me go. I
adopted this plan because I did not know whether they
were friends or foes, as we had many Mexican lanceros
in our service. I reached the city, put up my horse, and
entered the Bella Union Hotel; had taken a wash, and
walked up to a mirror to comb my hair, when I noticed
an apparent tear or jagged hole in the breast of my new
uniform, with white cotton padding protruding, and, as
I was turning from the glass, still looking at my uniform, I discovered another white place still, down under
my arm, when the truth flashed through my mind that
one of the two bullets fired while I was stooping to pick
up the brooches, had passed between my arm and body,
penetrating my uniform, and my horse jumping and
pulling away from me at the same time, prevented me
from noticing the concussion or jar from the bullet.

I exhibited the rent to some brother officers, and told
them of the occurrence, when one of them asked me if
my horse was not struck, causing him to jump and run
away from me as he did. I said I had not examined
him. We went to the stable, and upon examination we
found that a bullet had passed across his rump, cutting
about half the thickness of the ball, making an ugly
wound about four inches long. While we were yet conversing, a courier arrived from Tacuba, stating that a
band of guerrillas had murdered a major and captain,

who were returning from the city, having just been paid off. I then congratulated myself upon the precaution I had adopted when charging through their ranks a few minutes before the murder.

Major Young and a party of officers being about to return to Puebla, I joined the party, making six of us, all told. We set out on a return trip, and about six o'clock in the evening we arrived at a little wayside inn or half-way place, in the foot-hills of the Popocatepetl, at or near the entrance of the pass across the mountains by way of Rio Frio. At this place we found a small number of Frians and others in a state of great excitement. On inquiry, we learned the following facts: Lieutenant Marsden and wife, with an escort of three mounted men, while on their way to the City of Mexico, and within half a mile of that place, were assaulted; the lieutenant was lassoed, pulled from his horse, and dragged to death, and at the time of the lassoing a volley was fired from the brush, wounding one of the soldiers in the side and breaking one horse's leg, while the assailants rushed in, seized the lady's horse by the bridle, and soon disappeared in the hills, with the lady a prisoner. The other soldiers, with their wounded companion, reached the station, and the party returned and found the body of the lieutenant partly stripped and rifled of all valuables. The body was bruised and mutilated, and in a horrible condition.

We soon determined to pursue the villains, and rescue the lady if possible. From what we could learn, there were not more than a dozen of them at most. Our little party numbered six, and the two troopers swelled our efficient force to eight. There was one old peon, who

informed us that he knew the location of one guerrilla
rendezvous; that it was at an old *hacienda* among some
spurs of the mountains about seven miles distant; and
he offered his services as guide. By half-past seven we
were all in the saddle, and commenced a rapid ride over
broken ground, where spurs of the mountains were projecting into the valley, sometimes riding through an
open pine wood, sometimes over open ground, until our
guide informed us that we were close to the place, when
we dismounted and left our horses in charge of one of
our party. The rest of us commenced a stealthy march
upon the old adobe, which stood upon the bank of a
small mountain stream.

We gained the rear of the building and discovered a
large orange orchard at our left. Coming up close to
the house, there was light proceeding from a broken
window. We ventured a short distance from the window, and after a hasty consultation, we cocked our carbines, and five of us were to approach the window, that
being as many as could do execution through the narrow casement, and that only by firing over each other's
shoulders, while two gained the front, where we expected
them to fly to make their escape. When all was ready,
the signal was given, and we simultaneously discharged
our five carbines in their midst. At that instant a terrific scream was heard inside. It was by a woman. As
we had anticipated, there was a rush for the front door,
where we heard two more shots in rapid succession.
We sprang to the front, saber in hand; but the guerrillas
were tearing through the orchard like frightened deer.
Upon entering the house, our passage was obstructed by
a dead "greaser" in the doorway. On entering, we

found three on the floor, two in the last agonies of death, and the other wounded in the chest, undoubtedly fatally. We next looked for the woman, whom we found in an adjoining room, seated upon a stool and tied hand and foot. We released her, and, on searching, found her horse, where there were several other horses. We saddled her horse and also one for the prisoner, and were soon ready for our return march. Some suggested that we should burn the house; but this I opposed, as the probable owner of it was doubtless not a party to the transaction or had any knowledge of its perpetration. We left the three dead Mexicans where they were lying, mounted our horses, and were soon on the trail homeward. We had ridden about a mile on our homeward route, when a shot was fired in the rear of our little command. The two troopers who had charge of the wounded Mexican came riding up, and said the prisoner had escaped. We readily understood how the escape was made, and that probably a bullet through his brain had aided him on his way.

The next morning, after giving the remains of Marsden as decent a burial as the condition of things would admit, we took our departure and were again on our way to Puebla. After consultation with Mrs. Marsden, we took her under our charge, and with us she returned to Rio Frio, where she had some acquaintances in the command stationed at that place. We saw her safely in charge of her friends, when we again pursued our journey without further adventure, till within a few miles of Puebla.

It was dark and we were hastening on to reach the city that night, when, in the distance, we heard what we thought to be the rattle of musketry in the city. We could hear it clearly and distinctly. We hurried up, believing that there was a general engagement, and each was cudgeling his brain to know how he should find his respective command; and more than once I had exclaimed, in my anxiety, "What the d—l has become of the artillery?" We dashed along at a rapid rate, and entered the city. The firing seeming to be at the lower end of the city, near the plaza; we rode as near as we dared, and then commenced a reconnoisance to learn which were the American forces and which the Mexican, when, in a short time, to our entire disgust, we learned that the men had secured a great quantity of those large Mexican fire-crackers, the report of which was about equal to that of a musket, and two regiments had pitched into each other in good earnest with the fire-crackers; "this, and nothing more."

CHAPTER XX.

MEMOIRS OF THE MEXICAN WAR—CONTINUED.

OUR command had now their regular station at Puebla, placed there as a portion of the defense of that city. This is a most lovely place, situated as it is upon the high table-lands about six thousand feet above the level of the ocean, in the midst of a vast plain, with brooks and rivulets of pure water running through it, and surrounded by snow-capped mountains. To the west is Mount Popocatepetl and the White Lady, on the same range. To the southeast is the Orizaba, with its spire-peak, already mentioned. In this same valley are situated the ancient city and pyramids of Cholula. There are also beautiful mineral springs between the city and that place, sending a flood of sulphur and other mineral waters through the valley, a portion of which is brought to Puebla, by way of aqueducts and canals, where it is used for bathing purposes.

I have seen, in the city of Puebla, a most beautiful picture of the founding of that town by the angels, some with their tape-lines measuring off the ground, and showing a lovely stream running through its site, while four other angels are descending from heaven and bearing to earth the cathedral of Puebla, one at each corner of the immense edifice. It is firmly believed by the ignorant Mexicans that the cathedral was erected in a single night by the angels, and a contradiction on that subject renders them very hostile, notwithstanding the fact that it took more than fifty years to complete the structure, while the "northern barbarians" would have completed the work in five or six years. I was told by parties who pretended to know, that the entire cost of the edifice was something over sixteen million dollars.

There were, at the time I sojourned there, about 80,-000 inhabitants in the city, and a prettier, cleaner city I never saw, containing every evidence of wealth and luxury. The buildings and architecture compared favorably with those of the City of Mexico; but not-withstanding its wealth and beauty, over two-thirds of the whole wealth in buildings and lands is owned by the churches, of which, I believe, there were eighty-seven; in fact, it is the great city of churches. I do not believe there was ever three minutes, day or night, in which you could not hear the ringing of bells. In Puebla the churches are not confined to a single bell; but the most of them are furnished with from three to a dozen, and the cathedral contains twenty-four, the largest of which is over twelve feet across the chime, and can only be rung by means of a windlass attached to the clapper. But among the bells, there was one that was more efficient than all the rest, that would knock every Mexican flat to the earth, as far as its sound could be heard; this was the bishop's bell. I have seen some of the more devout drop upon the street and absolutely lick the pavement. Puebla, next to Cholula, is the cradle of the church. Our command was quartered in the convent of St. Augustus, and I here, as at the City of Mexico, became quite a favorite with the padres by reason of my moderation, demanding no more room for the men than was necessary. There were a great many nuns and a great many children in this institution. The children were foundlings, of course.

We had been stationed but a short time in this convent, when one day I felt a severe pain in my throat, the glands about my neck becoming very much inflamed, and I made complaint to our surgeon, Dr. W. B. Whitesides, who was my bosom friend and who had saved me once at Tampico. I told him I was suffering very much, and if it was popular to die of sore throat, I believed that it would kill me. The doctor did not seem to know anything about the disease. My throat continued to swell until it and my chin were even, and I kept scolding about it and rubbing it with opodeldoc and other powerful liniments that I found among the doctor's medicines. At length it became so swollen that I could scarcely breathe at all. Night came on and

I˙got a big hop poultice and wrapped it around my throat and went to my cot. I gradually became easier and dropped off into a sleep, and when I awoke the next morning I was much better. But before the next morning there were three dead officers laid out in my quarters from the same disease.

There were few attractions in the city for wild, adventurous spirits; but there was one never-failing source of enjoyment, and that was the Passo, or species of plaza. There were beautiful walks, choice shrubbery, fragrant flowers, and bright, sparkling fountains. One evening, as Lieutenant Poleon and myself were walking in the Passo, we discovered two men in what appeared to be a deadly combat, one being armed with a saber, the other with a heavy knife, resembling, in breadth and weight, a butcher's cleaver. We stepped up each behind one of the combatants and pulled them asunder, and arrested both of them. They yielded to the arrest and we marched them into quarters and placed them under guard. The one with the saber turned out to be a member of the Mexican police force; the other a noted cut-throat. The policeman died at the end of two days, and I had the satisfaction of seeing the other hanged.

The monotony of the city finally became unendurable, and one fine morning in the month of April, I rode out of town, resolved upon an adventure of some kind. I went out of the city on a well-traveled road, not knowing to what point it led. ·In fact I never thought of making an inquiry; but it led through a lovely plain, well-settled, with large and handsome houses and well-cultivated fields, bearing orange groves, bananas, plantains, alfalfa, and waving grain, while here and there were bright, sparkling brooks, wending their way over a pebbly bed to the river in the distance. In a word, it presented a prospect that the lover of the beautiful would treasure in mind.

I continued my ride to a distance of at least sixteen or eighteen miles, seeing nothing but peons and laborers of different grades; but presently, in the distance, and at the edge of a grove, I noticed what first seemed to be a low grove of small bushes, with a most singular foliage; I continued to ride in that direction, and the nearer I approached, the more singular the appearance. But in a few minutes the mystery was solved; it was a group of lances stuck in the ground with their streamers waving in the breeze; and I had no sooner discovered the character of the object of my curiosity than the lanceros had discovered and made me out. While I sat on my horse watching them, the group of lances were hurriedly pulled up from the earth and in the hands of Mexican warriors; and, each mounting a mustang, disclos:d the fact that a regiment of lanceros had been luxuriating in the shade of the grove, their horses secreted in the grove, and all taking a rest. As soon as they were mounted, they made a furious dash across the field for the highway, where I sat upon my horse looking at them as they advanced. I would have told them, if I had had an opportunity, that they need not hurry so on my account. They must have held me in high respect; for when I drew my saber and waved them a salute, they returned it by the discharge of a hundred escopets. I did not wait for further compliments, but concluded I would go back home. I was mounted on my favorite horse, which was fleet as the wind; and although they were traveling after me at a rapid rate, old Selim soon increased the distance between them and me.

As soon as I was entirely safe from their careless shooting, on coming to a little eminence, I wheeled my horse and again waved my saber at them, when they made another vigorous dash for me, when I retreated again in good order. I thus amused myself beckoning them on to follow me for several miles, until passing a *hacienda*, where I saw two men rushing out, each having an escopet in hand to cut off my retreat, when I put my horse on a dead run, dropped my rein upon his neck, and as I passed them discharged my two pistols at them, while at the same moment they fired at me; but as far as I could see, this new danger rather accelerated my speed. I soon increased the distance between us, and continued to hold it until within about three miles of the city, when they gave up the chase. I then rode back a short distance toward them and beckoned them on, but could not induce them to follow me further, when I rode slowly into town, feeling well satisfied with my day's adventure.

About this time Lieutenant Conkling and myself were taken down with Mexican rheumatism. It is one of those diseases that seems to be peculiar to the highlands and table-lands of Mexico, and it is one of the most terrible and painful diseases that ever afflicted humanity. There are hundreds of men in Puebla whose limbs are drawn into all conceivable shapes. I have seen some poor creatures stalking through the streets with their shoulders drawn down at right angles with their legs; others crawling along the streets upon all fours. I suffered in every limb and joint the most excruciating agony; and this continued, day and night, for several weeks. The doctors could give me no relief. It was entirely new to our surgeons, and beyond their control. Conkling would lie in his hammock and exclaim, "Oh God! Norton; what shall I do?" I, on the other side, "Oh God! Conkling; what shall I do?" At last we called in the padres to our aid, as they professed medical skill. They prepared a strong ointment and anointed us from head to foot. I don't know what effect it may have had on our souls, but this I do know, it did not help our bodies in the least.

We became cross, irritable, and reckless. I recollect that it was a little cool, and I sent my servant out to get a pottery charcoal furnace to warm the room. My man got it up, kindled and ready for a warming process; but it did not work to suit friend Conkling. He picked it up, walked to the balcony and threw it down on the sidewalk, to the infinite amusement of a crowd of beggarly peons, and sent his servant out for another. He brought it in, and started the fire, when I deliberately picked it up and dashed it from the balcony to the street and immediately sent for another, which was brought, but shared the same fate as the first and second. We amused ourselves and the street Arabs in this way for a couple of hours, until we had smashed up some twelve or fifteen, when that sport became monotonous (the furnaces only cost about eight cents apiece) and we commenced throwing them *clacos* (copper cents) to see them rush and pile up to get them, until we began to think the street Arabs were getting more fun out of it than we were. The crowd increased until it became a perfect throng, men, women, and children all piling into one heap, when a general scramble would ensue.

· We next began to heat the *clacos*. We would make them red hot, and then throw them to the sidewalk, and it was rare sport to see them grab them and then drop them, until at length they hit upon an expedient· They would pick them up with the corners of their blankets in their hands, this preventing them from burning themselves. We ran this for some time, until it began to be stale, when we got another crotchet in our heads. We heated a shovelful of *clacos*, and dropped them down from the balcony, and when the general rush was made, we emptied a pailful of flour over them. By this time the street was blockaded for several rods by all classes of the community, all seeming to enjoy the joke. They would look up at us and call out "*mas clacos.*" We proceeded to heat another shovelful and prepared a pail of flour and a pail of water; and first we threw the *clacos*, secondly the flour, and closely following it a pail of water, and when we got through I think they were the worst-looking set of devils I ever saw. Our sufferings did not in the least diminish, and we racked our brains for new diversion to kill time and drown pain.

One afternoon I was suffering outrageously, and I felt discouraged and desperate. I dressed myself in full uniform, ordered my horse (old Selim), and rode out of the city alone (I never did take my servant, as I would not subject any one else to the risks I ran in those wild rides). I took the road for Cholula, without any definite idea how far I would ride, or where I would eventually bring up. When some five or six miles from the city, I began to meet peons, packing large sacks of wood on their backs, going to Puebla. They viewed me with perfect amazement, and one of them exclaimed, "*Donde va V. Señor?"* I replied, "Almost anywhere." They informed me in their lingo that there were many cut-throats and robbers, and that unless I returned, I would be killed. But, as I saw nothing alarming, I continued on my course, passing *en route* many ranches and *haciendas*, until the pyramid of Cholula broke upon my vision. As I neared the place, it loomed up like some small mountain, and anything but the pyramid of Cholula pictured in my old school geography. But the nearer I approached it, the more regular seemed the formation, and what I at first took to be cavities and an irregular surface, proved to be the spiral drive that winds to the top. The road leading from Puebla to the ancient city of Cholula passes to the north of the pyramid, and, as it were, through a small gap in a ridge that runs north from it, which it was evident to me had some day been a portion of the pyramid, and that it had fallen and stretched its length on the plain. But more of this in the future.

I could not with any safety dismount; consequently I did not try to examine the pyramid, but rode straight on to the city, which, like Puebla, is situated on a vast plain; in fact, the country is one immense plain from the base of the Popocatepetl Mountains to the foot-hills of the Orizaba Mountains. I rode straight down the main street of the dilapidated city until I reached the plaza, which lay on the north side of the street. When at that point, I drew rein on my favorite and took a survey of the place. The sun was just sinking behind the crest of the Popocatepetl Mountains at the time. The Mexicans who watched my advent into the town seemed staring more in the direction I had come than at me, when a series of howls and whistles reached me from the populace I soon discovered what it meant. They at first were looking to see where my companions or escorts were; and seeing none, then for the rush and capture, or the death of me. I quietly watched the excitement for a few moments, when I drew my saber, whirled it a few times over my head, in the last rays of the setting sun, released old Selim, and in a few minutes the city and its excitement were far in the distance, and in less than two hours I was safely in my quarters, without further adventure.

When I asserted that I had visited the city of Cholula alone, my statement was far from being credited by my fellow-officers who had visited it in company with a strong expedition organized for that purpose. But I soon convinced them of the truth of my statement by minutely describing the road by streams, hills, and bridges, the location of the pyramid, and more than all, the plaza and some burned buildings on the north side of it, when they with one accord said, "He must have been there." Conkling, who lay upon his cot groaning, exclaimed, "Yes, if he says he has been there, you may depend upon it, as the d—d fool goes everywhere safely, when one of us would get his throat cut."

A surprise met me on my arrival at quarters, that was very pleasant in some respects and mortifying in others. The officer said that a young man had called to see me who seemed to have some important business with me, and said that he would be back in a short time. I was not kept in suspense long, for the visitor was presently announced, and to my astonishment my youngest brother, John, whom I had left at home in charge of affairs, seized me by the hand, the tears rushing to his eyes as he did so. The story was soon told. The old abolition party, who opposed the war, and threw all possible obstacles in the way to prevent parties from volunteering and to oppress those who had volunteered, had got up a scheme against me that frightened my people at home, and John had set out at once to seek me and communicate the facts. I knew that the whole thing amounted to nothing, and cast it at once from my mind. But my brother had been hired by the Government as a teamster to go through to the City of Mexico, and was under charge of the quartermaster, conducting the train. They were to continue their march the next morning, and poor brother John thought that he was to be separated from me immediately. I accompanied him to their camp, sought out the quartermaster, and told him that I wanted that teamster and would furnish him another to drive in his place. The exchange was made, and I took my brother under my immediate charge and kept him with me to the close of the war.

Our Mexican rheumatism still continued to afflict us. But there was residing in Puebla an artisan who worked gilt ornaments, and whom I had served by filling a commission entrusted to me on my trip to the City of Mexico, and who had through me become acquainted with several of our officers, after which he often visited our quarters. On being informed of our condition, he called on me and said if I would furnish the cost of the medicine he would provide a remedy that would cure us. I did not have much confidence in it, but in our extremity we were prepared to try almost anything. He bought the medicine; it was a transparent liquid and very penetrating, and was almost strong enough to blister. In this we both bathed our limbs, and the result was that in less than ten days we were entirely cured of the dreadful scourge.

14

CHAPTER XXI.

MEMOIRS OF THE MEXICAN WAR—CONTINUED.

IN Mexico, the ideas of family residences are unlike our own notions. We prefer living on the ground floor of our residences; they like to live as high up as they can get. My quarters in Puebla were in the third story of an extensive building, with stairs leading to the roof. I could not utilize one-half of the vast structure, so I assigned quite a large portion of it to officers of our regiment. There are, as a general thing, ornamental balconies at each story of the buildings; and that was the case with our quarters. Immediately across the street from us lived an aristocratic Castilian, whose name I learned was Queretaro. He was President of the Mexican Senate, and was absent on his official business. We formed a kind of eye acquaintance with the family from the opposite balconies, and in a short time I was honored with a visit by a boy about fourteen years old. He informed me that his name was Edwardo Queretaro, and the son of the gentleman who lived across the way. He had picked up a very few words of English, and with my few words of Spanish, we managed to understand each other very well. He was delighted with our military trappings, such as sabers, sashes, epaulets, and many other things which were new and strange to him; and, in return, I was much pleased with young Edwardo. He was very expert with the lasso, and we amused ourselves hours at a time by his throwing the lasso and my attempting to guard against it with my saber; but I must say I found it impossible to parry and protect myself against his skill. He would sometimes catch me around my neck, and if I happened to step, perhaps he would catch me by the foot; and, when all other parts were guarded, he would frequently catch me by the sword arm.

Things continued in this way about three weeks, only Edwardo became so attached to me that he was with me two-thirds of the time. At length he became very solicitous that I should visit him. I assured him that I could not on his invitation, as I was an entire stranger to his family; but before this time he had told me the family at home was composed of his mother, a sister nine years old, and his Aunt Amelia, who was twenty years old. In three or four days after this, Edwardo told me his aunt wished me to visit them. I told him if I visited their house the invitation must come from his mother. The next day he informed me that his mother wished me to visit them. Consequently I resolved to do so, as I could not doubt that they were ladies and moved in the best society. I took my interpreter and went over, and was introduced by the boy to his mother and aunt, as his friend. I remained an hour and was delighted with the ladies; but it was hard to tell who were the most disgusted with my interpreter, the ladies or myself. He all the time indulged in a twaddle about himself, and failed to interpret one-half of what we wished to say to each other. When the time came for leave-taking, they warmly insisted on my coming again, and in these words, that the house was mine. In return, I assured them that I would avail myself of their kind invitation, and that I should bring no interpreter, but that they should all act as my interpreter.

In the first interview they asked me if I was married, and I assured them that I was. But the next day Edwardo asked the same question of Lieutenant Conkling, and of other officers; they, supposing that they were playing into my hand, assured him that I was not married, and was only joking with them when I pretended to be married. So when I called again, several days afterwards, I was warmly received by the whole family, and more especially so by Miss Amelia, who took upon herself the task of teaching me to speak their language, and no one ever had a more zealous teacher. I would frequently get off some Mexican phrases, when she would check me and say, "*Este no bussna; este lingua lotros indu.*" Time rolled on, and somehow when not on duty I found myself with my friends most of the time. I was not slow to learn that my little Amelia was becoming very fond of me, and, in fact, too fond for her own peace of mind. I often said to her, "You must not be too fond of me, for I have a wife at home." She only laughed at me, and said that she had caught me at my trick; that I was not married; for all the officers said so; that I was only fooling her. I found it impossible to convince the poor girl against her will; therefore things went along in their own way.

Amelia was very pretty. She was of medium height, well formed, with a light and elastic step. In complexion she was a blonde, with a full, deep, blue eye, and as fair as a lily; but I do not pretend to dwell on her perfection, further than to distinguish her from the "greaser" horde. I had introduced her to a few superior officers, and it was amusing to me to hear Amelia's perfections set forth by them. The Spanish are a very jealous race, and she seemed to think I would be of the same organization; for she would pass the open window or step to the blinds every minute during their call, for fear I might be jealous of her. During our acquaintance I fell ill. When they heard the fact they sent Edwardo over to my quarters and insisted that I should come to their house, where I could have better attention than I could at my own quarters. I finally complied with their wishes, and was with them for over three weeks, and though Amelia was waited upon by her own servants, she would not allow a servant to wait upon me. Everything that I needed came from her own hand.

As I convalesced, one morning I took a walk in the Passo, and had a little chat with an early walker who, as well as myself, was out to take the air. She was a young Mexican girl of the better class. She arranged a button-hole bouquet and pinned it on the breast of my uniform. On my return I met Amelia, and as soon as she saw the flowers her eyes flashed with fury. She sprang to my breast like a tigress, seized the flowers, dashed them on the floor, stamped them beneath her little feet, and exclaimed in her own language, "You have no love for me." She seized her diamond-handled stiletto, passed it to me, and exclaimed, "Here; kill me; I have nothing to live for." I finally got her quieted down, and asked her what she meant; that I was not conscious of having done anything to offend her or any injustice to her. She said that a woman had placed those flowers on my breast. I admitted it, but assured her that I gave the matter no consideration, and did not know that it meant anything more than a little coquetry. But I then, for the first time, learned that the Spanish language of flowers is more read and better understood than ours.

After I had quite recovered my health, and was about to return to my own quarters, I told her that they had been at a large outlay for me, and I wished to compensate them for my trouble and expense while there. Amelia treated my offer with contempt and scorn at first, but soon changed to a flood of tears and assured me that money was the least of her care; that she had plenty of money; she threw me her keys, saying, "Here are the keys of my coffer, if you want money, help yourself; I do not want yours; I did not take care of you for money." She was an heiress; she and her brother owned three large *haciendas*, and one fine day she asked me to visit one of them with her. I entered one of their clumsy carriages, and we drove out there. I was amused and yet perplexed at her, for all that was to be seen or enjoyed was us and ours. The place was a lovely one; the buildings were magnificent, situated upon a lovely plateau of about one thousand acres. They were of adobe, containing an inner court with plats of grass and fountains inside. The whole was inclosed with a high adobe wall, with broken glass cemented in the top, which all the way around inclosed the premises. This was for protection against the assaults of ladrones and guerrillas. It was just the place where a man, with that beautiful creature, might content himself to while away a life-time. She wished me to visit her other two *haciendas;* but I never went out to see them. The whole family were good and kind people to me, and at the close of the war, when the order came for us to take up our line of march, I hardly knew how to break the news to Amelia; for the four months of our acquaintance seemed to her, so she told me, to be as one bright vision.

But alas! the parting had to come. I left my Amelia in her sister-in-law's arms, in a swoon, and have never seen nor heard of her from that day to this. But think not that I left her without a pang of remorse, not for any perfidy on my part, for I never deceived her, but my principal regret was that she loved me so fondly.

CHAPTER XXII.

MEMOIRS OF THE MEXICAN WAR—CONTINUED.

DURING the time I was stationed at. Puebla we had had little active service more than scouting and keeping that place and the surrounding country in subjection. Many of the officers who had never visited the pyramids of Cholula were anxious to do so, and at length we raised a company of commissioned and non-commissioned officers, amounting to about seventy-five or eighty, and one fine morning set out to visit the pyramid and city of Cholula. We swept over the level plains, and two hours and a half brought us to the city, where I was, on my second visit, in a condition to take notes of the place and surroundings, and soon learned what I had failed to discover on my first visit, that Cholula was the head-quarters of the Catholic clergy. As we all rode up to the plaza, I noticed a large number of boys, about one hundred and sixty, all swinging censers, and, at the head, two mitred priests. They were in two files and presented quite an imposing sight. It must have been some holiday with them. There was a ditch between us and them; I clapped spurs to old Selim, we scaled the ditch, and in less time than I am writing it, were at the

head of the procession. The priests left their flocks in
great consternation. I drew my saber and bade the
youngsters (who ranged from fourteen to eighteen years)
forward march. They were headed for a large cathedral. I marched them along to the side of the building,
when I gave the order, " File left; march." When they
reached the door, I again ordered them, " Single file;
march." They entered the building, and I sat upon my
horse until the last one had disappeared, when I sheathed
my sword, released my horse, and joined my companions.
Some of them wanted to know what I meant. I told
them that I just wanted to see how it would seem to
command Mexicans.

We then made a general circuit of the town; but could
see but small evidence of that grandeur we read of at
the time of the Spanish conquest. There were no moss-
covered piles or mound walls to impress the minds of the
traveler that it had ever been the seat of a mighty
empire or the home of kings, outside of the vast ruins
of its pyramids; and to this I never gave my attention.
I obtained through my interpreter, from an aged Mexican, this tradition: When the pyramid was intact, it was
very high; and long ago the city of Cholula was destroyed
by a vast flow of lava from the crater of the Popocatepetl, situated some thirty-six miles west of the city; that
Cholula was afterwards rebuilt, and, as there was no hill
to escape to, the people built the pyramid to have a
retreat in case of another inundation from the fiery flood;
that after it had stood for many years, there came a
great earthquake and shook it down; that before the
earthquake the Popocatepetl was in an active state of
eruption, with the lava streams flowing to the valley, and

thousands had already taken possession of the pyramid as a protection against the burning flood that was approaching the valley; and that at the time of the earthquake they were buried beneath the huge pile or crushed by its fall.

I am aware that some historians speak of a second and smaller pyramid at Cholula; but as for myself I saw but one, and what their imagination has pictured to be a small pyramid, I am fully satisfied is but a portion of the great and only one. On a close examination, I am convinced that the pyramid of Cholula was once at least three times as high as it is now, and that it has fallen to the north and left quite a long mound, which, if solid, would be a cone with its base to the standing part of the pyramid. I was more fully convinced on examining the corresponding parts of the pyramid and comparing them with the fallen portion. It is asserted by most writers on the subject that the pyramid is built of unburned brick; as to the truth or falsity of this allegation, I cannot say, as I could at no point discover any shape of adobe or brick; but the principal ingredient forming this immense pile is a hard clay, resembling in texture the adobe used by the Mexicans in constructing their houses; but it is no harder than the uncultivated earth of the valley in summer; but there is one thing that I think is not noticed by any writer, and that is that mingled with the general mass composing the pyramid are thousands and probably millions of small images of everything that walks, hops, creeps, swims, and flies, that is known to that country. I commenced digging with a short sword, and in an hour's time I had dug out of the standing pyramid and *debris* of the fallen portion, at least fifty images. They were composed of pottery were well burned and in a perfect state of preservation. There were deer, bears, wolves, coons, foxes, fish, crocodiles, serpents, lizards, monkeys, parrots, ducks, geese, swan, chickens, elks, and innumerable types of the human family, giving additional proof that the fallen remains were but a part and parcel of the original pyramid; the images were alike mingled in the component parts of both. I carefully preserved the images that I had taken out, and brought them home with me to Illinois. Among the balance of my curiosities, over thirty years' absence has scattered them to the winds and robbed me of my relics, at least so far as I know.

The location of the town of Cholula was well chosen, the soil in the vicinity is fertile and productive, with brooks of clean, fresh water wending through the valley; and while I say that the town was never of the magnitude that writers claim for it, yet there are evidences to show that it has been much larger and more flourishing than it is at the present time. After having spent the day in investigating the town and pyramid of Cholula, our company returned to Puebla without accident or adventure further than related.

At the entry of the Americans into Puebla, or the "city of churches," the immense wealth of the clergy has been hastily considered, the wealth consisting of gold and silver plate, ornaments, and jewels, which amounted in value to many millions of dollars. This wealth found hiding-places inside and outside of the city limits at the time of the capitulation of the city to the Americans. The bishop had a palatial mansion about three miles south of the city, where it was confidently asserted, and doubtless with truth, that great masses of the church wealth was deposited, and probably a more fitting place could not have been selected. I had ofttimes listened to the tales told me regarding the beauty of the grounds and magnificent buildings, and curiosity prompted me, on one of my wild rambles, to visit the place. It was a pleasant summer day and the gates of the grounds were open. I first met a menial who told me in their language "to leave." I assured him that I would do no harm; that I merely wished to see the grounds. He was inexorable, and seized my horse by the bit and attempted to turn him about. At this, I drew my saber and told him to let go my rein or I would cut his arm off. He accordingly released his hold on my bridle.

At this juncture a padre came up, who said "that the grounds were private and strangers were not admitted." I apologized and said I was attracted to the spot by the beauty of the grounds and had no idea of interfering with private property, and it was sufficient for me to know that the public were excluded. Whereupon the padre very courteously invited me to dismount, and ordered the peon to take charge of my horse. We walked together over the most artistically arranged grounds that I had ever visited since my arrival on Mexican soil. There was a beautiful grove of orange trees loaded with ripe, yellow oranges, interspersed with green fruit and blossoms. On the other side of the walk was a large grove of lemon and lime trees; and further along the walk was on one side a grove of olives, while upon the other side were bananas and other fruits. At the end of the walk we came to the baths, which were supplied by a large sulphur spring, and, on invitation of the padre, I treated myself to a refreshing bath. The cautious padre continued to walk in the shrubbery while I took my bath, when he again joined me; but I observed an equal precaution by keeping my sword and side arms close by me. When fully dressed, we again sauntered around the grounds, keeping in the shade, where I spent over two hours in a state of perfect bliss, and while there I could not help noticing the great strength of the gates and towers. On approaching the building, I recollected the stories regarding the great church wealth therein deposited. I returned to quarters, where I freely conversed with my fellow-officers about the place of my adventure, when the matter was dropped and almost forgotten by me.

Probably about four weeks after the adventure last narrated, one night about nine o'clock the colonel's orderly came to my quarters with a note requesting me to call at the colonel's quarters forthwith, on a matter of importance. I complied with the request. On my arrival there I found about twenty-five commissioned officers in attendance, who I soon learned had been called together for a business meeting, which had been for some little time in session; and when introduced, I was requested to pledge myself upon the honor of an American officer that, in case I should not be in sympathy with the move about being inaugurated, I would not expose the scheme, or the name of any individual connected with it. To this I gave a qualified consent, stating that unless there was something treasonable in it, or involving my honor as a man, I would remain silent and ignorant of everything that occurred there that evening.

Upon this promise I was let into the secret of the meeting, or rather organization, which I found to be as follows: They had learned, by information entirely reliable, that the diamonds and most valuable portion of the church wealth at Puebla had been collected together and deposited at the bishop's *hacienda;* that some time before, the padre had been corrupted by some of the officers, and at their instigation had wound himself into the good graces of the bishop and the attaches of his *hacienda*, and now was resident there; that he, for a stipulated fee, was to give the parties in the plot access to the inside as well as outside, and that it was, in reality, a kind of second Gibraltar; that there was an abundance of arms and ammunition, and about twenty resolute men to use them; that the plan, as far as developed, was that every one there was to make one of a party to attack and rob the bishop's *hacienda;* that each one was to take a soldier's uniform to be worn on the occasion; and that no one was to wear any insignia of rank that could expose them in case of disaster or accident; that each was to arm himself with a musket and bayonet, with forty rounds of mixed ammunition in his cartridge box; that the expedition should be conducted on foot; that the parties should leave the city at the hour of eleven o'clock at night, in squads not to exceed three or four at most, and were to meet at a well-known point outside the city, about one mile distant.

All this was minutely detailed to me, showing that their plans had been well matured, and they further assured me that in case success crowned our efforts we should all be millionaires; that there had been several meetings, and the thing had been fully discussed; that the attempt was to be made at a time when the bishop was sure to be at home, of which we would be informed by the venial old priest; and when once in possession of the bishop, the rest would be easy. " But," said I, " about the old priest; supposing he betrays you ? " That they did not fear, as the arrangement was made that he was to meet them outside the gate, and accompany them, and that he had been admonished that the first signs of treachery on his part would decide his fate; that they had held several meetings, and thus far had their plans matured, and that their only trouble would be to make their way to the underground vaults, where they were informed that the treasure was deposited. " But," said they, " we have come to the conclusion that if we could catch the old bishop, by the threat of cold steel, we might easily persuade him to draw the bolts that conceal the hidden treasures." I was further informed they had been discussing the question as to who should lead the expedition, and that they had unanimously chosen me in case I would join them in the enterprise.

I was perfectly astounded at the idea of the thing, and the cool atrocity contemplated, as well as the proposition that I should become the leader of a band of thieves; for I could not bring myself to look upon it in any other light. I told them that under any other circumstances I should be very thankful to them for the honor that such an appointment would confer, but that I could not thank them for such an offer of preference, and that, under no circumstances, could I be induced to take any part in the matter; that I held a commission under one of the proudest Governments in the world,

and that full faith and confidence were reposed in me
by my country; and that I would faithfully discharge
my duty as a soldier of the great American republic,
and would never bring a stain upon the grand escutcheon
of our nation; that I thought the whole thing was ill-
advised, and that upon serious reflection I did not believe
that one of them would for a moment think of carrying
the plot into execution. If I had been astonished at
the narration of the scheme in which they were engaged,
I was more astonished at the result of my remarks. I
saw that I had awakened them to the enormity of the
offense they were about to commit. I assured them the
secret was safe as far as I was concerned; that if they
persisted in carrying out their plan, I should feel myself
bound by my promise; but I begged them, for sake of
their own self-respect and for the sake of the reputation
of the army and our country, to abandon the enterprise
and forget it; but, if remembered at all, to be only as a
fevered dream.

I took leave of the party, returned to my quarters,
and that was the last of the expedition; but since that
time and since the close of the war, I have ofttimes been
thanked by my companions for the stand I took on that
occasion.

CHAPTER XXIII.

MEMOIRS OF THE MEXICAN WAR—CONTINUED.

ABOUT the latter part of April, 1848, as the war was drawing to a close, there was a considerable force of Mexican and American deserters assembled in a large *hacienda*, on the east side of the Orizaba Mountains, and were making constant incursions into the surrounding settlements, robbing Mexicans and small detachments of troops, and we came to the conclusion that it was necessary to dislodge them. For this purpose a small volunteer force from the command stationed at Puebla determined to perform that service. The volunteer command consisted of about two companies of the Sixth Illinois Infantry, which, under Colonel Collins, composed the expedition. We were to be guided by a woman and her son, who claimed to know the country and the exact location of the robbers' den, which was said to be some forty miles from Puebla. Accordingly the command took up its line of march about daylight, under the guidance of the woman and her son. Lieutenant Poleon and myself were to be of the expedition, but were detained in settling up some matters in connection with a court-martial held on the previous day, until about nine o'clock in the morning. But, having learned that the command would pass *en route* through Tepeaca, about twenty-five miles distant, we mounted our horses and followed after the command; and, after a ride of about fifteen miles, we began to overtake a few stragglers in the rear.

The first whom we overtook were Lebenstein and a

wild Irishman, whom we called the "flying dispatch." A Mexican was pleading with the Irishman to give him his *serape* (a blanket with a hole in the center to go over the head). I said to him, "Have you got the Mexican's blanket?" seeing he had a Mexican *serape* hanging over his arm. He replied, "No; shure, I have not." I asked, "Where did you get that blanket?" "And is it the blanket you mane? Shure, I bought it of Captain Wight, and gave him two dollars and a quarther for it." About this time another "greaser" crawled out of the brush, and, "*Si Señor, la serape es el otros hombres.*" I turned to Lebenstein and asked him if that was the Mexican's blanket. He answered by an inclination of the head, I turned to the "flying dispatch," and advised him to give the Mexican his blanket. Whereupon he threw it at the Mexican, and exclaimed, "Take it, ye murdersome thafe, and bad luck to the day I iver came to Mexico, to be robbed by a graser." We ordered them to close up on the rear, and riding on soon gained the front, and arrived at Tepeaca about three o'clock in the afternoon, where we encamped for the night.

We were within the walls of a town of considerable size, all of whose inhabitants were hostile to us, and before we were settled in our quarters, news was brought in from the rear that one man had been picked off and killed by the Mexican marauders. Some eight or ten of us remounted our horses, and rode back to where we found the man shot and his skull crushed in by a rock. Continuing our ride to the rear, we immediately gave chase, but took no prisoners. Captain Armstrong (not of our command), one of the party, was slightly wounded in the leg by an escopet ball. We returned to

15

the town, where before midnight there was an alarm, and our sentinels were driven in and a general assault made upon our camp; but we soon repulsed them with but slight loss on either side, one of our men being shot in the shoulder, and three of the Mexicans killed.

The next morning we resumed our march for our destination. We marched all day until night, when we began to suspect our guides. The woman and young man were called to a counsel, when they declared they were lost. We placed them under guard and continued our march, soon coming to a Mexican hamlet, where we found that we were within two leagues of the place we were seeking. We pressed a Mexican into our service as guide, and continued our march, which had become very laborious; the roads were rocky and we were winding up through ravines and continuously up the spurs of the Orizaba, and ere we were aware, our last guide had deserted us; but we continued to follow the road, when about two A. M. we came in front of a large *hacienda*, where we halted to make further inquiries. I had dismounted and thrown myself upon the ground near the walls of the place, holding my horse by the bits, when all of a sudden I heard the report of a gun above me, and a bullet struck the ground about three feet from me. My horse sprang back and jerked me to my feet, and about this time the bullets from the *hacienda* were rattling around like hail, and it did not take us long to learn two things: First, that we had found the place we were looking for; second, that they had been notified that we were coming.

It was useless for us to return their fire, as they were wholly protected by the walls. The officers held a hasty

consultation, and we resolved to force the gate. Colonel
Collins took no command, but placed Capt. C. L. Wight
first, and myself second, in command. Wight ordered
the squad to seize a large bowlder and batter the gate.
They did so for half a minute, when they found they
would have to get something heavier, and had stepped
from the front of the gate when a perfect blaze of fire
came through the third paneling of the gate, between
the heavy framework. I ordered up a platoon and
delivered a volley back at them, and ordered the rear to
reload; then ordered the second platoon up and delivered the second volley through the gate. By this time
Captain Wight had found a large square timber to use
as a battering ram, and as all those before the gate were
stooping to raise the timber, the Mexicans delivered
another volley through the gate, just high enough to go
over their backs, one of the bullets striking a man in
the rank beyond. I ordered the men up by platoons
and gave them two more volleys through the panels,
which effectually silenced them. Captain Wight then
plied the battering ram so vigorously that the gate
yielded, and we rushed into the hall and through into
the court yard, where the last of the Mexicans were
scaling the rear walls. Their leader was a fat Mexican,
who slipped and fell back; a dozen muskets were leveled
on him in an instant, but Captain Wight and myself
threw ourselves between the Mexican and our men, and
that saved his life. We made him and several others
prisoners, and were soon in complete possession of their
stronghold.

I forgot to state that during the first firing our surgeon
came rushing up to me and said, " My horse has broken

from me, and run in that direction," indicating by pointing his finger. I charged off in the direction indicated,
and had not ridden more than one hundred yards when
a gun cracked beneath a bush, a bullet came whizzing
past my ear, and a Mexican started to run! I charged
after him and delivered my holster fire. He evidently
was a guerrilla chief, as he wore a very rich pancho. I
had it for many years; it was stolen from me in Placerville in 1863. I did not find the surgeon's horse. We
erected a temporary barricade at the front entrance
where we had broken down the gate, placed our sentinels, and quartered for the balance of the night. The
Mexicans and deserters kept up a desultory firing all
night from the brush and outer walls; we could easily
distinguish the Mexican shots from the whiz of the
American cartridge in possession of the deserters. The
old don that we had captured, after finding that he was
in no immediate danger, became quite cheerful and
communicative, informing us that his name was Pedro
Sanchez; that a scout had been sent from Tepeaca
informing him that a band of Americans was *en route*
to attack and sack his *hacienda*, and that he had made
such hasty preparations for its defense as he could in
the short time allotted to him.

Thus we learned to a certainty that we had been
betrayed by our guides. The old man denied that he was
a robber or that he had harbored any deserters, but that
there was a band of Americans about four miles from
their encampment in the mountains. The truth may as
well be told here; we had expected to capture a booty
of at least forty thousand dollars at this *hacienda*, of
which the inhabitants had been robbed. The premises

were searched, but no strong box or money was to be found. With the notice they had of course that was taken care of. The next morning they restored the doctor's horse and surgical instruments, and we took the old don to Puebla for examination, turning him over to the Mexican authorities, the news having reached us that a peace had been concluded at Queretaro.

I found a very remarkable picture hanging on the wall. It was in a heavy black ebony frame with French glass in front of it. I mashed the glass and took the picture. It was worked on silk, and was a marvel of artistic needle-work. I made inquiries of the old don regarding the picture, telling him at the same time that I had robbed his establishment of that alone, as I did not believe that either he or his kind had much use for the Holy Virgin. He said the picture was quite famous for its antiquity; that it had been wrought by the nuns of the convent of San Domingo in 1675, and was taken by his father in a raid on the City of Mexico, about thirty years before. I have ever since cherished the picture as a choice gem of antiquity, and have preserved it in all my wanderings, and it is now hanging in my parlor. The silk upon which it is wrought is cracking and giving way under the destroying hand of time.

But I soon had something of more importance to attract my attention than Mexican works of art, or pretty señoras. It soon became a fixed fact and known to all, that the great war which had been raging between the republic of Mexico and the United States of America had come to a close, and preparations had to be made for evacuating the Mexican territory.

About the last of May, 1848, as quartermaster, I received orders to prepare my supply train for the march; to turn over all my camp and garrison equipages, not imperatively necessary for the march, to the quartermaster-general, that they might be destroyed; to prepare a supply wagon for each company, and one for officers' baggage of each company; also, as acting assistant commissary of subsistence, to accumulate such provision as was necessary for supply on the route; and as ordnance officer, to turn over all arms to the general department and take receipts therefor. I had about forty-eight hours to accomplish this pretty little duty, which would have employed a Hercules for a week; but I was young, active, and energetic, hardly knowing what fatigue was, and I never slept from the time I received the order until we were on the march. But a little incident occurred, just as we were ready to take up our line of march, which I ought not to omit. I was in my saddle (and so were most of the infantry officers, many of them having purchased Mexican horses) when I discovered that the baggage wagon of Company K, Second Illinois Volunteers, had disappeared. I rode up to the captain of that company and rather authoritatively demanded what had become of the wagon. He replied that he had ordered it to drive on. I addressed a coarse remark to him, and demanded what right he had to order the wagons to drive on. He replied with a taunt. Our sabers sprang from their scabbards the same instant and we made a rush at each other. We had just crossed swords, when Lieutenant-Colonel Hicks threw his blade between ours, and ordered us both under arrest, and took our swords. Here everything came to a standstill, as I was the moving spirit of the command, and could not be immediately replaced. The consequence was, the captain was returned to the rear. The lieutenant-colonel returned my sword to me, remarking at the same time that I had very much to vex me and he could hardly blame me. The captain was kept under arrest for several days, and then discharged. The truth of the matter is, he was wrong, and I was insolent, and both of us deserved punishment.

At this time I was discharging the threefold duties of acting quartermaster, acting assistant commissary of subsistence, and ordnance officer of my regiment and six attached companies; and I now took charge of Col. Charles Bruff's brigade, he having been breveted brigadier-general, and we were all of General Patterson's division, of which Colonel Wyncoop was the acting officer. Bruff's brigade took the advance, and I soon discovered that many of the men who had been taken from the hospitals, and others from having lain long in camp, were giving out on the march, and it was necessary that we have more transportation. Consequently, I started for the rear, to make arrangements for the wagons. I then made a ride which I deemed a somewhat famous one, making one hundred and thirty miles, and only out of the saddle long enough to change horses. I had left the quartermaster's arrangements in the hands of my quartermaster-sergeant, so far as the Illinois Volunteers regiment was concerned. On my return late at night, I found my quartermaster-sergeant under arrest, by order of Col. James Collins. On inquiry I found that a lieutenant had attempted to force himself into one of the sick wagons. The quartermaster-sergeant had resisted his effort. The sergeant drew his pistol on him, and on complaint of the lieutenant, Collins had ordered the arrest. Having heard the whole facts of the case, I went directly to the colonel and requested him to release the sergeant, as his services were indispensable to me on the march, and that Sergeant Norris was only carrying out my orders; that before leaving I had directed him to keep all persons out of the wagons excepting those who already occupied them, they then being crowded. In reply he very pompously inquired what authority I had to issue orders. I retorted that I had my appointment as brigade quartermaster. He said, "I will let you know that I command this regiment, and the wagons, and will say who shall ride or who shall not ride." I again retorted, " Yes; and with all due respect, you may also drive them, but I shall hold you responsible for all damages that occur to the service through your interference with my duties."

The next morning I was out as usual, at three o'clock, waking all the wagon masters excepting those of Collin's regiment, and directing them to wake the teamsters to feed and harness. All was ready at half-past five o'clock, when we took up our line of march, leaving Colonel Collins and regiment in camp, who began to stir about the time the rest of the command was starting. I informed Colonel Bruff as to what I had done, and the reason for my action. He said I was right; that if Colonel Collins saw fit to take the responsibility of interfering with my department, the safe way for me was to let him alone. I replied to Bruff that Colonel Collins had a right to interfere in my business, as he was my superior officer, but he was responsible to the Government for any injury accruing to the service from such interference, and that I intended to report him in case any damage accrued. It was not long after this conversation when an orderly rode up to me with a note from Colonel Collins, requesting me to return and take charge of the regiment, and bring it up to the rest of the command. I handed Bruff the note, and said, " General, if you order me to go, I will go; otherwise Colonel Collins must come in person and make the request." He laughingly remarked, " Do as you please, it is not my quarrel." I then penned a note to Colonel Collins, to the effect that if he would come to the front, we would negotiate. In the course of a couple of hours, the old colonel put in an appearance. It was soon arranged that he was to release Norris, my quartermaster-sergeant, and I again took charge of the regiment. I found two wagons broken down, and the balance of the wagons that I had procured the day before were filled with soldiers who thought that poor riding was better than the best walking. I ordered them out, and placed some timber under the hind axles of the broken wagons, and loaded them with hard beef and other light articles, and managed to get through the *pedregal* at the pass of Alahoya, where we camped for the night, and where I made arrangements for the balance of the trip, leaving the broken wagons, and reported them broken down and rendered useless by the interference of Colonel Collins in the quartermaster's department. For which the colonel never forgave me to the day of his death.

Nothing further occurred of importance until our arrival in Vera Cruz, when one of my wagon masters came riding up to me, bare-headed, with a deep sword cut in his forehead, the blood running down his face and neck. He saluted, and said, " This, captain, is what I got for obeying your orders." I asked him to explain, when he said that he was taking his train of wagons to the

custom house for distribution, according to my orders,
when Capt. Harvey Lee rode up and ordered the
driver of his company wagon to break the line and drive
immediately to his quarters, and when the wagon master
resisted his order, he drew his sword and gave him the
wound (which was a very serious one).   On hearing this
recital, I put spurs to my horse and rode off in pursuit
of Lee.   I soon found him, and at once denounced him
as a dastard and a coward.   We both drew and would
have settled the matter right there, but for the interference of a number of officers present.   I then rode off,
and preferred charges against Lee.   But the yellow fever
had just broken out in Vera Cruz, and the army was
ready and anxious to embark for home, and the charges
would necessarily involve a trial which would detain us
and other officers for several days, and at the earnest
solicitation of the officers I withdrew the charges and
allowed Lee to be discharged from arrest; which was
done with great reluctance on my part, as it was a das-
tardly act on the part of the captain.   I have never since
heard of the poor wounded wagon master, but if he is still
alive, and this should by chance meet his eye, he will see
that, though from the condition of things I could not
avenge his wrongs, at least I have not forgotten them.
And as to Capt. Harvey Lee, I never saw him again until
I had been several years in California, practicing my
profession as attorney, when to my surprise I found that
he and myself were employed on the opposite sides of a
case.   I learned from him that he had been practicing
law in Benicia; and in justice to the dead, I will here
say that when I called him a coward, I did not believe it
myself.   I think he was a brave man, but with much of
the tyrant in his composition.

CHAPTER XXIV.

MEMOIRS OF THE MEXICAN WAR—CONTINUED.

WE arrived in Vera Cruz about the 12th of June, 1848. Now all was hubbub and confusion. On the breaking up of the army of occupation of Mexico, a commissioner had been sent from Washington to assign ships for the transportation of the various commands to New Orleans, and, as acting commissary of subsistence, there was assigned to me the charge of a ship. Accordingly I reported myself to the commissioner for that purpose. The commissioner asked for the date of my appointment. On examining it he said, "Yours is the senior appointment of all who have applied, and hence you will have the choice of ships." Now Captain Blanding was the acting commissary-general of the command, and had gone aboard of the *Massachusetts* the flag-ship, with General Patterson, without reporting himself to the commissioner. A brilliant idea struck me. I replied, "I will take charge of the *Massachusetts*, the flag-ship." Without a word, the invoice of supplies of that ship was made out to me and I receipted for the same.

With my receipts in my pocket, and sailing orders for the ship, I repaired to the wharf, where Captain Daniels, quartermaster-general, was superintending the embarkation. After warmly thanking me for the efficient service I had rendered him, he remarked to me, " I believe you are also commissary of subsistence." I replied in the affirmative, when he asked me what ship I took charge of. I replied, " The *Massachusetts*." He said,

"I guess you must be mistaken; Captain Blanding, as commissary-general, will take charge of that." I corrected him by saying that his was the mistake and not mine; that I had receipted for the stores and held the nvoice. I further explained the circumstances to him. The captain laughed heartily, and seemed to think it one of the best jokes of the campaign.

In this connection I may be permitted to say that to Captain Daniels' efforts the army was more indebted for the safe-conduct of the camp and baggage equipments of the army, from the City of Mexico to Vera Cruz, than to any other one officer. He was active, energetic, and untiring in his line of duty. And, by the way, I met Captain Daniels in San Francisco about two years ago, and I could hardly bring myself to realize in the old, decrepit, and hoary veteran before me, the active, untiring Captain Daniels of the army in Mexico, in 1848. But the hand of time rests heavily on all of us, and the probabilities are that he discovered as great a change in me as I did in him.

But to return to my narrative. The captain said, "I will send you a board with flying colors, in my best cutter. But I want you, if possible, to report yourself to the captain of the ship *Massachusetts*, and when we meet in New Orleans, tell me how Blanding took the matter." I gave him my promise, shook his hand, threw a last look back upon Vera Cruz, entered the boat, and was soon skimming over the bright water to the ship, which lay anchored in the roadstead. When I came on board the ship, I saw General Patterson, Captain Blanding, and a person whom I supposed to be the captain of the *Massachusetts*, all in conversation upon the quarter-deck

I approached the trio, and after saluting the general and Captain Blanding, I turned to the captain of the ship, and said, "Have I the honor of addressing the captain of this ship?" He replied, "I am the captain." The general then stepped forward and formally introduced me. I then said to the captain, "I have the honor of reporting myself as commissary of this ship." When Blanding stepped forward and said, "Not quite so fast, Captain Norton. I am commissary here." I saluted, and replied, "I believe not, Captain Blanding." He changed color, and said with some asperity, "What the devil do you mean, Norton?" I again repeated that I thought I was commissary of the ship; adding, that at least I had receipted for the stores on board, and held the invoice of them, at the same time producing my papers, which, of course, ended the controversy. At which the general burst into a hearty laugh, and said, "Well, Captain Blanding, this is a good joke on you." Captain Blanding replied, "Well, general, give him full command, and we will go below and play chess during the voyage." I was at once installed in my new position, every order being sustained by the general.

We had a pleasant trip across the Gulf of Mexico, and up the river to New Orleans. After we had landed, the officers generally took up their quarters at the St. Charles Hotel. There I met General Taylor, Stephen A. Douglas, and many other notables. We had a jolly time. Some one of the officers referred to the joke of the "green sucker" as applied to myself—and heretofore explained—when Stephen A. Douglas remarked that "a few years ago, the 'green suckers' would come floating down the Mississippi with their flat-boats loaded with corn and potatoes, and when the question was asked, 'Where did you come from?' the timid reply was, dropping the head, 'I come from Eelanois.' But now you ask one of those 'suckers,' 'Where do you come from?' and he will throw back his head, look you square in the eye, and exclaim, 'I hail from Illinois, sir.'" And, after the achievements of the Illinois troops at Buena Vista, Cerro Gordo, and the City of Mexico, no man need to be ashamed that he hailed from the "Sucker State."

Our command was sent up the river a short distance, and formed an encampment until they were discharged and paid off. And the first thing we knew, there came a gang of sharpers from the city, waylaying by their runners every soldier who had received his pay and discharge, inveigling him into some low groggery or den, where they would get him drunk and for a few dollars get him to sign away his discharge, with an agreement and power of attorney to collect back pay, and bounty, and all rights and interests that the soldier had in expectancy on account of services rendered the Government. This was reported at. head-quarters, and we received an order to arrest them and turn them over to the civil authorities, as swindlers. General Taylor remarked, "I think that as they, just at this time, seem anxious to dabble in military affairs, we will give them a small experience, just to initiate them; see that they are 'bucked and gagged' for four hours each." And in less than two hours there were nine of them rolled up, each chewing a bayonet. This caused quite a sensation among the civilians; but they were soon pacified on Taylor's informing them that, without warrant of law, he would protect the soldiers, and that sooner 'than see them robbed in that way, in defiance of civil law, he would declare the city under martial law, and thus protect them from, a band of thieves. After this I heard no complaint of the militia punishment, neither was there any occasion for further arrest.

During our stay in New Orleans, Uncle Sam must have footed up some pretty good bills; for about a week all was mirth and hilarity in the city. Parties were given by the aristocracy of New Orleans ‹ very night, and the military officers were all welcome guests; and all of the wealthiest inhabitants seemed to vie with each other in showing the returned soldiers that they were welcome home. But their glorification came to an end and vanished like a bright elysian dream, for then came the fraternal hand-shaking and heart-burning of separation. The different commands were each sent home on their proper lines of travel, and in many instances the parting was like that of the nearest and dearest of kin, to say nothing of the hearts that were left and brought away from New Orleans through love's passion during our short stay there. There was a general order left in New Orleans that no expense be spared in transporting men and officers to their homes. Accordingly there was an agreement entered into with Captain Taylor, of the steamer *Illinois*, to take our regiment up the river to Alton   The captain agreed to transport us to that point and give us *en route* the best the market afforded; for the men, twenty dollars each, and officers, thirty-six dollars each, wines and liquors included. We spent a glorious Fourth in New Orleans; on the 5th we were all aboard and assigned our state-rooms, and on the 6th we stemmed the tide up the river for St. Louis and Alton.

We steamed up the Mississippi for two days without an incident worth mentioning. The third day a circum-stance occurred that marred the hilarity and harmony of the remainder of the trip. The command was under the charge of Lieutenant-Colonel Hicks, a small, wiry man, weighing about one hundred and thirty pounds, while Captain Taylor was a man that stood something over six feet, and weighing about two hundred and twenty pounds. Hicks had boxed up some specimens of earthenware and other novelties that could be easily broken; and it appeared he had given the captain especial caution regarding them, and the captain had promised to see that they were carefully handled. I was in the cabin playing a game of cards, when I heard a great noise and excitement on the lower or boiler deck, and the word was passed up that Colonel Hicks and the captain were fighting. I dropped my cards, sprang to my feet, and rushed out to the forward deck, when I saw Hicks com-ing up the stairs, looking somewhat pale, followed by the captain.

I said, "Colonel, what is the matter?" "Well," he replied, "when I put my boxes on board, I told the captain that I wanted them handled carefully, which he promised me should be done, but when below I saw the men on the lower deck knocking them about in such a manner as to break everything in them. I called the captain's attention to it, and reminded him of his promise to me. He indignantly asserted that I had told him nothing of the kind, and I called him a liar." At this the captain sprang forward and exclaimed, "And why did you call me a liar?" Upon which the colonel re-torted, "Because you are one." The words had scarcely escaped his lips, before the two men were together again. I shoved the captain back, saying, "If you are spoiling for a fight, select a man of your own size." At this, the captain with a bound literally sprang over our heads, exclaiming, "I will let you know that I am one of the red-heads!"

I now discovered that the colonel had an ugly cut on his forehead. He then called out, "Norton, where are your pistols?" I ran and got my holster pistols and placed myself in the gang-way, the captain having run to the stern of the boat, as I supposed to arm himself. At this time the mate and other officers of the boat came up to me and said, "For God's sake, help us to stop this." I replied, "Take care of your captain; I will vouch for the colonel." I continued, "The captain has doubtless gone to arm himself, and as soon as he returns, I shall shoot him." The mate rushed off to the stern of the boat, but presently returned and informed me that the captain would not again interfere with the colonel; and, further, that he was then washing himself.

Thus ended what bade fair to be a most bloody fight, as there was a large crew of hands on the boat. But on our side there were over three hundred soldiers, well armed. The colonel and the captain could not meet after this, except as strangers, and it became necessary for the management of affairs that each should be represented. The result was, I took command, at the request of the colonel, and the mate represented the captain, and everything went along as usual. In due time we arrived at St. Louis. I made arrangements for the boat to stop at St. Louis for half an hour, as it became necessary for me to report to Captain Lyon, after-

16

ward General Lyon, then quartermaster of that post. On returning to the levee, I noticed a first-class steamer backing out into the stream. I bawled out, "What are you doing? Who will debark those men if I am left?" The wheels were reversed, and the boat stood in the stream. I said, "Send a boat ashore and fetch me on board." In a few minutes I was on her deck. Looking about I discovered that the decks were strewed with pigs of lead, and at a glance I saw that it was not our boat. I rushed to the captain and informed him of my mistake. The boat was headed up stream. I said, "Never mind, you can land me at Alton. The captain exclaimed, "The devil! I am going to New Orleans." I said, "Then put me ashore." They again chopped about, and landed me. On looking about, I saw our boat, and the officers and men laughing, having discovered my mistake. I was soon on board, and before nightfall the whole command was safely landed at Alton, where, in a few days, all were discharged and I returned to St. Charles, where I met my family, and the congratulations of my fellow-citizens, when I laid aside my sword and returned to private life.

On my arrival at Geneva, in Kane County, Illinois, I heard the cannon boom at St. Charles—a distance of two miles—and in a very short time a carriage arrived for myself and wife (whom I had met at Geneva), with a large delegation of my fellow-citizens, who escorted me home to St. Charles. On arriving at the west end of the bridge across Fox River, there was a densely packed crowd, and I thought I had never found the bridge so long, as we were two hours in crossing it, a distance of about four hundred feet. And I had by this

time learned that gilt buttons and epaulets were at a
premium in St. Charles. Bonfires blazed in the evening
and impromptu speeches were made, with a grand ball
at night. In a word, it was a most gratifying reunion,
for the most of my company had returned before myself,
as I had to remain in Alton some weeks before I could
get my official reports made out and forwarded to Washington. I was warmly grasped by the hand by fathers
and mothers of young men who went out with me, saying, "When you took my son away, he was wild and
wayward; but you have returned him a perfect gentleman." With tears in their eyes, they thanked me for their
improvement. And I found that many letters had pre-
ceded me from the sick and wounded soldiers, even
exaggerating the kindness they claimed to have received
at my hands. But as for that, I will let the subjoined
letter from Colonel Hicks, of Mt. Vernon, Illinois, speak
for me:—

MT. VERNON, Ill., April 24, 1856.

*My worthy and ever to be remembered and respected
old friend, Capt. L. A. Norton:* It was with pleasure,
indeed, that I, yesterday, read your kind letter of the
13th of August. When I ·looked at the superscription,
I was somewhat surprised. I knew the handwriting,
but seeing it was sent from California, was a thing I was
not looking for. On the receipt of your letter, how
vividly my mind was carried back to that long and
tedious campaign that we made together. And how
many reminiscences presented themselves to my mind.
How fresh it brought to my mind the many sufferings we
had to witness and endure. When you spoke of the couch
of the sick soldier, tears involuntarily rose in my eyes.

Poor fellows! how many of them have reached out their hands to me, when I could feel the wet, clammy sweat on them and know it was the last, but would try to encourage them in the hour of death. In fancy I see them now, as we did then, on their beds of straw or blankets, laid on a stone or brick floor. We, however, have the proud gratification of knowing that they were never deserted or neglected by us for a single moment, when it was in our power to render them assistance. Our personal attention was always at their command; and it affords me pleasure to be able to say of a truth, that I received more aid from you than from any other one officer of my command in ministering to the wants of the poor fellows; and those who survive fully appreciate it, and the friends and relatives of those who did not return, often refer to our kindness bestowed upon them when living. In fact, their friends treat me with more kindness than I actually deserve. I am treated more like a father than a stranger, by them. You ask, then, if my thirst for military honor and glory ceased with the close of that war. It did, to a certain extent; but, should I ask you the same question, with your constitution, energy, and dash, I well know what the answer would be. . . .

I want you to let me hear from you often; for it does my heart good to keep up a correspondence with you. Let us keep it up. After wishing you health, wealth, and happiness, I subscribe myself, your old and sincere friend and companion-in-arms,   S. G. HICKS.

CHAPTER XXV.

SUBDUING A NOTORIOUS "BULLY."

ON my return from Mexico I found my little wife much improved in health. I met her in Geneva, the county seat of Kane County, Illinois, at the residence of her parents, where I remained several days with her before taking her home to St. Charles. About two days after my arrival home, an incident happened that made me quite notorious in the northern portion of the State, and although it may make me appear as a braggart and boaster, yet this history would be incomplete without the story.

I must preface it by saying that on my arrival in Du Page County, Illinois, I made the acquaintance of a young fellow by the name of Frederick Lord, a son of Dr. Lord; I think I was about one year his senior. It was the custom of that country every Saturday afternoon to meet on the common and wrestle, and all who ever knew me in my younger days can testify that I was an expert wrestler; in fact, I threw all the young men in that vicinity. I was light, but tall and very active. On the other hand Fred Lord was a powerfully built young fellow, but with my skill and action I could always handle him. Our acquaintance extended over a period of more than ten years. When Fred had matured he was a perfect giant, standing six feet six inches and weighing two hundred and sixty pounds; and for about four or five years before the Mexican War he had been leading a very dissolute life, horse-racing, gambling, and bullying his way through the world to that extent that he had become the terror of several counties.

After I had taken my departure for the seat of war, Fred volunteered and went out as a private; and owing to his natural insubordination, he had been frequently punished, and had imbibed such a hatred to army officers that when he returned home he declared that he had whipped every officer of the army in Mexico that he had met after the disbanding of the troops, and he intended to whip Norton and Conkling (one of my lieutenants who lived in St. Charles), and then he would be satisfied; Fred and I had always been friendly, and there was no cause for the threat. But when it was reported to me, I sent him word that he had better commence on me, as I was the smaller of the two, and perhaps when he had whipped me he might not want to attack the other.

It was Monday morning, and the Circuit Court of Kane County was to commence its session that day. The Geneva Hotel was packed with people, and about eight o'clock I walked over to the hotel to get my morning "cocktail." I met J. Y. Scammonds (author of "Scammond's Reports") and an eminent attorney from Chicago by the name of Brown. After some conversation, Scammonds asked me if I made the acquaintance of General Taylor (the men were canvassing for Taylor). I informed them that I had. They asked me when I had last seen him. I replied that I left Taylor at the St. Charles Hotel in New Orleans, on the 29th of June last. Just as I made the reply, Fred Lord stepped out of the parlor, where he had been carrying on a flirtation with some girls, and said, "Where do you say you saw General Taylor last?" I repeated, "In New Orleans, on the 29th of June last." He said, "General Taylor was not in New Orleans on the 29th of June last." I replied,

"Permit me to tell you, you are a liar, sir!" At this he sprang upon me and struck at me.

I attempted to fend the blow, and at the same time threw my foot back to kick him; but his arm was so heavy and the blow so powerful that I did not entirely escape. He struck the upper part of my forehead, my head striking some one in the crowd. Bringing my foot back to kick him threw me from my balance and made it a very pretty knockdown. But it was of such a nature that it did not in the least stun me. He knew that if he whipped me he must work lively, and at once bent over me, and, thrusting his hand in my face, attempted to gouge my eye out. His thumb nail missed my eye but cut my eyebrow. At this I grabbed his neck-tie with my left hand, took a twist and sprang up, raising him with me, and when we struck the floor again it was fourteen feet (by measurement) distant through the crowd.

I retained my grip on his throat, coming on top of him; but he had thrown his immense legs tight about my loins and had clutched both hands tight in my hair, where he held me as in a vise, while my right hand was at liberty until it was all stove up. (I remember they applied oil of wormwood after the fight, to take the swelling out.) Finally I thought to myself, I can't get to strike your face to spoil that, but I will mark you anyway. So I reached up and clawed down his face a couple of times. It looked very badly for a while. At this stage of the game I found his hands getting very loose in my hair, and some one in the crowd said, "Take Norton off; see how black Fred is in the face," when a man by the name of McMear caught a fire-poker and declared that he would kill the first man who interfered; that Norton could whale Fred the best day he ever saw. (Fred had once pounded McMear very badly.) I continued to choke him; his hands and legs had become quite loose, and I was about to spring from him and stamp him to pieces, when old Uncle Jimmie Brown, the landlord (whom no one would strike), exclaimed, " Take him off, he is killing the man."

At this the crowd concluded to release Fred. They caught hold of me and in attempting to pull me off they pulled Fred up to a sitting posture, but could not get my hand free from his neck-tie; so they procured a knife and cut the tie, and after throwing a few pails of water over him, he came to, and evinced himself satisfied. Though a powerful man myself, I look upon my victory as a mere accident, as I could not compare with him in physical powers. But the accident had its effect. I have many times been in a crowd and have heard men say, " That is the man who whipped Fred Lord."

In this connection I may add that, after a time, Fred made his way out to the Missouri River and, at Traders' Point, married a French lady who was possessed of quite a fortune; but he soon went through with that, and when I was on my way to California I stopped a few days with my brother, who lived but a short distance from Traders' Point, and he and Fred were very good friends. My brother told me that Fred was at the Point, and was in company with a big half-breed Indian burning lime; that he had often expressed a desire to see me, saying that I had served him right, for he had no cause of quarrel with me. So I finally decided to go down to the Point with my brother and call on Fred.

When we arrived at the Point and inquired for him, some of his crowd said he had been gambling the night before and was across the street taking a sleep. I went over, the crowd following me. (I suppose my brother had told them about the affair.) I found him fast asleep, and as I walked up to him, he looked like a great giant. He was dressed in buckskin, in regular frontiersman style, with a revolver and knife in his belt. I shook him and called out, "Fred." He awoke, looked me full in the face and exclaimed, "Lew Norton, by G—d!" He sprang to his feet, took me by the hand and said, "Here, boys, is the only man that ever whaled me; and no man ever deserved it more than I did; let's go and take a drink."

I pursued my journey to California, but not more than three weeks after the occurrence above narrated, Fred got into a quarrel with and whipped his half-breed partner. The next day afterward, as he was hauling limestone to the kiln, the half-breed secreted himself in the brush near the road, with an old-fashioned Yager, and when Fred had got past him he fired, tearing an enormous hole through the vitals of his victim. Fred turned his head and exclaimed, "D—n you, I would make you pay for that if I could live an hour." He then fell over on his load and expired in a few minutes.

CHAPTER XXVI.

THE RESTORATION OF A STOLEN CORPSE.

WHEN I returned from the Mexican War I had large unsettled accounts with the United States Government, and pending the settlement I entered the law office of W. D. Barry, Esq., at St. Charles, and commenced the study of law. During my absence in the service, Dr. Richards had established his medical institute at St. Charles, and, by the way, from that establishment were turned out some of the most eminent practitioners of our day, among whom are Dr. Boice, of Santa Rosa, Dr. Obed Harvey, and others.

I had heard many complaints in regard to resurrectionists and body-snatching throughout the adjoining country, and one day I was awakened from my studies by a party rushing in and informing me that Professor Richards and John Rood, one of the students, had been shot by a mob, or company of riflemen from De Kalb County, numbering about eighty. I dropped my book and, on inquiry, learned that a young married woman, the daughter of a respected farmer by the name of Churchill, had suddenly died in full flesh, and that the body had been stolen, the effect of which was to craze the mother and so exasperate the father and his neighbors that, in their wrath, they had armed themselves and, in a perfectly organized state, had marched upon the institute and demanded from Richards the remains of their dead. Richards and the students indignantly denied having the remains, or knowing aught of them. This denial was anything but satisfactory to them, although I have reasons for believing that Richards did not know much about the affair at the time, the whole matter having been a little private enterprise of George Richards, son of the professor, and one John Rood, a student.

The crowd, however, persisted in the demand, and became very clamorous, while Richards and Rood, who stood with their guns in their hands in the door, became very insolent, Richards telling the father of the deceased that if they did not leave he would have a better subject. At this, several shots were fired almost simultaneously by both parties. Richards was struck by a rifle ball in the right hand, while his shot-gun was still raised, the bullet passing through just below the knuckles, out at the wrist, and then penetrating his right shoulder, close to the chest. Rood was also struck by a rifle ball on the right side, the ball following a rib round to the back, not entering the chest. Rood survived five or six days only, the concussion having caused such internal injuries that mortification ended the chapter of his life.

On my arrival upon the ground, I found the sheriff of the county and several prominent citizens attempting to quiet the then exasperated rioters, who were determined to demolish the buildings, and amid the howl and fury it was next to impossible to be heard. Several attempts having been made by the sheriff and others to calm them, I saw the condition of things at a glance, sprang upon a horse-block and, after several efforts, succeeded in making myself heard. I told them that, as citizens, we deeply felt and acknowledged the outrage that had been committed, and that they had our fullest sympathy; that we were ready and willing, in every legitimate manner, to aid them in prosecuting the search for the body; but we could not, and would not, suffer them to go into the destruction of property to gratify revenge. I then said, " I have this proposition to make you: select from your body a committee of five to search the premises, and every bolt and bar shall yield to your touch, and if the body is here you surely can find it." From the crowd there was a universal acclaim that the proposition was fair. They selected their committee. I called Professor Hall, son-in-law of Richards, to bring the keys of the establishment. The sheriff, Hall, and myself went through the whole establishment, prosecuting the most vigilant search, not neglecting out-buildings, barns, and stables, but nothing was to be found. The day was now far advanced. The search was abandoned and the crowd retired. The institution was broken up and Richards was removed to Chicago; but this did not end the excitement. The public press was full of reports and comments and dire vengeance was threatened to all who were suspected of having a hand in the outrage. On the other hand, Richards had at once commenced suit for damages, and retained W. D. Barry, my preceptor, as counsel. All this had occurred in less than a week from the time of the outrage, when one day Judge Barry came into the office, evidently with something on his mind. He walked the floor for a few minutes, when he suddenly turned to me and said, "Norton, I know your sympathy is with those people. Now I will give you a chance to show it. You have been to the wars and have seen many men killed and have had much to do with dead folks. I want to restore that body, but I have not the nerve to do it. You are a clerk in the office and they cannot put you upon the stand as a witness. I have made every preparation; will you do it?"

I unhesitatingly agreed to do anything that I could to restore the body. He then gave me these instructions. "At twelve o'clock to-night, go to a certain point [describing it] in town, and you will find a span of horses and a spring-wagon, with a shovel in the wagon. Take the horses and first drive to Geneva [this was a town two miles below, on Fox River]; go to Danforth's shop, where two men will bring you a coffin. You need not speak. Then drive to Cedar Bluff [describing the point], where you will hitch the horses. On examination, you will see the white bones of a horse's head at the commencement of a path, and strewn along the path, you will find white bones until it leads you through the woods, to the head of a ravine, near Otto Perkins' fence; thence follow down the ravine about three-fourths of a mile, where you will find the tops of the bushes all broken in toward each other. There dig."

At midnight I was at the point, found the horses hitched, untied them, drove to Geneva; and to Danforth's shop. Two men emerged from the shop, carrying a coffin. They placed it in the wagon without a word. I glanced at it and saw that the lid was screwed down, when I remarked, "Bring a screw-driver." One of them soon returned and placed a screw-driver in the wagon, when, without another word, I drove back to Cedar Bluff, where I hitched the horses, and soon found the horse's skull, with other marks indicating my path through the woods. I followed it with the shovel on my back. I do not remember whether I whistled to keep up my courage or not; but as I am a poor whistler and a worse singer, I probably kept silent. I found the white bones, as Barry had told me, which I followed until I reached the head of a dark gulch, the one referred to in my instructions; thence down through the tangled brush and underwood until I came to the spot indicated, where the bushes were all broken in towards each other.

There was no moon, but a starlight night. Owing to the thick woods and heavy foliage overhead, it was very dark. When I commenced digging, I found the bed of the gulch very wet and muddy. I had not prosecuted my labors very long, until my shovel struck something yielding. I cleaned the dirt away as well as I could, put my hand down and got hold of a sack. I pulled it out, found that it contained the body, shut up like a jack-knife, having the limbs from the hips bent forward so that the face and feet were together. I took the body from the sack and found that the oozy mud had settled all over it. I wiped it off as best I could, shouldered it, and made my way back to Cedar Bluff. There was a small creek of pure water, and I washed the body clean   I found that they had cut through the skin and flesh on the forehead and skinned it down till it fell like a flap over the eyes. I placed it back as smoothly as I could, preparatory to putting it into the coffin; but here was a dilemma! No one had thought of a shroud, and I could not think of placing the body in the coffin in a nude state. While revolving the matter in my mind, I happened to think of my outer shirt. I at once pulled it off and put it on the corpse. I then gathered some moss, placed it in the coffin for a pillow, placed the body in the coffin, screwed down the lid, and drove the wagon back where I found it, according to directions.

Now, I do not believe that I am more cowardly than most of the human family, and probably as far removed from superstition as any one; but when I found myself away in the woods, in the depth of night, with all its surrounding gloom, trudging along with a cold, clammy corpse on my back, I plead guilty to having felt a kind of involuntary shudder pass over me, an undefined something—not fear, but a species of desolation and awe wholly indescribable.

As I started in to give a simple recital of facts, I have wandered a little; but please excuse the digression. After hitching the horses where I found them, I pushed on toward home, but could not repress my curiosity to dodge around a corner and watch to see what would become of the wagon. I saw a man unhitch the horses and drive through Fox River at the ford, making his way west in the direction of the home of the distressed parents and friends of the deceased. I returned home and thought I would slip into bed and that my wife would not discover the missing shirt; but not so. She threw her arm over me and exclaimed, "Oh! my God, Lewis; what has become of your shirt!" I was compelled to deceive her and pretend that I had been out fishing; that it had caught fire and I had to tear it off.

Two days elapsed, when news came from De Kalb County that the missing body had been restored; that it was found in a coffin, sitting on the father's porch, and that there was great rejoicing. But there was one feature they could not understand—the body had a man's shirt on, for a shroud! The friends proposed to remove it, and put a different shroud on the corpse before the interment; but the mother interposed and exclaimed, "No! no! the hand that placed it there was a friendly hand, and it will be a charm that will protect my child."

When my wife heard the story, she remarked to me, "That, my dear, was your shirt; and had they removed it, they would have found your name on the bottom of it." There are many living, doubtless, even in this State, who knew of the occurrence and have often heard the query, "Who restored the body?" and, as it is no longer a secret, and after the lapse of a third of a century, I give the world the facts.

CHAPTER XXVII.

DEPARTURE FOR CALIFORNIA.

I CONTINUED reading law and was admitted to the Bar of the Superior Court of Illinois, before Trumble, Treat, and John Dean Caton. At this time my wife's health was so poor that she remained with her mother constantly. A household counsel was called, and it was finally arranged that I should let her remain with her mother. I divided my property with her, paid for a divorce, and prepared to leave for California. (This was my second trip, the first being uneventful.)

Before leaving for Mexico my wife's uncle came to me and, with tears in his eyes, said, "I have to ask a favor of you, and I hate to do it, as I know how much you have lost by assisting your friends; but I was sued in the circuit court, have there lost my case, and want to appeal to the Supreme Court. I have a meritorious defense to the action, and am assured by my attorney that

I can beat the case, and you shall never lose a dollar by me if I have to sell the last thing I have to pay up. I went on his bonds and paid no attention to the case after.

Now I had paid every cent that I was indebted, had started my teams a week before, and had told everybody that I should start myself the next Thursday, when I was brought up standing by an officer serving me with a summons—suit brought upon the appeal bond. I went immediately to Howard and asked him what it meant, reminding him of his promise. He assured me that he meant all that he had promised, and in-order to protect his bondsmen had turned over all his property exempt from forced sale to Dearborn, the sheriff, to pay judgment and costs of suit.

At this time there was a Democratic Convention at Springfield, the State capital, about eighty miles distant, and the sheriff, county judge, and in fact nearly all the county officers, were in attendance as delegates. Howard claimed to feel very badly over the matter, while Farnsworth, the opposing attorney, gave me to understand that unless I settled the matter before leaving, a State's warrant would be issued against me for leaving the State without paying my debts. The county judge being absent, they would of course hold me a prisoner until he returned, which would be about ten days, when I could be released by showing that I was leaving an abundance of property to pay any judgment which they might obtain against me. I refused to pay the debt of Howard, and they swore out a bench warrant. Howard went to Farnsworth and stated his arrangement with the sheriff, and asked him not to proceed against me.

17

His reply was that I had the money, and he intended to make me pay it before I left. Howard reported to me what Farnsworth said, and I told him to pay no further attention to the matter; that I should leave Thursday at noon, and that, unfortunately for Mr. Farnsworth, there were not men enough in St. Charles to arrest me. I sent a similar notice to Farnsworth.

The affair was generally talked of, and I had the sympathy of the community. I then went to Randal, the under-sheriff, and said, "Randal, I have lived among you for twelve years and have tried to be a good citizen; a child could at any time have arrested me. Now you hold papers for my arrest, but this is such a bare-faced imposition that I will never submit to an arrest on the warrant you hold while I have life to resist, so do not attempt it." He replied, "Captain, if that is your resolution, I am sick." Farnsworth then went to Geneva, the county seat, and got two deputy sheriffs to come up to arrest me. They called on Randal for the papers, but, after some conversation with him, they were taken suddenly ill and did not make the attempt.

Time passed on until Thursday noon, when I mounted my horse, in full uniform, my sword by my side and my pistols in the holsters, and rode around town, taking leave of my friends. I then turned my horse's head to the west, rode across Fox River, and ascended the hill on the west side. As I passed Mr. Farnsworth's office (now General Farnsworth) he was standing in the door. I raised my cap and said, "Good-by, Farnsworth; I told you I should leave to-day at twelve o'clock." He said, "Then you are really going? Good-by, and God bless you!" When on top of the hill, which commanded a fine view of the town, I sat upon my horse and waved my handkerchief to my friends who stood watching me from street corners and balconies, and then pursued my journey.

I had rode less than a mile when I noticed a couple of men on horseback, loitering along the road ahead of me. I immediately recognized them; they were two constables—one, Orange Bayard, whom I had rendered many essential services; the other's name I do not remember. I readily comprehended their business. I spurred up my horse and rode up between them, and as I approached them I said, "How are you, gentlemen? Well, Orange, which way are you bound to-day?" He replied, "We are going out into the Bur settlement." I said, "Are you not afraid to ride unprotected in this murderous country?" to which they returned rather a cynical laugh.

Now my road, in a short distance from where we were, turned to the right and theirs to the left. I said, "As you are friends of mine I will ride over to the Bur settlement with you, and protect you; but I wish you to keep a little in advance. So I rode with them five or six miles to the Bur settlement to where there was a by-road which led across the country and joined my road, some distance ahead. I said, "Now, gentlemen, I think you are safe, but you ride on and I will wait here a few minutes and watch to see that no harm befalls you, when I shall go my own way, as I am bound for California." I waited until they had rode beyond all danger to me, when I sped swiftly along on my own route, and in a couple of hours joined my company.

CHAPTER XXVIII.

THE JOURNEY AS FAR AS CARSON VALLEY.

I HAD two four-horse wagons, and our party organized, calling ourselves the "Rough and Ready Company," of which I was unanimously elected captain. We pushed along all right to the Missouri River without any serious difficulty. But on arriving at Traders' Point, where we were to cross the river, we found an immense crowd waiting transportation across the stream. There was but one small scow, which would only convey a single wagon at a time, and at that rate it would take about six weeks to ferry the crowd across the river. But the man (Stokes by name) who owned the boat entered into an agreement with us that he would, with our aid, build another boat, and my company was to be crossed first.

There was also a large Missourian company with ox-teams waiting, and I noticed that they were also working on a new boat; and at length it leaked out that Stokes was playing us falsely, and had made the same promise to the Missourians that he had to us. Ours was but a small company, thirteen wagons, and we said nothing, but kept to work. The boat was completed and launched, and before it was through its oscillations I sprang into the stern and seized the rudder. My men, who understood the situation, sprang into the boat with their poles, and I gave the order to shove down to a second landing (only a few yards) where one of our wagons was ready to come aboard. All was so well arranged that before the other party was aware, our first wagon was on the boat, and we ran across the river and landed it. Returning, we ran up to the landing to receive another wagon, when to my surprise there was a big Missouri wagon, with a crowd of men ready to run it aboard. They had driven our men and wagon-aside intending to put their company across ahead of ours. The wagon contained sixty hundred weight of corn, for feed on the plains, and as it came rushing down the bank, I exclaimed, "Push off, boys!" They did so, and as the boat moved out of the way, the wagon .plunged into the river.

I called to our boys on the bank to bring a wagon to the other landing. They did so; but before we got it on the boat a crowd from the Missouri company came to take possession of the boat, and a powerful-looking young man, who claimed that I, as commissary, had issued him rations in Mexico, was at the head. I took my position near the bow of the boat, and told the parties to keep off; that we had an arrangement with Stokes that we should be the first to cross on the new boat, when Red-shirt gave me the lie. Somehow his foot slipped and he fell on the side of the boat. The next moment I felt some one buckling a belt around me, and I discovered a revolver in one side and a knife in the other. I raised the revolver, and fully persuaded the crowd to stand back until the boys could run the wagon on the boat.

As my red-shirted friend stepped overboard, I looked around to see if I was alone in the muss, when I saw Sponable and J. L. Mack, who were both powerful men. As I looked around, they exclaimed, "Give them h—l, Cap., we are here." I stood to the helm all that night, and the next day until ten o'clock, when our wagons were all landed.   I then restored the boat to Stokes, and paid him a dollar apiece for ferriage of the wagons, which I should not have done, as his duplicity got us all into trouble.

Now all went well with us until, far out on the plains, they began to find fault with me as captain of the train. And it was not long until there was not a man, woman, or child but what knew more about encamping and camp-life generally than I did.   There was constant quarrel-ing and bickering among them, with innumerable lies, which prejudiced them one against another until the best of friends were ready to fight.   At length we over-took some Dutchmen, with several head of cattle, and the Indians were hanging on their flanks.   These men, for some cause, had been separated from their company; I have forgotten how it happened, but I saw that the Indians intended to rob and probably murder them.   I told them that I would regulate our travel to their pace until they could fall in with some other company, or to a place where it was safe for them to encamp until they should be overtaken by ox-teams.

This proposition met with a most stubborn opposition by my company.   Some asserted that I was crazy, to take those Dutchmen on my back, and others proposed to depose me and elect a man by the name of White, who had crossed the plains before.   I was indignant to think that my company wanted to leave the unprotected men to their fate, and told them to go on, if they were disposed to do so, but I would remain with the Dutch-men and share their fate.

We continued our journey for two days, when I think they had decided to elect White that night, and the next day to push on and leave me and the Dutchmen. But about noon we came to Shell Creek, where we found about three hundred Indians gathered on the bank of the Platte River., We had to cross Shell Creek near its junction with the river, where there was quite a grove of cottonwoods along the banks of the creek. The principal band of Indians was on the west side of the creek, between where we had to cross and the river, while the squaws were further along on the bank of the river. About seventy or eighty Indians had swung to the rear of our company, thus completely hemming us in. I saw that they meant mischief, as their bows were all strung and the wipers were out of their rifles.

White's team was in advance, and some of the chiefs stopped him, and said they wanted toll for going through their country. White gave them five or six dollars and they let him go on, which he did, and kept going. The next one was Fred Parker. The Indian said, "Me chief; me want money." Parker replied, pointing to me, "That is our chief; go to him if you want money." I was dressed in uniform as a United States officer, and rode with my sword on, and my pistols in the holsters. I did this at the request of the company, as the Indians had great respect for army officers. The chief started to make his demands on me, when I drew my sword and charging to the rear ordered the Indians, who were closing in upon us, to leave the road and take to the river bank, when their spokesman, in fair English, told me that they had as good a right to travel the road as I had.

At this I called to the company in advance to seize their rifles, and form in line. At the same time I whipped out a pistol, rode right up to the Indians, and told them to leave the road or I would fire. They reluctantly moved off to the river. I then charged back to the front and met the chief, who handed me a paper (extorted, doubtless, from some one) stating that he was a good chief. I threw his paper on the ground, told him we had given them corn in payment for the right to go through their country (which was true), and that they were forked-tongued, bad Indians, and then ordered him to the rear of our wagons. He refused to go, upon which I welted him across the shoulders with the flat of my sword, which made Mr. Indian move as directed. When I had started him I rode right in among the band, and, with the flat of my sword, drove them like a flock of sheep to the rear. All this time I had thirty men in line with cocked rifles. I expected to be killed, but I knew it was the only chance to save the company. When I had driven them across Shell Creek, I ordered the wagons to advance, keeping a rear guard to protect us until we got out of the way of the Shell Creek Indians. Late in the afternoon we overtook White, and that night we encamped in a short loop of the Platte, where I could defend our position, with our wagons drawn up in front as breastworks. There was no talk of an election of a new captain that night, nor did I ever hear the subject mentioned afterwards. But our valiant would-be captain, White, became the butt of the company.

We continued our weary march across the plains with the usual experiences that have been written and re-written, and in the course of time we reached Carson Valley, poor and jaded—that is to say, those of us who were not left on the desert to feed the wolves and buzzards.

CHAPTER XXIX:

RELIEF TRAIN—A FRIGHT—CROSSING THE MOUNTAINS.

WE had passed the sink of the Carson River and were proceeding up that stream, when we came to an encampment in a very pleasant valley, and on inquiry learned that it was a relief train sent out from California to aid the immigration. We encamped but a short distance from the relief train, and I walked over to the camp to make some inquiries regarding their object and the nature of their supplies. I was soon introduced to Gen. James Estel, who I learned was first in command. I found him very affable, and apparently ready and willing to do all in his power to aid immigrants. The supplies, he informed me, were intended for those who had no money to purchase what they needed.

He then introduced me to Gen. J. W. Denver, General Price, and some others holding subordinate positions. I then informed him that we could not claim to be without funds, yet we needed some articles for the use of some of our party who were sick, for which I was ready and willing to pay. General Estel said, "We cannot take pay, but that is all right; make out your requisition." I said, "General, shall I make my requisition in bulk or by ration?" He replied, "Oh, make it out in detail." I went to camp and made a regular requisition in accordance with the regulations of the United States army, as follows: Twenty men, ten days' tea, 200; twenty men, ten days' coffee, 200; twenty men, ten days' sugar, 200— and so on until the requisition was filled. I chose William Brophey, a shrewd fellow, and told him to take a team and go down to the supply camp and give my requisition to General Estel and mark what occurred. In about two hours Brophey returned, and made his report as follows:—

"I presented your requisition to General Estel as you directed. He took it and commenced reading, 'Twenty men, ten days' tea, total two hundred pounds; coffee, twenty men, ten days, total two hundred pounds;' and so on through the requisition, reading all pounds. Finally the old general said, 'I don't understand this; take it to General Denver.' I handed it to General Denver, who it seems was issuing commissary, and he read it the same as General Estel,—instead of number of rations, as carried out, he read it all pounds. But they were puzzled to know why you had put all two hundred pounds —tea, coffee, pickles, and potatoes. They called in General Price; he read it the same. They finally said to me, 'Is your captain a military man?' I informed them he was; that he had served almost fourteen months in Mexico, and then added, 'I think the captain intends the two hundred at the right hand as the total number of rations, and not pounds.' General Estel said, 'Ah! yes, yes, I understand it; twenty men, ten days, two hundred rations; yes, yes, that's all right; General Denver, issue the rations.'"

General Denver did issue the rations, and in addition, I received a very polite note from General Estel, saying that they had issued on my requisition, but they were sorry that, owing to their limited means, they were not able to fill it. And now the cream of the joke was, they had issued at least four times what my requisition called for; thus proving to my satisfaction that the military lights of California, whatever they might be in other respects, did not know the value of a regulation ration. In after time I had lots of fun with Estel regarding the commissary department of his expedition for the relief of immigrants on the plains, in 1852. But the next year, in Sacramento City, we compromised the ration business. I was never to tell the story on him, and he was to treat whenever we met.

We rested a few days where we met the relief train, and continued our journey. Nothing of importance occurred until we reached the lower end of Carson Valley, I think it was the first day out from Mormon Gulch, when I got about the greatest fright of my life. We found several camps in the valley where there were wounded men, whose wounds had been inflicted by Indians in their attacks on immigrants. From them we learned that the Indians were very hostile in the valley, and also learned that the attacks had been made from the willows and timber growing along the banks of the river.

Now the only grass for our stock was in the valley lying along the river, and the stock must have feed; we were compelled to let our teams graze there or they would starve. We turned them out about sunset to graze for the night. But when I called for volunteers to guard the stock next to the river, I could not find a man who was willing to take that dangerous position. I finally told the men that I would take that post myself. Accordingly I repaired to the spot, and continued to march between the stock and the brush, with my holster pistols. The animals were scattered along the valley for about half a mile, and I concluded to march up and down between them and the brush until midnight.

In making my beat I returned to the lower end, where
I found that some of the horses were close to the edge
of the brush.   I went around to start them back, when
all of a sudden I saw the willows commence shaking
and bending right in front of me.   My first thought, of
course, was Indians.   I cocked my pistols, presented
them at the point of commotion, and commenced running backwards, expecting momentarily to feel the point
of an arrow.   Presently I struck my heel against a little
hillock and keeled over on the ground.   I did not attempt
to rise, but kept my eyes steadily fixed on the brush.
But the shaking of the brush soon stopped, and I saw
one of my horses walking out onto the open ground.
In an instant I recognized the cause of my fright.   To
the horse was attached a long lariat, which had got
caught in the willows, causing the commotion.   I got up,
and after thinking over my ludicrous position, I had to
laugh over the farce, but thought I would keep it to myself.   The next morning I was congratulated by my men
on having my scalp-lock preserved; but the joke was too
good to keep, and in a few days I related my adventure,
which caused great merriment in camp.

We continued our journey to the upper end of the
valley, where there were some settlers.   Here I found
Captains Bolch and Parker, with a drove of cattle which
they had brought across the plains; and they had encamped to rest the stock.   I made an arrangement with
them to leave my teams and wagons in their care, and
took my riding-horse and joined a company of horsemen to cross the mountains to California by way of old
Emigrant Cañon, where hundreds of wagons had passed.
And such a road!   Many places the wagons had to be

lifted over big bowlders, three or four feet high.. After getting through the cañon proper, we reached a lovely valley, through which a beautiful mountain stream flowed, one of the sources of Carson River. The valley was a regular amphitheater, the mountain walls reaching nearly three-fourths of the way around it. All was green and beautiful in the valley, while the lofty range that surrounds it was capped in perpetual snow.

I wandered up a small stream at the east end of the valley, where I discovered immense deposits of marble. The marble bowlders in the head of the stream had been washed for ages by the water as it had been poured upon them by the rushing mountain torrent, until they had received a polish that could not be surpassed by the most ingenious workman, bringing to view all their inherent beauties. Whether the quarry has since been utilized or not, I have never learned.

From this place we wended our way up a steep mountain until we reached the summit of the Sierras. We had passed the summit but a short distance when we came into an immense field of small red flowers, many of them just peeping up through the snow. I mention this because these hardy little plants were the only things, save the mountain forests, that gave any evidence of vegetable life to relieve the eye in this desolate waste.

We now commenced descending the mountain by an easy grade towards the Pacific, and that night reached Leak Springs, where we encamped with a large crowd of immigrants, all bound for the valleys in California. This was the point I had reached in 1850, when I was compelled to return, owing to a family of friends having lost a husband and father by death. I have omitted reference to that trip in this history, as there were but few events worth noting, and I have designed to record only the most remarkable events in my life.

As already stated, at Leak Springs we encamped for the night, with many other immigrants. There was a station at this place, a mere booth of brush and shakes. Under the counter and about one foot from the top was a shelf, upon which was a large cheese and many other things, and under this was the proprietor's sleeping bunk, or, rather, a nest. Now at that time the western slope of the mountains was filled with grizzly bears; and during the night a large grizzly came into the place, ate up the big cheese, and made off, without awaking the proprietor. This is rather a hard story, but I know it to be a fact. I saw the mess he had made by scattering crumbs, and also the print of his immense feet in the soft earth, as well as the nest where the man slept. A lucky thing it was for the store-keeper that he did not awake while old bruin was taking his meal.

This may strike the eye of some one who was present at the time, as many beside myself had ocular demonstration of the fact. It occurred about the first of September, 1852.

Nothing further worthy of note occurred, and I arrived safely in old "Hangtown" (now Placerville). Of course at that day I thought of nothing but money, and I firmly expected, with my superior genius, that I would make the rivers and gulches yield up their treasures in untold thousands. But there was something to be done. My teams were yet in Carson Valley, and I must get them over the mountains, and dispose of them before finally settling down. Accordingly, after selling my "alkalied" horse, and purchasing what I supposed to be a fresh one, I prepared to resume my travels.

CHAPTER XXX.

INITIATED AS A MOUNTAINEER.

IN a previous chapter, the reader will remember that I incidentally mentioned having met Gen. J. W. Denver in Carson Valley. After my arrival in Placerville, I became more intimately acquainted with him. He was at that time smarting under the effect of the duel between himself and young Nelson, editor of the *Alta California*, which resulted in the death of the latter gentleman

When I spoke of having to return to Carson Valley, he also expressed an anxiety to make a trip across the mountains; and it was finally agreed that he should return to San Francisco to enlist a party of friends who he thought would like to go along, and among them was a young lawyer, whose name, I think, was Snyder. He was a man of great promise, but was fast going to a drunkard's grave, and the excursion was as much to get him sobered up as for any other purpose. We had set the fourth day of July as the time for leaving Placerville.

We were going to cross by the Johnson Cut-off, a mere bridle train across the mountains, where even the fallen timber was not cut from the trail. The entire route was an unbroken wild, inhabited only by grizzly bears, California lions, and wild Indians.

Well, the day arrived for starting, but the night before I had received a line from Denver saying that his party could not get ready for, some time to come. But I had made full preparations for the trip, purchased what I supposed to be a fresh pony, got my blankets, and a little sack of provisions, revolvers, and some hooks and lines. Thus equipped, I could not wait, as my horse would soon "eat his head off" in those days; and, besides, I was anxious for my teams. Consequently, I set out on my journey alone. At about twelve o'clock I crossed the American River (south fork) at Bartlett's Bridge, that being the last trading-post on the route.

I commenced ascending the mountain on the opposite side and had nearly reached the summit, when I met a lot of my acquaintances who had crossed the plains with me to Carson Valley, and were footing it over the mountains. Their provisions had given out, and they were nearly starved. Well, I opened my provision kit, and before their appetites were satisfied, they and myself had exhausted my slender store. I then took leave of them, and started on my lonely trail, with nearly one hundred miles of unbroken forest before me, without an ounce of provisions, my revolver and hooks and lines being my only dependence wherewith to gain a sustenance. I jogged along on my pony, as I supposed all right, when all of a sudden he gave out. Although he was fat and apparently in good condition, he refused to carry me further, and would have lain down had I not dismounted. I soon discovered that he had been recently alkalied, and hence the deceptive appearance. I let him rest a little, then drove him before me, with nothing on him but my blankets and saddle, and we made a few miles only before the sun went down and darkness came creeping over us. We were threading our way through a dense forest of lofty pines, redwood, and mountain cedar, whose tops reached some three hundred feet into the air, and in the gray light giving a dense gloom to all surroundings; but at length I thought I saw an opening through the trees to the left of the trail. I led my horse in that direction, and soon came to a creek with several acres of open ground, and found an abundance of food for my used-up horse. I removed the blankets and saddle, and tied him where he could get all he wanted of food and water.

I now began to look about for a place to sleep. I found a fallen tree about five feet in diameter, with large slabs of bark that had fallen from the log. I also found some dry poles and placed them one end on the ground, with the other leaning against the log; then I laid the bark on the poles, thus making for myself a shelter. I had plenty of matches, and could have built a fire; but then came the question, was it policy to do that? It was true it would keep off wild beasts; but, on the other hand, it would attract the attention of Indians if they were about, and I chose to risk savage beasts rather than savage men. So, with my saddle for a pillow, I crept into my frail shelter, and placing my revolver under my head, was soon in a sound sleep, from which I was awakened about ten or eleven o'clock by the cracking of brush. I grasped my pistols and listened; it seemed to be approaching me. I sat up, watching further developments, when, all of a sudden, something larger than a dog sprang upon the log about forty feet from me. I leveled my pistol and fired, when the beast did some good running. I did not then know, but afterwards ascertained that it was a California lion. But that shot rang through the little valley and far into the mountains, and if there were any Indians about they would be sure to hear the report, and perhaps see the

18

flash. Hence, it was necessary to change my quarters, which I did by crawling under the lee of another fallen tree, not so good a place as the first, where I spent the rest of the night in peace.

Next morning I was up with the sun, saddled my pony, which had had a good feed, tied my blankets to the saddle, and once more finding the trail, prosecuted my journey. I could travel only at a pace of about two miles an hour, on account of the horse (which I wished to save), but I trudged on until about nine o'clock, when I felt very hungry, having had no supper and no breakfast as yet. In an opening among the pines, where the sun's rays penetrated, I found some grasshoppers, which I pocketed and went my way. About noon I came upon the bank of the south fork of the American River, at what is now known as Strawberry Valley, where I got out my fishing tackle and grasshoppers, and soon caught trout enough for a good meal. I built a fire, and roasted and ate trout until I felt like a new man. They were excellent, although I had no salt for them.

Between two and three o'clock in the afternoon, I again resumed my journey, the trail following up the river; but, as before, my progress was very slow, sometimes leading and sometimes driving my horse before me. About an hour before sundown, finding good grass for my horse, and a chasm in the rocks for my own nest, I concluded to camp for the night. So I cut a fishing pole, went down to the stream and took out enough trout for my supper, which I roasted as before. By this time it had grown quite dark. My den was between a rift in the rocks, about three feet in width, and some ten or twelve feet long, the bottom being a natural receptacle

for leaves and small twigs, which had accumulated to
such a depth as to make me a nice, soft bed. I now
commenced to roll in a quantity of loose rocks to fill the
chasm at my head, which was about five feet deep, and
then to cover the top with green brush, which I cut with
my Bowie-knife. When my nest was completed it was
quite dark, and I seated myself upon a rock to survey
the scene, which was the most gloomy (yet in some respects sublime) that I ever gazed upon. The eye could
not reach the lofty heads of the monarchs of the forest
that surrounded me; in front of me, not fifty yards distant, were three pyramids, to which Cleopatra's Needle
would be as a cambric needle to a crow-bar, rising
abruptly from the valley to a· height of seven or eight
hundred feet, while every brush and old stump of a tree
was transformed into an Indian, and every rock that rose
above the surface wore the garb of a grizzly bear or a
crouching panther, and the sense of loneliness that crept
over me called to mind Cowper's verse:—

> " Oh, solitude ! where are the charms
> That sages have found in thy face ?
> Better live in the midst of alarms
> Than reign in this horrible place."

Nevertheless, I got a good night's sleep, and was out
early in the morning with my rod and line, pulling out
the finny denizens of the stream until I had plenty of
provisions for my onward trip. I got my breakfast, and
about nine o'clock went back to my grotto to get my
blankets and prepare for my journey. But on my approach I discovered that my possession was disputed and
my claim had been jumped, for within three feet of the
entrance lay, coiled in the sun, a huge rattlesnake, which
warned me on my approach. Here was an enemy I had

not even thought of; but since that time, in traversing those same mountains, I found them plenty, large, and vicious. I attacked my enemy with a club; the contest was short, and I was soon in peaceable possession of my den. The snake was something over four feet long (which is a good size, even for the mountains).

Again I was under way, and about noon I crossed the river at what is now known as Slippery Ford, and followed the trail along the north bank of a small creek (which empties into the river) for several miles. As I was leading my horse along I saw ahead of me some small animal coming in the path directly toward me. I halted, drew my revolver, and when it got within about thirty feet of me I fired, shooting it through the head. It fell in the path; I hastened forward and discovered it to be a large groundhog. It would weigh, when dressed, ten or twelve pounds. I soon removed the entrails, letting the skin remain on to keep the meat from getting dirty, and hung him on the saddle to balance my string of fish; then who was happier than I ?

But it soon become camping-time again. There was plenty of grass on the banks of the creek, and in looking around I soon found a long, hollow tree, which at some time had been burned out at the roots, leaving a doorway into which I could crawl. Here I resolved to pass the night. As the night closed in it became very cold, as I was then high up the mountains, in fact, upon the summit of the Sierras; and in order to keep warm, was compelled to build a fire in front of my hole in the tree, in defiance of the savages. But I very properly reasoned that they would not be likely to camp where it was so cold.

I found my scalp all right in the morning, and my horse where I had left him; and, after breakfast, I again pushed forward. But before noon, I met some packers and purchased a piece of salt, half as large as a hen's egg, for fifty cents. Then I was fixed! A couple of miles farther brought me to where I commenced my descent from the mountains; and before sundown I was in Lake Valley and across the first summit. Here I met a lot of immigrants packing through. They had plenty of crackers, but no meat. Hence a bargain was soon struck; my groundhog was put in the camp-kettle and stewing in short order, and we all had a feast that night. They cooked the most of my trout for breakfast, I reserving a few for an emergency and taking my pockets full of crackers.

I camped the next night at the lower end of Lake Valley, and the day after reached Mormon Station, *via* Dyit's Ravine, in Carson Valley, where I joined a band of old mountaineers, who extended to me the right hand of fellowship and considered me duly initiated. Since that time I have scoured those mountains most effectually, and when Green Yarnell and myself wanted to start a grizzly bear from his lair, we always went to North Peavine for him; and when I have shown my first night's habitation alongside of the old log to the boys, they always declared that I must have been hunting grizzlies, as it was the worst place in the mountains for grizzly bears.

CHAPTER XXXI.

ANOTHER TRIP FROM CARSON TO PLACERVILLE.

ON arriving in Carson Valley, I again met my old friends Bolch and Parker; found that my teams had sufficiently improved to be able to cross the mountains, and had arranged to start in a few days on the return to Placerville, with my wagons. One day as Captain Parker and myself were talking with one of the men who owned the toll-bridge across the south branch of Carson River, away up near Emigrant Cañon, some immigrant wagons came up where we were conversing. The bridgeman stepped up to one of the immigrants and said, " I am one of the owners of the toll-bridge about five miles ahead, and I want you to pay your toll here." The man hesitated a little and then, while taking out his purse, asked the tollman how he should know but that he might find a man again at the gate who would demand toll. The fellow assured him that he would find no one at the bridge, as the Indians were troublesome in that vicinity, and the owners had left and come to the valley. There being two travelers together, the other man asked, " Have you a charter for your bridge?" The bridgeman replied in the affirmative, when the immigrant paid his toll and went on.

As they left, the tollman addressed himself to Parker, saying, "If those fellows had asked me to show my charter [clapping his hand on his revolver, suggestively] I would have shown it to them." Presently the fellow went away, when I remarked to Parker, " When I start across the mountains with my teams, I will make that gentleman show his charter, or else I will not pay to cross his bridge." In a few days I was ready to start, leaving Bolch and Parker with their stock in the valley, to follow in a short time.

Joseph Stone drove one of my teams and a young man, whose name I do not remember, drove the others. We went on until we reached the aforesaid bridge, or rather two of them close together, when my boastful toll-taker came out and demanded his toll. I said, " Sir, have you a charter authorizing you to receive toll for the crossing of these bridges?" He hesitated a moment, and then said, "No, I have not." " Then," said I, " I will not pay to cross." At this his partner stepped out of the toll-house. The first one pulled out a long spring dirk-knife and commenced whittling as he talked, leaning up against a long pole that laid in two crotches, making a barrier to prevent driving across the bridge. He said he had no charter; that the bridge was not in California, as the lines had not been run. I asked, "Why, then, did you not get a charter from Brigham Young? I have been recognizing his charters ever since we reached Utah." I then peremptorily demanded, " Get away from there and take down that pole, so I can cross, or I will pitch it into the river." He replied, "You must not touch that pole, and you cannot cross this bridge unless you pay your toll, as this is our property; you shall not interfere with it, and we will defend it." I retorted, " Look below your bridge; do you not see that it is placed exactly over the immigrant ford? I want you to remove your nuisance at once, or I shall drive over it." He again replied that I could not cross the bridge without paying toll.

I then stepped forward and pitched the pole into the stream and called out, " Drive on, boys." I remained with our two heroes, one of whom said that if they knew my name they would prosecute me; that I had taken the advantage of them and forced the·bridge by superior numbers. In reply I said, " I do not think I have much the advantage of you, there are two of you and but one of me, as my teamsters are entirely beyond my reach for aid. ·So I do not see where the advantage comes in. But," said I, " listen to me; in this matter I have not acted without an object. So far as my name is concerned, you shall have that." I handed him my card, saying, " I shall be found in Placerville whenever you want me, and now for my reasons." I then referred to the boast of some days before to Parker, about showing their charter, and also told them what I had said to Parker regarding their charter; and clapping my hand on my pistol, I said, " I always carry a pass for all such charters as yours, and wish you to learn this lesson: it is the easiest thing in the world for a man to be mistaken. You undoubtedly can boast of being 'old forty-niners,' and imagine that all the immigrants are a set of submissive cowards; but to rectify that mistake, I want you to distinctly recollect that I am an immigrant!"

During our controversy, a couple of packers came along and crossed the bridge, going to Carson Valley; of course they met the immigrant trains and told them that the bridge had been forced, and after that no one would pay toll. The next day the fellows burned their bridge and left, and I never saw them afterward. But, by the way, when I came up to the wagons, which were awaiting me about two hundred yards distant, I found

my friend Joe Stone with my old rifle cocked and a
bead drawn on the bridgemen. When I asked for an
explanation, he said, "I did not know but they would
shoot you as you walked away from them, and I did not
intend to allow that."

We proceeded on our journey, and in time, without
further adventure, we reached Placerville, which, outside
of San Francisco, was then the town of the State. The
streets were crowded with people of all classes, and all
nationalities, and all professions. Men of industrious
habits were generally in the mines, and those who lived
by their wits were looking for a chance to make money
by adapting themselves to anything that might be
learned easy. Lawyers found a very fair field for their
wits in defending mining suits, under the district mining
laws, and physicians were generally employed in their
legitimate profession. But the preachers; ah! there
came the rub; what should they do? There were no
churches; at that day the body was to be cared for, but
the soul was seldom thought of. Hence, like black
Othello, they had to own their occupation.gone. And
I have seen many a divine change the pulpit for the
monte table or the faro bank, while another would get
up and air his eloquence in a gambling hell, warning the
occupants of their wicked ways, and if he happened to
take with the crowd, he would reap a rich harvest for
the labor thus bestowed. I was intimate with one of
that class, who often remarked to me that preaching was
easier than handling the pick and shovel.

CHAPTER XXXII.

MY EXPERIENCE AS A MINER.

AFTER disposing of my teams, Joe Stone and myself went down on the south fork of the American River, where we purchased a claim and went to work mining. The sun was very hot and the shade was cool and pleasant, and Joe was a good hand to tell stories; consequently sometimes the claim did not pay very well, and we came to the conclusion that the thing would not pay anyhow. So I bought Joe out, and he sought other fields of labor. I soon sold the claim and took up other claims, all of which I sold to "forty-niners." I would not sell an immigrant a claim.

After making a few thousand dollars by the sale of claims, I finally located what was known as Prospect Flat, or rather that was what I named it. I had erected a cabin and struck moderate pay. Doctor Morse, P. F. Adams, and several others were with me. They had nowhere else to go. Winter came on—the terrible winter of 1852–53. The whole crowd was sick, save "Doc." and myself, and he and I worked our mine to feed the sick ones. It paid tolerably well, and when we cleared up for the night the only question was, Have we made enough to-day to purchase grub for the crowd? when we would shoulder our picks and make for the cabin, through the slush of snow and mud, all dripping wet.

Thus we worked the whole winter to supply our comrades with necessary food; and we were doing well at that, as all that winter flour was a dollar a pound; bacon, a dollar and a half a pound; potatoes, one dollar, and everything in proportion. These high prices were caused, not by any scarcity or sudden rise in provisions in San Francisco or the valleys, but owing to the impassable condition of the roads. To transport by wagons was impossible, and pack animals would in many instances mire down; hence much of the provision was brought in on men's backs, many men finding that making pack animals of themselves paid better than mining. However, the winter wore away and spring, with all its poetry of birds and flowers, once more dawned upon us, and with it the usual prices for provisions. The sick boys, having regained their health once more, resumed their picks and shovels.

But about this time an incident occurred which caused me to change my occupation. I had organized a mining district known as Prospect Flat Mining District, and had taken up a claim in a gulch; but there were three men working a claim below mine, and I could not get fall enough to work my claim until they had worked theirs out; so I put just the required amount of work on my claim to hold it under the district laws. But when the men below me had worked up the gulch to the boundary of my claim, they did not respect it, but continued to work right along. I remonstrated with them, but they would not listen to anything I said. I then notified them that I should call a miners' meeting to decide who the claim belonged to. They said they did not care for me nor the miners' meeting. They declared that they would not attend the meeting, and that they would work the claim or die over it; that they came from "Old Kentuck by G—d." I told them that I didn't come from "Old Kentuck," and that, like all my race, I was a coward; but they had better be more careful, as an invasion of my rights might make a lion of me.

On Saturday night I attended the miners' meeting, and introduced my evidence showing that I had done the requisite amount of labor to hold the claim, when the miners decided the case in my favor and offered to send a committee to place me in possession of my claim on Monday morning. I told them that in case I wanted a committee to place me in possession I would call upon them; but I would ask the president of the meeting to let the secretary go with me, and read the proceedings of the meeting to the adverse party.

Accordingly on Monday morning I was on the ground, with my pick, shovel, and long-tom, at work uncovering a space to get to the wash dirt. Charley Barney, a friend, accompanied the secretary and myself; and in about half an hour my antagonists put in an appearance. They came right upon the ground and commenced work with me. I quietly notified them that I should not pay them for their labor, and they returned the compliment, telling me that they would not pay me for mine. I told them that unless the Government paid me I should not expect any pay.

After thus working for a time, the secretary having in the meantime read the decision of the meeting giving me the ground, I said to Charley Barney, "Charley, will you help me to set my tom?" We took the tom and jumped down into the trench where they had worked to, which was about four feet deep, with a straight face up to where they had quit work. As we jumped down and took the tom with us, one of the contestants, the leader of the three, a well-made man and six feet high, sprang upon the rocks above us with a bright new pick in his hand, and it was difficult to say whether his black and flashing eyes or the pick shone the brightest. He raised the pick and exclaimed, " D—n you, come out of there or I will pin you to the rock." Charley was down in the ditch; I glanced up and saw a small projecting point about half-way up the face of the rock; I caught fire and said, " Yes, I will come out." I sprang, placed my toe on the projection, and before he was aware of my intention, I was at his side, and my head was above the point of his pick. He attempted to raise it to strike, when, like a flash, I threw my left arm around him, seized his pick with my right hand, and tearing it from its grasp, threw it down into the ditch. And as he attempted to slip his hand into his pocket, I momentarily relaxed my hold of his waist and again threw my arm around him, pinioning his arm at his side. I felt that the man was as a child in my grasp.

At this moment one of his partners rushed up and with one of the long-handled mining shovels struck at me a terrific blow. As quick as thought I threw the man I was holding right under the descending shovel, which must have split his head open had not Dr. Morse, the secretary, caught another shovel and raised it so as to receive the blow in time to save my man's life. When the fellow saw what he would have done, he turned deathly pale and sank down upon the grass, making no further effort to aid his friend. But an over-grown fellow that would have weighed over two hundred pounds, the third partner, stepped up with a spade in his hand and said, " Release that man or I will split your head open."

But by this.time I was ready for almost anything, and the shovels did not seem to me to be more than so many straws whirled about my head; and as he advanced on me, I exclaimed, " You coward, you dare not strike any one," and dealt him a kick that wilted him at my feet. Then my " companion-in-arms " began to come to his reason and asked me to let him go, as the claim was not worth fighting for. I told him that. he should have thought of that sooner! " But," I said, " you have a plaything in your side-pocket that I want for a minute." He, without further resistance, permitted me to put my hand into his pocket and take out his revolver. I removed the caps, threw it out onto the bank, and told them all to get out of there. They helped out the man I had kicked, and all marched off, leaving their tools, for which they returned in three or four days.

As for myself, in jerking the pick away from the fellow (whose name I afterwards learned was Hendricks), I had so strained my right wrist that I could no longer use it. Hence I quit mining and went to San Francisco to purchase a law library. I called on my friend E. D. Baker, who was then practicing law with Judge Crockett, and they kindly assisted me in selecting my books, when I returned to Placerville, stuck out my shingle, and commenced the practice of law. But it was many months before my arm got well, as the muscles were badly strained.

CHAPTER XXXIII.

LAWYER AND MERCHANT—UNCLE BILLY'S LARCENY.

AFTER practicing a while, I was compelled to take a stock of goods, on which I had advanced money, and for some time I ran an auction and commission business, in connection with my legal profession. But after trying to conduct both for a time, I came to the conclusion that I had too many irons in the fire, and disposed of my goods.

But while I was still trying to conduct a mercantile business in connection with the legal profession, a happy-faced old gentleman came into my store one day and wished to know if my name was Norton. I informed him that it was. "Well," said the old gentleman, "I have got into a little trouble and John Frink told me to come and employ you and you would get me out of it." I replied that I thanked my friend Frink for his confidence in my ability. I then asked him his name. He said his name was Billy Sutton, but they all called him Uncle Billy. "Well," I said, "Uncle Billy, what is the nature of your case?" He replied, "They have arrested me for stealing Aunty Crowley's turkey." I said, "Well, Uncle Billy, did you steal Aunty Crowley's turkey?" He said, "Yes." "Well," said I, "can they prove it?" "Yes," said he, "there was a man with me when I took it, and they have got him for a witness." "Well," said I, "how do you expect me to clear you when they have an eye-witness to your guilt?" He said, "I don't know, only Frink told me to employ you and you would get me out of it." I then interrogated him further and found that he had been to Placerville and got "pretty full," and in returning to his cabin he saw the turkey on the fence and concluded, "just for a lark," to take the turkey, and himself and friends would have a "bit of a feast," never thinking that the turkey was worth five dollars.   He told the young man who was with him to wait and he would get the turkey. He said it was all done, by moonlight.   He got the turkey and they made their way home; but the turkey being a good fat one, it was rather heavy and he got his friend to help him carry it.

The turkey was taken home and cooked, the boys undoubtedly enjoying the feast.   But after a time the young fellow "leaked," and Aunty Crowley, learning what had been the fate of her turkey, made complaint and had Uncle Billy arrested for stealing it; and he was then under an arrest and permitted to come and get counsel, the boys having bailed him; for, as I afterwards learned, they all liked Uncle Billy, and he was anything but a thief.

I soon found that they had the young man who was with Uncle Billy under summons as a witness and were keeping a close lookout for him.   The justice who issued the warrant of arrest was Esquire Vernon, of upper Placerville.   He was an old hard-shell Baptist deacon, and was very much down on any infraction of the criminal code.   I accompanied my man, Uncle Billy, up to the room where I found the court, Johnson, prosecuting attorney, Cock-eyed Jack Johnson, an assistant (being a good friend of Aunty Crowley), and the constable (L. B. Hopkins, I believe), Hopkins or Charley Tureman; but I am satisfied it was Hopkins. (Now, friend Hopkins, if this meets your eye, please excuse me, for you know it is every word true.)

Well, Johnson (the prosecutor), who was one of those well-bred, pompous men, with a great corporosity, sat back in his chair, with his thumbs in the sides of his vest, believing that he had the case dead; but for once he was destined to learn that "dead things sometimes crawl."

I walked up to the justice, to whom I was an entire stranger, and asked to see the papers in the case. He passed them over to me, I examined them, saw that they were all in form, that the charge was petit larceny for feloniously taking, stealing, and carrying away one turkey, being the property of Mary Ann Crowley, of the price and value of five dollars, all of which was, etc.

I asked that the prisoner be arraigned, and he pleaded not guilty. I had before this time had Uncle Billy point out to me the witness, who sat on a bench not far from the door. I said, "Your honor, we will take a jury in this case." A *venire* was issued and Hopkins went out to summon the jury. As soon as he was gone, I stepped along to where the witness sat, gave him a tip and walked downstairs. He was not long in following. When we got to the bottom of the stairs, I remarked, " Well, you are the witness who is going to swear against Uncle Billy to send him to jail." He began to half whimper and said, " I did not want to, but they made me do it." I now remarked that it was unfortunate, as I understood from Uncle Billy that he had carried the turkey part of the way. He said, "Yes, I carried it a piece." " Well," said I, "if you send Uncle Billy below for stealing the turkey, I shall have to send you along to keep him company; for, if he is guilty, you are *particeps crim-*

19

inis."   He said, " What is that ? " I answered, "A party
to the guilt."   " Well," he said, " what can I do ? "   I
remarked that, as a witness, I could have nothing to say
to him ; but were he to employ me as his counsel, I could
tell him what to do.   He said, " Then I employ you as
my counsel."

There was a round hill less than half a mile distant,
and on the other side was what was known as Long
Cañon, that led off in a westerly direction, very brushy
and rough.   I said to him, "All right; I will act as your
counsel.   Do you see the top of that hill, yonder ? "
" Yes," said he.   " Then let that portion of the flour-
sack on the opposite side to your face disappear behind
that hill as soon as your legs and God will let it be done."
He said, " They will see me."   I replied that the coast
was clear, and bade him go.   And it was one of the
prettiest against time (uphill at that) that I ever saw.

I immediately walked upstairs.   Cock-eye Johnson
(or Jack Johnson) saw me return alone, when he exclaimed, " Where is the witness ?   I will bet a hundred
dollars that cuss has run him off."   At this he looked
through the window, through which I was watching the
progress of my friend, when he exclaimed, " Yes; by G—d,
there he goes ! "   Hopkins had just stepped into the
room, when he and Jack Johnson took after him; but
my young racer soon distanced them and they returned
panting.   (Don't think that L. B. was then the venerable, white-whiskered Hopkins of to-day, in San Francisco;
oh ! no; he was spry as a cat and lively as an eel.)

Then the prosecuting attorney arose in dignity and
addressed the court, asking for a continuance of the case,
as I had undoubtedly tampered with the witness and

run him off, and if he could prove it on me, he would disbar me, and I would never appear again in court as an
attorney.   When he was done, I arose to oppose the
motion for a continuance, and urged the court to discharge the prisoner for want of prosecution.   I further
remarked that "the gentleman prosecuting the case
pompously tells you, if he could only prove that I ran
young Whitman off, he would disbar me and that I would
never appear again as an attorney in court.   Now, your
honor, I ran him off—I did! but mark ye, not as a witness, but advising him as an attorney to a client.   I
found that if any one had stolen Aunty Crowley's turkey
it was young Whitman who was guilty; and as his attorney, I advised him to run, and I am happy to say he
took my advice to the letter and carried out my instructions admirably.   Now, let the gentleman disbar me if
he can."   The court was indignant and gave a continuance for two days (that being the extent of one continuance, and not more than six days in all).

The same day of the race, in the evening, I received a
note from my runaway client, then at Coloma (ten miles
distant), asking me when he could come back; he was
afraid some one would jump his claim.   I wrote to him
to stay there, as he valued his liberty, until I told him
to come, and that I would look out for his claim (which
I did).

The two days elapsed and no witness!   I again
moved to discharge the prisoner.   Johnson asked for
another continuance of two days, which was granted.
At the end of the two days, I demanded trial; but the
court granted continuance till the statute of rights was
exhausted, and no witness being heard of, I forced them

to trial. They introduced Aunty Crowley, who swore to
the loss of the turkey, ownership and value. They
introduced several witnesses whose testimony was unimportant (mostly hearsay), and when the prosecution was
through with the examination, I would ask the witness
if he knew anything about Aunty Crowley's stealing
Uncle Billy's turkey, etc. Thus the case went to the
jury, who acquitted Uncle Billy without leaving the
jury box, to the great chagrin of the justice and prosecuting attorney. I then directed Uncle Billy to go and
pay Aunty Crowley for her turkey and make his most
humble apology for the outrage; all of which he did, and
with such good effect that the old lady afterwards declared
that she did not believe Uncle Billy ever intended
to steal her turkey; that he was one of the most pleasant gentlemen that she had ever met; and had she but
known him then as she did now, she would never have
mentioned it, for it was nothing but a little freak, and that
when it was over he would have come and paid for the
turkey; that was what Mr. Sutton would have done.

Well, Uncle Billy was one of the fortunate miners.
His claim turned out to be one of the richest in that
section of the country, and, as Uncle Billy often renewed
his visit to the widow's, some of the miners were
wicked enough to assert that one of two things was
certain: that Uncle Billy either was paying for the turkey in installments, or else he was hanging around
to steal another. But it turned out different from what
they expected; for at the end of six months Uncle
Billy stole the widow, turkeys and all; and true to her
opinion of Uncle Billy's honesty, she brought no action
for the last larceny.

CHAPTER XXXIV.

AN EXCITING HORSE-STEALING CASE.

ABOUT the time of the occurrence mentioned in the preceding chapter, a party by the name of Higgins came to me and wanted to retain me to defend him and three associates, charged with stealing eight head of mules and horses. The parties had been arrested in Placerville, but the offense was charged to have been committed in Sacramento County; hence, under the statute, the prisoners would have to be tried in that county, and be examined for committal before the nearest and most accessible justice. I allowed myself to be retained for their defense, and the whole city was very indignant to think that I would defend them—even threatening to hang the prisoners and their attorney with them. Threats were freely exchanged, and finally the officers in charge of the prisoners, in their zeal, boasted that they would take the prisoners before N. Greene Curtis, who was then recorder of Sacramento City, where they would be prosecuted by James Hardy, the "bull-dog" prosecuting attorney, and Norton would get into deep water, where he could neither wade nor swim.

I came to the conclusion that I would block their little game, if possible, and get an examination before the first justice that we came to in Sacramento County. The officers were going to take the prisoners down by stage, at five o'clock in the morning. I went to the livery stables to procure a team to go to Salmon Falls, but to my surprise I could not get a team or horse, for love or money.   So I determined to take it on foot, being in the full vigor of manhood and very active, and at two o'clock in the morning I started out.   Now Salmon Falls did not lie on the Sacramento road, but on the American River, some three or four miles north of the road.   My plan was to get to the Falls in time to get out a warrant against the officers for kidnapping, before the stage should pass that point.   I continued my journey at a rapid pace for about twelve miles, when I became very sick, as a consequence of want of rest, having been up two nights before, studying up the case. I was compelled to abandon my scheme and stop at a hotel, at a stage station, and go to bed, requesting the landlord to call me on the arrival of the stage.

When the stage arrived I got aboard, and found my four prisoners, with their hands bound behind them, in charge of two officers.   I had subsequently learned that the next hotel was kept by a justice of the peace of Sacramento County, and finding an opportunity to whisper to one of the prisoners, whose name was Wilson, I told him to tell the rest of the boys, when he came to the hotel, to insist on getting out to get a drink.   Accordingly, on arriving at the house, they all claimed to be very thirsty and were permitted to get out of the stage and go into the house for a drink.   I followed the officers with their prisoners into the bar room, and asked the landlord, "Are you a justice of the peace of Sacramento County?"   He answered. "Yes." I asked, "Are you duly elected and qualified?"   He replied, "I am."   I further inquired, "Are you ready to take jurisdiction of this case?"   He answered, "Yes."

I then turned to the officers and prisoners and said,

"This is the nearest and most accessible justice in Sacramento County;" and to the prisoners, "You have a right to your examination here, and if you go any farther you are fools; you have a right to resist, and if these men take you any farther by force they are no longer officers but kidnappers." Upon this the officers ordered the prisoners into the stage; but they refused to go. One of the officers, named Murphy, drew his revolver, swearing that he would shoot them down if they did not get aboard. But before he could make a further demonstration, I covered him with a cocked revolver, and told him to put up that iron, as he should not draw a pistol on a bound man. He then put up his pistol, when both officers swore that they had started to take the prisoners to Sacramento, and to Sacramento they were going to take them. The prisoners were all young, athletic fellows, and there ensued one of the most lively struggles I had ever seen. The officers took them one at a time and bound their feet, and by main force piled them into the coach, when we continued our journey.

On our arrival at Sacramento the prisoners were taken before Judge Curtis, recorder of the city, whereupon I moved to dismiss the prisoners, as the court had no jurisdiction of the case, and the court sustained my motion. Hardy, the prosecuting attorney, asked the police to guard the prisoners until he could make a new complaint; but in the hurry of writing his complaint, he omitted to state the venue, and I again moved that the case be dismissed, as the prisoners might have stolen the horses in South America, where that court would have no jurisdiction.

The prisoners were again discharged, and were again

guarded by the officers until Hardy drew another complaint, and they were once more arrested. Not having the name of the prosecutor before him, he omitted
to insert his name in the complaint, and I took it up
and read, " Blank paper being duly sworn, deposes and
says"—and added, " I suppose your honor cares to hear
no more of this. I move that the prisoners be discharged." The order was made, dismissing the prisoners, whereupon Hardy swore roundly, and dashed off
another complaint; this I examined, as before, and found
that he had omitted to attach any value to the stolen
property. I read the complaint to the court, and remarked that in order to maintain larceny the thing
taken must be of some value; if petit larceny, it must
be under the value of fifty dollars, and if grand larceny,
it must be over the value of fifty dollars; but as no
value was stated, the court must presume that the animals alleged to have been stolen were *feræ naturæ*.
Hence, no offense having been alleged, I asked that the
prisoners be discharged.

By this time Hardy had become perfectly cool, and
now said, " Gentlemen, I propose to draw up a complaint; " and he did. This time the document was in
every way sufficient, and I demanded an examination. The prosecution asked for a continuance. The
court, after argument, and on the showing of the
prosecution that there were four others engaged in the
larceny, that the officers were after them, and that there
was information that they had been arrested, decided
that the examination might go on, but should it appear
that there was evidence in the case which could not then
be obtained, then he would grant a continuance, giving
opportunity to produce it.

The examination was then opened, and the prosecution called Murphy, the constable, who was present at the arrest, to the stand. He swore that he was present and assisted in the arrest of the prisoners; that the horses and mules were not found in their possession, but that Higgins had confessed to the officers and parties connected with the arrest that they, the four prisoners, were implicated in the stealing, and that the animals were in possession of the other four partners in the matter. In cross-examining the witness I asked him if Higgins, on his first interrogation, had admitted the taking of the animals. He replied, "No; at first he denied it." I then asked him how he had come to admit it afterward. He said that they had put a rope around his neck, drew him up on a limb, and let him hang for a while, then let him down and asked him if he was ready to confess the crime. The accused again told them in reply that they had not taken the horses. Then the party proceeded again with the hanging, and continued the process until the third time, when a full confession was made, as heretofore sworn to. Upon this statement, I moved to strike out the entire testimony of the witness, as the confession had been extorted by duress. The motion was sustained. The witness also swore that the other four prisoners were in possession of the animals, and that they were expected to be in the next day ; whereupon the court continued the case, and sent the prisoners to the prison-brig to await the arrival of the other parties.

I made my way to the brig, and directed the prisoners that when their associates arrived they must be entire strangers to them, and leave the rest to me. I watched the arrival of the other prisoners, and found an opportunity to do a little whispering to one of them; told him that their companions were on the prison-brig, and that the only hope of all of them or any of them to escape was in being entire strangers to each other, and to tell his companions what I said.

My instructions were strictly carried out. The last lot enfiployed Abe Ward to defend them. He was, I think the most eloquent man I ever knew. I was also retained to assist him in their defense. I asked to sever in the examination, and to arraign the four men for whom I had first been employed as counsel, and continue their examination. There was no opposition and the examination proceeded. The prosecution immediately called the four parties last arrested; each one as he took the stand was asked if he knew the prisoners, and each answered that he had never seen them until they met them on the prison-brig, and knew nothing of them nor their antecedents. I again asked that the prisoners be discharged, and asked the court to furnish an escort of police to guard them out of the city, as they were threatened by a mob. The court granted the motion, I bade the poor devils good-by, and they departed.

But it was not thus with the other four; the property was found in their possession, and there was no means by which we could account for that possession; and Abe and myself, after fighting the thing for three days, had the satisfaction of seeing them held for trial, a result which I did not expect.

CHAPTER XXXV.

OPPOSITION TO LYNCH LAW.

IN the spring of 1853, society commenced forming, and as permanent settlements were made in and about the mines, the civil law began to be appealed to in the settlement of difficulties between the inhabitants of the country, and during that summer many of us concluded that the " Hangtown Oak " needed no further ornamenting with human bodies dangling from its limbs; accordingly we organized, some eighty in number, in the interest of law and order, and determined that promiscuous hanging should be stopped, and that the laws of the country should be enforced in all cases, criminal as well as civil.

A short time after this organization was consummated one Hughes, living on Hangtown Hill, near Coon Hollow, in a fit of jealousy, killed a man with an ax, both of the parties being drunk. The murderer was arrested and brought over to Placerville by the civil authorities, and lodged in Squire Doyle's office for examination. He had been there but a short time when the miners from Coon Hollow and the surrounding country gathered in and demanded the prisoner, which of course was refused. The parties to our organization were scattered through the crowd, and in an unorganized state. The justice's office was in a two-story building, on the second floor, with a balcony in front. The sheriff and myself were quietly left to guard the stairs, while several of our organization went out to hunt up the rest and organize. We stood upon the stairs while an infuriated mob, consisting of several thousand, were hooting and howling and demanding the prisoner. The sheriff and myself .firmly held our position, while the more desperate part of the mob was thronging the-lower part of the stairs, and crowding upon us with threats of violence unless we permitted them to pass.

A big butcher from Coon Hollow, who was in advance, attempted to wrest my arm from the banister where I had stretched it out to prevent their coming up, when I presented my pistol and told him that I would kill him unless he desisted. In this manner we held them back for about half an hour, when our boys were fully organized and made their way through the crowd. A portion of them took possession of the stairs to keep the crowd back, and the others stationed themselves in the court room to insure order, while the prisoner was having his preliminary examination.

Suddenly there was a bed-cord, with a noose, thrown over the prisoner's head, and the other end quickly thrown from the balcony down among the excited crowd. The prisoner was dragged up to the banisters of the balcony and in an instant more would have been over the balcony and down amongst the crowd, when R. M. Anderson (afterward lieutenant-governor of the State) jerked a Bowie-knife from his boot and cut the rope. We then hustled the prisoner into a small back room and thence up a back stairway, where he was disguised in a different suit of clothes, which had been smuggled in for the purpose.

We had in the meantime procured ten saddle-horses, which ten of our organization mounted and rode up in front of the justice's office. One man, of course, did not intend to ride any farther. After fully disguising the prisoner, he was slipped down the back way and through the store below into the street and amongst the crowd, which had entirely surrounded our horsemen; one rider slid from his horse and Hughes, the prisoner, was thrown into the saddle. At this he was recognized, and the cry from the mob rang out, "There he is! there he is!"

There was now at least ten thousand men in the crowd, which literally packed the plaza, and as they rushed forward every one of us on horseback drew our revolvers and presented them, when the crowd began to surge backwards; and the throng was so dense and the press so sudden that men were pushed with great violence through the store windows on the opposite side of the plaza, causing a fearful crash. We then, with the prisoner, taking advantage of the confusion, charged through the crowd and dashed off for Coloma, the county seat. We arrived safely, with our prisoner, and I do not think that any man was ever more anxious to get out of prison than he was to get safely in. To conclude this sketch, Hughes was tried, convicted, and hanged at the same time that Logan was hanged at Coloma, we having had a somewhat similar experience with Logan.

There was no more lynching in El Dorado County. The old Hangtown Oak was cut down and principally manufactured into canes, which are carefully kept in remembrance of the days of gold excitement, riot, and blood-shed.

CHAPTER XXXVI.

MYSTERIOUS ROBBERY, AND THE ROBBER'S CONFESSION.

AT the time referred to in the preceding chapter, I
was a widower, and had erected a nice dwelling-
house in the center of Placerville. Before erecting the
building I had boarded at the Eagle Hotel, kept by Mrs.
E. W. McKinstry, and, by the way, she had a history.
She had a fine education and commanding appearance,
was a lady in demeanor, and at the time of her marriage
with McKinstry was the widow of Professor Webb, of
Indianapolis, Indiana. She came to California in 1850,
with her husband, who soon sickened and died. She
was rather a devotee of the church. Being left with but
little means, she was compelled to do something for the
maintenance of herself and little child, and engaged in
baking pies. Having the sympathy of the community
generally, she was extensively patronized, and at the
end of two years had accumulated about nine thousand
dollars in gold-dust, when a man by the name of Mc-
Kinstry, rather pleasing in appearance, having the reputation of being wealthy, was introduced to her by the
clergyman of her church as being a good and pious
man. He was represented as one that would make her
happy and be a father to her child, and his suit was so
insidiously pressed that she was at length induced to
marry him.

The marriage proved to be an unfortunate and un-
happy one for her. It came to light that the preacher
was an unscrupulous villain, and that McKinstry, in order
to induce him to further his interests, had paid him five

hundred dollars. This was the common report, and it reached her after the marriage. She also discovered that the Eagle Hotel, which McKinstry was erecting and which was then about completed, was mortgaged for nearly all that it was worth; and in fact, when his debts were paid, he was not worth a dollar. Being a woman of more than ordinary intellect, and McKinstry being a weak but unscrupulous man, she resolved to make the best of a bad matter, paid off the incumbrances upon the house with her own money, took a deed to the property in her own name, and managed it herself.

She conducted the hotel about two years, when, from excitement and excessive labor, she had very much wrecked her constitution and nerves, and she and her husband had lived a "cat and dog life." At length she found an opportunity to rent the hotel, and sought another residence. McKinstry came to me and proposed that if I would let them go into my house, which was well furnished, I should have my room and board with them as rent, to which I readily consented.

They had remained several months in my house, when the Kern River gold excitement arose, and McKinstry decided to go to the new mines. He asked me if it would be agreeable to have his family remain in my house while he was absent, about four months. I at first objected to the arrangement, but on his insisting I finally acceded to his wishes, and his wife and her little son, some twelve years of age, continued to reside in the house.

When McKinstry had been absent some two months, two or three letters arrived from his mother and other friends, who resided in the East. Woman-like, his wife opened the letters, and discovered that he had been writing defamatory and scurrilous letters in regard to her, at times when they had been having their quarrels. These letters were of the most infamous character. as evidenced by the replies. She came to me crying and showed me the letters, and declared she would never live another day with a man who would write such letters about his wife.

Time rolled on, and McKinstry did not return until the expiration of eight months. During this time my sister and her husband, one Dr. Alexander, a man whom she had married at Oshkosh, Wisconsin, and who was keeping a large drug store there at the time, visited me at Placerville. They had been there some two weeks, when I thought it would be a good opportunity, they remaining in the house with Mrs. McKinstry, for me to go and visit a ranch for which I had traded property in Placerville. It was situated in Monterey County, and the trip occupied about ten days.

On my return home I found Mrs. McKinstry almost crazy, from the fact that she had been robbed, the night before, of all her gold-dust, amounting to about seven thousand dollars, including a lot of fine specimens and ·some valuable jewelry. Her gold-dust was· stored in bottles, while the specimens and jewelry were in a small tin box, and as at that day there were no safes or places of deposit, when McKinstry left she requested me to secrete her gold-dust and jewelry. She had made this request because of an attempted robbery a few nights after her husband had left home. It was between nine and ten o'clock, just before I had retired to bed, Mrs. McKinstry having gone to bed. She and Livey, her son, slept on the first floor, and the boy came running up to my room half dressed, and said they heard some noise at their bedroom window.

I quietly slipped out around the house, and as I turned the corner I received a blow from a slung shot, or some other missile, that made me "see stars." The blow did not knock me down, but staggered me. I turned and ran into the house for my rifle, and rushed out again, but could see no one. However, on examination, I found a wash-tub turned bottom side up beneath their window, with a bar lying across it. So the next day Mrs. Mc-Kinstry requested me to secrete her dust, specimens, and jewelry. I took the gold-dust in the bottles, ripped off a portion of the lining in the kitchen and slipped the bottles in between the wash-board and the studding, and carefully put back the lining as before. It was a story-an l-a-half house, with box cornice. I took the box of jewelry and specimens to my room and slipped them in between the plate and the rafters, down into the box cornice.

On the night of the robbery, Dr. Alexander had invited my sister and Mrs. McKinstry and son to go to the theater. They had gone from the house some little distance, when Dr. Alexander remarked that he had forgotten his purse, having left it in the pocket of another pair of pants, and he returned to the house to get it. He was gone but a few minutes when he joined the party again and they together proceeded to the theater. On their return home, on entering the house the first thing noticed was that the lining in the kitchen was slit, and next the gold missing. Mrs. McKinstry went into her bedroom to take off her wraps, and there found

20

the lining slit in every direction, as in the kitchen where the dust had been, and she exclaimed, "Oh, my God! I wonder if they have got my specimens and jewelry too!" Telling the doctor where they had been secreted, he made search and soon reported that they were all gone.

These were the circumstances attending the robbery, and the woman was almost frantic over her losses. I did not know what to think about it, but had a vague idea that no stranger could have committed the robbery, as she did not believe she had confided to any person where the money was hid. But as fate would have it, McKinstry had arrived the same evening that I did. It struck me as possible that he might have come to town the night before, and in their absence had perpetrated the robbery. And yet I could not conceive how it was possible for him to have any idea where the treasure was hid. His wife refused to have anything to say to him when he returned further than to inform him of the infamous letters she had received.

My suspicions were divided between Alexander and McKinstry. However, I said nothing to any person as to my ideas of the matter, but went quietly, after dark, and scattered ashes upon the paths leading to and from the house, so that in case anybody should go in or out they would leave the impress of their feet upon the paths. I believed that if any person about the premises had taken the money it would have been secreted at no great distance from the house. The next morning I examined my traps of ashes and discovered that no person had entered or left the house by any of the regular avenues. On the following morning I commenced a close search of the yard, which was of ample dimensions. In this search I was joined by the doctor, my sister, Mrs. McKinstry, and her little boy. After prosecuting the search about two hours, I took quite a long pole and went to a shallow well in the lot, which was about eight feet in depth, containing nearly two feet of water.

There had been an old wash-tub sunk in the well, by placing some stones in it, to keep it from falling to pieces by the drought. I commenced punching into the well and also into the tub with the pole, to see whether I could feel anything in the bottom, when the doctor, some distance off, exclaimed, "I have found it! I have found it!" I immediately left the well and went over to where he was, and found that he had turned over a flat stone beneath which were two big toads. He commenced laughing, and turned it off as a capital joke. I did not return to the well, and we soon abandoned our search in the yard.

Time passed by, and when it became known that the money was stolen, speculation became rife as to who were the guilty parties. In a short time Dr. Alexander and his wife moved to Santa Clara County, and there established themselves in a hotel. When they left and had got as far as Stockton I procured a warrant of arrest and had them and everything about them thoroughly searched; but there were no traces giving any evidence to hold them.

When the affair had been thoroughly discussed by the community at large, and all the circumstances of the robbery were known, it was generally believed that I had been at the bottom of the robbery; that I had got Alexander and his wife there, had disclosed to them the location of the money, and had gone away on purpose while they should perpetrate the 'eed, and that I was to share in the booty. The circumstances were so suspicious that I became completely under the ban, and knew no way to extricate myself. Mrs. McKinstry was urged to have me arrested; but she would as soon think that she had stolen the money herself as that I had committed the theft, or had any hand in it.

McKinstry continued to come around, and he and his wife were in a perpetual quarrel, she utterly refusing to live with him. Finally Mrs. McKinstry requested me to institute suit for a bill of divorce on the ground of extreme cruelty, he having struck her and choked her on several occasions. This I declined to do, on account of my having been mixed up in her affairs, but I advised her to get a good lawyer and proceed to obtain a bill if she so wished. She took my advice, employed W. H. Brumfield, and procured a bill. But before proceeding she left my house and occupied a room in her hotel. There were several parties, including some of the first men of the town, who proposed to marry her; but their proposals being rejected, and finding that she thought a great deal of me, and considering previous circumstances, I proposed, was accepted, and married her.

We had lived together about a year, when I received a letter from my sister, Mrs. Alexander, stating that Alexander was the robber; that he had confessed the whole thing to her. He said that on one occasion the cat had attempted to get through the lining of the house where a small hole had been gnawed by a mouse, which caused Mrs. McKinstry to become quite excited and rush for the cat to drive it away. And knowing that she had the gold-dust stored away, it struck him at once that this was the place where it was secreted; so one day when his wife and Mrs. McKinstry were absent, he ripped off the lining and discovered the gold. He replaced the lining, and the night they went to the theater, when he returned on the plea of forgetting his purse, he cut the lining, then ran into her room and cut the lining there. He then took the bottles and set them out under a tree near the house, and again joined them and went to the theater. On their return to the house, when Mrs. Mc-Kinstry discovered that her dust was gone, and spoke of her specimens and jewelry, telling him where they were, he concealed the box in his coat pocket and reported them gone. He then immediately went out to "hunt for the robbers," taking the occasion to pour the gold-dust into a handkerchief, tie it up and throw it into the well.

He further stated that I had come very near finding it, and had he not attracted my attention by unearthing the toads, I would have found the treasure; and as it was, I punched several holes in the handkerchief. But a few days afterward, when all were absent, he ventured to take the dust out of the well and put it and the specimens all into a buckskin sack together, hiding the jewelry under some of the top stones of the well. In case of accident the dust and specimens could not then be so readily identified. He therefore hid the buckskin sack outside the yard. But a few nights afterward, when the women thought he was down town, he took the dust and carried it to Prospect Flat, about four miles from Placerville, and buried it in the bank of the South Fork Canal, under the end of the bridge where the road crossed.

My sister then went on to say that she told her husband that unless he immediately restored the stolen property, she would leave him, as she could not live with a thief; and that she would notify me at once. But he begged of her not to write to me; that he would go and get the gold and place it where I could get it. He wanted to go to San Francisco and get supplies for the hotel, and while on that business he said he would go up and make the restoration. He left home to get the supplies, but never returned.

After his wife discovered that he was not coming back, she wrote to me, giving me the foregoing information, that we might go and find the gold. The first thing I did was to go to the old well. I lifted a few stones, and soon found the jewelry. I then took the old tub out of the well and there found the truth of Alexander's assertion that I had punched holes in his handkerchief, as there was about seventy-three dollars' worth of the gold-dust left in the tub. I then got my brother William to accompany me, and went in the night to the South Fork Canal, to the place described, and made a vigorous search for the money; but we found nothing. We then went into the ditch and into the water in hopes of finding the prize, supposing that it might have slid down from the bank into the ditch, but were again unsuccessful. We then made arrangements with the ditch-tender at Negro Hill to shut off the water at night and give us an opportunity to hunt. But, to make a long story short, we never found the dust, and the only conclusion we could arrive at was that Alexander had carried it off. Subsequently my wife lost her little boy, when she became nearly broken-hearted; and, having been for some years afflicted with tape-worm, she sank by degrees and died at the end of four years after our marriage.

CHAPTER XXXVII.

PLACERVILLE GUARDS—COUNTY SEAT CONTEST.

THERE had been considerable difficulty on the plains from the frequent attacks of Indians upon the immigrant trains; and it was thought proper at Placerville to raise a military company to be ready in case their assistance should be demanded.   Consequently, under the order of Governor Bigler, I proceeded to raise and organize a company, known as the "Placerville Guards," and was commissioned captain.   It being the third military company raised in the State, we were attached to no other command.   We were uniformed and armed by the State, were well drilled, and maintained our organization about two years, having been called out on many occasions to preserve order in times of excitement.   Amongst other special duties, we were called out to act as guard at the execution of Mickey Free and Crane.   We also received orders to proceed to San Francisco, on behalf of the State government, in the vigilance committee affair; but some opponents of the move stole our arms, and thereby stopped the expedition, after which I resigned my command, but not until the trouble was over and the arms had been restored.

Placerville at this day was one of the leading cities of the State, and there was a great contest between it and Coloma, Placerville claiming that the county seat should be located there instead of at Coloma.   There was no doubt that a large portion of the voting population was in favor of Placerville, but the county officers were nearly all located at Coloma, most of them being compelled to reside there by statute regulation, and having their property there, they were very much opposed to having the county seat removed. John Conness and other leading citizens of Georgetown were in full sympathy with Coloma, while the western part of the county was rather inclined to be neutral.

We were in the habit each year of circulating petitions to present to the legislature, asking an act of that body removing the county seat from Coloma to Placerville, and each year I was called upon to canvass the northern part of the county. My beat included Georgetown, and I knew that the leading men of that place were opposed to the removal. So, upon the occasion to which I now refer, I went to every tunnel and cañon, around the place, where the miners did not care a cent whether the county seat was at Placerville or Coloma, or whether or not we had any county seat at all. Soliciting in this way, I obtained a large list of names, and about the third day entered the town, where I obtained but very few signatures.

In the evening I went to the hotel and put up for the night, and between eight and nine o'clock I was called upon by a deputation from Mr. Conness and others, requesting me to call upon them, as they were holding an impromptu meeting. I walked over to the hall where they were assembled, and there found Conness and several other leading magnates of the town, about fifty in all. When I inquired their pleasure, Mr. Conness informed me that I had been reported as a spy in camp and as I was a military man I probably knew the fate of spies in general, when taken, and, though they did not intend to inflict the extreme penalty on me, they wished to know my business there. I replied, "By Heaven, they lie who say I come as a secret spy;" and continued, "I am here, gentlemen, circulating a petition asking our legislature to pass a law removing the county seat of El Dorado County from Coloma to Placerville, and I hope, gentlemen, you will all sign it." He replied, "Oh, no, we can't do that, but I will tell you what we will do; if you will submit a bill for the division of the county, and for one county seat to be located at George-town, and the other at Placerville, we will all sign your petition."

I saw their trap, and knowing that the people of El Dorado County were bitterly opposed to a division of the county, I replied, "Mr. Conness, I am not blessed with such pleasing powers; I haven't even the honor of belonging to the county seat committee; but if you will kindly put your proposition in writing, under the signa-tures of your committee here, I will submit it to our county seat committee for their action. Then they "put their foot in it," and drew up and signed their proposi-tion.

I returned to the hotel at once, paid my bill, mounted my horse and was off. I arrived at Placerville about midnight, immediately called up Dr. Obed Harvey, and the committee soon assembled. I then produced the proposition of the Georgetown committee for their action. They said, "Well, what do you want to do about it ? What do you wish us to do?" I said, "Give it an emphatic refusal, by resolution." They could not see what object there was in it. I told them that the fate of our petition in the western townships of the county depended upon prompt action. They finally appointed me as one of the county seat committee, and then appointed me as a committee of one to reply to the proposition.

I drew up a resolution refusing to comply with the request of the Georgetown committee, rushed to the printing office, and had a thousand extras struck off; and at half-past four in the morning was in my saddle, and with about half a dozen of our most enterprising citizens, rode through Diamond Springs distributing the extras containing the proposition of Georgetown and the refusal of the county seat committee at Placerville. When we arrived at Mud Springs we met Mr. Conness, who, with his crowd from Georgetown, was assiduously distributing the news that the Placerville county seat committee were going in for a division of the county. When we came up they positively denied having ever made such a proposition, and that the extras were all a lie; whereupon I pulled out Mr. Conness' proposition, in his own handwriting, and showed the truth of our statements. Mr. Conness and his crowd sneaked back to Georgetown, and the result was that we got the signatures of three-fourths of all the voters of the southern and western parts of the county.

The legislature was soon afterward convened, Conness being a member, and the petitions were presented. Now the rule in presenting petitions was that each party should verify under oath the genuineness of the signatures; so when Mr. Conness, who was opposed to the movement, was reported to have said that the petition from Georgetown was a libel and a forgery, and that he had said it to John O'Connell, of course all eyes were turned upon me to know what I would say or do. I wrote a very few lines, of which the following is a substantial copy:—

"To the Honorable John Conness, Legislative Hall, Sacramento City:—I have been informed that you stated on the floor of the legislature that the petition purporting to come from the people of Georgetown was a libel and a forgery. I hope that the Honorable John Conness did not so say. If he did, I say that John Conness is a liar, a paltroon, and a coward, and if he takes exceptions to this I refer him to my friend Dr. Keene, of the Senate."

I passed the note to the county seat committee, with instructions to do with it as they pleased. Everybody was crying out, "A duel!" and I expected myself that I should have to stand up to the rack; but, to my surprise, at the end of two days I received a note from Mr. Conness, in which he denied having used the language, but stated, "What I did say was that I did not see the names of any of the prominent citizens of Georgetown on the petition, and I thought there must be some mistake about its being a petition from the citizens of Georgetown; and this I did not say on the floor of the legislature, but I said it to an intimate friend, John O'Connell, and did not expect him to tell it."

The next day I received another letter from Conness, stating, among other things, that when I came to know him better, perhaps I would not think him as big a liar as I then did. The petitions were presented to the legislature and the best that the friends of Placerville could do was to get a bill passed submitting the location of the county seat to a vote of the people of the county at a special election, the day being fixed by the legislature.

.During the interim both parties were electioneering their best. The night before the election I was in Clarksville at the western boundary of the county, when a courier brought me a note, saying, "Hasten to White Oak Township; Constantine Hicks is preparing to practice a mammoth fraud upon the ballots of that precinct." I accordingly lost no time in getting upon the ground. Now there was a valley about one mile wide, through which the road ran, crossing the valley at right angles. Hicks kept a hotel on the hill on the east side of the valley, and there was another hotel on the hill on the west side of the valley, the two houses being one mile apart. The note I had received informed me that the committee had sent a man over from Placerville to assist me in guarding the polls. I came in on the west side and stopped at that hotel to observe how things were going. I there met Gage, who was drunk as a fool. He staggered up to me and, with a drunken hiccough, said, "We have got Hicks; he is all right." I looked at him and replied, "I guess Hicks has got you." I then charged him not to touch another drop of liquor until the polls closed the next day. He promised that he would not. The sun had set before my arrival; I saw by the notices of election that the place of holding the polls was fixed at Hicks', but written underneath was, "Changed to this place, by order of the board of supervisors." But no one had signed the writing to show authority for the change. I then directed Gage to return to Hicks' and stay all night, which he did.

The next morning I was up in good time, and believing that there was no danger excepting where Hicks was, I walked over to his place, where I found Hick and Gage together. I engaged Hicks in conversation for some time, when he remarked, "It is eight o'clock and time the polls were open." We walked together to the other hotel, where he got a cigar-box, cut a hole in it and made a ballot-box of it, and placed it upon the table. I suggested that the board be formed, as I wished to vote. After Hicks and some others present had held a whispered consultation, Hicks remarked to me that they had no statute there; that he had sent a man down to Red Cañon to a justice of the peace to get a statute.

Presently a big, rough, blustering fellow came in and personally addressing me, said, "What the h—l are you doing here? We miners generally do as we please; we don't want any of your kind sneaking about here." I replied, "I can't help what you want, I shall sneak around as long as I please." He retorted, "I'll be d—d if you do," and commenced drawing his six-shooter. I immediately covered him with a cocked revolver and told him to "put that thing back." He proceeded to do so, when another one, pretending to be drunk, staggered up to the table where the ballot-box stood, brought down his fist and smashed it to pieces, saying, "D—n the ballot-box! who wants an election?"

During the confusion I had lost track of Hicks, and rushing to the door, I looked down the road and there I saw Hicks on his little black mare, going at the top of her speed, being near his own place. I started right away after him as fast as I could travel; but when I got there I found the polls open and parties proceeding with the voting. I hurried to the polls and tendered my vote, and counting the votes said, "Gentlemen, my vote

stands number fifteen, and recollect it is now just half-
past eight o'clock; and farther, the statute requires that
you number your votes." A man by the name of
Dr. Rexford, and who was Hicks' father-in-law, was
one of the two tallying clerks. He immediately commenced at one, and numbered the votes up to mine,
which was fifteen. At this moment Hicks and Gage
walked up to the polls (Hicks had been showing Gage
some of his fine stock), when Hicks, seeing what the old
man had just done, gave him a withering look. The old
man instantly drew his coat-sleeve across the figures he
had just made, blotting them, and declined numbering any more votes. Names were recorded on a
large number of sheets of paper, that lay underneath the
paper on which they were keeping tally. Hicks gave
me a nudge to walk with him, and when we were beyond
earshot of the others, he laughingly said, " Norton,
d—n you, you have caught me; I can't outgeneral you
but I have the numerical force, and I shall keep my
contract with Coloma. I agreed to give them a thousand votes from this precinct, for which they are to pay
me one thousand dollars. I don't give a d—n for them
after I have got my money; so you may as well keep
quiet and let me have the money."

We returned to the house; I sauntered around and
went into an unoccupied room where there was a table
and several benches, with papers scattered over the floor.
It looked as though there had been some caucasing done
there. I examined the papers on the floor and discovered some long slips of passenger lists cut from newspapers. I quietly gathered them up and put them in my
pocket, and again mingled with the crowd around the
polls.

Now the White Oak precinct would legitimately poll from one hundred and sixty to one hundred and eighty votes. I stepped to the table where they were voting, stuck my fingers beneath the sheets where the legitimate votes were recorded and raised them up, showing sheet after sheet with long lists of names. I said to the board, "Are you going to count these out on me to-night?" They hung their heads, but made no reply.

At the proper time the polls were closed, and they commenced counting the votes, turning back to the commencement of the spurious list. I then remarked to them again, "Gentlemen, before I would be guilty of such an action as this, I would suffer my right arm to be cut off at the shoulder." They made no reply, but went on with their count. Hicks gave to Coloma his one thousand votes, and something over. During the progress of the count I noticed several names which I had on the steamboat list in my pocket.

Placerville was beaten, when charges of fraud were brought before the grand jury against Constantine Hicks and the election board of White Oak Township. I was summoned before the grand jury and made my statement. I told the jurors that if they would examine the returns (one copy of which had to be filed, and as the old doctor's was the only one that was legible, it had been forwarded), at about number 850 on the poll-list, they would find where they commenced numbering from one to fifteen votes, and that the figures would be blurred upon the paper by something having been rubbed over them while they were yet wet; and at this point the legitimate voting had commenced. The grand jury sent for the list and upon examination found it just as I had

stated.   I then produced the steamboat list, which I had
carefully saved, and which gave the grand jury infinite
amusement in following up the long list of names on the
steamboat list and finding them all recorded as voters of
White Oak Township.

It is needless to say that the grand jury found a true
bill against Hicks and his associates, but the case never
came to a trial.   The county judge and the district
attorney were residents of Coloma, with their interests
all centered in that place, and when the case was called
for trial, the district attorney moved to enter a *nolle pros*,
which the court sustained.   Thus ended the Hicks
swindle.

The next year Placerville was again before the legislature with sufficient influence to get another bill passed
submitting the county seat question to a vote of the
people of the county, when from some strange influence
Hicks had become converted from the errors of his way,
and White Oak Township cast a very large vote for
Placerville, which, having a majority of the votes cast,
was declared to be, and still is, the county seat of El
Dorado County.

CHAPTER XXXVIII.

A TRIP TO MONTEREY COUNTY.

IN a previous chapter I have incidentally mentioned a
business tour to Monterey County, and I will now
devote a short chapter to some incidents of the trip.
It was in the summer of 1853, while I was living at
Placerville, that a man came in from South San Juan,

Monterey County, and proposed trading me a ranch near South San Juan, for some property interest at Placerville. I got some information that satisfied me as to the character of the ranch. The trade was made, and in the course of time I was desirous of visiting my investment. Accordingly, I proceeded to make my arrangements for the trip, extensive of course, and consisting of my horse, saddle, bridle, and a heavy double blanket. To this outfit I added a small amount of dried beef and crackers, to be used in certain emergencies, which emergencies were not likely to arise while skirting the foot-hills through the mining country which I would pass going to Stockton. My horse was my favorite and pet. No better companion was needed, as I think Billy knew more than one-half of the human family. I never had to carry a lariat to tie him with. I would always turn him loose when I wanted him to feed, and should he get scared, night or day, he would "make a bee-line" for me. I remember on one occasion, while on this trip, I turned him out to grass and had lain down under the shade of a cotton-wood tree and gone to sleep. When I awoke, Billy, having finished his repast, was standing with his head over me, dreaming.

But as I did not start in to write the history of my horse, I will proceed with my story. I had passed Stockton, and in making inquiries as to the route was informed that I had better, probably, cross at Firebaugh's Ferry and go down to and through the San Juan Valley. But there was a shorter, though dangerous route; I could cross by a ferry higher up the San Joaquin, pass up the southerly bank of that

21

stream about thirty miles, and then strike across the
valley to the San Luis Rancho, and go through the
Pacheco or Robber's Pass to South San Juan.   Feeling
a little the spirit of adventure, and having Billy under
me and a good revolver at my side, making three of
us, I thought we were quite equal to any dangers that I
was likely to encounter; hence I was resolved to take
the shortest cut.   I came to the river, at what was
called, I believe, the Woods Ferry, where there was a
crazy old scow with a line across the river by which to
pull the boat across the stream.   Myself, Billy, and the
ferryman all aboard, we started across; but when in the
midst of the stream, the line parted and down the
stream we went; but we hung to the shore line, which,
with the current, swung us towards the bank, upon the
side from which we started.   But presently we came in
contact with some flood-wood lodged in the top of a
prostrate tree which had fallen into the stream, the roots
of which were still fast in the bank.   The current was
strong, the stream being narrow at this point, and, as the
boat struck the current, the upper side was drawn under,
precipitating Billy into the stream; but he soon made
the same shore whence we had come, while the ferryman
and myself scrambled upon the flood-wood and brush,
thence to the fallen tree, and walked to the shore, the
only catastrophe to me thus far being the slight wetting
of my blanket.

The ferryman had a small skiff in which he said he
could get me across; but how about the horse?   I informed him that Billy would take care of himself.   I
removed the saddle, bridle, and blankets, put them into
the skiff, and we were soon on the opposite shore.   As

soon as we were landed, I called to Billy, who was un-
concernedly grazing. As soon as he heard my voice he
looked up, and seeing me on the opposite shore, he
plunged in and soon joined us. I followed up the stream
for several miles without seeing a house or habitation of
any kind; but at length I came to two quite large wooden
structures, and I believe there was a post-office there. I
am sure of one thing, at least, I broke my fast at that
place.

I continued up the stream for a long distance, in
search of a certain unoccupied house, where I was to
leave the river and strike across the plain to the San
Luis Rancho. After many miles of travel, I concluded I
must soon reach a habitation, as I saw far in the distance
a large flock of sheep, as I supposed; but, on a nearer
approach, I discovered that they were not sheep, but
antelope; in fact, it was the largest band of antelope I
ever saw. But in course of time, without further adventure, I came to the old house and there found a trail
leading across the valley, said to be twenty-one miles, to
the San Luis Rancho. I had not rode far until I saw a
vast band of wild horses that came running directly
towards me. They came to within twenty or thirty rods
of me, with heads and tails in the air, snorting and playing. Then they commenced running around me and
fairly encircled me, but always keeping at a respectful
distance. This operation they kept up for an hour or
more, when they beat a hasty retreat towards the San
Luis Rancho, at which place I arrived just before sunset.

There I found a boy about twelve years of age, who
spoke very good English. I asked him if I could turn
my horse out to feed and stay all night at the ranch. He

informed me that I could, and showed me where to
turn my horse out. I noticed that there was a very nice
house on the place, and another quite large but rough
structure. He took me to the latter place and told me
that was the men's quarter, and that I could get my
supper there. When he left me I walked round the
premises, and noticed some very long poles, or small-
sized trees, with the bark peeled off, placed in crotches
set in the ground. Each of these poles was from sixty
to seventy feet long, lying in the crotches horizontally
and parallel with each other. I could not imagine what
they were for; but presently up rode a Mexican, armed
with revolver and knife. Dismounting he took off the
saddle and put it on one of these smooth poles; then
came another and another until the poles were filled
with saddles, and before the night fairly closed in, there
were swarming around the yard fifty or sixty as positive
specimens of Mexican bandits as one ever saw, all
armed like the first. I was astonished and scared. In
fact, I did not know what to do. The boy came
around, and I asked him who owned the place. He
informed me that his father owned it. I asked his father's name. He told me that it was Joaquin Balara.
That was sufficient. Joaquin Murietta had just been
killed and a part of his band captured, and the name
Joaquin was all I sought to know. But what was I to
do? The "Robber's Pass" lay before me through the
mountains. Escape would be impossible. At last I
concluded that the only thing that I could do was to take
my chances among them. I had in my life wormed out
of many a tight spot, and perhaps I might, by hook or
crook, get out of that. But one thing I had resolved

upon, and that was, if attacked, I would sell my life as dearly as possible.

In a short time there were immense kettles of bacon and beans produced, with tin plates to eat from, and tin cups for coffee, and bread but no butter. I joined in and made a very satisfactory meal. The crowd soon commenced singing, and seemed to heartily enjoy themselves. I could understand much of their conversation, but when they addressed me, I pretended not to understand one word. The evening wore on, and I began to look for a place to roost. I noticed that there was a space under the stairs about seven feet long, where my head would be close to one wall, my feet to the stairs, and a wall back of me, leaving only the front for an attack. Between nine and ten o'clock all had retired, the greater number going up-stairs. I was very tired from the day's exertions, and about ten or eleven o'clock I forgot myself, and was disappointed to awake in the morning without having my throat cut.

I got up and started out, and in a short time the boy of the previous evening came around. I then for the first time made inquiry as to those men. Before this I had not deemed an inquiry necessary. I thought I understood what they were. But the young fellow soon enlightened me. He said they were his father's rancheros; that his father had about 10,000 head of sheep and 10,000 head of cattle, and about 8,000 horses; that the reason the men were so heavily armed was to protect the sheep and calves from the wild beasts. He then showed me the skins of wolves, panthers, California lions, and two grizzly bears. This showed me the necessity of arming the men, and that I had been "badly sold," and had my fright all for nothing. The boy said that he had been going to school in San Francisco, where he learned English; that he was going to be a lawyer. I informed him that I was a lawyer. He left me, but in a short time he returned and invited me to go to the house; his father wanted to see me. I accompanied him and he introduced me to his father, who apologized for not inviting me to the house the night before, saying he had come home late in the evening. Joaquin Balara was a fine-looking man of about forty years, a Castilian. He invited me to breakfast. He had two or three other guests, and the boy, acting as my interpreter, told his father where I was going. He informed me that it would be very unsafe for me to go through the pass alone, as several men had been killed in that pass, which gave it the name of the " Robber's Pass." In fact, but a few days before, a man was found hanging to a tree. But as one of his guests was to go through that morning, and he was going to furnish him an escort, I could accompany them in safety; an offer of which I very willingly availed myself.

We had a very pleasant trip. My companion gave me the benefit of what little English he possessed; while, in exchange, I gave him my best Spanish. After we reached the valley lying between the foot-hills and San Juan, we struck a forest of mustard in which a man on horseback could have easily got lost had it not been for the trail. I was on a fair-sized horse, but the mustard was several feet above my head and very thick on the ground. After passing through that, we reached the wild-oats country, and the oats were so rank in many places that they had fallen down. From the appearance of the country, there must have been several thousand acres that would have produced, when harvested, forty or fifty bushels to the acre.

From this valley I crossed a rolling country for a short distance, when I brought up at San Juan, which then consisted of a hotel, store, and blacksmith shop. I put up my horse, and, as I had a four or five days' beard on my face, my next inquiry was for a barber. The landlord informed me that there was no barber in town, but the blacksmith would shave me. I walked over to the shop and asked him if he shaved. He was a Frenchman, and answered, "Oh yas, I shaves sometimes." And when he had drawn his hot iron on the anvil, he threw down his hammer and tongs and directed me to sit down on the little bench used for sharpening horseshoe nails, when he took from the jamb of his forge a huge razor. It looked more like a cleaver than a razor, and I never knew whether the blacksmith forged it out or whether it was Vulcan's first attempt at edge tools before the siege of Tróy. At least, it was a hard-looking specimen. He gave it a few rakes over a strop nailed to the wall, daubed some lather on my face, and commenced operations. The first rake over my face brought the beard out by the roots, with my tears, which had the effect to make me jump about a foot from my seat; then another and another in rapid succession, when I exclaimed in no very gentle voice, "For God's sake, hold on!" and he said, "Vat ish de matter—he bool?" "Pull," roared I, "pull is no name for it!" "Oh vell I trish another." He then took down its twin brother, went through the same whetting process as before, and again commenced work, when I

again brought him to a parley by asking him if he was
tired.   He replied, "Oh no, me not tired."   I then asked
him if he was sure the handle would not break; for, if it
did, we would be in a bad fix.   He assured me that it
was strong, and that there was no danger, and proceeded.
In time, what he had not cut off he had pulled out by
the roots, or so tangled down as to hide its bushy appearance, and concluded his labors, leaving me sitting on
the bench.   After demanding and receiving his two bits,
he proceeded with his blacksmithing, as calmly as though
he had not tried to commit murder.   "Well," I said,
"what about washing this lather from my face?"   After
some instructions as to locality, I found an old tin
wash-dish outside of the shop, with comb and towel to
match the rest of the operations.   When I had washed
and snagged out my hair, I gathered up a club and returned to the hotel, went for the landlord and threatened
him with annihilation.   He readily comprehended the
joke, and said I was not the only one who had threatened his life for the same offense.

I took a run over the rancho, placed it in the hands of
an agent, and returned to Placerville by the same route
that I came, having a narrow escape from a set of cut-
throats on returning through the Pacheco Pass.

I will here take occasion to say that, in 1883, on a
journey from Los-Angeles to San-Francisco, as we came
flying along on a Southern Pacific Railroad train, I could
but wonder at the change in the San Joaquin Valley.
Now, as we approached, it opened out before us in all
its beauty and grandeur—with its snug and cozy farm-
houses, and cities, towns, and villages on every side.
Yes, thirty years have changed the face of the entire
valley.

CHAPTER XXXIX.

DISTRICT ATTORNEY IN WESTERN UTAH.

IN 1855, the Mormons came into Carson Valley in force to make a settlement, claiming it to be a portion of Utah. They organized and established themselves in Carson County. Elder Orson Hyde was sent out as the leading spirit of the enterprise, and, by the way, they could not have sent a better man for the position. The third judicial district of Utah was organized, and W. W. Drummond was appointed judge of the United States district court. Orson Hyde was elected probate judge, but they had no district attorney, and Hyde came to Placerville and insisted upon my taking the appointment. I consented and accompanied him to Carson Valley.

Genoa was a little center, where Col. John Reese resided; there was a store, a saw and grist-mill, and the place was dignified with the title of the village of Genoa. On our arrival I found some two hundred Mormons camped, with tents, covered wagons, and shanties. I soon found myself surrounded with Mormons, and my blankets, saddle-bags, overcoat, and traps generally were stripped from my horse and thrown down in a large tent which, from the appearance of things, seemed to be the tent of Hyde; and all seemed ready to perform the duties of body-guard generally to Hyde. They rushed around and soon had a substantial meal prepared, to which the elder and myself did ample justice.

After dinner I went back to the big tent (which, by the way, was subdivided), and commenced looking for my baggage, as I wanted a cigar from my saddle-bags. But imagine my surprise and chagrin, for on examination there was not a vestige of my plunder where I had left it, or in sight. I did not know what to do. I did not feel like coming out and getting into a row with the *Mormons the first thing on my arrival, and Hyde had gone out among his people to attend to some of his many duties. Well, I was perplexed, but concluded on the whole to forego my cigar and await the return of Hyde. On his return I rather shamefacedly told the elder that my things had all disappeared and I could not imagine what had become of them. I noticed a broad grin overspread the old man's face, when he remarked that we would go and see if we could find them. On entering the tent he addressed one of the lackeys and asked him what was done with the gentleman's things. He immediately led the way to a small room partitioned off with canvas. Upon one side of the room was a long pole on two crotches set in the ground, and there, neatly brushed, hung all my clothes, saddle-bags, and fixtures; and I soon discovered that I was not a subject to be robbed by the Mormons, but rather to be treated as a favored guest.

This was in the latter part of August, 1855. The weather was warm, and the old elder, or rather the probate judge of Carson County, and myself stowed ourselves away in the tent, rolled in our blankets for the night. We had not lain long before we had a realizing sense that there were about as many fleas as there were grains of sand under us, and that we were surrounded and covered with them to that extent that we were compelled to beat a hasty retreat and seek other quarters.

There was a small hay-stack near by, of which we took possession. We shook our clothing and blankets and again turned in; but it was no go. The old judge could not stand the assault as well as I could; he had a buffalo rore, and he finally got up, divested himself of every stitch of clothing, and rolled himself in his robe, the flesh side next to his body, and then curled down on the hay and was soon asleep. But as for myself, I had no alternative but to surrender at discretion and submit to the torture until morning. How the Mormons stood it I do not know.

Now there was a beautiful cold mountain stream flowing through the place, running and sparkling over its sandy bed, and a large bowlder had parted the stream a short distance above our quarters, and left a little island of sand about ten feet wide and twenty feet long, with a nice flow of water each side of it. I told the judge that I thought we might yet get the best of the fleas; that we could put a couple of armfuls of hay in the stream long enough to get the fleas out of it, then take it out onto the little islet, spread it out in the sun and let it dry; then soak our blankets for an hour, wring them out and let them dry; then put some poles and brush on the sand and put our hay onto that, and thus fortify against the fleas.

The idea struck the old judge favorably, and before night his slaves had carried the whole thing out to perfection, and it proved a success. And before the week had elapsed there were at least a dozen little islands with similar sleeping arrangements in the stream, made by throwing in rocks above and sand below. It worked well, but it was one of the inventions for which I never applied for a patent.

After a time our court was fairly organized, and when the business of the term was concluded, Orson Hyde and myself had become fast friends. I found that the old man possessed a fine intellect, and a kind and genial disposition, all backed up by a liberal education. He had a versatile mind, and was possessed of great energy of character. This was about the time when there was quite a dispute regarding the location of the line between California and Utah. The old man and myself took observations by the north star, not through a goose-quill, but an instrument about as simple. I say *we* took observations; well, he took the observations and I looked on. We lay by the same camp-fire and slept under the same blankets, and Mormon elder as he was, I learned to love the old man. In fact I have heard him preach ofttimes; his text was always from the Bible, and was always of that instructive character that would interest intelligent hearers. And during all the time I was with him I never heard him preach one of their doctrinal sermons. In fact, I got the statement from the Mormons, that he had such differences with the church that he had withdrawn on two or three different occasions, but each time the leaders had pursued him until the matter had been fixed up between them. The following extracts of letters will show something of the feelings he entertained towards me:—

CAPT. L. A. NORTON—*My Dear Sir:* . . . To illustrate the present state of political affairs, allow me here to relate an anecdote. Several years ago, a young lawyer in the little town of K——, in Ohio, by the

name of N. M., got very drunk, and cast anchor under
the lee of a worm fence by the roadside, to snooze off
the great quantity of steam which the fire of alcohol
had raised or caused to generate in his boiler. After
enjoying this repose for a time, he was abruptly disturbed in his spirit dreams by the rough "hallo" of a passing stranger. "Get up here," said the stranger, "who are
you?" The inebriate answered (rubbing his eyes and
scratching his head, with an occasional yawn), "When
I lay down here, I was N. M., the young lawyer; but
now I don't know whether I'm Joe Smith, the prophet,
or Sidney Rigdon, his spokesman." The old political
landmarks are broken down, and the lines of distinction
cannot be traced. A general *melee* ensues, in which
every participant "goes it on his own hook," hardly knowing who he is or what he is. Who or what will come out
best, time must determine. Meanwhile, for one, I will be
only a looker-on, and take items—watch the signs of the
times and of the weather, which, by the by, has generally been very cold and dry here, though for the last
week we have had a little rain and considerable snow.

Our citizens bitterly complain about paying one-half
per cent county tax upon a very low assessment, and one-
fourth per cent territorial tax even after our legislature has
appropriated the territorial tax to the use and benefit
of this new county. The citizens here are rather generous and public-spirited! You may expect to see Carson County "excelsior" under this order of things.
They still claim, that is, some of them, that they are in
California, though the line has been correctly established,
I believe. At the Lawson diggings, manifestly in California, they claim that they are in Utah, for the sole pur-

pose of dodging taxation.   In my late trip to that region, I took observations every night from the north star, not exactly "through a goose-quill," but with instruments nearly as simple, and am confident they are in California. The truth of the matter is this: the eastern range of the Sierra Nevada Mountains is the natural boundary and ought to be adopted.   Then the expense and trouble of a survey would be avoided.   Indeed, it is already the legal boundary for a long distance.   But the trouble is, we do not intend to pay taxes, if we can possibly dodge that bowlder.   Anyway, between wind and water, between California and Utah, you must not touch our purse.   We are lords of the soil.

   I am a conscientious Mormon.   I live and practice that religion, expect to live and die in that faith, because I believe it to be true; and whatever faults its professors may have, however exaggerated, shakes my faith no more than the murders, thefts, robberies, and the vast catalogue of crimes that come in every week's papers from the Golden State, shakes yours in the political economy or code of California enactments.   I believe that the only crime (if crime it is) that the good people of this county can lay to my charge is, that I am a Mormon.   Some, however, care nothing about it.   Others think it a damning sin to be suffered in the midst of their profanity, general gambling, and horse-racing on the Sabbath and other days.   Still, the people are kind and neighborly.   But I have been very careful not to dishonor any of these entertainments, by being a participant, or even to be present; and I never intend to dishonor any such amusements, here or elsewhere, by my presence, when I can reasonably avoid it.   If mine is the only house of prayer in all western Utah, it may be a digression from the practice worthy to be an exception.

But I must stop talking to you so freely about things directly and indirectly connected with my religion, lest some may think, from the liberty I take with you in writing, that you also are a little tinctured with Mormonism. But the freedom that I have indulged in with you arises from that natural friendship which I feel towards every frank and generous-minded man who, if he prefer to eat his goose, is equally willing that I should eat my turkey. On this principle alone have I reason to claim a reciprocal affinity.

If, however, any man can take the good old-fashioned Bible, which all Christendom extols (but not too highly), and point out to me my error, philosophically and scripturally, he will bring me under an obligation which I should be happy to discharge by a renunciation of that error.　　　　Respectfully, your obedient servant,

ORSON HYDE.

GENOA, February 28, 1856.

CAPT. L. A. NORTON—*My Dear Sir:* . . . Having been confined since last Christmas-day with frozen (or rather thawed) feet, I may be thought a little childish. Well, if any poor fellow has a right to be childish, I can assert my claim with many painful reasons, for thawed feet are far more severe and tedious than frozen ones; so your generosity, I am sure, will make all necessary allowance, and indulge me while I quote a Mormon poem illustrative of some of the foregoing—especially as the poetic organ stands prominently developed in the cap-stone of your own superstructure:—

" O my Father, thou that dwellest
    In the high and glorious place!
When shall I regain thy presence,
    And again behold thy face?
In thy holy habitation
    Did my spirit once reside?
In my first primeval childhood
    Was I nurtured near thy side?

"For a wise and glorious purpose
    Thou hast placed me here on earth,
And withheld the recollection
    Of my former friends and birth;
Yet ofttimes a secret something
    Whispered, You're a stranger here;
And I felt that I had wandered
    From a more exalted sphere.

" I had learned to call thee, Father,
    Through thy Spirit from on high;
But until the key of knowledge
    Was restored, I knew not why.
In the heavens are parents single?
    No! the thought makes reason stare;
Truth is reason; truth eternal
    Tells me I've a mother there.

" When I leave this frail existence,
    When I lay this mortal by,
Father, mother, may I meet you
    In your royal court on high?
Then, at length, when I've completed
    All you sent me forth to do,
With your mutual approbation,
    Let me come and dwell with you."

When the number of spirits destined from the beginning to emigrate to this world, ere the morning stars
sang together or the sons of God shouted for joy, shall
have obtained earthly tabernacles, or bodies of flesh and
blood (and God grant that the purity, integrity, and de-
votion of thy conjugal atmosphere may be such as to
invite a liberal number of the higher orders or grades of
those spirits to seek an earthly home with you), then
will be completed the great revolution of nations and
kingdoms, and the kingdom of our God cover the earth

as the waters cover the vast deep! To this crowning climax is the present disturbed political state of affairs throughout the world, as a faithful index, now pointing.

The tide of immigration to this lower world has not been (mathematically speaking) in a ratio equal to the square of the distance from the creation (counting time for distance), in consequence of, perhaps, the know-nothings of California, who, I believe, are opposed to the influx of foreigners, preferring a life of "single blessedness," through the strange desire for gold, and who thereby check the tide of immigration by practically carrying out their principles. Add to this the great drawback by premature deaths in wars, etc. Yet wisdom, justified by her children, may have disclosed a partial remedy. But why should I trouble you with that which may generally be considered a delusive fancy? I will not trespass further with this subject. Forgive the foregoing!

The last mail brought us the long-looked-for message of President Pierce. I consider it a good one—plain, pertinent, reasonable, dignified, and true. On the subject of our foreign relations, his reasoning is unostentatious, clear, generous, firm, and conclusive. His remarks touching home affairs are highly conciliatory and just— even such as we might expect from a father who felt a deep solicitude for the welfare of every part of his family. In short, it is just such a message as the condition of the country, both at home and abroad, requires. In many sections, President Pierce has not had credit for his talent, ability, and statesmanship, to which the evidences in his late message justly entitle him.

But that the interests and honor of the American people should be so ingloriously tampered with at the

22

present critical state of affairs, by the political factions
now in Washington, to whom that interest and honor
have been generously and sacredly confided, is humiliat-
ing and mortifying in the extreme! Quite too many
are eager to carve out of the Constitution portions which
their own selfish and disordered appetites may direct
them to appropriate to personal aggrandizement or sectional party interests, while the great *Magna Charta*,
the broad shield of American liberty, the entire Constitution, is picked, mangled, perforated, and preyed upon
until it becomes a scarecrow to the infatuated, a burlesque in the eyes of strangers, a deep wound to the
spirits of its departed framers, and a cause of mourning
in every American heart.

There appears to be no lack of courage to defend
party politics and interests; but who, and how many
among them all, possess courage enough to yield a point,
and "stoop a little to conquer"? There is one striking
instance on record clearly demonstrating that by yielding a most essential point both honor and the desired
object were obtained. In the days of Solomon,. the
wise king of Israel, two women claimed an infant child
as its mother. Of course only one of the women could
be its mother. Hence a serious dispute arose, the final
adjustment of which was referred to the king. He called
for a sword to divide the child, with a proposition to give
half to each claimant, as it was so very difficult to determine to which of the women it really did belong.
She who was not the mother would not yield, but consented to take half the child inasmuch as she could not
have it all. She sanctioned the proposal of Solomon!
But the other, with all the tender sympathies that swell

a mother's heart, said, I yield my claim! Let not the
king divide the child, but give it all to the other woman!
God bless the real mother! Did she not get her child
by yielding all her claim? And did she not gratefully
and fondly bear it away amid the gratulations of an admiring crowd? I " reckon " she did.

If our political men at Washington had really drawn
from the breast of the Constitution the pure milk of
sound policy, and had been raised to political manhood
by its kindly nourishing properties, could they be so
tardy in organizing the House? Why profess friendship for the Constitution and deny the rights which it
secures?

I was born and raised in the free States of the North,
and have no personal predilection in favor of slavery.
Yet the terms of the original compact, to which the
North and the South voluntarily subscribed, ought not
to lose their binding force upon either party, only by the
voluntary consent of both. Through all the extension
of territory subsequently acquired by the mutual exertions and enterprise of the northern and southern States,
the rights of the South should run parallel with those of
the North. Take it up on one side and down on the
other, and I can see no injustice or inequality in allow-
ing the citizens of each new State to determine, by vote,
whether it shall be a free or a slave State. Any other
course would savor too strongly of foreign legislation.
The Yankees of the North are about as quick to take
up the line of march towards a new territory as the
slave-holders of the South. If they are not, it is their
own fault.

It is agreed that liberty is national, and slavery sectional. Hence slavery should not exist. I believe that corn and wheat raising is national; but cotton and rice growing, I think, is sectional. Must we, therefore, be deprived of our rice puddings—our shirts, hose, pants, and a hundred and one other articles of common use manufactured from cotton? It may be asked if it is not lawful and right, in this age of progress, to reform abuses by remodeling the internal policy of the Government. It certainly is when there exists a reasonable prospect of bettering the condition of the country. But when certain ruin is likely to attend the enterprise, it can be with no very benevolent or charitable design that it is set on foot. If I had a son who was born with a hair lip, it would be criminal rashness to cut off his head to reform his personal appearance. To effect a reform against the decree of Providence and our own plighted faith, to say the best of it, is the investment of an ill-grounded political piety in a sinking fund. Fair play and equal rights are the principles of high-minded and liberal men. When these fail to stand in the ascendant, it may be regarded as a painful proof of the downward tend-ency of everything that can shed a glory on the American name.

But for years I have marked the tide of events, and carefully noted the progress of affairs; and have beheld, in the foreground, with painful anxiety, the crisis that must be met. I have also contemplated in sorrow and regret some of the causes that have indirectly and prov-identially led to the present political embarrassments that now threaten to afflict the country—causes which, though on record, are measurably lost sight of and for-gotten by the nation; and yet, if fresh in the memory of all, they probably would not be believed.

I am no politician; still I can hardly avoid entertaining some views upon every subject that commends itself to my attention. If you shall consider them to contain anything curious, amusing, or beneficial, you are at liberty to use them as you may deem proper.

It becomes every man to act well his part, in these as well as in all other times, in the sphere in which he is destined to move—praying that an overruling Providence may guide our destiny in mercy, and crown the efforts of the just with glorious victory!

Till I see you, believe me as ever your friend and obedient servant, ORSON HYDE.

CHAPTER XL.

REMOVAL TO HEALDSBURG—THE SQUATTER WAR.

I HAD built up quite a practice in the valley, and one day as I was on the floor addressing a jury in the United States district court, a friend stepped up to me and said, " Give them h—l, Norton, you are gone in at home." When I had finished my argument, I asked my friend what he meant. He replied, " Placerville is entirely wiped out by fire; nothing has been saved." I returned home, and learned that a fire had broken out near the Carey House, at the foot of Main Street, at the west end of the city, and as the town was in a cañon running nearly east and west, and there being a strong west wind, and everything very dry, the flames would leap forty and fifty feet from building to building, firing the roofs, and in less than thirty minutes the town was all in flames. It was Sunday, and my wife was in church, not far from my office. She rushed to the office, and with the assistance of a few friends had secured the most of my library, conveying the books to the rear of the building into a mining tunnel. My house was situated on a hill outside of the town, and was safe. But my entire block of buildings on Main Street, that I had just finished at a cost of thirteen thousand dollars, was entirely destroyed, and I was left with my library and one thousand dollars (my fee in the case I was trying) and with three thousand dollars owing me from T. B. Andrian & Co., mill men, to be paid in lumber. There was no insurance in those days in Placerville.

This fire occurred on the 5th of July, 1856. In the course of a couple of months I had filled the burned space in my tract with a block of cheap buildings, and again continued my business till the summer·of 1857, when I found that many of the mines were exhausted, and that Placerville had seen its best days. And I had further become satisfied that every blow struck in a mining county was exhausting the native wealth of the county, while each blow struck in an agricultural county was increasing its wealth. Hence I was resolved to seek a location in an agricultural region, and having favorable reports from Sonoma County, I made up my mind to visit that quarter with a view to finding a location. Having relatives living in Green Valley, Sonoma County, I mounted my horse and set out for that point. I had paid them a flying visit in 1855, but saw very little of the country. On my second visit I spent a short time with my friends and in the coast country, when A. J. Steele, my brother-in-law, suggested that we visit the Geysers, which we accordingly did.

Returning from this tour, I became favorably impressed with the then small hamlet of Healdsburg, and the broad acres of Dry Creek and Russian River bottom-land lying on each side of the town site, while the little town itself was embowered in and overshadowed by a luxuriant shade of native oaks, with its varied and picturesque scenery, with water as pure as ever flowed from a crystal fountain, a healthful climate, without sand-flies, gnats, or mosquitoes to afflict humanity. I resolved to settle in Healdsburg, and take my chances to make a living at my profession. Among the first to renew an acquaintance at this place was "old man" Forsee, with whom I had been acquainted in El Dorado County. The old man informed me that there was a fine opening in Sonoma County, but that I must not go in with the land-grabbers. This was all new to me, and I was led to make inquiries as to what he meant by land-grabbers, when he proceeded to inform me that the country was covered with spurious grants, purporting to be Mexican grants, but which were all fraudulent; and that he (Forsee) had united himself with the settlers to resist the claimants under Mexican title, both legally and forcibly.

Judge Forsee also said that the Fitch or Sotoyome Rancho was a fraud, that the patent issued therefor was a fraud, that on two sides there were no boundaries, etc., etc. I visited Santa Rosa for the purpose of learning the facts from the records, when, instead of finding the grant without boundaries, I found the entire estate de-fined by the most substantial lines, and that the United States patent had been on record for more than five years. I returned to Healdsburg and opened an office, and soon found that all legal proceedings at this place amounted to a grand "comedy of errors,"—deeds embracing sales of both real and personal property, one-half of them without a seal, many without acknowledgments, etc.

The first case in which I was engaged was, The People of the State of California *vs.* Charles P. McPherson, charged with an assault with a deadly weapon. I was employed on the defense, and one James Reynolds (now dead) was prosecutor. The justice, instead of sitting as a committing magistrate, took jurisdiction of the case to try it. I did not demur to the jurisdiction of the court. The evidence disclosed the fact that my client had, in the town of Geyserville, struck the complaining witness with a small stick, about one inch in diameter; but, unfortunately, there was a large-sized splitting chisel at one end of it, used for splitting iron in a blacksmith shop. I convinced the jury that it was not among the deadly weapons described in the statute, and my man was acquitted on that charge, but, under the advice of his counsel, McPherson pleaded guilty to an assault and battery. Receipts of first month's practice, thirty dollars.

About this time a gentleman stepped into the office and introduced himself as Egbert Judson, of San Francisco, and said: " I am part owner and agent of the new Sotoyome Rancho. The ranch is covered with redwood timber, and is only valuable for the timber, and I am being robbed by more than a hundred trespassers, who are cutting down and carrying away my timber in lumber, pickets, shakes, rails, and for other uses. The entire valley has been and is being fenced from my land. I started up here to see if I could do anything to save it. I stated my object to Col. S. H. Fitch, on the boat coming up, and told him that I was going to see if I could employ some attorney in Santa Rosa who would try and save my property. He replied that the man I wanted was in Healdsburg, that he knew you well, having served through the Mexican War with you, and if you undertook it you would accomplish it or die trying. He at the same time remarked that the squatters were a set of desperate men, and that he expected they would kill any one who should attempt to stop their trespassing. I told him that his assurances were truly refreshing, nevertheless, for a reasonable consideration, I would undertake it. After having fixed on a compensation, I said: "Go back to San Francisco; you are afraid of these men, and within two weeks you will find your worst fears realized, or I will be in possession of your land."

Judson returned to San Francisco, and I was in somewhat of a quandary how to commence my task, being fully alive to the magnitude of the undertaking; I was aware that about a month before my arrival in Healdsburg, a mob had taken and destroyed the field notes of Surveyor-General Tracy, gave him four hours to leave or hang, and that a like mob had chased Dr. L. C. Frisbie, he only escaping by being mounted on a fleet horse, and from the known character of some with whom I had to deal, I could scarcely hope to come out of the contest alive. First I thought I had better commence in the district court and call to my aid a sheriff's *posse comitatus*, and again I feared that that course would induce the trespassers to think that I was personally afraid of them; but a notice from them two days after my appointment, decided my course of action.

The notice which I received informed me that, if I dared to show myself in the redwoods, I would be hanged to the first tree. Accordingly the next day I loaded myself down with iron and steel, got a horse, and started for the redwoods alone, having previously learned that their leader was a six-foot-and-a-half Irishman, a perfect giant, by the name of McCabe, who would sally forth from his mountain hiding-place, come to Healdsburg, get half drunk, whip out the town, and return to the redwoods, where he had his family. On my approach to the redwoods I inquired for McCabe's shanty, and on reaching it I found him seated on his shaving-horse making shingles. I dismounted, hitched my horse, advanced toward him and said, " Is your name McCabe ? " He. replied in the affirmative. I added, " Fighting McCabe ? " " They call me so some-times." I then said, " Well, sir, I am that detested Judson's agent that you propose to hang to the nearest limb, and have come to surrender myself for execution; my name is Norton." He dallied a moment with his drawing-knife and then said, " Suppose we carry our threat into execution ? " I made answer that no doubt they had force enough in the woods to do it, but there would be some of them that would not be worth hang-ing by the time it was done. He then queried, " Well, Norton, what do you propose to do with us ? " I replied, " Mack, I intend to put every devil of you out of the woods, unless you carry your threat into execution." He was silent for a minute, then said: " Well, you look and act as if you meant all you say." I answered,

" I mean every word of it." " Well," said he, " in case I
leave, how long will you give a fellow to get off with his
stealings ? " I said, " How long do you want, Mack ? "
He replied, " A week or ten days." I asked, " Is two
weeks sufficient ? " He replied, " It is." " Will you
leave at that time?" "I will." I said, "That is enough
between gentlemen." Mack left according to agreement.

I then went out into the woods where the axes were
cracking on every side, some chopping, some splitting
rails, others sawing bolts; in fact, it was a busy place.
When I approached them I asked what they thought
they were doing there, if they did not know they were
trespassers? They wanted to know who I was and
what business I had there. I answered, "I am the
agent of Egbert Judson, the owner of this land and timber, and I forbid you to cut another stick, and intend to
make you pay for the trespass already committed. They
commenced to gather around me, using the most in-
sulting language; one of them, pointing to a large limb
on a spreading oak, said, " We will give you just two
minutes to get out of this, and, unless you are gone by
that time, we will string you up to that limb." I drew
a revolver and cocked it, and told them to keep their
distance, that I would kill the first one that attempted
to advance. I then asked them to give me their names,
as I intended to prosecute them, each and every devil.
They gave me a laughable list, which I will not attempt
to copy here. After informing them that they were a
set of cowardly scoundrels and not a gentleman in the
crowd, I left them and returned to Healdsburg.

Johnson Ireland was the justice of the peace, and a
firm, positive, honest man; and being satisfied that I

could trust him, I brought about a hundred suits, using all the *aliases* I could think of, placed the papers in the hands of an officer, with instructions to serve on all he could find in the woods, except my Irish giant, and to obtain their real names if possible. The actions were for trespass upon personal property, for taking and carrying away posts, rails, pickets, etc. I think the officer got service on sixty-two persons. The cases were set for hearing at twelve o'clock noon. The parties did not arrive in time, and I took a default against the crowd; but at two o'clock in the afternoon of the same day, as I was seated in my office (which was on the second floor over a store on West Street) conversing with a friend, I heard some one hallooing on the street. I walked to the balcony and saw that the street was crowded with men.

Their spokesman called out, " Well, old fellow, there is a friend of mine up in the redwoods who wants to compromise with you." I inquired his friend's name. He replied: " D—n you, if you want his name find it out the way you found ours." I said, " It is very unkind in you not to give your friend's name, but as the business of the day is over with me, I will attend to it; I think, however, you are mistaken in your man. It is not Norton you are hunting; it is Surveyor-General Tracy, or Dr. Frisbie that you are after; but as you will not give your friend's name, I will accompany you to see him. I will go with one of you, two of you, or three of you, or I will go with your crowd; or I will be fairer still, I will agree to come down there and whale any one of you so blind that your wife will not know you when you get home again. I know your kind better than you know yourselves." Instead of rushing for me, as my friend had anticipated, they commenced gathering in knots, and at the end of an hour there was not one of them on the street. Thus ended their first and last attempt to mob me.

My next adventure was in removing squatters from the east side of Russian River. Judson had sent a man by the name of A. J. Soules with a flock of sheep on his own land on the Sotoyome Rancho, to pasture. The squatters (numbering sixteen families) went and removed Soules and the sheep from the grant, admonishing him that it would not be safe to return. Judgment in ejectment was obtained against those men in the federal court at San Francisco, but no one had dared to attempt to enforce it. Having been successful in driving the trespassers from the redwoods, Judson came to the conclusion that perhaps I might gain possession of his other land. After consultation, I directed him to send me a deputy from the United States marshal's office, with the writs of ejectment, which he did. We went over to the field of our new labors about five o'clock in the evening, having previously sent them notice of my intention to remove them unless they would enter into a lease, and recognize our title. We found them all at the house where we proposed to commence, all armed with knives or pistols. Over an hour was consumed in trying to get the party to sign a lease, but to no purpose. The evening was chilly, and I could not think of throwing a woman and small children out at that time of the evening. Accordingly, I told them that I would be there at eight o'clock the following morning to put them out. At the appointed hour we were on hand, and found them all there. I again tendered the lease, which was refused. I cocked my revolver, took my position in the gateway, and directed the marshal to throw the goods out of the house, which he proceeded to do. They made a demonstration as though they intended to make a rush. I warned them to keep back. The marshal got all out but the woman. He came to the door and said, "I cannot get this woman out." I told him to take my revolver and keep the men back, and I would attend to her. I walked in, found her seated in the middle of the floor, and said, "Madame, it becomes my unpleasant duty to remove you," at the same time stepping quickly to her back, bending over and putting my hands beneath her so as to carry her out. She sprang to her feet, exclaiming, "I guess I can go out myself." After the woman had surrendered the citadel, the man (whose name, I believe, was Weber) remarked that, if it were not too late, he would sign the lease. I replied that it was never too late for me to ameliorate the condition of my fellow-man, and handed him the lease, which he signed. We then went from house to house and all the occupants signed leases. Thus Judson was restored to his land on the old Soto-yome Rancho.

CHAPTER XLI.

THE SQUATTER WAR—CONTINUED.

THE Russian River and Dry Creek valleys at this time were nearly all in the hands of the squatters, which territory was covered with Mexican grants, as follows: Sotoyome or Fitch Grant, eight leagues; New Soto-yome, three leagues; the Tzabaco Grant, containing

something over four leagues. The titles were all con-
firmed, and patents issued and on record. Notwithstanding all this, the squatters in possession had their
secret leagues all over the county, and forcibly resisted
all efforts to dispossess them, and the law seemed to
be entirely a dead letter; actions in ejectment were prosecuted to judgment; writs of restriction were issued and
placed in the hands of officers, but resistance was made
by armed force; the military was called out—a requisition for the militia on one side, and Captain Forsee
mustering two thousand squatters on the other side.
Parties would be evicted one day, and the next morning would find them in possession of the same premises
they had been ejected from the day before. Two thousand men had met and confronted each other in blood-
less combat; both parties marched and countermarched
until the farce was played out. By express command
of the sheriff, I was excluded from these wars, and the
affair was finally left where it commenced. Though
the fairest domain on which the sun ever shone, yet
people shunned it, as there was no title or undisputed
possession.

Things were in this condition when Dr. L. C. Frisbie
of Vallejo, employed me to look after his interests in the
Sotoyome Rancho. I took his business in hand, and
succeeded in making some sales and getting along pretty
smoothly for a few months; but it became necessary to
bring several suits in ejectment, which I prosecuted to
judgment. One of them was against Riland Arbuckle,
on a portion of the Sotoyome Rancho, and as he was a
boastful, blowing fellow, I thought I would go for him
first. The sheriff dispossessed the party, and levied upon

a quantity of sacked barley, which we removed to the house for safety. The squatters said they would not resist the officer, but that Arbuckle should be placed in possession again before morning, and that old Norton had better leave with the sheriff if he knew what was good for him. I, however, thought differently. My client was not there, and I had determined to try strength of nerve with them, and had secured the services of seven young men to aid me. We were all supplied with double-barreled shot-guns and plenty of ammunition. The sheriff had retired, and about a dozen of the squatters lingered for a time. I had gone out to reconnoiter the premises, when they commenced talking very rough to the boys, telling them that they had better leave, as every one of them would be killed before morning, etc. The boys were telling them that they were not there to fight, but merely to hold possession under the law. In the early part of the conversation I had slipped up behind a large oak tree where I could hear every word that passed, and at this juncture I sprang from my concealment and exclaimed, "You are a bombastic set of cowards; you have dared me to hold these premises; now go home and rally your forces for your night attack; you will find 'old Norton' at his post." My boys all bustled up and told them to go or they would boot them, and finally bluffed the fellows from the ground; but on riding off they called back that we would see them again before morning.

We then made breast-works of the sacks of barley in the house, with loop-holes through the thin siding, and before it was quite dark I placed patrols up and down the road with instructions, if they should see the enemy approach in force, to retreat to our fortification and notify us; but if the enemy advanced too fast, they were to fire a revolver as a signal and make good their retreat. About eleven o'clock I heard the discharge of a revolver, and the two outposts came rushing in and said there was a large company of horsemen rapidly approaching. I formed the command outside of the house, under a large laurel tree, where it was quite dark. I ordered them to drop down upon their faces on the ground. On came the horsemen, from eighty to one hundred strong. When they got opposite to us and about four rods distant, I ordered, " Ready! " All the locks clicked audibly. I said, " Reserve your fire till they attempt to cross the fence." The horsemen wavered for a moment, then with a right-about-face made equally as good time in getting away as they did in coming. I was satisfied that we had not seen the last of them, and in consequence of this impression I kept a vigilant watch. About two o'clock in the morning one of my sentinels came running in and said there was a large crowd creeping along the fence. I ordered my force to keep perfectly quiet. I took my old rifle that I had had in camp, and skulked along the fence to within about a hundred yards of the foremost of the approaching party, when I slipped out and fired a shot about ten feet over their heads. At this there was another general stampede, and we were again in peaceable possession of the Arbuckle place.

I continued to eject the squatters from Frisbie's tracts, with greater or less resistance, until I had reduced the whole to possession. It now seemed to be the general opinion that I was the only one who could successfully

23

cope with squatters, and John N. Bailhache, as one of the Fitch heirs, or rather tenant by courtesy, having married Miss Josephine Fitch, had a large tract of land covered by squatters, and had made many futile attempts to expel them.   They had become so well organized, and so confident of their ability to forcibly hold the premises, that they actually paraded the streets of Healdsburg, both men and women, with music and banners waving, and seemed to think that if they could only get rid of Bailhache they would be secure in their homes. In accordance with this idea, they made a raid on him and forced him to secrete himself in the Raney Hotel. Seeing his danger, I marched out with a cocked revolver in each hand, meeting the mob, and persuaded them that I was the man they wanted, and not Bailhache; but they came to the conclusion that they did not want either of us, and retired, still holding forcible possession of his lands.   Mr. Bailhache about this time discovered that he had business at Fort Yuma; so he moved his family to Santa Rosa and departed.

A few months afterward I received a letter and power of attorney from Mr. Bailhache at Fort Yuma, giving me full authority to enter upon any and all his lands in Sonoma County, and expel squatters, etc.   I commenced operations under this power, but not until after I had convinced the sheriff that his was not much of an office anyhow, and he had agreed to turn it over to his under-sheriff in case he could furnish the necessary bonds, which I believe were about thirty thousand dollars; and I agreed to furnish ten thousand, in consideration of having the privilege of selecting my own deputy for Healdsburg.   This was carried out, and I chose J. D. Bins, and adopted a new system of warfare. I put in teams and went to work hauling off the fencing from the farms on the west side of Dry Creek, thus rendering the land useless to the holders. This drove them to desperation. The teams had been hauling all day, and at evening when they were coming in with the last load for the day, as they were approaching Dry Creek, my team being in the rear with five or six men upon the wagon, my brother among the number, two shots from rifles were discharged in rapid succession, and a bullet from one of them struck a Mr. Ferguson just above the knee, and running down the leg shattered the bones in a terrible manner; it was a death shot. My brother drove him to town as fast as possible, but he never rallied from the nervous shock, and died the next day.

Until this murderous attack I had not been thoroughly aroused, but after the death and burial of young Ferguson I took a *posse* of ten men, all thoroughly armed, and went with them in person. Stationing a few outposts to prevent any further shooting from the brush, I commenced throwing out goods from the houses and burning the buildings to the ground. In this way I went from house to house, until I burned down all the dwellings on the Bailhache premises occupied by squatters. They followed us up *en masse,* and at length one of them said, "I would like to know who sets those buildings on fire; I would make them smart legally." I replied, "What, you appeal to the law, who have so long trampled law and justice beneath your feet! You shall be gratified!" I said, "Jim Brown, fire that house." The house was soon in flames. I then said to the squatters, "Now take your legal remedy." Brown (a brother of Mayor Brown, of

Santa Rosa) was indicte , but a *nol. pros.* was entered in the case, as the house was mine, and I having authorized the act; there being no property of others in it, nor no living being, under our statute the act was legal. Some of the houses were goo1 two-story buildings, but I treated them as I would have done a lot of rats' nests; under the circumstances there was no alternative.

Although 'I had reduced the dwellings to smouldering ruiqs, the squatters continued to hang around, like the French soldiers around a burning Moscow, until the elements drove them away to the hills, where some of them put up temporary abodes on the adjacent Government land. In our attempt to keep the raiders from the different places. we had only been successful in gaining possession of a small portion, and in order to perpetuate my possession, I commenced repairing the fences, and on two or three occasions in the night they fired them. But I was ever on the alert, and discovered the fire in time to prevent much damage.

My next effort was to find some one who would dare take possession of· some one of the places. At last I found a man by the name of Peacock, a powerful, resolute fellow, who proposed to purchase a piece of the land which a man by the name of Clark had been claiming, and whose house had been burned down. He contracted and entered into possession, and guarded a fine lot of hay, a volunteer crop growing on the place. The hay had matured and he had cut and cocked it, but in the meantime, contrary to my counsel, he had made great friends with and confidents of the squatters who had been evicted, and among other things told them that he was going to see my brother the next day, to

get his team to bale hay, and should be absent that
night. I strongly opposed it, while he assured me that
everything would be safe, but did not convince me. I
was on the watch, and about two o'clock in the morning I discovered a bright light arising from the neighborhood of Peacock's hay. I rushed around, awakened
Bailhache, Ransom Powell, and two or three others,
and started for the scene of the fire. We succeeded in
saving about one-third of the hay.

On Peacock's return it was impossible to convince
him that the Prouses had any hand in this, or that they
knew anything of it. He continued his former relations
with them for about a month after this time, having
gone to board with them. One day a dispute arose at
the dinner table, and the two Prouse brothers set upon
him, one of them armed with something that the evidence afterwards disclosed as being somewhat like a
butcher's cleaver. They cut and hacked Peacock up in
a terrible manner, so that for a long time his life was
despaired of. For this offense I had Daniel Prouse sent
to the penitentiary, and we continued to hold possession.
The land being desirable farming land, others, seeing that our title could be maintained, commenced purchasing; and thus Bailhache was restored to his possession, which put an end to the squatter difficulty on
the Sotoyome Rancho.

CHAPTER XLII.

THE SQUATTER WAR—CONTINUED.

ABOUT this time I was requested to take charge of the Tzabaco Rancho, by John B. Frisbie and W. H. Patterson, of San Francisco, sending the request by James Clark, then sheriff of Sonoma County, who held writs of ejectment against all the settlers on the Russian River side of the grant. I had been acting for them for more than two years as their agent, selling and leasing the Dry Creek portion, where they met with but little opposition to their title. But before stating my action on the Russian River Valley, I must state one incident that occurred on the Dry Creek portion. I had been up Dry Creek serving some notices on parties who had not paid up, and was returning, mounted on a gentle little mare; and while jogging along, right opposite the widow Bell's old place, where there was an old watering trough and spring at a large redwood stump, surrounded by a dense growth of redwood sprouts, a shot was fired. I felt a concussion, and at the same instant my mare made a jump sideways, nearly throwing me from my saddle. I recovered myself and dismounted.

I saw the brush wiggle and shake, and made for the point. The party took to his heels, running through the thick brush and up a very steep hill, and I only got a sight of his back. He wore a bluish-gray coat and a low black hat, and was rather a short man, and that was all I could tell of my would-be assassin. I was unarmed and had no way of stopping him. On examination, I discovered that the bullet had passed through both sides

of my vest, having entered the right side high in the
breast, passing through my outer shirt, in front, and out
at the left side.   This was at a time when strangers
thought us a set of desperadoes here, and there was but
little said about it, as I did not wish to add to our reputation in that line.   When I came in I showed it to Bailhache, D. F. Spurr, and, may be, two or three more.   I
still have the vest, and if this reaches the eye of the
perpetrator of the deed he may congratulate himself on
the fact that I could not recognize him.

And now to the squatters on the Russian River side
of the grant, hostile almost to a man.   When the sheriff
informed me that he was under my instructions, I told
him to go home and if I needed him I would let him
know.   I then wrote to Frisbie and Patterson, and told
them that in case I entered upon the hazard of attempting to manage the squatters, they must give me an un-
conditional power to survey, segregate, and sell all the
lands upon such terms and time as I should deem proper,
being accountable to no one for my actions in its disposition.   They immediately sent me the power, which
was communicated to the settlers in a very exaggerated
manner, they being led to believe that I would eject them
from their homes without an opportunity of purchasing
at any price.   Whereupon their secret organization met,
I having two trusty friends in that organization, who
hastened to me and communicated to me so much of
the proceedings as in their judgment was necessary to
preserve my life.   I was told by them that it was determined in counsel that my death was essential in order
to defeat the measures about to be carried into effect;
and they had adopted a resolution that if I ever showed

myself upon the Tzabaco Rancho I was to be killed like
a snake by whoever discovered me; and in addition to
this, they balloted to see whose duty it was to be my
special executioner and hunt me out and kill me.   These
men begged of me, under the circumstances, not to come
onto the grant.   I fully comprehended the fact that the
settlers were in a state of desperation, as we held one
judgment over them in the sum of ten thousand dollars,
for use and occupation of the premises, and another
judgment of ten thousand dollars obtained on injunction
bond, making a total of twenty thousand dollars; together with writs of ejectment against every one of
them.

     After due reflection, I resolved to "beard the lion in
his den," and to fight the devil with fire, and when I was
all ready, I hitched my pony to the buggy, and started
for the Tzabaco Rancho.   After placing a quart bottle
of old Bourbon under the buggy seat, and arming myself in case of trouble, I drove to the ranch, which is
about six miles from Healdsburg, following the Geyserville road, and adjoining the Sotoyome Rancho on the
west.   I drove up opposite the house of one Captain
Vessor, then living close to the line, and saw the old
captain in his yard hewing out a plow-beam.   I stopped
my horse, and called out, "Captain Vessor, will you step
this way?"   He dropped his ax, and came to the road;
when about five or six feet from the buggy he raised his
spectacles, and recognizing me, he instantly became as
black as a thunder-cloud.   I jumped out of the buggy,
and confronting him, said, "I am informed that you men
have in solemn conclave determined to shoot and scalp
me if I ever came on this grant, and as shooting is a

game that two may play at, I will commence now," at
the same time running my hand under the buggy seat.
The old captain threw up both hands and commenced
running backwards, exclaiming, "Don't, don't." "I'll
be hanged, if I don't !" said I, at the same time bringing
the whisky bottle to bear upon him. A pleasurable
sensation, after the most abject fear, wrought another
change in the captain, when he laughingly exclaimed:
"Oh, God! you might have shot me with that long ago."
I then gave the old man a "shot in the neck," and bade
him get into the buggy; but I frankly told him that I was
through joking and meant business; that for the present
he was my prisoner, and must go with me. He very
reluctantly complied and I drove to Geyserville, only
holding him hostage to insure my own safety.

At this place I met Dr. Ely, who I had good reason
to believe was the brains and managing man of the
squatters, he being a man of intellect, and a fair-minded,
reasonable man upon all subjects excepting the one at
issue. I dismissed Vessor, "shot" Ely, and took him in
the buggy, and continued my journey through the Tzabaco
Rancho. I informed the doctor that I came up to sell
them their lands, and that I proposed to give every man
a reasonable chance of paying for the farm I sold him.
I was aware that the lands had been held too high; that
the owners were honest in their convictions of the value
of the land, but were mistaken; and for that reason
I had refused to take the agency until they gave me
carte blanche to dispose of them according to my own
judgment. " But," he said, with apparent surprise, "you
do not propose to sell me my place ?" "Why not ?" I
asked. He replied, " I have always heard that you said

you would not sell my place, but had selected it for yourself." " That," said I, " is just as true as many other things you have heard about me. I am a Western man, and am anxious to see every man have his home, and will sell to you just the same as to the rest." " But," said he, " if disposed to purchase, how can we? We are bankrupts; with the twenty thousand dollars judgments hanging over us, we can do nothing." I told him that it was not necessary to tell me that they were bankrupts, for I knew it; and continued, " It is not necessary to tell me that you are a set of ruined and desperate men; I know it. It is not necessary for you to say, in case I attempt to execute the writs of ejectment which I hold against you, that these fair domains will be left blackened ruins, and that the inhabitants will retire to their mountain fastnesses and wage war against human nature at large, for I already know it, and in my present action have given due heed to it all; yet I am going to sell every man of you your farms, and as fast as you purchase I shall wipe the judgment out against the purchaser and again place you in the position of freemen."

The doctor frankly admitted that if that was my intention, then I had been greatly misrepresented to them. I told him that, having unlimited power, I intended to be a benefactor and not an oppressor of the people. The doctor took me at my word, rode through the settlement with me, and advised the settlers to purchase their homes, which seemed to them unusual advice. I notified them that, on the following Thursday, I would be at Captain Vessor's for the purpose of going with them over every man's place, and fixing a price upon it per acre.

I was there at the time appointed, and met the entire settlement, and went over every place, fixing my price upon the land as I passed over, and to my surprise and satisfaction every one of them thought that I had put a fair price upon his neighbor's land, but had got his a *little too high.* The result was that every man purchased his farm within the ensuing six weeks, paying one-fourth down and getting three years to pay the balance, at one per cent per month interest. And what was still more satisfactory, by the enlargement of time of payment, all succeeded in paying for their farms, and thus ended the squatter war that had been kept up for over seven years in the northern portion of this county.

But before dismissing the subject I must say, in justification of these men, that the most of them, in my judgment, were honest in their convictions that the claimants either had no title to the lands, or if they had a title it was fraudulent; and that many of them to-day are among our most respected and prominent citizens. Our old feuds are now looked upon as a feverish and disturbing dream, or treated as a subject of mirth, and as for myself, the most of the men who once wanted to see my throat cut are among my warmest friends. I will here append a set of resolutions, expressing their feelings toward me after our fight was over:—

"At a meeting of the citizens of Washington Township, and on the 'Tzabaco Grant,' held this day, without distinction of party, the following preamble and resolutions were unanimously adopted:—

"WHEREAS, It having become known to us that statements are being publicly made to the effect that Capt L. A. Norton, of Healdsburg, is regarded with unfriendly feelings by the citizens and settlers of this township, and knowing such statements to be wholly untrue and unjust to Captain Norton, it is hereby

"*Resolved*, That we recognize in Capt. L. A. Norton, a gentleman of great firmness of purpose, and energy in the discharge of duty; entirely impartial as agent between grant holders and settlers—and that his courtesy and friendship as evinced toward all who wished to secure their homes, demand and receive our hearty approbation and respect, and that we entertain for him none but the kindliest feelings.

"*Resolved*, That all statements and assertions made in relation to Capt. L. A. Norton in connection with ourselves, which are not in accordance with the above, are untrue, and very unjust to both Captain Norton and ourselves.

"*Resolved*, That the Secretary forward a copy of the proceedings of this meeting to the *Sonoma Democrat*, and one to the *Russian River Flag*, requesting them to publish the same.

"(Signed)   DOWNING LAMB, *President.*

"ELISHA ELY, *Secretary.*"

I can now look back with surprise at many of my foolhardy adventures while engaged as Egbert Judson's agent on the Sotoyome Rancho. I had occasion to cross Russian River to look after his interests and went over in the morning, crossing the ferry then owned by a man by the name of Kibbe. It was lowering weather when I went over, and as the day advanced it set in a drizzling rain. I was absent the whole day, and as I came back at night to the river it was getting a little dusky. The ferry-boat was kept on the opposite side of the river. I commenced hallooing for the boat, but no one paid any attention to me. I know they must have heard me, for I could hear them talking on the opposite side; could hear the chopping of wood at the house. Well I hallooed and bawled at them until I got tired' and began to consider what I was to do. There was no house nearer than the Fitches, and they were entire strangers to me.

The river was much swollen by recent rains and the flood-wood was coming down the stream pretty freely. I was somewhat wet by the falling rain, and at last made up my mind to attempt. to ford the stream. I hunted out a long pole to brace myself from the lower side and waded into the swift current, I continued to wade, bracing myself with the pole, and in that manner I made my way across. In the middle of the stream the water came up to the points of my shoulders; it was late in the season, the water was very cold, and I got badly chilled. I was a strict temperance man, but one druggist insisted on fixing me up a dose, which I took. I thought for awhile there was a small-sized volcano inside of me, and for a time I felt pretty boozy. The next morning I drew up a complaint against Kibbe and was about proceeding against him for damages, when he came into my office, in company with Mr. Hugh Patton, and wanted me to hold on and not prosecute my action. He said the river was so high that it was dangerous to run the ferry-boat owing to the flood-wood. I told him that I thought his defense would be a poor one, when it was shown that I had waded the stream. Mr. Patton informed me that he was about buying the ferry, and if I would stop my action no one should ever again be put to a similar annoyance, and it should never cost me a cent to cross while he owned it. I didn't accept his last offer, but I stayed the action.

CHAPTER XLIII.

CLIPPINGS.

[From the "History of Sonoma County."]

IN 1861 or '62 there was a regiment of volunteers organized in Kane County, Illinois. They met in companies at Batavia to perfect the organization; they first proceeded to elect their major; second, their lieu-

tenant-colonel, when, on motion, a recess of fifteen minutes was taken, when it was proposed that the health of
Captain Norton be drank standing, which was informally
carried out. When the meeting resumed business it
was moved and carried that Capt. L. A. Norton be
elected colonel of the regiment by acclamation, which
motion was put and carried unanimously. Whereupon
Capt. P. J. Burchell moved that a copy of the proceedings of this meeting be forwarded to Colonel Norton, by
its secretary, with the request that he come home and
take charge of his regiment, which his situation in this
county forbade him doing, for at that time the captain
(or more legitimately the colonel) had his hands full at
home. We are informed by reliable persons that the
northern part of Sonoma County is much indebted to
the firmness and energy of the colonel in keeping down
an outbreak, as that portion of the county boasted a
strong secession element, and when it was asserted that
no recruits to join the Federal army would ever live to
cross Russian River, he organized and secretly drilled
the Union forces, and was at all times ready to meet the
threatened outbreak. And when it was said that no
Union flag should ever float in Healdsburg, he went
immediately to Petaluma, purchased one, placed it on
the top of his carriage, carried it through the country
to Healdsburg, and nailed it to his balcony, where it
continued to wave. When it was reported that a rebel
flag was floating from the top of a high tree, between
Santa Rosa and Sonoma, Norton made it his business
to go down there, in open day, climb the tree and remove
the flag. And we are informed that it is now in the
possession of Mrs. Molloy, of San Francisco, the colonel.

having presented the same to Dr. E. B. Molloy, now deceased. The colonel still practices his profession in Healdsburg, and we believe he possesses the confidence of the whole community, as a careful, honest, and able member of the bar. ____

[From the San Francisco *Alta California.*]

" HEALDSBURG, November 12, 1861.

"EDITORS ALTA: On yesterday the citizens of our town were called to the banks of Russian River to witness the launching of a small boat, built by Mr. Johnson, for the trial of Capt. L. A. Norton's newly invented wheel.

" The boat is nineteen feet long with four feet beam; the wheels are four feet in diameter, with eight buckets each. Each bucket is composed of five paddles, which are perpendicular to the shaft, worked by simple machinery, so that each bucket is a full, solid bucket, by the folding together of the paddles when it strikes the water; and on leaving the water it is again thrown open, lifting no dead water, nor offering any resistance to the air until it is ready to perform labor again.

" When a large crowd had convened at the place, the craft was named by Mr. Norton after W. W. Stow of San Francisco, who was present, and made a few brief remarks. The *W. W. Stow* was then launched upon the water, and propelled by two men, at a crank on the shaft. She moved off gracefully, amid the cheers of the crowd, and the thrilling music of the Russian River Brass Band, which attended to enliven the occasion. After she had run up and down the river for several hours, exhibiting great speed and beauty and regularity of motion, the crowd dispersed, satisfied that the new wheel must undoubtedly prove a success, and that it is the very thing for which the world has been experimenting for the last thirty years.   ____   W. A. M."

Subsequently the annexed notice appeared in the "City Items" department of the same journal:—

"NOVEL EXHIBITION—ANOTHER CALIFORNIA INVENTION.—Quite a number of persons on Steuart Street wharf, yesterday afternoon, were surprised at seeing a Whitehall boat shoot from under the pier propelled by muscle brought to bear on a pair of novel paddle-wheels. It appears that a Mr. Norton, of Sonoma County, has for some years past been endeavoring to improve upon the present paddle-wheels. He believes that his invention is calculated to effect the needed improvements in these respects, viz., that whilst the speed of the ordinary paddle-wheel is limited, this is limitless, and that to any extent the power can be applied, in like proportion will additional speed be obtained. Furthermore, he contends that his wheel avoids not only the lift, but drag of back water. The wheel is composed of a series of paddles forming a bucket, the paddles being hung upon pivots, and opened and closed by a shackle-bar, which has a friction roller on each end, fastened to the bucket by knees.

"The wheel, whilst undergoing the rotary motion, brings the friction roller in' contact with cams, which open and close the bucket. The moment the latter has performed its labor, the paddles make the open revolution until they again touch the water. The inventor contends that in navigating the ocean in a heavy sea, the dead force which the ordinary steamship wheel has to encounter is completely avoided, as the vessel will sit on an even keel, and never submerge one wheel so as to retard its speed.

"The experiment tried yesterday seemed successful so far as the working of the wheels and speed are concerned. The two men at the crank propelled the craft quite as fast as two oarsmen another boat, with which a trial of speed was had.

"The inventor has filed his caveat, and formally applied for a patent. A model is now being constructed in this city."

CHAPTER XLIV.

A VISIT TO THE EAST.

SINCE the events recorded in the foregoing chapters, I made, in 1874, a lengthy tour to the East, visiting the scenes of my early life and adventures in Canada, and also many of the States of the Union. I kept a diary of my travels, and the prominent occurrences of the journey, from which I take the facts herein set forth.

I started out of San Francisco on "All Fools' Day" on an eastern-bound train. Among the passengers was a Mrs. G. and her little son, aged about eight years. Her husband, who was an official of Alameda County, sought · an introduction, and placed his wife and son under my care. We were soon settled in one of the commodious palace cars, and all within the car soon became acquainted and, in fact, constituted a little social community. In reading, talking, playing cards, and looking from the windows at the various external objects

24

that caught the fancy, the time passed pleasantly as we rolled slowly along; for, here let me say, I was very much disappointed as to the speed in crossing the continent by rail. I don't think they averaged twenty miles an hour. We had crossed the American Alps, had doubled Cape Horn, and on the second day were steaming up the Humboldt River, without a remarkable incident on our trip.

When we arrived at the county seat of Humboldt County, and when the cars stopped at the depot, the conductor walked through the cars and announced that we had twenty minutes to exercise our limbs. I asked Mrs. G. if she would like to walk out, and she replied in the affirmative. I looked at my watch, and we walked to the court house, less than a five minutes' walk, exchanged a few words with the clerk, and started back, when the whistle blew, the bell rang, and away went the cars. The woman was perfectly frantic, and screamed, "My child! my child!" I consoled her as well as possible, telling her that I would telegraph to the next station and have the boy and baggage left. In the meantime the cars had gone out of sight and hearing. I had restored the lady to quiet, and was meditating a suit against the company for damage, when to my surprise the cars hove in sight, and some one on the back step was waving a handkerchief most furiously. We rushed on and were soon on board again.

Then came the secret: The first day out, a small specimen of California's best production passed from my possession to that of the negro steward, with the understanding that he was to consult my best interests while it should be my good fortune to travel in his society; and when it was announced that I was left, he made a furious dash at the bell-rope, pulling it in two the first effort. He then rushed through the cars, reached the engine, and yelled to the engineer, " *You mus' go back! two ladies left, and two suckin' babies on board.*" Such an appeal couldn't be resisted, and the train backed up. I shall never regret what I invested in that nigger.

I will not attempt to describe a route that has already been described a hundred times, but will content myself with a truthful detail of what came under my observation as a traveler, that has not been chronicled by more able pens. The journey was without accident or further mishap until we reached Aurora, Kane County, Illinois, where I left the train to visit my old home at St. Charles, on Fox River. I returned to St. Charles after an absence of twenty-two years, almost to a day. I entered the town an entire stranger, knowing no face that I met and none knowing me. I had an intimate friend, one Colonel Burchell, who, at the time of my leaving St. Charles, was a merchant, and had rendered me many favors. I left him an active business man in manhood's prime. I was informed that he now kept the St. Charles Hotel. Accordingly I put up at that house, and found my friend of other days a decrepit old man, whom I could not recognize as being my old friend of twenty-two years before. I engaged him in conversation; ate supper with him and a half dozen former friends, but none knew me. Presently the conversation turned on California, and " Captain Norton " was the first one inquired for. I told Burchell that I knew him very well; that he lived in my town, and, after answering many inquiries regarding him, I remarked that I didn't suppose they could recognize Norton now, if they were to meet him. But they all declared that they would know him the minute they put their eyes on him. After amusing myself for some time in this way, I presented my card to Burchell, and, to the astonishment of the crowd, declared that I was the veritable Norton that they were all going to recognize.

I next went to the office where I had read law and met my old preceptor, Judge Barry. He also had grown very old. He asked me to be seated. I told him that I had a little matter of business that I wished to call his personal attention to, and handed him my card. The old man looked at the card, and then at me. In a moment he dropped the card, sprang forward, seized me by both hands, and exclaimed, "Great God, Norton, is this you!" He then commenced rubbing my head and running around me like a child. The news soon spread that I had returned, and then dozens of acquaintances of former years came rushing in, calling me by name, whose faces were as strange to me as though I had never seen them before. There was but one among all of them that I could have recognized; that was my old friend, W. G. Conkling, who served as lieutenant with me through the Mexican War (now Major Conkling). We were as brothers through that long and trying campaign, and our relations were so intimate that time and change could not deface that recollection. I spent three days, among the happiest of my life, with old friends at St. Charles, making at least twenty promises to dine, visit, or lodge with my old friends. I absolutely had to run away to prosecute my journey.

Leaving St. Charles, Illinois, I descended Fox River, one of the most lovely streams in the world, to its confluence with the Illinois, passing the cities of Aurora and Oswego and many other lovely towns on its banks. Then, going through Ottawa and crossing the Illinois and Vermilion Rivers, I visited the great coal-fields of the West at Streater, La Salle County, Illinois. This place is but about four years old, and contains from six thousand to seven thousand inhabitants. It very much reminds the California traveler of a mining town in 1852. It is principally a wooden town, sprung up as by magic, and bright new shanties meet the eye in all directions. They seem to have a well organized city government and all is one wild rush and bustle. There are now five railroads centering in the town, with coal-cars leaving in all directions, while the various hoisting works, propelled by steam, are tugging and puffing on all sides. There are three distinct strata of coal, lying from eighty to four hundred feet below the surface.

From this region I retraced my steps to Aurora, and went thence to Chicago. I will give but little space to a description of this great mart of the West, as, especially since its recent disaster, it has so often been described that all who read know what Chicago was before and at the time of the great fire. All that it is necessary to say here is that it has arisen from its ashes more beautiful than before, and all the evidences that are left of its calamity are here and there a scar that looks as though there had been a local fire. Chicago is the shining light of the West. It owes its present existence to the East, to whom it is mortgaged. There are two places that the traveler should be sure to visit—the tunnel under the Chicago River and the Lake Water Works.

I cannot leave the great West without speaking generally of the improvements of the great Mississippi
Basin. I visited Chicago in the fall of 1837 for the first
time, when but a boy. It was but a small village then·
The frame of the old United States House had just been
raised at the west end· of Randolph Bridge. Colonel
Bobion lived near the old fort on the lake shore, in his
log-cabin lined inside with birch bark, and Lake Street
was a first-class mud-hole. Now (1874) the city boasts
about a quarter million inhabitants. At the time to
which I refer, the whole country lying between the great
lakes and the base of the Rocky Mountains was comparatively an unbroken wild, with only here and there
the rudely-built shelter of the early pioneer or hunter,
and the only guides from the settlements to their new
homes were the trails left by General Scott's troops and
the brands of their camp-fires while marching to chastise the hostile tribes of the West. But what a change!
The human mind can hardly comprehend it. In the
short space of thirty-seven years this mighty empire
of the West has sprung into existence. And what a
change even from twenty years ago, where the little
"balloon frame" or log-cabin, with a hovel for stock,
covered with straw or prairie grass, where the fierce
winds of our Western winters would penetrate every
pore as they howled over the vast prairies, without a tree
or bush to check them! Now, where stood the lowly
cabin, you may see a noble building two or three stories
in height with a beautiful observatory covering its top;
and where stood the straw-thatched hovel, you may see
clustered splendid granaries and stock barns, all well
sheltered and protected with a fine, thrifty grove of

timber. Add to that a thick hedge of Osage orange or thorn surrounding the whole premises, and you have the present appearance of the home of the thrifty Western farmer. One of the most memorable changes that meets the eye of the traveler who has not visited the West for many years, is the great increase of timber. The farmers, who in many parts of the West have impoverished their farms by constant cropping, have been compelled to change their tactics, and are now grazing them with dairy cows. The consequence is that at a distance of every eight or ten miles, there is a steam cheese and butter factory. By the change referred to, the farmer is restoring the land to its former richness, and I was informed that it pays better than grain raising. While the war has had the effect in the East of making the rich richer, and the poor poorer, the West has felt a general impetus that has reached all classes.

I continued my journey eastward by the Michigan Central road, April 11. It was exceedingly cold in Chicago when I left. It seemed as though the north wind from Lake Michigan would cut a Californian in two, and, in fact, I had not been out of sight of snow from the time I reached the summit of the Sierra. I reached Detroit about two o'clock Sunday morning, April 12. Detroit is a splendid city. It is beautifully located on the St. Clair River, and is among the oldest towns of America, settled by the French. This is the town that was surrendered to the British by General Hull, in the war of 1812, at the time of "Hull's Surrender." There is a very fine depot there, and the city contains many beautiful public buildings, handsomely flagged sidewalks, and many ornamental trees.

The city contains about one hundred thousand inhabitants, but the old French stock is pretty well worked out.

On the morning of the 13th I crossed the St. Clair River into Upper Canada, taking the Grand Trunk road, and arrived in London about four o'clock in the afternoon. Again in London! After an absence of thirty-seven years I was again visiting the spot where I had been a prisoner for nine months, indicted for high treason, and banished from her Britannic majesty's dominions during my natural life. I left, a boy in my seventeenth year; I returned, a gray-headed man! At my banishment I had left many warm friends in London. "Where are they now?" was the first question that came to my mind on my return, for among those friends were some who had watched over the sick couch of the young rebel and to whose kind care perhaps I owed my life. I asked an old settler of London, "Where is O'Brien, the merchant?" He replied, "He is dead!" "And Mrs. O'Brien?" "Also dead!" "Where is Sam Parks, the former keeper of the London prison?" "Dead!" "And his wife?" "She is also dead!" None who had lifted a hand or voice in my defense were left. It was one universal reply, "Dead, all dead!"

But there was one thing to console me: times had so changed in the Dominion that the old Tory party of 1836–37 was at a discount, and the reform party was in power, the British Government having granted a general amnesty, and conceded every reform asked by that party. I next visited the old prison where I had lain so long, but there the hand of time had made no change. I found everything in the rooms where I had been incarcerated just as it was the day I left them. There was the old bullet-hole through the floor that we had reamed out to enable us to send our dispatches to the upper rooms, which were also filled with prisoners. I showed the officials who visited the rooms with me that the window sills were all cut out below, around the heads of the spikes; that the gratings of our windows were loosened (with the apertures closed with chewed bread to hide our work) in such a manner that the bars could be removed in fifteen minutes; that nothing but the sentinels around the walls had prevented our escape, and many other things that excited the mirth of the officials of the present time. When it was generally known who I was, the prominent citizens seemed to take an interest in me, and made my visit of a week in London a very pleasant one. London is a flourishing city, supported by oil refineries, manufacturing the crude oils obtained in the western district, together with a large agricultural country around the place.

CHAPTER XLV.

VISIT TO THE EAST—OLD-TIME HAUNTS.

BEFORE my final departure from London (Canada), I went up to Westminster, where I had left four uncles and about thirty cousins. In fact, Westminster Street was settled by Nortons and their descendants; but among all the kin that I had left, only one remained to tell the fate and whereabouts of the rest. This was Frank D. Norton. He was wealthy and a prince among good fellows, and spared no pains to make me enjoy my visit with him. We rode around the country and visited old haunts of my youth, but I could see very little to remind me of that long ago; for then the clearings were small and the forests immense; the fields were stumpy and the hay and grain crops had to be cut with the old-fashioned sickle, scythe, and cradle. Now, scarcely a stump is to be seen, and those vast primeval forests have almost wholly disappeared before the stroke of the axman. Those who never experienced it cannot for a moment appreciate or imagine the change. Where I had ofttimes looked from a small eminence for the cows, where the range of vision was less than half a mile, I could now stand and look away north to the shores of Lake Huron, forty or fifty miles distant, the forests that once obscured the view having been almost entirely swept away. The only timber now standing, where every acre of land was once covered by a heavy forest growth, is the sugar maple, rail timber, and occasionally a small wood lot for fuel, which is now valuable—in fact, more valuable than agricultural land.

This general clearing up of the country has given it an entirely new face. Those who have seen the emigrant who crossed the plains from '49 to '60, before going to the barber shop and after his return from it, may, from that metamorphosis, form some faint idea of the change in the face of a timber country by being shorn of its forests. The climate of Upper Canada has also greatly changed since cutting off the timber. There used to be but little wind before the country was cleared up, and now it is swept by heavy and frequent winds from the northern lakes. The land in Canada West, like that of the Western States, is much worn, and the farmers are resuscitating the soil by going into the dairy business. The Canadas are now shipping to England thousands of tons of cheese yearly. The soil is naturally good in Canada West, taking it as a whole, and were it not for the long, cold winters, it would be a desirable country to live in, for at the present time they have a very liberal system of Government—no inflation, everything reasonable; and their paper commands coin everywhere. Among other good things at my cousin's, I found them at the height of sugar-making, which permitted me to enjoy some of the sweets of other days. The sugar was as sweet as ever, but the girls—well, an old man of family cannot, and ought not, expect to find them as sweet as when he was a young beau.

Taking leave of my "coz.," I took a side train, connecting with the Grand Trunk at St. Mary's, and after a few hours' ride brought up at Toronto. We made no stay at this place, farther than the usual halt for meals, but even this enabled me to discover that Toronto had grown much since I last saw it. Indeed, it is now a very pretty city, the site sloping to the south with a gentle descent to the lake shore. From Toronto our trip to Prescott was performed in the night. Passing Kingston and other noted points, we arrived at Prescott at the break of day, at which place we changed cars for Ottawa, the seat of the Dominion Government. Ottawa is situated on the Grand Ottawa River, some ninety miles above the confluence of that river with the St. Lawrence. The city is divided into the upper and lower towns by the Rideau Canal, which gives an internal communication between Kingston and Lake Ontario and the Ottawa River. This town has been selected by the

Home (British) Government for the permanent seat of the Canadian Legislature. The scenery is not surpassed by any in America, unless by that of California. Prescott and Ottawa are also connected by the Ottawa and Prescott Railroad, which taps the Grand Trunk at Prescott. There is also a daily line of steamers up and down the river during the summer months.

The Russell House is a fine hotel, situated in the center of the town in juxtaposition with the Sappers' Bridge, the Rideau Canal, Parliament House, etc. A few minutes take the traveler to the suspension bridge, from which a fine view of the city can be obtained, as well as of the celebrated Chaudier Falls, which are almost a second Niagara. The Government timber slide, Table Rock, suspension bridge, etc., are well worthy of note by the tourist.

Returning by way of Prescott, I crossed the St. Lawrence River to Ogdensburg, New York. This is a city of considerable trade. It is an old town founded by Colonel Ogden, an Englishman of great wealth. There is an amusing anecdote connected with the early settlement of the place, calculated in some degree to illustrate the different ideas of the English and Americans as to the relations of master and servant. After Ogden had founded his town and was yet largely engaged in building, business called him back to England and he left an Englishman in charge of his works, who held the common English ideas of the servile condition of the common laborer. The hands were principally brought from England, but through sickness or some other cause, it became necessary to hire a few native Americans. Among them was a little American to mix mortar. He didn't exactly satisfy the old John Bull boss, who expressed his disapprobation in rather forcible terms, to which little Yank sharply replied, when the boss, with great indignation exclaimed, "Give me none of your impudence, sir, or I will cane you!" "You attempt to cane me," said the man, "and I will stamp you into this mortar bed." The Englishman struck him with his cane, and the man kept his word. The old boss crawled out of the mortar, made his way to an attorney and wanted to know his remedy. "Who struck first?" inquired the lawyer. "Is that the question you ask me? Why, sir, he gave me some insolence and I caned him." "That being the case," said the attorney, "you committed the first assault, and if he will drop it you had better let it rest. If not, you had better give him something to settle it." Johnny Bull was indignantly leaving the office when he was informed that he owed a fee of five dollars. He paid the charge, and when he went back to where the mortarman was, the latter asked, "Have you a warrant for me?" Being answered in the negative, "Then," said the man, "I will have one for you." "Ah, never mind, here is a sovereign to treat your friends with."

In time Ogden returned and was riding out with the old boss in his coach, when they met a Yankee teamster who gave one-half of the road. "How different," said Colonel Ogden, "in England a teamster would give the whole road and take off his hat to a gentleman." "Ah," replied the boss, "but in this country he will pull off his coat instead of his hat." The mortarman had taught him something.

We left Ogdensburg at one o'clock in the afternoon

and arrived at Malone the same evening, passing Potsdam and other small places on the way. I had now arrived at the base of my communications, and heard from home for the first time since leaving London. On leaving home I had directed all my correspondence to be sent to Wm. P. Cantwell, Esq., of Malone, New York. He and I were little children together at Norton Creek, Lower Canada. Thomas Cantwell, his father, was among the earliest settlers at " The Creek." He was our merchant and, in fact, the main man of the place. He was noted for his integrity, and commanded the respect of all who knew him, and prospered as such men should. Where even the advantages of a common school education were denied to many, Mr. Cantwell's children were sent abroad to school and received liberal education. My friend, Wm. P., chose the profession of law and is now a successful lawyer, standing at the head of his profession in Malone, and, like his father, noted for his integrity as well as his ability. He is blessed with an amiable wife and family, with all the home comforts and endearing associations that make home happy. Though my visit with them was a very short one, it was of that pleasing character that will ever keep its remembrance fresh in my mind. Mr. Cantwell's family could tell me more about my old home than all others combined, but I hastened forward that I might see for myself. I was then about forty miles from my old home at Norton Creek, in Lower Canada. I took the cars for the Summit, and from that place I hired a buggy to take me across the line into Canada, to the little town of Franklin, where I remained a couple of days to visit friends and get shelter from a snow-storm that was then raging. This was about the twentieth of April, and while others thought the weather reasonably mild, I was compelled to hunt the hot side of the stove to keep warm.

At Franklin I chartered a buggy to take me to Norton Creek. And now I was to visit a place, after an absence of forty years, the most cherished to me of all spots on earth. It was there I had spent my childhood's hours, and there centered all that was pleasant to reflect upon; it was my thoughts by day and dreams by night. Every play-ground was vivid in my memory and the enthusiasm which I felt upon the subject I cannot better express than in the words of Norton the poet:—

> Canada's wilds my early home,
> I think of thee where'er I roam!
> The lonely crag to me endeared,
> Its mossy brow my childhood cheered;
> The rising hill, the creek, the dell,
> The ancient tree, the pond, the well—
> All these endeared that land to me,
> Home of my youth and infancy!

But what a disappointment was in wait for me! When I came into the range of my childhood's acquaintance the first place I recognized was the Proper farm, where I requested my driver to wait until I made a reconnoissance of the premises. My rap at the door was answered by a French woman who couldn't speak a word of English, but she called her son, who spoke English. I asked him who lived there. He informed me that it was the widow St. John. I then asked him where the folks had gone who lived there before them. He didn't know; he was born on the place, raised there to manhood, and never heard of any other person having owned it but his father.

I then determined to go to Mr. Seivers', two miles further on, and make that my head-quarters while I remained in the vicinity, remembering that forty years ago they kept a very respectable hotel and but one mile distant from my father's farm—my early home. We trudged along through a slushy mixture of snow and mud until we reached the Seivers place, but here I was again disappointed. The old sign was gone and the house much smaller than when I left that country. I entered the house and inquired for Mr. Seivers. Quite an old lady answered me that her son would be in in a minute. I asked, "Is this Mrs. Seivers?" She answered in the affirmative. I then asked her if they kept a hotel, and she replied that they did not. I told her that I was a stranger wishing to spend a few days in that neighborhood, and would like to stay with them. She said they were not prepared to keep travelers. I insisted upon staying, and told her that any accommodations would answer me. In the meantime her son came in, and I saw that I was likely to fail in my efforts, when I made the fact known that I was a son of Lewis Norton. I needed no further passport, and a nice, clean room was assigned me. On inquiry, I found that the former house had been burned down and replaced by the present smaller one; that old man Seivers and wife had both been dead for many years, and that the old lady before me was the wife of John Seivers, who was a young married man when I left Lower Canada; that he also was dead, after having raised a large family of children, who were all married off and now had families of half-grown Canadians in their turn. Our school-house was near by and on the Seivers farm. I noticed that the building looked smaller than when I went to school there, and they informed me that it also had been burned, and replaced by a smaller one. I may as well say here, that the whole country for many miles has been filled up by French people, the former inhabitants having died or removed to some other parts; and that everything is on the retrograde, it being a cold, rocky, desolate clime.

After becoming domiciled in my temporary home, I set out on foot to visit the old homestead. I well knew every foot of the ground, and a fifteen minutes' walk brought me to the corner of our old field; but to my amazement I found the field a forest! It was covered with a thick growth of cedars, six and eight inches in diameter and from forty to fifty feet in height. I took the second look at the old rock monument at the corner, and satisfied myself that I was not mistaken as to locality. The next search was for my father's cooper shop, which used to stand close by. All traces of it were gone, except a few foundation stones that marked the spot where it had stood. I next pushed my way through the cedar forest for the old house; but alas! the house had not only disappeared, but all evidences that a human habitation had ever been there. A stone quarry had been opened precisely where the house had stood. When a child I had set out an orchard of apples, which, when we left, had grown to be quite respectable little trees. I had since always thought I would like to revisit the old orchard to see how it flourished, and my longings were now to be gratified. But when I reached the lot, not an apple tree was there, nor the slightest evidence that there ever had been one planted on the ground. I

25

then went in search of the old spring, to get a drink from the old fountain. But alas! no spring was to be found. I knew its location, within a rod or two, but the winter was breaking, and every little hole and hollow being filled with water, it was impossible to distinguish the spring from the pools of rain-water.

While I was meditating upon the general change, mortified, sick, and dispirited to see all of my high hopes and bright dreams of a pleasant visit to my old home dashed to the earth, a stern-visaged, hard-faced old woman made her appearance upon the scene, looking for her sheep. She seemed to look upon me with surprise and distrust. I stepped up to her and said, " My good woman, can you tell me who owns these premises? " " 'Tis meself, shure, but me husband is over the hill at the house beyont. I'll show you." I followed the crone and found that the portion of the farm which was a forest when I left was now cleared up, cultivated and contained the residence of the family. At dark I returned to my friend Seivers', with years of romance and bright dreams dashed to the earth by an experience of a couple of hours.

I wandered in the neighborhood of Norton Creek a week before it was generally known who I was, and I learned that all kinds of surmises and supicions had been entertained as to who and what I was. I found once in a while an old citizen who remembered our family, but everything on the face of nature was so radically changed that I could not have recognized the place had I been set down there without explanations. The stream had been dammed below, entirely changing its features; the big marsh—my old fishing ground further up the stream—had been drained and was at this time cultivated farms. And even the white sandstone rocks had seemed to allow their faces to grow dark and dirty. The whortleberry bushes had disappeared from their seams, and the wintergreen was no longer to be found. At the end of the week—the last of April— we had a heavy snow-storm. I took a sleigh-ride of several miles, with bells, robes, cold toes and fingers; with ears tied up to keep them warm—in short, enjoyed all the pleasures of a sleigh-ride in a Northern winter.

Coming to the conclusion that I had had enough of my old Canada home, I began to think about emigrating again. I was told that I could take the stage and go to St. Rama, whence I could go by rail to Montreal. The stage passed Mr. Seivers' at about five o'clock in the morning. I was accordingly up, dressed and ready for the trip. The "stage" came! I found that it consisted of a one-horse buggy, with a lantern lashed on the dash-board and a little French pony in the fills. As it happened, it wasn't loaded; that is to say, the only seat for a passenger was vacant, but the driver insisted that he couldn't take me, owing to the condition of the roads. I paid but little attention to his remonstrances, piled in my valise and lunch-basket and directed him to drive on. In course of time I reached St. Rama without accident, took the cars and safely arrived at Montreal to await the final breaking up of winter.

CHAPTER XLVI.

VISIT TO THE EAST—MONTREAL.

WELL, here I am in Montreal, one of the prettiest cities in North America; and how little we Americans know of it! It is the largest and most populous city, in fact the commercial metropolis, of British North America. Situated upon an island, at the base of Mt. Royal, it occupies a very commanding position. The island is from twenty-five to thirty miles long, by ten or twelve broad. Montreal possesses all the advantages both of an inland and a commercial city. It is accessible to steamships and other vessels of three thousand tons burden, and, commanding the trade of the canals and lakes, its position with reference to Quebec, Ontario, the Great West, New York, Boston, Portland, Albany, Nova Scotia, Newfoundland, Prince Edward Island, and many minor points, makes it, by water and railroad communication, a great center and commercial emporium. They have gone largely into manufacturing in Montreal. The city was founded in 1642 and for many years bore the name of Ville Marie, having been originally settled by the French, and for a long time it was the head-quarters of the French forces in Canada, but was surrendered to the English in 1763.

I have not started out to write up the history of Montreal, but cannot in justice dismiss the subject until I have partially described two of the most magnificent works of art upon the American continent, viz., Notre Dame, and Victoria Bridge. Notre Dame, the parish church, was commenced in 1823, and was fifteen years in course of construction. The ground structure is 300 by 150 feet and is 260 feet from basement to the top of the towers, which is reached by 356 steps. The structure is stone and its walls are of massive proportions. It contains a bell, the third in size that was ever cast, weighing 24,780 pounds and costing $25,000. The church contains 1,500 pews. The building was constructed by one O'Donald, as architect and builder, at a cost of $1,500,000. O'Donald was a Protestant, but in after life embraced the Catholic faith. His remains now lie under his structure in the church vault. From the top of the towers of this church you have a magnificent view of all the lower part of the city and the shores of the St. Lawrence for miles.

The Victoria Bridge spans the St. Lawrence at Montreal. The cost of this bridge was $6,250,000. It contains 25,000 tons of stone and 7,500 tons of iron. The iron superstructure is supported on twenty-four piers and two abutments. The center span is 330 feet, and there are twelve spans each side of the center, 242 feet each; extreme length, including the abutments, 7,000 feet; height of the bridge above low water, sixty feet in the center, descending towards each end at the rate of one inch in 130 feet. The contents of the masonry are 3,000,000 cubic feet; weight of iron in the tubes, 8,000 tons. The tubes through which the railroad trains pass, are at the middle span twenty-two feet high and sixteen feet wide, and at the extreme ends nineteen feet high and sixteen feet wide. The total length from the river banks is 10,284 feet, or a little less than two miles.

I shall not attempt to describe the public buildings,

many of which are perfect models of architectural beauty, but will content myself by saying that there is in Montreal a greater display of Italian marble, Scotch granite, and Ohio sandstone than in any city I visited on my trip. Montreal is a city of boundless wealth and squalid misery; of rich clergy and poor laity; of silver-mounted hacks and ragged beggars. No place in the city is exempt from beggars.

Leaving Montreal by cars, we crossed Victoria Bridge and took the railroad for St. John's, that being the point where I expected to connect with the Vermont Central road, on which my fare was paid to Boston, Massachusetts. I presented my ticket and the conductor refused to recognize it, owing to the fact that it was but a branch road of the Vermont Central and leased to outside parties. I refused to pay and the conductor said he would have to put me off. I told him that was all right, but that he must forcibly expel me from the cars; that I shouldn't resist, but wished to reserve my legal rights. He treated me very gentlemanly, but said that under the rules he would have to put me off at the next station. In the meantime he conversed with the Hon. M. Mower, of the Canadian Parliament, in regard to the matter. Mr. Mower admitted that the conductor's instructions would require him to put me off, but he thought the company would finally be compelled to transport me over their road, and perhaps be mulcted in damages for their refusal to take me through, and for expelling me from the cars. Mr. Mower informed me that he was personally acquainted with the conductor and knew him to be an honorable man, etc. He also said that the managing agent of the road was at the next regular

station, some twenty miles distant; that he also was
a fair-minded man, and that if I would pay my fare
under protest he would insure me a favorable consideration of my case before the managing agent of the road;
so through his influence, I was prevailed upon to pay my
fare, under protest, to the main line of the road. On
our arrival I exhibited my through ticket to Boston and
a fair statement of the case was made, when the agent
directed the conductor to refund my money, as my
ticket called for my transportation over any part of the
road to the point of destination.

CHAPTER XLVII.

VISIT TO THE EAST—BOSTON—THE HUDSON.

I HAD now crossed the Vermont line. We passed
along the foot of Lake Champlain, up Onion and
White Rivers, crossed the Green Mountains to the east
of the Camel's Back, crossed New Hampshire, passing
through Concord, Lowell, and many other places of note,
and reached Boston about eleven o'clock at night. As to
the country embraced in the trip from Montreal to Boston, it appeared that the inhabitants had first tried
agriculture, then grazing and stock-raising, and finally,
in many places, they were abandoning the soil to a second
growth of timber, and gathering themselves up into
manufacturing villages and cities, resorting to the
mechanical arts and manufacturing almost exclusively
for a living. They seemed to have come to the conclusion that they could not compete with the more favored
portions of the United States in agricultural pursuits.

Hence we must not judge too harshly of the land of basswood hams and wooden nutmegs.

My arrival at so late an hour in the night was the most unfortunate of all the incidents attending my advent in Boston. The next morning I sallied forth to reconnoiter the city. Coming in so late I had not observed any landmarks, but with a bold spirit of adventure I pushed along through the labyrinth of buildings, without a blazed tree, chart, or compass, with the intention of finding the docks, that I might get a view of Massachusetts Bay and Boston Harbor, where there was a great tea party about a century since. A smart walk of half an hour brought me—not to the docks, but to the place from where I started.

Having procured fresh directions, I again started out on my search. This time, after an hour's ramble, I found myself at West End, instead of at the docks. Here I made more inquiries, and among them I asked whether there was any street or road that led out of Boston except the railroad by which I entered the city. I was told to go to Bowdoin Square, where I could gain the information. I took the direction pointed out for Bowdoin Square and followed the devious streets for another half hour, but finding nothing that looked to me like a square, and meeting a street-car, I jumped aboard and asked the conductor where that car was going. He informed me that it was going to Bowdoin Square. This I thought was a point gained; but after several twists and turns I came to the conclusion that I was again duped, and that the car was returning by another route to the point where I had got on. I was about leaving it for the purpose of throwing myself under the protection of the police, when a gentleman on board to whom I had disclosed my troubles (who, by the by, was a Californian) told me to keep my seat, as the car was really going to Bowdoin Square, and that we were on one of the straightest streets in Boston.

In a short time we arrived at what I should call five points, where all alighted from the car. I asked my friend if this was what they called Bowdoin Square, and he said it was. I was somewhat surprised, as I had brought up at the same place three or four times in the course of my ramble, but never would have taken it to be a *square*. In this strait I came to the conclusion that money was no object, and asked my new California acquaintance if he couldn't be induced for a' compensation to act as my guide to aid me in getting out of the city. In hopes of reaching his sympathy I told him that I was a married man, had left a wife and several small children in California, that I was their sole dependence for a living, and if he left me I was satisfied that I never again would clasp them to my bosom, but would perish on the cow-paths of Boston in vain endeavors to find my way once more to the borders of civilization. He being a true Californian, his sympathies were aroused and he kindly offered me such assistance as he could give; but he doubted his ability to act as a guide, for want of experience, as he had been but two years in Boston acting as delivery agent of an express company. However, between my guide's experience and the street railroads, I got along pretty well. We found Boston Harbor, and in order to get a good view, ascended Bunker Hill Monument, from which the harbor, bay, navy yard, and much of the city are seen to a good advantage.

I don't propose to describe the monument, as every school-child not only knows all about Bunker Hill Monument (which is not on Bunker Hill at all, by the way), but everything else in and about Boston, and much that never was there, for the innumerable presses of Boston, continually harping. upon its beauties, have made it rather an ideal than a real city. They have told the world not what it was in fact, but what their imaginations picture it. In claiming that the picture of Boston is generally overdrawn, do not understand me to say that Boston is not a great city, and that there are not many things in it worthy of admiration. But to return to Bunker Hill Monument. It costs the visitor twenty cents for admittance, and ten cents for a little "guide" of two leaves about one and one-half by two inches, not costing one-fourth of a cent each, making a charge of thirty cents to enable an Englishman to see the place where his ancestors were slain, or the American to see the place where the immortal Warren and his compatriots fell. This fee must produce a revenue of more than two hundred dollars per day. By what authority is this toll demanded? and to what fund do the proceeds belong? If I mistake not, the ground was a gift to the public, for the purpose to which it has been appropriated, by the Masonic fraternity, and the building fund, or the larger portion thereof, was raised by public subscription, the residue having been obtained through the influence of the ladies by subscription and other ways. If I am mistaken in the above statement, I beg pardon; if not, I reiterate the question, Who has a right to demand a fee from the visitor, further than enough to provide a fund for keeping the monument and grounds in proper repair?

From what I had read of Boston I had been led to believe that I should find a city of granite, marble, and brick, but, on the contrary, I found more common wooden structures than in any city of its population through which I passed on my journey. Boston Common is a very pretty place, though much smaller than I had expected to find it. It was pretty in its natural state and has been much beautified by art. Connected as it is with the National Gardens, it makes a very fine pleasure-ground; but were I the manager of the premises, I should either remove the tombs which it contains or make a cemetery of the whole.

But there is one thing for which I give the Bostonians credit: instead of paying men to cut down, dig up, and destroy the old forest trees on the public grounds (as our wise men of Healdsburg did), they have carefully protected, cultivated, hooped, and canvased the old monarchs of the forest, preserving them as landmarks of early days. Faneuil Hall still stands, well preserved. As unpretending as its appearance may seem, it was the nest where was hatched the bird that wrested a people's rights from the grip of the British Lion. The State House stands fronting the Common, and is a fine structure. The legislature was in session, and the Rotunda was closed to visitors, but by the kindness of the sergeant-at-arms I was permitted to visit it. He also furnished me a guide. From the top of this building I had a fine view of the city and its surroundings, and my guide pointed out many objects of interest.

From Boston I went west by the way of Springfield to Albany, New York. Along that route I found, as a general thing, that agriculture, as in New Hampshire

and parts of Vermont, was being neglected, while mechanical arts and manufactures were carried on with
great spirit and seeming success.   I took this route for a
threefold purpose, viz., to see the famous Hoosac Tunnel, visit my old friends, Mr. and Mrs. H. W. Dickenson,
and to descend the Hudson by a day boat to enjoy the
beauties of its far-famed scenery.   The two former objects were abandoned, owing to the incompleted state of
the tunnel.   I arrived at Albany about one o'clock in
the morning, paid a hackman a dollar to take me half
a square to a hotel, and awoke the next morning to find
myself on the shore of the Hudson for the first time in
my life.

Albany, the capital of New York State, is a flourishing city at the head of navigation on the Hudson River.
It is the oldest city in the United States.   The first
white man who ever visited the spot where Albany now
stands was Hendricke Chrystance, who was sent up
the river to explore by Henry Hudson, in 1610.   Between the Indians and the Dutch the place boasted a
multitude of names, but in the year 1664, it was named
Albany, in honor of James, Duke of York and Albany,
who afterwards ascended the English throne as James
II.   The town was incorporated as a city in 1686, under
Governor Dougan's administration.   A portion of the
town is situated upon the flat running to the water's
edge and a portion on the bank, which rises about one
hundred and fifty feet above the water.

The present capitol is situated at the head of State
Street, on a fine elevation overlooking the whole of the
lower portion of the city.   This building was erected
about 1835, and is now (1874) being eclipsed by a more

imposing structure, which is well advanced towards completion—the " new capitol." At this place the Hudson is spanned by two fine bridges, with draws to allow water craft to pass, although Albany may really be considered at the head of navigation of the Hudson. I had some difficulty in finding a steamer running through to New York, as the summer boats were not yet making their regular trips; but perseverance at length crowned my efforts with success, and I was soon floating down that lovely river.

A Hogg, a Scott, a Burns, and others, in their brilliant productions with pen and pencil, have made classic each tiny stream, every heath-clad hill and shady glen of Scotland, while farther south the early poets have sung the praises of the Po, the Rhine, Tiber, and Danube, until they have become as familiar to the present generation as household words; but on visiting those scenes the traveler frequently finds that the genius of the poet has overdone his subject. But here the case is completely reversed; nature has seemed to mock the genius of man; for no human pencil can paint, nor the pen of mortal describe, the beauties of the Hudson. And where an Irving, a Willis, a Clark, and a Drake have failed, with their descriptive powers, to paint this lovely panorama of nature, I should not attempt it. Lovers of the beautiful seek the banks of the Hudson that their senses may drink in their beauties, but the tongue can never express them. We passed the magnificent residences of Church, the great artist, Longfellow, Washington Irving, and many others whose fame is world-wide.

The banks of the Hudson are completely lined with cities, villages, and lovely country seats. Prominent among the former are Hudson, Catskill, Poughkeepsie, and Newport. It is hard to say which is to be most admired, the lovely green slopes and elevated banks above the highlands or the wild mountain scenery that the highlands present. We also passed West Point, the seat of our National Military School, which is on a beautiful site. It had been my determination on leaving home to visit my old friend, Josiah Hasbrouck, at New Paltz, but I had become so bewildered and lost in the many objects of interest that, before I was aware of the fact, I had passed the landing many miles, and was consequently denied a visit from which I had anticipated much pleasure.

CHAPTER XLVIII.

VISIT TO THE EAST—NEW YORK.

ON. the second day after leaving Albany we landed on Manhattan Island, which contains the great storehouse of the world, and I was soon lost in the swaying and jostling masses on Broadway. I put up at the St. Nicholas, and was not long in finding out that in New York style costs as much as living.

The next morning after breakfast I thought I would take a "promenade down Broadway" and call upon my banker. I had not proceeded on my walk more than two blocks when I was accosted by a gentleman who evinced great pleasure in meeting me. He rushed up furiously, seized me by the hand and exclaimed, "How are you, Mr. Jones," or some other name which I do not now remember. I remarked to him that he had probably mistaken his man; ·that that was not my name, and

further, that I didn't recognize him. " Is it possible that
I am mistaken," he exclaimed; "is not your name so
and so, and do you not live in Cincinnati?" · I assured
him that he hadn't guessed my name, and that I didn't
live in Cincinnati. He begged my pardon, but remarked
that I must be some near kin to his friend, as he never
saw two men look so much alike. "My name is Jonas
Collins," he added; "what may be your name?" I told
him that was the "old thing," and that he'd better be off.
He mingled with the crowd and was soon lost to my
gaze.

I pursued my way, chuckling to myself on his dis-
comfiture, as I had from my infancy heard of New
York sharps, and longed for the day when they would
have an opportunity to try their skill on me, believing
that there was one man at least that was invulnerable to
their arts. I walked along in a very happy frame of
mind, exulting over my victory, when a young man of
prepossessing appearance and manner rushed from the
throng of pedestrians and exclaimed, " Captain Norton,
how do you do! when did you leave San Francisco?"
I took his extended hand, but told him that he had the
advantage of me; that I failed to remember him·
"Why," said he, "don't you know David, of the Western Union Telegraph Company, of San Francisco?"
I replied that I didn't remember him; that there were
about a dozen of the boys and I should fail to recognize
any one of them. He said he knew me very well, having met me often in San Francisco. I told him that I was
pleased to meet him, or, in fact, any one from California.
He said that he had just got in the night before; was
putting up at the Astor House, and asked me where I

was going. I told him I was going down to the First
National Bank to draw some money. He then informed
me that he had come on to New York for the purpose
of settling a little matter; that his grandmother had died
and left him a small annuity; that he had bought a
ticket in a lottery and was informed that he had drawn
a prize; that he was hunting the place to draw his money;
that it was somewhere near where we then were (he
thought it was just around the corner), and if I would
accompany him he would go to the bank with me after
he had got his money. I consented to do so, and we
soon found the number.

We were admitted by a negro usher into the presence
of the lottery man, who was seated behind a long table.
He arose and David presented his ticket. The man
remarked, " I suppose you think you have drawn a fortune." The young man replied that he didn't know how
much he had drawn. The lottery man said, " You have
drawn $401," and handed the young man eight fifty-dollar
greenbacks and a ticket, saying, as he did so, " This
dollar ticket is all the percentage that the company has
in this matter, and that ticket will be drawn at the large
hall on Tuesday next." " I shall not be here on Tuesday," said David, " I am going right back to California."
I said, " What do you care about the dollar ticket?" and
he answered that he would like to know whether it drew
anything or not. The lottery man suggested, " Perhaps
your friend will be here." David turned to me and asked
if I would be in the city on Tuesday. I replied that I
should, and would see if his ticket drew anything, and
report on my return to San Francisco.

But the lottery man remarked that he had the scheme

of the drawing and that if David preferred, he could
have a private drawing then and there; that they did so
sometimes where men were going to leave the city.
After an exhibition of his scheme, it was agreed that
David should avail himself of the private drawing.
Among other things it was explained that where the
party throwing the dice threw any number other than a
prize number, it was called a "star," and the party
neither won nor lost, but would be compelled to represent the ticket by putting up a dollar first, and then
doubling the sum as often as he threw "stars," and that
the money so put up was not forfeited, but at the end of
seven throws the party putting up took all of his money
so put up, together with his prize in case the ticket won.
David threw a "star" and "antied" his dollar; the second throw was the same and he put up two dollars; the
third throw was another "star," and he put up four dollars.   Each time that David put up the engineer of the
game gave him a ticket.   After the third throw David
remarked that he seemed to be out of luck and asked
me to throw for him.   I did so and won eight dollars.
He seemed pleased and requested me to throw again, he
putting up eight dollars to "represent."   I threw again,
and won four hundred dollars.   The money was paid,
two hundred dollars on each ticket, to abide the issue of
the throwing; but we were informed that we must come
up twenty dollars apiece.   I was inclined to draw out,
but David offered to put up for me, assuring me that he
" saw into it," and that under any contingency we were
to take down the money that we "represented" with.   I
told him that I couldn't permit him to put up for me, so
I put up the twenty dollars.   I threw and it was a "star."

26

I then proposed to the lottery man to let him keep the two hundred which he claimed I had won and I would take down the twenty dollars and quit. To this he wouldn't agree, and said that in case I quit I forfeited the twenty dollars. I then thought I began to "see into it" myself, so I put up twenty dollars more and again threw a "star." It then required eighty dollars. I laid down a one hundred dollar greenback and threw —still another "star." The lottery man said that it now required five hundred dollars to "represent," and went on to explain. I told him it was unnecessary, as I understood it; that I had the change. I took up the one hundred dollar bill and carefully laid it in my pocket-book, where I had laid the two twenties before it, and put my hand in my hip pocket for the "change." Drawing out a six-shooter, I cocked it and covered the two worthies, informing them that if they moved a muscle I would blow the top of their heads off. The lottery sharp cried out, "Let me explain!" but I told him that it was my turn to explain; that they had simply mistaken their man; that they had got me into their den to rob me, but hawks as they were their claws were too short to get away with a California chicken. Again admonishing them to keep their seats, for if they moved it would make me very nervous and I couldn't be responsible for what might happen, I kept them covered, backed to the door, bade them good-morning and left, having learned that I was not so much smarter than the rest of the human family as I had thought myself, and that I, too, could be taken in by a Broadway confidence man.

It was sometime before I could really realize that I

was treading the streets of a city of a million inhabitants, the pride of our Republic and the admiration of the world. In 1656, New York (then New Amsterdam) contained but 1,000 inhabitants; in 1750 it contained 10,000, and the entire colonies but 1,000,000; in 1800 the city contained 60,489; in 1840, 312,706, and now (in 1874), it is estimated that it contains over one million. The island upon which New York is situated has an area of but $21\frac{3}{4}$ square miles, or 13,600 acres. As previously stated, this city is little less than a mammoth store-house, the people locking up at night and leaving for their residences in the surrounding country, some nearly thirty miles distant, and returning to business in the morning. It is utterly impossible for any one to appreciate the extent of the New York trade without seeing it, and then the mind can scarcely comprehend it.

Through the kindness of the manager of that mammoth establishment, I was shown through Stewart's wholesale house, from basement to uppermost room. I think it is six stories high, with a large elevator to hoist up and let down customers. The retail store covers an entire block, and I believe the wholesale house does also —at any rate it is very large. One floor is filled with domestics, another with prints, another with woolen fabrics, carpets, etc., another with silks, fancy goods, etc. Mr. Stewart consumes the entire product of fourteen large factories of cotton fabrics. When I was there the store contained between $8,000,000 and $10,000,000 worth of goods; so I was informed by the foreman. I next visited the retail store, which is six stories high, exclusive of the basement, and has street entrances on all four sides. I do not know how to make one understand its magnitude better than by saying that the pay-roll shows over 2,000 clerks in the one store, and I think, at a reasonable estimate, there were at least 8,000 people in the store when I was there.

I next visited the gold rooms on Wall Street, to see the "bulls" and "bears" fight, and to me it was a very great curiosity. In fact, after having visited as many lunatic asylums as I have, had I been set down in the gallery blindfolded, and had the bandage removed from my eyes, I should have taken them for a set of maniacs, and should have fully expected to see them pitch into one another and fight to the death. Such shouting, screaming, shaking of fists and fingers, jostling and pushing, I never before saw without its ending in a fight. I was asked by a friend who sat at my side, what I thought of it. I told him if they were in California a commission of lunacy would be issued against the whole crowd and they would be landed in the Stockton asylum in less than twenty-four hours. Nevertheless there was method in their madness, for they seemed to understand one another perfectly.

In my first day's exploration of New York, I owed much to Mr. Steinhart, of the firm of Dinkelspiel, Bloom & Co. I had expected to meet my old friend, Joseph Bloom, in New York, but in this I was disappointed, as he had left for California two days before my arrival; but Mr. Steinhart was master of the situation, and rendered me all the assistance that I could have asked of my friend, for which I felt very grateful. Among the public grounds which I visited in New York —all of which are very beautiful—were Central Park, Union Square, Madison Square, Steuben Square, and

Castle Garden. I spent the most of two days in Central Park. It is not only extensive in its dimensions, but it is lovely in the extreme. Art has made it what it is, for to divest it of the twelve million dollars expended on it, it would be rather a sorry place. But the New Yorkers seemed to go on the principle that the more crooked the stick the finer the cane, and in Central Park they have verified the saying. Where the lake is (inside the park) was once a low marsh, covered with such a thick growth of brambles, rank grass, and weeds as to be an almost impenetrable jungle, a secure hiding-place for wild beasts and bad men.` At the northeast end of the lake is the cave. This is a small concern, but I was informed by J. H. Parsell, a native of New York, that before the ground was purchased by the city it was the rendezvous of a desperate gang of robbers who infested the city and completely baffled the police. Long and fruitless were the searches for the hiding-place of the outlaws and their plunder; but when the city cleared off the ground, they found the cave, which turned out to be the robbers' den, as many evidences were left of the fact in the way of remnants of stolen goods, etc.

Croton River has been a God-send to New York City. I do not know what they would have done without it. That stream has been brought into New York by canals and aqueducts, and is now emptied into what is known as the old and new Croton Lakes, both of which are artificial excavations. I could not learn the area of either, but they are both large ponds of water and are indispensable to the comfort and beauty of the city. I shall attempt no description of buildings, further than to say that the new post-office is of most ample proportions,

and overtops all its surroundings. Its dome may be
seen from all surrounding elevations. The two abutments, or towers, of the East River bridge look like the
Colossus of Rhodes broken in two near his hips, and his
legs left standing, one on Manhattan and the other on
Long Island.

Among the curiosities that I visited in New York (for
I can only mention some of the most prominent) was
Barnum's hippodrome, which was the wonder of the day·
It had been open but three weeks and I was informed
by good authority that it had taken in over sixty thousand dollars. It had the effect of closing the theaters
and other places of amusement. California's favorite,
McCullough, was then in New York, performing with
scarcely a corporal's guard attending. The hippodrome
is an immense institution; it ·is to ordinary circuses and
theaters what a steam locomotive would be to a hand-
cart.   .

At the end of four days I had visited various points
of interest in New York, from Castle Garden to Sixty-
fifth Street, north and south, and from North to East
Rivers, east and west; had made the discovery . that
Manhattan Island was divided up into one hundred and
forty-one thousand, four hundred and eighty-six lots, and
that of that number, about sixty-two thousand contained
buildings of some kind. I then turned my attention to
the surroundings of New York. Sunday* morning, instead of going to Brooklyn to hear Beecher explain the
m st approved mode of "nest hiding," I took the boat
for Staten Island. I had no acquaintance on the boat,
and having met with so many rebuffs from men of whom
I had made inquiries, by their going down into their

shells like so many clams, it was with a good deal of diffidence that I approached a gentleman and made some inquiries in regard to Governor's Island and the fortifications in the bay. To my grateful surprise I not only got a civil answer, but found the gentleman ready and even anxious to give me all the information in his power (and, by the way, he was well informed). He pointed out every object of interest on our route to Staten Island —the numerous store-houses, wharves, fortifications, and public buildings.

On further inquiry I found that my new friend (for such he proved himself), was John H. Parsell, of the New York City Post-office. From this urbane gentleman I obtained more valuable information in regard to New York and its surroundings than from any other source. On our return he accompanied me into the city, pointed out many relics of Revolutionary days, instructed me in my future researches, and gracefully extended me all those delicate attentions that can only be found in a heart of refinement and a mind of enlarged views. He even followed me with his kindness, promptly forwarding all my letters after I had left. New York.

I visited in detail, Jersey City, Hoboken, Williamsburg, Hell Gate, Blackwell's Island, Governor's Island, and Brooklyn. The last named is one of New York's lodging-houses. Brooklyn is a large city, containing about five hundred thousand inhabitants, and is famous for its fine avenues, public grounds, and the far-famed Greenwood Cemetery. The highest point of Greenwood commands a pretty view of Governor's Island and the . southern portion of New York. I had heard so much about the beauties of Greenwood Cemetery that I had supposed it must be a pretty place by nature ánd extensively beautified by art; but on visiting it I found that naturally it was one of the roughest places imaginable, but I honor the judgment of the parties in selecting it as a cemetery, as it never could have been made worth a cent for anything else. So far as art goes, she has attempted to make up for the defects of nature by expending many millions of dollars—not to tell what departed friends were, but what they ought to have been.

Prospect Park is a lovely place from its natural beauties, and its elevated position gives a perfect view of the eastern slope of Long Island, Coney Island, and the surrounding country. The Brooklyn people are firmly in the faith that in a few years it will eclipse Central Park. Taking New York and its surroundings as a whole, the American people may justly be proud of the great metropolis.

CHAPTER XLIX.

VISIT TO THE EAST—PHILADELPHIA AND BALTIMORE.

AFTER having spent eight days in New York, and familiarized myself with the city, and having visited both Barnum's great hippodrome and the old Bowery theater, besides various works of art and many other places of interest, I resumed my journey, passing through New Jersey, Delaware, Pennsylvania, and Maryland, my objective point being Washington. The route lay through an undulating country, showing great thrift in an agricultural point of view.

We rushed on "o'er river, plain, and hill," until we reached Philadelphia—the "Quaker City." It is situated on the Delaware River, a short distance above the bay of the same name. The selection of the town site gives evidence of good taste, as it is located in the midst of a rich agricultural district and commands superior advantages as a seaport. There are many historic memories that cling to the old town, and I regretted that I had no more time to spend there. I was much disappointed in not finding my old friend, General Patterson, who was out of town. The city extends along the Delaware River from five to six miles and extends west to and beyond the Schuylkill River. It is the second city in population in the United States, containing some seven hundred thousand inhabitants. Though it is about ninety-six miles from the ocean, by the river, the tide flows some distance above the city. The soil in and about the city is generally of a gravelly character, yet there are some bold rocks in the immediate vicinity. The old State House (now Independence Hall) is still standing and well preserved. The old bell that first rang out the joyful notes of the birth of the American Republic still has a tongue to speak. It was in this hall that the Declaration of Independence was signed, and it was also the nation's capitol, with a slight intermission, up to 1800, when the capital was removed to Washington. The old capitol stands near the center of the city, and Philadelphia may justly be proud of her relic of continental days.

At Philadelphia the water off the pier-heads is from forty to fifty feet deep, and the shoalest place on the bar below the city is nineteen feet at low tide, which allows

ships of the largest tonnage to safely approach their
docks, giving the city both a domestic and foreign trade.
The streets are all of reasonable width, and some of
them are very wide and beautiful. Broad Street, I believe, is one hundred and thirteen feet in width. The
original idea of William Penn was carried out and the
streets of the additions, like those of the first survey,
cross each other at right angles. The Schuylkill Mountains (we would call them foot-hills here) approach very
near to the city. Among other things, Philadelphia can
boast no less than seven squares or parks, ranging from
thirty-five acres downwards; and many of them are very
beautifully ornamented. I learned for the first time that
Philadelphia was the last resting-place of Benjamin
Franklin, America's great statesman and philosopher.
His grave is in the cemetery at Christ's Church, and is
quite unpretending when compared with many in Greenwood Cemetery whose inmates are only known by the
amount of money expended over their remains.

Girard College is a grand institution, and some of its
regulations coincide with my notions. One is that when
the student leaves college he must be bound out to learn
some useful trade or profession. The structure is of
enormous proportions. The building alone was erected
at a cost of over two million dollars, together with an
immense outlay of money on the surroundings and fixtures, with a large fund to run the institution. All tui-
tion there is free.

Another great beauty of Philadelphia is its fine
water works. Though it has no Croton River, or
stream that can be brought on a sufficient elevation to
water the city, yet I have hardly found a city better sup-

plied with water; and this is all accomplished by steam power. The largest among the water works is the Farmington works. The water is elevated ninety-two feet, into a large reservoir, or basin, from whence it is conducted through pipes into every part of the city. Penn, after receiving his grant from Charles II. and sending a colony ahead, came to America in 1682, and no reflective mind can visit Philadelphia without coming to the conclusion that the man who could enter a new and wilderness country and use the judgment that he did in founding and laying out a city, was competent to rule an empire. The old Dutch stock is yet to be found in Pennsylvania, and many Quakers in Philadelphia, although they seem to have outlived their early prejudices, and more closely adapt themselves to present customs.

The whole route from Philadelphia to Baltimore presents to the traveler a bright and lively picture. The soil seems to be generally productive and the whole line of road is studded with fine buildings, orchards, lawns, parks, and all the conveniences that should surround happy homes. On arriving at the depot I could understand what to me before was a mystery; that is, how it was possible for the Baltimoreans to so seriously annoy the Massachusetts Regiment in the cars while passing through that city at the commencement of the Rebellion. I found that the locomotive was detached and a large number of horses hitched to the cars to draw them up a steep incline, about a mile and a half, to the second depot. Hence the opportunity for the prolonged attacks with paving-stones and brickbats. This route is still adhered to by the Pennsylvania Central Railroad. Although the grade seems steep, I think it might be traveled by steam power, but a city ordinance, I understand, forbids it. The Baltimore and Ohio road passes through a tunnel under the city.

Baltimore claims to be the third city in point of population in the United States. Such *was* undoubtedly the case, but I do not think the claim well founded at the present time, as the whole population cannot exceed four hundred and fifty thousand. The location of the city is a pleasant one. It is situated upon an arm of the Patapsco River on sloping ground, gently rising from the water to an elevation, at the highest point, of perhaps one hundred feet. It is on tide water and, like Philadelphia, has a large shipping trade. There is considerable manufacturing at Baltimore, and the shell-fish trade is conducted with greater vigor and success than in any city of the Union. There are piles of oyster shells in various parts of the city that in height and extent would rival the famous Pyramid of Cholula. The city is one vast pile of brick and mortar. Here are the finest pressed brick I ever saw.

I can say but little of the public buildings, as I could not afford the time to make a general survey of the city, although there were two structures that came particularly under my notice. One was Washington's Monument and the other the Vernon Church. They are both situated on a commanding eminence, and from the top of the monument you have a beautiful view of both the city and harbor. The monument is round, one hundred and eighty feet in height, built of granite with a colossal statue of Washington on top. The Vernon Church (Episcopal) is the prettiest thing of the kind I ever saw.

It is built in the Gothic style, small and compact; its colorings are lively and tastefully arranged, and everything about it presents an unusually pleasing aspect; so much so that no person of ordinary observation could pass it without being attracted by its beauties. The city hall is a noble building of white marble; but I did not enter it, and consequently had to judge from exterior appearances. My time was up, the whistle blew, and I was soon on board the cars and rapidly moving over the country that divides Baltimore and Washington, arriving at the latter place about six o'clock in the evening.

In penning this I am not unmindful that it must meet the eye of many who have visited our national capital, among whom may be some who hold different views of Washington City from mine; but I always exercise the right of seeing with my own eyes, and I give my own estimates of men and manners. When I arrived at my hotel (Willard's) I was soon surrounded by darkey porters who vied with each other to see who should get my luggage and quarter. My experience had been, during the whole trip, that if a man didn't make up his mind to bleed freely, he had better dodge first-class hotels. The one who takes your valise expects his quarter; the one who brushes your dusty back counts on a "piece;" the one who takes your soiled linen to the laundry looks for his fee, and the one who returns it expects you to "see" him; you ring for a pitcher of ice-water and it costs you some fractional currency; the hand that manages the elevator becomes very sore unless it receives a "shin plaster;" the waiter at table cannot hear or understand your order unless you open his understanding by opening your purse—in a word, you must subsidize every lackey that comes in contact with you, or you are looked upon as a cipher. But I could not learn whether subsidies were first introduced into Washington by negro servants or Government officials.   .

Montreal, New York, and Washington are, in my estimation, the three prettiest cities that I visited. They show more taste and architectural beauty, with wide streets and white walls, less filth and more life, without that somber appearance that characterizes many cities of our Union. I had often heard Baltimore praised for its pretty women, but I saw none there. At the time I could not account for it, but on arriving at Washington the mystery was solved; for when I saw the array of beauty there I came to the conclusion that the pretty women had all moved to Washington during the session of Congress.

After dinner I ventured out into the strange city. It was a clear, pleasant night, with brilliant moon, which made it nearly as light as day. I looked up the long avenue to Capitol Hill, and there before me, like a specter in white, stood the national capitol, with its lofty dome extending its dark shadow along the background, resembling a stern warrior posted as a sentinel, with his plume unstirred by a single breeze, keeping his night watch over that lovely city lying below, which was lit up by thousands of gas jets, and mirth and pleasure held their revels. Government officials, clerks, and employes have completed their labors for the day and are now out in force. Gray-headed statesmen, pleasure seekers, and gallants are now to be seen threading their way through the beautiful grounds and parks, escorting the softer sex of all ages and conditions, ranging from the most transcendent beauty down to mere bundles of paint and powder. Some are seated in retired nooks beneath lovely green shades, where the moonbeams never stray. Near a babbling fountain, where the voice is almost drowned by the sound of many waters, may be seen sighing lovers pouring their plaints into ears of willing listeners. In these public grounds there are lovely walks for the pedestrian, drives for those who cannot afford to walk, seats for those who cannot stand, shade for the retiring, and lights for the student.

> "For oh! if there be an Elysium on earth,
> It is this, it is this."

The public buildings in Washington are all white. The capitol, post-office department, and some others are at the east end of the city, while the President's mansion and the remainder of the public buildings are at the west end, near the Potomac River. Millions upon millions of public money have been expended to make Washington what it is; but this is as it should be; we have a national reputation to sustain, and how could it better be done than by beautifying our capital and grounds.

I cannot convince myself that the site for the Washington monument was wisely chosen. It is situated upon a point (once an island) commanding an extensive view of the Potomac River and western shore; but the ground where the monument stands is so much lower than the capitol grounds and those of the other public buildings that the monument, from a land view, is entirely dwarfed when compared with its surroundings. The monument is an imposing structure. Washington City would be admired in any country for its beautiful streets and avenues, had it no other attractions. There is a large negro population, though from their servile position they attract but little notice.

The next morning I called on my friends J. K. Luttrell and Frank Page, both faithful representatives of our State in Congress. I was much annoyed to learn that they were not friends, not even on speaking terms, and that the subject of their disagreement was such that I could offer no mediation ; and this was rendered still more vexatious to me, as I found them both apparently laboring faithfully (but each in his own way) for the interests of their constituency. Mr. Page was domiciled at Washington, had his family with him, his own house, carriage and complete outfit for driving and entertaining friends and guests. In calling at his house I was made to feel as though I was once more among friends. As to the quarters of Luttrell, they seemed unpretending and looked more like the workshop of the laborious student and statesman than a hall of pleasure ; and I was not long in finding out that he was a general favorite in Congress, and that the defeat of many of his prominent measures for California was neither owing to his want of perseverance or popularity, but was rather owing to a combination in the East against the entire delegation from the Pacific slope. Luttrell seemed to know everybody and perfectly confused me with introductions to notable characters whom I could not describe were I disposed to make the attempt.

I had long had a desire to see Gen. Ben Butler, and it was now gratified. He was quietly listening to the debate, and looked as placid and innocent as a child. I was told by those who know him that he is one of the most affable and gentlemanly members of our national legislature. I had never supposed that there were a great many listeners to Congressional speeches, unless upon great occasions, though I had never thought that there was such a scanty auditory as I found, nor that men would talk for hours to reporters and bare walls. Upon expressing my surprise, I was informed by an old Congressman that those speeches were not made for members, but for the constituents at home.

I saw the negro orator, Fred Douglass. I should suppose from his complexion, that he probably is a quadroon and that he owes his intelligence to white ancestors; at least, he has more ability than full-blooded negroes ever fall heir to. His head is as white as a sheet, and age seems to be telling upon him. I also met Gen. J. W. Denver, an old Californian, who told me that he was practicing law in Ohio. Senator Cole was also at the capitol, looking as though he was very much at home in its halls. But enough of this, for I met no one in Washington unknown to fame—even Grant is known throughout the land—and they are all "written up" by more able pens than mine, and as this is a simple story of a traveler I leave biography to others.

From the time I left home it had been my intention to visit Mount Vernon. I accordingly took passage on a steamer that made daily trips to that sacred place. I believe we started about seven o'clock in the morning and returned at four in the afternoon, and that the dis-

27

tance is about twenty-five or thirty miles from Washington. It was a lovely morning as we steamed down that wide and beautiful river. There was not a ripple on the water and it reflected objects from its smooth surface with all the truthfulness of a mirror. We swept down past Alexandria and numerous fortifications on either shore, and in due time landed at Mount Vernon. A beautiful custom here strikes the visitor. Every steamer that passes down the river commences tolling its bell before reaching Washington's burial place, and continues the solemn tolling until the vessel has passed the spot. Mount Vernon is on the west bank of the Potomac, on a high commanding point. The river, whose general course is north and south, then makes a bend to the west, which gives a grand view up and down the stream. The close observer will soon learn on landing at Mount Vernon that, though he is standing, as it were, on holy ground, though pressing the soil so often trod by the "father of his country," yet there is but little there that Washington could recognize, were he permitted to pay it a visit; for the evidences of former neglect and recent repairs are too apparent at every glance to admit of doubt or contradiction. The late improvements have been made by the Ladies' Mount Vernon Association. Washington's tomb is between the house and river. It is large, but unpretending, and is composed of brick-work with iron gratings in front. It contains the remains of others of the family, besides several graves and monuments near by, of other noted persons. The residence is a common two-story building, with porches above and below. Some books and paintings of the Washington family still remain in the house. The grounds have been well laid out and cultivated; the trees are numerous, and many of them native forest productions; but the great attraction is the fact of its being the last residence and final resting-place of the great American hero and father of a nation. We spent a pleasant day and returned to Washington City in the evening, without accident or remarkable incident outside of the objects of our visit.

CHAPTER L.

A VISIT TO THE EAST—"ON TO RICHMOND!"

AFTER having taken the principal cities of the Union by storm (for up to this time there had been but little fair weather), and wishing to emulate the heroes of other days, I was determined to push my conquests south. Accordingly on the 24th of May, 1874, after arming myself with a box of cigars, a flask of old Bourbon and a box of Brandreth's pills, I opened the campaign by chartering a steamer (or at least two dollars and a half's worth of one) and steamed boldly down the Potomac, passing Alexandria and other places of less note. In about two hours and a half we landed at Quantico, where we took the cars for Richmond. Whether from our approach or some other cause, I found the country pretty generally deserted, excepting by a few contrabands who attacked the train, but by bestowing quarters they were easily captured. The country through which we passed at some time had been cultivated and very well improved, but the

land seemed to have been worn out and the farms neglected. The soil had never been of a very good quality,
being generally a gravelly ridge covered with yellow
pine timber. In many places the yellow pine had
sprung up on lands that had once been cultivated, and
had attained a growth of from eight to ten inches in
diameter. In some instances they were clearing off the
second forest, preparatory to cultivation.

In due time we reached Fredericksburg, a small town
pleasantly located on the south bank of the Rappahan-
nock. It was at this point that Joe Hooker made his
big fight, and where Stonewall Jackson and many other
brave men fell; but not a sign is left to tell of that sanguinary struggle; not a fortification, trench, or earthwork
is now to be seen. I took the town entirely by surprise, as there was not a soul in the place aware of my
approach. There were but two shots fired, and those
were fired by me. I shot Mr. Barbour, an old citizen of
Fredericksburg, and his companion. Both shots took
effect in the neck, and the enemy surrendered at discretion. After the capture we were soon on board the
cars and arrived at Richmond about four o'clock in the
afternoon, where a short struggle ensued, but I was
again victorious. The city surrendered and I established my head-quarters in the Ballard and Exchange,
having accomplished in one day what cost the United
States two years of bloody war and untold millions of
treasure to do, and that "without the loss of a man on
our side." I wonder if history will do me justice.

Richmond is a beautiful city. On entering it, the
cars ran out to the bridge spanning the James River,
and before me, spread out for nearly half a mile in

width, lay that lovely stream, rushing, bounding, and dashing its spray upon the monster granite bowlders that impeded its course. Here is one of the first water powers in the world. It is practically unlimited, both in fall and volume of water. The banks are of that character that the water may be raised to any necessary height. Richmond has been noted for its superior flour. There were originally four large flouring mills, of which two remain. One was destroyed by fire during the rebellion and the remains of another were still smoking when I was there. But not one-thousandth part of the water-power has ever been employed. The city is situated on the north bank of the river, right at the foot of the rapids, to which point steamers of a large class run up. The country around Richmond is fertile, especially the James River bottom below and south of the city. It is something like two hundred feet from the bed of the river to the top of the bank, which then spreads out into a level plain. The water to supply the city is taken from the river, two miles above. Its abundance permits the people to enjoy many miniature lakes and playing fountains. Evergreens, beautiful shade trees, green velvet lawns, and sparkling fountains make the large and fine grounds around the State House seem a perfect paradise.

During my visit to Richmond I tried to trace some evidences of the great struggle, but in vain. There is scarcely a mark or a scar left to give evidence of the sanguinary conflicts that raged in and about the city. My first and greatest curiosity was to visit the old Libby prison, which is situated between Cary Street and the river. I found it now, as it was before the war, an enor-

mous tobacco factory, everything intact and doing a
flourishing business; the only change in it was a few new
posts, Eastern visitors having carried the original posts
off, piece-meal, by way of relics. I next visited Castle
Thunder, and found a well-built machine shop—"this
and nothing more." Washington's residence stands on
the main street of the city, carefully protected, and held
intact as a relic of continental days. I noticed at this
place, as in other parts of the South, that every evidence
of the rebellion, so far as it was possible, had been ob-
literated. The visitor may take the line of the great
seven days' fight and follow it clear down to Malvern
Hill, and he will see nothing to evidence it excepting the
graves of those who fell in that long and bloody action.
There is one monument erected to the memory of the
Confederate dead. It is obelisk-shaped, built of rough
stone, and I should think about sixty feet high, without
mortar or cement. Evergreen vines are being trained
around it.

While all reasonable efforts have been made to oblit-
erate the recollections of our late civil strife, it is pleasing to see how carefully everything has been preserved
that relates to the great Revolution of our forefathers.
Not only the residence of Washington is faithfully preserved, but standing on Libby Hill is the venerable
St. John's Church, in which Patrick Henry delivered his
philippics against the English Government, and where
with matchless eloquence he urged our patriotic sires to
take up arms in defense of infant liberty. It is true
the church is somewhat like the boy's jackknife which
had been rehandled and rebladed, yet it was the knife
his grandsire gave him. St. John's Church, though

sided, floored, and roofed several times, no doubt (as it
is a wooden building), is yet preserved and exhibited
with great pride by the Richmondites as the sacred
place that gave out inspiration to the heroes who threw
off King George's yoke.

In the State House grounds stands the finest eques-
trian statue of Washington that I saw on my journey,
and, it is said, the finest in the world. Around on the
projecting pedestal, stands, in life size, Virginia's statesmen and heroes. Among them are Patrick Henry,
Thomas Jefferson, Crawford, Mason, and several others.
But it would take a large pedestal to contain the statues
of all the great men Virginia has produced. Inside the
State House there are many things that to the lovers of
early American history are worthy of observation.
There is a great mass of documents relating to revolutionary days which reach back even to the first settlement of America, for be it remembered that the city
of Richmond is one of the oldest cities of America.
Among other things in the State House, I found the
parole of honor of Lord Cornwallis, upon which he was
released for exchange. It was dated October 28, 1781,
and permitted Cornwallis to return to England either
by way of New York or Baltimore, and he pledged his
honor to report himself for exchange any place dictated
by His Excellency, George Washington, commander-in-
chief of the United States forces. I also saw, preserved
under glass, the original draft of the Declaration of
Rights, by Mason. There are also many ancient books
there preserved, and some of them are great curiosities.
One was published over five hundred years ago—of
course before the art of printing, but I am certain that

with all our improvements, nothing at this day would be better executed, and it was hard for me to realize that it was possible to execute a work with such uniformity of letter and neatness of execution. The Virginians will exhibit to you with equal pride the rock, about seven miles below the city, on which John Smith's head was laid for execution when rescued by Pocahontas.

But, by the way, speaking of water puts a man in mind of fishing. I have a fine production of the art and genius of this same John Smith. It is nothing less than a correct and well-executed engraved map of the survey of the State of Virginia, made by him. The survey was made while in the colony and the map was engraved at London, England. Smith did not live to enjoy the fruits of his labor or to even exhibit to the people of England his map of the new world; but a traveler discovered the plate among some old rubbish that was being exposed for sale at auction, and bought it. The copy in my possession was kindly presented me by the superintendent of public printing in Virginia —Mr. Walker.

The mass of the inhabitants of Richmond are negroes, or more or less mixed with negro blood. I found them employed as barbers, mechanics of different kinds, house servants and common laborers, but I never in one instance saw one of them in a store, either as clerk or principal; and the matter struck me as being so strange that I gave it my particular attention. Notwithstanding the great negro majority in Richmond, the city officers are all Democrats, many of the negroes esteeming the carpet-baggers worse than do the whites;

and many of the negroes, if their declarations are to be taken as true, regret the change from slavery to freedom. They told me that when they could get work it was all very nice, but when they got out of employment, or were sick, they had no home and were driven to do things which they did not like to do. On the other hand, when they were with their masters they always had a home and no care. I almost universally heard them speaking of their old masters with pride and reverence, and showing a warm attachment for them, just as the whites boast of the name of their ancestors. I would frequently ask them why they did not return to their old masters and live with them, and the reply nearly always was, "Massa is dead," or, "Massa is poor now." I further learned that where the former master is living, there is generally a good feeling between him and his former slave, and in many instances where the negro is out of a home he falls back on his old master until he can do better. But what is most refreshing is to see the plug-hatted colored politician strut and swell, and to see with what contempt they look down upon "de po' foolish nigga." I was informed by the business men of Richmond that the city has not been in as prosperous a condition for many years as it is at the present time.

I had intended going farther south, but was dissuaded from my purpose by the Richmond people, who assured me that my trip would be anything but pleasant or instructive. The seasons are just about as early in Richmond as they are in this part of California. Richmond, with her boundless water-power, her advantages as a shipping point, together with a fertile country surrounding it, has a future surpassed by few cities in the United States; and I think, if from any cause I should be compelled to run away from this country, the officers of the law might look for me in Richmond with a good prospect of finding me.

On Sunday morning I ascended the hill and took a last look at the city of Richmond, packed my traps, bade good-by to the Ballard and Exchange Hotel, and at half-past one o'clock took the cars on my back track, arriving in Washington about six in the evening.

CHAPTER LI.

A VISIT TO THE EAST—HOMEWARD BOUND.

I HAD now become very anxious (I do not like to say homesick) about home, and took my way through Harrisburg, Pittsburg, Columbus, and "all intermediate points" to Cincinnati. I would like to tell you something about the city of Pittsburg, but the smoke was so dense that it was absolutely impossible to see enough to form any opinion further than to say that coal, smoke, and iron were the principal things with which I came in contact. As to Columbus, it is only remarkable from the fact that it is the capital of Ohio. We landed from the cars at Cincinnati in the night, and I probably never shall know just how I did get in, as we went a great distance around the city before the hackmen assailed us; but at last I brought up at the Burnett House, where I got good accommodations at four and a half dollars per day. I remained but one day, although I regretted that

I could not get my own consent to stay longer. The city is built in a bend, between the river and the bluffs. The bench, or valley, is a complete amphitheater, and I do not know whether the ground was formed for the city or the city for the ground; but one thing is certain, the city just fills the space and is a good fit.

I went to see the inclined plane that is constructed to ascend the bluff overlooking the city. It is so arranged that when one car runs up the steep incline another runs down, operating like a couple of well buckets, one at each end of the rope. The rope is made of wire and is about an inch and a half thick. The motive power is a large steam engine on the hill. The enterprise is still young, although they have a large pavilion, restaurant, saloons, etc., and the place is intended to be to Cincinnati what Woodward's Garden is to San Francisco, with some exceptions. From this elevated position you have a magnificent view of the city which lies at your feet, and a long stretch of the Kentucky shore. Standing on this commanding position, it is difficult to realize that three hundred thousand inhabitants are at once beneath the vision's range. Cincinnati is a great horse market, and many hundreds of fine horses are sold there daily. Real estate was very low while I was there, magnificent brown stone fronts being sold at auction. The city has a very fine park, several public squares, and many handsome public buildings.

As I am homeward bound, my route lies through the southern part of Indiana after leaving Ohio. This portion of Indiana has been heavily timbered, and the soil does not compare very favorably with the middle, or prairie, portion of the State. We passed Vincennes,

crossed the Wabash River, ran through Illinois, crossing
the Kaskaskia River at Carlisle, and arrived at St. Louis
about six o'clock in the evening. The next morning I
was not long in discovering that the St. Louis of 1848
was completely lost in the St. Louis of 1874; and I, too,
was lost where I was once well acquainted. Everything
had so changed in appearance that the Planters' House
did not seem to stand on the same ground that it did
twenty-six years ago. The grand steel bridge spanning
the Mississippi River is a magnificent work of art, and
the descriptions that have been published are not exaggerated. Being a traveler I was permitted to go onto
the bridge the day before it was opened to the public,
and I had a fine opportunity to examine the beautiful
structure. The Mississippi steamers pass under its immense arches, but the noblest of them are compelled to
make their obeisance as they pass under the spans, by
lowering a part of their smoke-stacks, which is done by
ingenious hinge arrangements and cable chains attached
to the top of the pipe. The lowering and raising are
done by steam power. On the St. Louis side the bridge
extends up to Third Street, and over it passes all busses,
street-cars, teams, and foot passengers; while the railroad
trains come under the city by way of a tunnel and enter
the bridge below, or, if you please, on the first story.
St. Louis has very respectable parks and public gardens.
The largest, as well as I remember, contains about thirty-
eight acres, and is very well ornamented by way of shade
trees and works of art.

Leaving St. Louis we traveled across Missouri, visiting
Kansas City on our route, but in reaching that point we
passed through a level, fertile, and what looked like a

very sickly country, as green pools and ponds of water were standing all along the route. Kansas City is located on the Kansas frontier, in Jackson County, Missouri, on the south bank of the Missouri River, just below the mouth of the Kansas River, and is about fourteen miles from Independence. It is on elevated ground, and I should think it a healthy location. It is well laid out, the streets being wide, and the most of the buildings are of brick. There are churches representing almost every Christian creed.

From this point I made a night trip to Omaha, arriving there about ten o'clock in the morning, after some delays on the east side of the Missouri River. About eleven we were on our way for California, having been fortunate enough to secure a good lower section in the palace sleeping-car. We rolled along over every variety of country of which the mind could conceive, but the general topography was barren and uninteresting after leaving the Platte River.

When I left home for my Eastern visit, I left behind me green fields and buds and blossoms of spring; but on nearing the Sierra I merged from spring into winter, and continued to encounter winter weather through Nevada, Utah, and, in fact, through all the Western States, Upper and Lower Canada, Vermont, New Hampshire, and Massachusetts. I found spring again in New York City, and it continued until I reached Richmond, where I found summer, which held on until I reached Omaha, when I again came into the season of spring. This lasted until I came to the Sierra Nevada on my homeward journey, and there I found my third winter in one year. But on commencing the descent of the western slope of the Sierra, what a change! and with what pride the old Californian would exclaim to those who were visiting this State for the first time, "This is our country!"

As far as the eye could extend, we could see spreading out before us the ripe, waving fields of grain, gently undulating in one of California's soft and delicious breezes, reflecting back its rich golden hue in the brilliant rays of a California summer sun. The passengers were perfectly delighted, each calling the attention of fellow travelers to the opposite side of the cars, and each believing that he or she had discovered a prospect surpassing in loveliness all others. To those who had never witnessed it before the sight was equaled only by that of Balboa on discovering the Pacific. Presently we came in full view of the Sacramento River. From our elevated position it looked like a silver thread winding its way through bright green pastures until it lost itself in the distant windings among the foot-hills of Mount Diablo, which are kissed by the ever restless waves of San Pablo Bay. In this instance Campbell is wrong. "Distance" does not "lend enchantment to the view," for as we approached Sacramento the scene became more lovely still. Broad, spreading vineyards, well-cultivated gardens, orchards loaded with fruit, long and shady avenues, and palatial residences were constantly passing before us in this beautiful panorama. All on board seemed not only happy, but jubilant.

We arrived at Sacramento, the capital of California, and, after twenty minutes for lunch, were off again on the southern route for San Francisco. This route gave us an excellent view of California's capitol, and as I viewed that massive pile, with its ample and lofty dome

I could say with honest pride that, after a travel of over eight thousand miles, it was the finest public structure I had seen, the national capitol alone excepted. Passing through the city of Stockton, and other towns, we arrived in San Francisco at seven o'clock in the evening.

CHAPTER LII.

MY CALIFORNIA HOME.

" Breathes there a man with soul so dead
Who never to himself has said,
    This is my own, my native land !
Whose heart has ne'er within him burned,
As home his footsteps he has turned
    From wandering on a foreign strand ! "

HAVING led my California friends through a long journey over several States, and through the principal cities of the Union, I will now, as a closing scene, devote a short chapter to a description of my California home and its surroundings, for the benefit of my Eastern friends, to whom I hope it may not be entirely uninteresting. The last chapter closed with my arrival at San Francisco. That city I shall not attempt to describe. Though but twenty-five years old, it is the Hercules of the Pacific. In 1849 it was Yerba Buena. The pueblo of Yerba Buena contained the Mission Dolores and little more. Now, in 1874, it is the great mart of the Pacific, and boasts a population of two hundred thousand inhabitants. It would take a respectable volume instead of a single chapter to describe that flourishing city and its surroundings.

At San Francisco I met my family, and, after remaining a short time to enable them to finish up their visit,
one bright day in June we took passage in the steamer
Antelope and crossed the bay *en route* for Healdsburg.
There was not a breeze to ruffle the placid waters, and
we steamed along past Red Rock and the Two Brothers,
and in about two hours and a half arrived at Donahue,
where we took the cars for Healdsburg. On landing at
Donahue I was once more in old Sonoma County, with
familiar scenes surrounding me. About twelve miles
north and east lay the city of Sonoma, one of the oldest
towns in California; in fact, it was a place of some importance when San Francisco was the Yerba Buena of
Mexico, with little else than drifting sand-hills and an
occasional rocky cliff. At the time of the conquest of
California, during the Mexican War, Sonoma was a point
of considerable importance to the Americans, and it
was at this place that the famous Bear Flag was hoisted.

A ride of sixteen miles from Petaluma, through a very
pleasant valley, brings us to Santa Rosa. This fine little
city is situated near the center of the lovely valley of
that name. The surrounding country is generally fertile,
producing wheat, barley, oats, and all the family of root
vegetables in great abundance, but it is most remarkable
for its immense yields of hay. The valley lying between
Santa Rosa and Petaluma is very rich in soil, but rather
low, and it has received but little at the hands of art to
develop or to beautify its natural resources. The valley
was, unfortunately, a Mexican grant, and has never been
divided up into farms, but the whole constitutes an immense stock ranch. Santa Rosa is the county seat of
Sonoma County, and for the last two years has made a

rapid growth. It boasts a city government and is in a flourishing condition. It is sustained by its colleges and the agricultural pursuits of the neighborhood.

Fifteen miles in a northeasterly direction lies the town of Healdsburg, my home. Healdsburg is situated on the bank of Russian River, between that stream and Dry Creek. The land upon which the town is built is dry and gravelly, with the Russian River Valley on the east and the famous Dry Creek Valley west and north of the city. The town is also about two miles above the confluence of the two streams. No more lovely spot was ever selected for a town site. The soil in the valleys surrounding Healdsburg is probably the finest in the world, the banks of the Nile not excepted. And the best feature in the case is the fact that artificial fertilization is not needed, as nature has provided a fertilizer in the flood that visits us in our winter season. Sometimes it is much greater than it is at others, owing to the cañon some twelve miles below Healdsburg, which in a very heavy flood backs the water over our valleys to a depth of from three to four feet. There is then but little current and the rich vegetable deposits washed from the surrounding hills are allowed to settle on the surface of the ground. These floods run off very soon and never overflow the land more than from twenty-four to thirty-six hours, and, though the grain crops may be sowed, and all green, they are not injured, but frequently improved by their inundation.

Sonoma County is the garden of California, and Russian River and Dry Creek Valleys are the garden spots of Sonoma County. One remarkable feature is that since the county's earliest settlement we have never lost

28

a crop. Where we have sown we have always reaped a rich harvest, and in some instances we have harvested from sixty-five to seventy bushels of wheat to the acre, while the crops of Indian corn compare favorably with those raised on the American bottoms. Adjoining our valleys on the west is a fine forest of redwood, firs, and other valuable timber, which affords an abundant supply for fuel, fencing, lumber, and all other purposes. The water here is peculiarly good. It is pure, cold, and soft. There are gushing springs flowing from almost every hill, and throughout the valleys, water of the same quality may be obtained at the depth of from twelve to twenty feet. For washing purposes it is equally as good and pure as rain-water; hence no cisterns or saving of rain-water are ever indulged in here. Flowing from our hills and mountains are numerous spring brooks, full of speckled trout, where the angler finds fine sport, while in our mountains, bear of several varieties, deer, grouse, squirrels, and quail abound.

Healdsburg is within seventeen miles of the great Geyser Springs, over one of the finest mountain roads in the world. The view of the valley and streams below from this road beggars all description. Skaggs Springs are situated fourteen miles up one of the loveliest drives in the world. Lytton's Soda and Seltzer Springs are distant three miles from here. A large hotel is being built at these springs, and next year it will be opened to the public. This will at once become one of the most popular watering places in the State. Sulphur Flat Sulphur Spring is within two miles, Fitch Mountain Sulphur Spring within one mile and a half, and many others of less note are within a short distance of this place.

Our climate cannot be surpassed in the world. We have some hot days during the summer, but they are very few and easily endured when we take into consideration the fact that such a thing as a hot night is unknown with us. We can always sleep under a couple of blankets during the warmest summer nights; and we are never troubled with mosquitoes or gnats. The fogs and cold winds from the ocean have but little effect here, as the winds in crossing the Coast Range for about forty miles become so modified and softened as to be only cool and pleasant. During my long residence in this town, I have never known a case of chills and fever, or fever and ague, or any other malarious disease, unless brought here from some other part, and then it would soon disappear.

Our scenery is the admiration of all visitors. It is, in fact, one extensive valley from the bay to and far beyond Healdsburg. As the town is approached it seems an amphitheater surrounded in the background by lofty hills and mountains. At the east, just raising its high head and prominent nose above Fitch Mountain, may be seen Mount St. Helena, some fifteen miles distant. To the northeast is Pine Mountain, crowned with a dense forest, while north is Sulphur Peak, raising its bald head high above the surrounding hills. Fitch Mountain, within a mile of the city, is a prominent landmark by which we can for many miles around locate the exact position of Healdsburg. At the west the hills gradually rise until, far in the distance, between us and the ocean, they assume the magnitude of mountains and present to the eye one of the loveliest pictures imaginable. The first belt of hills, ranging from three to four miles distant, is studded with lofty fir and redwood trees, stationed on the summit equidistant from each other, looking like so many giant sentinels on those lofty watch-towers of nature to guard the valley below; and when the departing sun casts its golden light upon the elevated crests, throwing the lengthening shadows down the vale, no more lovely sight ever met human gaze.

CHAPTER LIII.

RETURN TO BUSINESS—MORE THRILLING INCIDENTS.

ON my return from the East, I once more settled down to my profession. As to my family relations, on the first day of September, 1865, I had married Miss Minnie Molloy, daughter of Dr. E. B. Molloy, and she proved a most kind and affectionate wife, wholly domestic in her nature, and, thanks to her parents, had been the recipient of a first-class education. Her affections were of that warm and engaging nature that she looked upon the happiness of her husband and children as her only aim in life. She bore three children, the eldest a girl. However, I held her but for the short space of six years, and her death left me with an infant boy eight months old. In the early months of our marriage an accident happened to me, which I will here record.

I was engaged on part of the plaintiff in the case of Bennet vs. Bennet, for divorce, having made an application for the custody of the children. The case was tried in Mendocino County, and it was necessary for four of us, the plaintiff, her two witnesses, and myself to go from Healdsburg to Ukiah, and that necessitated a two-

seated conveyance.   On application at the livery stable
I was informed that I could either have a thorough-
brace or a light two-seated carriage.   I told them that
I would take the carriage, but I wanted a true, steady
team, as there was no brake on the carriage.   Well, we
went to Ukiah, made our showing, and got an order of
court for the children, and were jubilant over our success.

As we were returning over the old toll-road on the west
side of Russian River, the high hills on our right and a
perpendicular precipice of thirty feet on the left, and a
roa !-bed of about fifteen feet, winding up the mountain,
on turning a bend, we suddenly met a team.   The bank
side was ours by right of way, but the other parties
took it, throwing us on the side next the precipice.
They halted to let me pass (I was driving), but as I
attempted to drive on I discovered the limb of an oak
tree projecting over the road, that came so far out as to
fence me off, so that I could not swing in behind them.
Coming to a halt, I told them to drive ahead; but before
they could understand what I wanted, my horses commenced backing, and the wagon pulled on them, inclin-
ing to run down the grade.   I readily comprehended
the situation and urged my horses to advance, striking
them with the whip; but the more I urged them, the
faster they backed.   At this place there was a bend in
the bank, forming a horseshoe, the toe running to the
precipice.   I saw that we were destined to go over the
precipice back foremost.   As the grade got steeper
in our downward descent, I whirled my horses, facing
the precipice, and noticed a jack-oak growing below the
precipice, whose branching, feathery top came up even
with the top of the bank.   It was now so steep that the

horses could not hold the wagon, and I plunged them into the top of-the tree (which was about eight inches in diameter at the butt), and down we went, head fore-most—horses, carriage, tree and all. The tree bent down with the weight, but as soon as the horses, car-riage, and passengers struck the bed of the creek below, the three passengers pitched out, and t e horses being on the ground, the tree, thus released, sprung back, throwing the carriage clear and pitching me some fifteen feet, head foremost, among the rocks. The next thing I knew the parties from the other wagon had hold of me, attempting to carry me out. I gained my feet, and, with their assistance, climbed to the road, where they got me into their wagon and drove me, with the rest, to MacDonald's Hotel, on the road, I believe about two miles. MacDonald got a mattress and spread it on a sidewalk running along the front of the hotel, where it was cool, and I was laid on it.

I had been there but a few minutes when I heard some one say that Bennet, the defendant in our case, had run off with the children, and it was supposed that he was taking them to Oregon. When I heard this I asked MacDonald if he had any brandy. He answered in the affirmative, when I asked for a glass. After drink-ing it, I dictated dispatches to Chief Burke, of San Francisco, and to the Sacramento police, and all was a blank for some time. The next thing that I realized was that Dr. Pike was present (the local physician). Word was sent to Healdsburg for Dr. O. S. Allen, my family physician, and Dr. Molloy, my father-in-law. On the way down the man reported the accident in Cloverdale, and Dr. Weaver, from the State of Nevada, a former partner of Dr. Allen, happened to be there; he said, "If one of Allen's patients is hurt, I must go and see him." The resident physician of Cloverdale hitched up his team, and they came up, and two hours later Drs. Allen and Molloy arrived, making five doctors in all. (Some will say that was enough to kill any man.)

They went to work in good earnest, gave me a thorough examination, found that two ribs had been stove in near the backbone, that the point of the left shoulder was broken, that my head was badly cut in several places and full of gravel-stones, and that the nervous system was badly shaken. My neck and all around the top of my shoulders assumed an inky blackness, but I had become entirely conscious. Night was coming on, and they were desirous of getting me into the house. They attempted to move me on the mattress, and carry me in, but the instant they commenced raising me on the mattress the breath would leave me, and I would faint, the pain was so excruciating. They had to leave me where I was, and I was compelled to remain there with an awning over me for three days, when I called MacDonald to me and asked him if he had any wide boards about the place, from sixteen to eighteen inches wide. He said that he had, when I asked him to cut off a piece seven feet long and bring it there. Some thought I was losing my mind, but he complied with my request. "Now," said I, "nail a bracket on one end, four inches high." He again complied. "Now," said I to Dr. Allen, "carefully shove that board under my mattress, and let the bracket come up to my feet." This was done. "Now," I continued, "go to my head and raise the board." I found that my plan was a success;

that lying on the stiff board I could be moved without any rack or pain. I lay at MacDonald's a week, when I was moved, with the aid of my board, to my home in Healdsburg, where I lay for nearly three months.

The doctors unanimously agreed that I would never get entirely over the injuries, but would be able to get around, and might survive for several years. But they were mistaken, as I have had occasion to try my manhood several times since, and could not see that I had lost much of my former elasticity.

Subsequent to the foregoing event, there was a desperate attempt made upon my life; I was seated in a chair, when the would-be assassin drew a cocked revolver, clapped it to my ear and fired. I saw the pressure of his fingers upon the trigger of the revolver, and throwing my head back and my hand up, the bullet crashed diagonally through the hand. I sprang to my feet and with my other hand reached for my revolver; but it was in the scabbard, buttoned down. My assailant had a long navy revolver, and continued his fire at close range, the muzzle of his pistol never four feet from me during the fire. He continued to fire in the most excited manner until he had emptied his weapon, when I had succeeded in getting my revolver with my one hand. He then started to run, when I hastily fired as he was about to escape through a door. I fired a little too quick, and just barked his neck with my bullet. I then sprang forward and drew a bead on his back as he was running; but from some cause the hammer of my revolver came down between the tubes. I cocked again, and would have got him before he escaped from the building, had it not been that a pretended friend sprang forward and

between us, exclaiming, "Here, Cap., take my pistol."
I subsequently learned that he too was in the plot to kill
me. He merely took that position to save his companion
in guilt. My assailant had attempted to get up a row
with me in the morning, on some trivial matter, and on
walking from me said significantly, "I will see you
again." These words put me so far on my guard as to
buckle on my revolver. I was afterwards told that the
squatters had agreed that, if he would kill me, he should
have five hundred dollars. Well, I followed him up, he
running and I pursuing, until I got two more shots, but
at long range, when I became so weak from loss of blood
that I could not follow further. He escaped from the
country, and was absent for something over a year.

This last occurrence left me in rather a bad situation,
having comparatively lost the use of my right hand by
a saber cut in the Mexican War, and now my left shattered by an assassin's bullet, left me crippled in both
hands. And this combination of circumstances has
clearly demonstrated to me that the old adage, "Truth
is stranger than fiction," has been verified. But this was
no secret; the whole town of Healdsburg well knew of
the affair, which occurred in the very place where this
is written; and there were over twenty persons in the
room when the would-be murderer commenced shooting.
I lay for three months with my hand-wound, and some
portion of the time in a critical condition; but at last it
healed, and I again continued my practice.

About a year after the death of my wife, I found it
necessary to again marry, as raising a family of small
children alone was anything but pleasant. Hence, on
the 14th of January, 1872, I married the daughter of

J. E. Turner, of Sacramento, who has proved an excellent mother to my children, which is the kindest thing that can be said of a step-mother. We have lived together for fifteen.years, and hope to live together many more.

CHAPTER LIV.

POLITICAL.

A S I have, in this volume, made no reference to my political creed, and as such a work would be incomplete without some allusion to that feature of my career, I here reproduce a short letter which has heretofore been published. This letter will not only explain itself, but will suffice to indicate my political predilections in a general way.

HEALDSBURG, CAL., June 27, 1868.

HON. JOHN BUSH, Placerville, Cal.—*Dear Sir:* When last in Placerville I promised to give you a letter explaining what you saw fit to denominate my "unreasonable course, politically," and in so doing I shall endeavor to be as brief as possible, and after a perusal of the statement of facts you will please inform me who has changed?

To begin: As an American I am proud of my country, and love its many glorious institutions; and hope that my highest ambition always shall be, as it always has been, to add to rather than diminish her honor and glory. .

At the Presidential election in 1860, as a Democrat, I supported that party. At the Charleston convention a portion split off from the party and organized what was known as the Baltimore convention. The Charleston convention nominated Stephen A. Douglas, who was a national man and a patriot; the Baltimore convention nominated a sectional ticket, and the Republicans did the same, and, as a national Democrat, I supported the regular nominee of the Democratic party. You know the result. Rebellion ensued, and I was found sustaining my country's flag—justifying any course that was found most expedient to crush treason and restore peace to the country. Of such a struggle as we passed through, the annals of history give no parallel; but like all other earthly things, it came to a close. During its existence the friends of the States in rebellion, as well as the rebels in arms, constantly proclaimed that they were "out of the Union," and all that they wanted was "to be let alone;" while on the other hand, Union men held that the rebellious States were not out of the Union, neither could they get out—that the federal compact could not be dissolved. This doctrine was advocated alike by the chief magistrate, Congress, statesmen, judges, clergy, and down to the soldier in arms. The murdered Lincoln, through Secretary Seward, in reply to the French Emperor, when the French proposed intervention, used this language: "No intervention is necessary; a portion of the States of this Union is in a state of rebellion against the legally constituted Government, and all that is necessary to a peace is for them to lay down their arms and return their delegations to Congress, when this war will cease of itself."

On the 8th of November, 1863, President Lincoln issued his proclamation, offering to send any seceded State a provisional governor when that State would make the request known by one-tenth of the votes, taking the vote of 1861 as a basis. This Congress tacitly or positively recognized—continuing from time to time to ratify the acts of Lincoln—and while this proclamation was in full force, and supported by the 4th Article of the Constitution of the United States, on an application of North Carolina, she having complied with the requisitions of the proclamation, Wm. Holden was appointed provisional governor of that State. W. L. Sharky was appointed provisional governor of Mississippi; June 17th, James Johnson was appointed governor of Georgia; June 17th, Andrew J. Hamilton was appointed governor of Texas; June 21st, Lewis E. Parsons was appointed for Alabama; June 30th, Benj. F. Perry was appointed for South Carolina; and July 13th of the same year, Wm. Marvin was appointed provisional governor of Florida. In all those States there was a thorough organization, in every instance compliance with the letter of the proclamation by declaring void the ordinance of secession, repudiating the Confederate debt, and adopting the constitutional amendment declaring slavery and involuntary servitude forever abolished, unless for crimes of which the party shall have been duly convicted. This mode of reconstruction was offered and accepted, and acted upon in good faith.

The South at this time was disarmed and powerless, while the conquerors possessed all the vast armament of the great American nation; hence no fear of treachery could reasonably be suspected, and hence the country had a right to rejoice in the happy termination of the fratricidal war, and a restoration of peace and tranquillity to our bleeding nation. Under this new organization the representatives of these reconstructed State govcrnments were sent to Congress, but failed to gain admittance to seats in that body. The first excuse was "disloyalty;" soon, however, that was wiped out by the election of men who bore the scars of many a well-contested field against the rebels, but to the surprise of all fair-thinking men they, too, were rejected; and when our Congress was pressed for a reason, they proclaimed that these States, formerly in rebellion, were all out of the Union, and consequently not entitled to representation. Thus they gave the lie to our former declarations "that the South was not out of the Union, and could not get out," thereby stultifying themselves, and asking every Union man to turn a political somersault. At this juncture, people less cool than Americans would have hurled such men from the high positions which they were daily disgracing, when a still worse state of anarchy would have ensued.

But, thank God, the people still forbore, and the horrid impositions of that body calling itself a Congress of the United States have continued. They have recklessly trampled the constitution under their feet at every turn. They have sent the bayonet in times of peace into the Southern States—overturned State governments in violation of the constitution (and these the governments they themselves had once recognized by the votes on the amendment to the constitution of the United States, and the only means by which that amendment carried), and have, for political purposes alone, disfranchised a large portion of the white, law-abiding voters, and enfranchised an ignorant, savage and lawless herd of blacks. By the aid of the Freedmen's Bureau they have placed thousands of emissaries in these ill-fated States to encourage the blacks in the most diabolical deeds of rapine and murder. This same Congress, to aid them without resistance to carry out their fraudulent and damnable designs, has attempted to cripple and control by unconstitutional acts and threats the co-ordinate departments of Government. They have threatened to impeach the Supreme Court for daring to act in its judicial capacity in declaring unconstitutional some of their measures. They attempted to impeach the President for no other offense than a firm opposition to their reckless and lawless course,—for being firm in his defense of constitutional government. They have legislated upon the local matters of sovereign States, in direct violation of the constitution. So reckless are they of former usages and the constitution adopted by our fathers, that they have absolutely attempted to abolish the office of President. In a word, they have in the most enlarged sense proved themselves traitors to our present institutions, and enemies to a republican form of government.

Now, my dear friend, you will do me the justice to admit that I denounced Jefferson Davis and his horde as rebels, and wished them punished as traitors for rebelling against the laws of the United States, though this rebellion was conducted by open enemies and brave men; then why should you think it inconsistent that I should oppose rebels and traitors to the institutions of our fathers, who have not manhood enough to decide their fate by the wager of battle, but who are fast accomplishing by fraud and evil legislation, what the former rebels failed to do by force of arms.

I can readily understand why you think me inconsistent; it is owing to your standpoint, and the reflection of a local glass. But when you change your position, and climb to the dome of the Temple of Freedom, take your stand between the goddess of liberty and justice, and then look through the national telescope of truth by the light of reason, aided by the reflection of the constitution, I believe you will not only discern that you are the one that is unreasonable, but will break your local glass and hasten to join me in preserving our country against a reign of tyranny and misrule, and that we may be permitted for many years to present our offerings together on the altar of constitutional liberty, with no broken fragments, but the whole United States of America. Till then, I have the honor to be

Your sincere friend, and obedient servant,

L. A. Norton.

CHAPTER LV. •

COMPLIMENTARY.

Philadelphia, Pa., 1200 Locust Street, July 26, 1880.

L. A. Norton, Esq.—*Dear Sir:* Your favor of the 26th ult. is duly received. I regret that among our losses by fire were your letters and many others. I very well remember our meeting at Vera Cruz, and our first meeting at the *hacienda* of Santa Anna at En Cerro. Your conduct at that time and your subsequent actions met my entire approval. And if I were going to the battle-field to-morrow I would be glad to have the Illinois volunteers under me, and you as commanding officer.

I am, dear sir, with great respect, sincerely yours,

R. Patterson.

THE above brief letter would be incomplete without some explanation. Our command, several thousand strong, was encamped on the bank of a lovely little stream which takes its rise in the Orizaba Mountains, rushing from the mountains in a tumbling and tumult-

uous torrent, then flowing placidly through the valley for
several miles, when it comes to an abrupt depression in
the valley and takes a perpendicular leap of one hundred and fifty feet. Our camp was some two or three
miles above this fall. We were a portion of General
Patterson's division, and his head-quarters were at Santa
Anna's *hacienda*, about a mile from our camp. The
imagination cannot picture a more lovely place. We
were waiting for the rest of the command to come up,
of which Colonel Winecoop, of Pennsylvania, was in
charge. Our extra stock was placed about twelve miles
down the river, on a rich bottom, for grazing, with a
small detachment (I believe about seventy-five in
number) to guard them. It being well known that the
treaty of peace had been signed and ratified, it was
thought there was little or no danger from the Mexicans.

Now it so happened that we needed some commissary
supplies, much of which had to be procured from the
country through which we passed, and in many instances
by forced purchase. That is, we would take what we
wanted and leave the owners a fair compensation in
coin. I had detailed a force of about one hundred and
fifty men and quite a wagon train, to go down the river
in quest of rations. I had proceeded about eight miles,
having left the direct line of the river and main valley,
and was some two miles east of it, among some low,
rolling hills and small valleys, when my advance
reported horsemen and lancers in our front. My force
were all mounted men. I halted immediately and sent
out a small scouting party, under cover of a brushy
hill. As the enemy evidently had not yet discovered
us, we had but little difficulty in getting their course.

They were traveling at right angles to us, down a narrow valley, and directly towards our stock encampment.

My scouts reported the party to be a battalion of lancers, from two hundred and fifty to three hundred strong. Their object was quite evident to me, and if I was to save our men and stock I must act promptly. I left ten men to guard the wagons and put the rest of the command in rapid motion, keeping behind the low hills; and when we broke upon the Mexicans over the brow of the hill, we were not five hundred feet from them. We charged for the center, dashed through, and, wheeling to the right and left, rolled their two flanks up like a scroll. They stood the shock for a moment, and ordered their fire with more coolness than I had expected; but they could not stand our carbine and holster fire, and broke and scattered in all directions. They left twenty-three upon the ground, seven dead and sixteen badly wounded—seven fatally. We had three killed and seven wounded, most of them slightly, and I lost my favorite horse. After the fight I ordered up the wagons, we loaded our dead and wounded, and the wounded Mexicans, into them, returned to camp, and reported to Colonel Collins (who was no friend of mine).

The affair caused a great commotion in camp. Colonel Collins ordered me under arrest for acts of war in time of peace, and I demanded to be taken before the commanding-general (Patterson). On inquiry, among the wounded Mexicans was found a lieutenant, who acknowledged that they had arranged to attack the camp and capture the stock. After a full hearing, the general dismissed the charge, highly complimented me, and said he wished they had more like me. And this is what

29

the old general meant when he said in the foregoing
letter, "Your conduct at that time and your subsequent
actions met my entire approval."

CHAPTER LVI.

A SEA VOYAGE TO SANTA BARBARA.   ·

IN a previous chapter I have incidentally referred to a
homeward trip from Los Angeles, through the San
Joaquin Valley, by rail.   In this I will give a short
sketch of my journey thither, down the coast.

I left Alameda, November 25, 1883, and took passage
on the steamer *Ancon*, which sailed at nine o'clock in the
morning, with a sharp wind from the northwest.   Contrary to our expectations, as we passed through the
Golden Gate the water was without a ripple, but when
fairly at sea, the wind being N. N. W., the vessel was
thrown into the trough of a long and heavy swell.   Erelong I saw the most vivacious and happy faces blanch,
while a general movement on deck led me to conclude
that all the passengers excepting myself had near and
dear acquaintances on board; for I saw ladies and gentlemen rushing into each other's arms.   Still I noticed
that the embraces bestowed had nothing of tenderness
or affection, since they generally fled from the embrace
of the first to the next they met.   I noticed, too, that
youth and age embraced each other alike as lovers,
while I remained a melancholy spectator of the scene,
burning tears fast running down my· face because no
one addressed me.   On reflection, I was consoled by
the discovery that I was on the windward side; hence

no one could conveniently rush to my arms, and those burning tears were caused by the spray that struck the side of the ship, giving me a liberal contribution. My first thought was to avoid this contribution by passing to the lee; but I soon discovered that on that side there was great business activity; men, women, and children were "casting up their accounts." While all seemed anxious for a settlement, they did not seem to succeed, as I saw them return to their state-rooms, singly. and in pairs, with infinite disgust depicted on their countenances. It was remarkable that their efforts seemed to destroy their appetite for dinner, the representatives at table being few in number. The captain, a young and good-looking fellow, seeming very wise and independent, sat at the head of the table, with his roast beef, carving-knife and fork, the dispenser of culinary blessing, but, withal, somewhat disconsolate, since all his "pullets" had "gone to roost," and only us poor devils, who were "placed before the mast," to serve. Of course I pitied him, and I would not have waited for a second invitation to take a seat next to him; but, unfortunately for him, I did not get a first.

The night was rough, but the morning was smooth and fair. The wind and waves had subsided and as general settlements seemed to have been obtained, all went "merry as a marriage bell." Of course we kept near the coast, which was rough and generally precipitous, while the valleys along the coast lay back of a bluff range, with small outlets to the shore. I found my notions of the bay and town of Monterey far from correct. The bay makes a deep, horseshoe-like indentation into the land. The town, instead of being at the toe of the shoe, is at the heel; and, to take the coast going down, it is three times as far by land as it is to sail across by water, from one heel of the shoe to the other.

From San Francisco to point Concepcion, our course is nearly south; at that point we turn directly east, and on that course we reach Santa Barbara, at which place we found ourselves on the second day out at eight o'clock in the evening. Before speaking of this place, I must refer to a very strange phenomenon which occurred at sunset, before our arrival. As thousands have heretofore written of the lovely sunsets at sea, the subject having been handled by wit, genius, and ability, in colors more than the sun itself ever presented, I shall not, at this late day, enter the arena and compete for the prize. And though it is of a sunset at sea that I speak, it is not the bare sight of seeing it lave its brilliant disk in the briny wave.

I heard an exclamation from one of the passengers: "Oh! look at the sun." I turned my eyes to the west, where a huge, bright golden block presented itself. It was perfectly square, and seemed to be about three feet across, and not more than ten minutes above the water. As I was watching and marveling at the strange appearance of the scene, the base of the perpendicular seemed stationary, while the upper portion commenced sinking until it presented the appearance of a large cheese, with the edge towards us. The lower portion or base then began to sink, while the upper portion appeared stationary till it formed the most perfect picture of a mammoth wash-bowl, with its broad top and graceful curving in and usual swell of the bowl, while there was the usual

and perfect flange around the bottom of the bowl,
which seemed to sit upon the water. It now commenced
elongating until it set in a long and fiery glow upon the
water. But this was not the last of it; for as the darkness gathered in the east, and in that direction all was
somber night, a soft pink tinge illuminated the western
sky, casting a soft, delicate light upon the shimmering
ripple of the ocean, which changed and flashed as if
beneath the rays of a noonday sun. In fact, the west
was so lit up that you could look in that direction until
the sea and sky united in the distance. The phenomenon of the western light continued after our arrival at
Santa Barbara, throwing a lovely light purple glow
over the mountains surrounding the town.

As before stated, the coast at Santa Barbara runs
nearly east and, west. The town is situated upon a
channel which separates the mainland from the four
islands that lie immediately north of the place some
twenty miles distant. These islands seem to form
almost a continuous belt, running nearly parallel with
the mainland, thus breaking, in a great degree, the fury
of southern storms. The town spreads out over the
mouth of the valley, where it reaches the ocean, extending up the valley about two miles. I should think the
ground rises, from the ocean to the upper end of the
town, about one hundred feet. The town is a good deal
scattered, covering an area usually occupied by a city
of 10,000 inhabitants, while it had at that time less than
5,000. What is peculiar is that the valley is not situated on any stream emptying into the ocean, and the
town is watered from Mission Cañon, the only water
upon which the inhabitants rely for fire or domestic uses;

but the supply seems plentiful. With the gradual rise from and slope to the ocean, and bathed by the first rays of the rising sun as he comes forth from his watery bed, and in close proximity, are the sloping foot-hills, with their grazing herds; and then, abruptly rising, is the rough and rugged Coast Range, giving a great variety of scenery. Here the millionaire may smoke his cigar on the veranda of the Arlington and drink in with pleasure the grand and varying prospect, while the poor invalid, who can illy spare the means to try the experiment of life or death, can first turn his eyes upon the ocean and cast forth his anchor of hope; or, if despair seizes upon him, he can from his chamber turn his eyes toward the old cathedral, with its Moorish towers, which seem to invite him to a comfortable last resting-place.

Yes, Santa Barbara is a pretty place; but she is a parasite, not living upon any innate resources of her own, but upon foreign substance. It will ever be the stopping-place of the invalid and the temporary home of the pleasure-seeker, while the denizens of the town will take good care that sojourners pay for all they get. But, on the whole, I think that in case one wants a holiday, there is no lovelier place to take it than in Santa Barbara. As to the inhabitants, they are about one-third native Californians, wholly strangers to energy or progress, still living as their fathers lived sixty years ago. The Arlington Hotel is the finest and, in my opinion, the best kept of any on the coast.

The valley in which Santa Barbara is situated is small, not more than eighteen miles long, with an average breadth of from two to two and one-fourth miles. I drove out to the place of my old friend Sherman Stowe, taking lunch with him; then to Colonel Hollister's, and then through the Cooper Ranch, thus taking in the entire length of the valley. Stowe, Hollister, Cooper, and Moore own the principal portion of the valley, and they all have lovely places, mostly fruit farms. Mr. Cooper's place is the most extensive. I believe he has 15,000 almond, 15,000 walnut, and 5,000 olive trees in full bearing, all protected by gum-tree wind-breaks. It is said that he makes the finest and purest olive oil in the world, and he puts it all in labeled bottles to avoid imposition. This is really a fruit valley. They can raise small grain and corn, in a word, all cereals; but the fruit interest largely predominates, and the great misfortune of the vall~y is that the land holdings are entirely too large for the area of country capable of culture.

I remained in Santa Barbara four days, leaving on December 1st for Santa Monica, and thence by rail to Los Angeles, returning home by the Southern Pacific Railroad route.

POEMS.

BY COLONEL L. A. NORTON.

TO MISS MINNIE MOLLOY, SANTA ROSA.

I AM thinking of thee, dear Minnie,
  I am thinking of thee now,
While thou art gently sleeping,
  With a calm and cloudless brow;
For 'tis noon of night, dear Minnie,
  And the fleecy clouds do fly,
Shown by the moon's uncertain light,
  Like some giant of the sky,
With just enough of borrowed light
  Sweetly resting on the plain,
To change each shadow to a sprite
  To people this earth again.
Among these sylphs I seem to see
  Little Minnie, bright and fair,
With her large and lustrous eyes,
  And her light-brown braids of hair.
Full well I know 'tis fancy all,
  Yet is it not sweet to feel
That fancy can somewhat supply
  What we so much wish was real?
So sleep, dear Minnie, gently sleep,
  With no shade upon thy brow.
There is one sentinel on his beat
  Who is thinking of thee now.

TO MY WIFE.

I AM thinking of thee, dear Emma,
  Alone thinking of thee;
While you in your home are waiting,
  And are watching for me.

You will claim it was a weakness,
  That I should never know;
But, my dear, it is a weakness
  I am proud to have you show.

You are never demonstrative,
  Or at least so you would seem,
But all through your seeming coldness,
  I see affections gleam.

So now, down life's path together,
  We hand in hand will roam,
Until time and age shall call us
  To dark oblivion's home.

But until we rest together,
  We'll make the best of life,
Though I make a rough old husband,
  You are a loving wife.

TO MARY.

MARY, I am now alone;
The midnight hour has long since flown,
Yet visions haunt my sleepless mind,
In search of what I cannot find.

Oh, vain the search; the efforts vain;
The prize I seek, I cannot gain;
For that I've sacrificed my rest,
And climbed the rugged mountain's breast.

I've stemmed the stream where torrents roll,
A terror to the bravest soul;
Panuca's course I've traced alone,
Where cities were long since o'ergrown

With a dense growth of chaparral,
Without a tongue their fate to tell;
Where panthers crouch and tigers growl;
Where leopards hide and lions howl;

Tarantulas, whose fatal sting
On man and beast destruction bring—
I've faced death in a thousand forms,
Mid battle's glare and frightful storms.

I've floated on the ocean's wave
When every surge my breast would lave;
From stranded ship I've sought the land
Where earthquakes shook the very sand.

rom battle-field I bear the scars
Those dealt me by the sons of Mars,
And all for what?   Why did I roam?
To trace each clime, why leave my home?

For happiness! but ah; to me
How transient must that name e'er be;
While hopeless here I journey on,
I feel, I know, I am alone.

Who see me smile can never know
The yet unfathomed depths of woe,
The anguish of this bitter strife
That rends my soul and poisons life.

For happier lots that have been cast,
They cannot feel the withering blast
That breaks my heart, that kills my frame,
And makes me loathe my very name!

But would to God my heart were steel,
To oppose the bitter pangs I feel,
And check the sigh that e'en would start
The very cords that bind my heart.

To one on earth the power is given
To make this hell eternal heaven;
If she would now but smile on me,
And bid me henceforth happy be!

RESPECTFULLY ADDRESSED TO ONE OF THE AMERICAN OFFICERS IN MEXICO.

"THIS Northern girl, I fear her not,
    Though brave and fair thou art;
  My shadow stands as sentinel
    To my loved captain's heart.

"That guarded palace mocks thy siege,
    Its gates thou canst not win;
  Go sighing round his home at night,
    But dare not enter in!

"He told me you were beautiful,
    But I am well content;
My form alone has charms for him,—
    He swore it when he went.

"Let welcome, in its softest tones,
    Its dearest secret tell,
Such welcome e'en cannot efface
    The sound of my farewell."

Thus spoke Amelia, sitting lone
    On Mexico's wild shore;
The foaming waves of that wide gulf
    Her dark eye traveled o'er.

She spoke it with a steadfast trust—
    Oh! trust that vain must prove;
She spoke it with the curling lip
    Of proud, triumphant love.

Poor girl! at that same sunset hour,
    In the distant Northern land,
The captain knelt and pressed his lips
    On a white, bejeweled hand,

Then clasped the lady in his arms—
    His vows of yore forgot;
His heart withdrew itself from hers,
    But Amelia knew it not.

TO MY TRUEST AND BEST FRIEND.

HOW sweet it is for us to know
That there are hearts that burn
With love for us, where'er we go,
And sigh for our return.
Then, though the world is cold and drear,
And gives the bosom pain,
We've but to turn to scenes more dear,
And all is bright again.

But sad must be the home of those
Condemned to live alone,
With none to cheer amid life's woes,
And none to call their own.
No season sweet of joy doth come
To shed its fragrance there;
No sunshine to disperse the gloom
That broods a dark despair.

The heart can ne'er be truly blest
Unless it can recline
On some congenial, faithful breast,
Where love's sweet tendrils twine.
Then we can brook life's many ills,
Its sorrow and its woe,
For love its soothing balm distils
To cheer us while below.

TO A. C. BARRY, ESQ.

ADIEU, dearest friend! I must bid you adieu.
I cannot, I will not, ask you longer to stay.

Remember there's one friend that ever is true,
And his heart is with you, wherever you stray.

With steps fast receding, when thy native shore,
Like some longed-for haven, shall burst on thy view,
When thy heart it shall throb like the cataract's roar,
To again greet thy friends that are constant and true,

Where beauty will smile and where maidens will love,
Where a fond mother will greet her wandering boy,
Where sounds that are soft as the coo-cooing dove
Will start tears of regret that will dampen the joy,

Thy heart will then heave for a friend that's not there,
With a pang that no vulgar affection can feel ;
A friend that thy weal or thy woe would fain share,
And a friend that loves thee with woman-like zeal.

Though barren and cold is the world without thee,
I can ask thee, in justice, no longer to stay.
But with thee, my friend, my heart ever shall be,
To blend with thy visions by night or by day.

May blessings of Deity rest on thy head,
To shield thee from sickness, harm, death, and the grave.
May Heaven combine to strengthen life's thread,
To shield thee, dear friend, from the merciless wave.

BLACK EYES.

SOME worship a brow that is ever serene,
Like the lifeless sky of a painted scene,
Where the sunshine sleeps and the clouds are still,
Just as calmly as gushes the mountain rill.

· There are hearts that can worship the soft, pale dye,
And passionless hue of a tame, blue eye;
But such eyes to me are too patient, too true;
I love not their sleepy, inanimate hue.
But give me the glance with the soul in its rays,
An eye that can flash, and a brow that can blaze.
For one, my dear girl, is the still, smooth lake,
That no winds can ruffle and no storms can shake;
The other, the foam of the cataract's dash,
The darker the water, the brighter the flash.

TO THE ONE FOR WHOM IT WAS INTENDED.

SOME are charmed with the view and passionate hue
    Of a dark and rolling eye,
But mine is the charm, without fear or alarm,
    Where all is calm as a·summer sky.

As deep as the sea, let that eye be to me,
    Then I know the affection is true;
I can read in that face, displeasure or grace,
    When lit up by an eye of blue.

If you wish to disclose your sorrows or woes
    To friends that are constant and true,
Take the clear open brow, requesting no vow,
    That's lit up with an eye of blue.

And if sympathy's tear should ever appear,
    You'll then take my statement as true;
Nines times out of ten, be it ladies or men,
    'Twill be found in an eye of blue.

Yet 'tis not the eye that can whimper or cry,
  When danger approaches in view,
But as firm as the arch, sustaining time's march,
  The eye of unfaltering blue.

An eye that is blue, a heart that is true,
  Shall hence be the drift of my dream;
And a lady most fair with lightish brown hair,   ·
  In song shall henceforth be my theme.

LINES TO MRS. ELIZABETH HALE.

THIS rose to me is passing fair,
  Fresh from the donor's hand;
Its fragrance floats as rich and rare
  As any in the land.

Upon the plain, the rose we hail,
  The daisies on the mount,
We pluck the lily from the vale,
  The cresses from the fount.

The glory of the morning fair,
  First hails us when we wake,
We're greeted by the violets rare,
  As morning walks we take.

And thus we find our path is spread
  With sweetness and perfume,
And odors of the flowerets shed
  Throughout the month of June.

30

But when they fade, the withered stalk
   Is shaken by each blast,
Each time enfeebled by the shock,
   In winter sinks at last.

An emblem this of man's sad fate,
   A floweret here below;
In spring he blooms with joy elate,
   And sinks in winter's snow.

The rose that blooms upon his cheek
   Will wither and decay,
When the fond pleasures that we seek
   By magic fade away.

It bends the stalk in silent gloom,
   All withered by the blast,
And, like the flower, cut down at noon,
   At evening's shade 'tis passed.

Unlike the rose, there's some below
   When earthly beauties fade,
Sweeter perfumes around them throw,
   Approaching evening shade.

And when the stalk is bleak and bare,
   Shook by winter of age,
A bright halo will hover there,
   That mocks to us the sage.

The word, with magic in its charms,
   That bids the soul aspire,
Snatches a brand from nature's arms,
   To light the poet's fire.

MIDNIGHT AND THE GRAVE.

THE lover's lute is hushed and still,
The moon has sought the western hill,
The breeze now holds its balmy breath,
All silent as the cells of death.
The nightingale, whose ceaseless note
Would seem to rend his tiny throat,
Now for a moment's hushed and still;
You scarce can hear the murmuring rill.
The dewdrop on the violet's brow
Would seem devoutly waiting now,
As if its fall upon the ground
Might break the silence thus profound;
Where midnight, with dark pinions spread
Her gloom o'er living and o'er dead—
A gloom that all erelong must feel,
Humanity's eternal seal;
Where innocence in silence sleeps,
Where guilt no more its vigils keeps,
Where toil and strife will be at rest,
Where peace will calm the troubled breast,
And where the high and low shall be
Forever on equality.
There glitt'ring wealth and boasted fame
'Shall, cank'ring, lose their worthless name,
By mouldering time beneath the sod,
And all true merit go to God.

On my return from Mexico at the close of the war,
our command was mustered out of service at Alton,
Illinois; but I was compelled to remain there a few days

to settle up some commissary and quartermaster claims.
One day I was riding out with some ladies, when Miss
Jane Young Harrison threw a rose of Sharon at me. I
picked up the flower and jestingly said, "I will return
this at the end of ten years," at the same time deposit-
ing the rose in my bosom, and thinking no more of it.
at the time; but when retiring at night, on divesting myself of my vest, the rose dropped to the floor. I picked
it up and threw it between the leaves of one of my
quartermaster account books, again forgetting all about
it for seven months, when one day, in turning over
the book, I discovered the flower pressed between the
leaves. I then concluded to keep my promise, and inclosed one little petal with the following lines:—

> One single leaf I send to thee,
> Of what in jest you threw at me.
> But when ten years have passed and flown,
> I'll then return to thee thy own.

My life for the ensuing ten years was adventurous and
somewhat roving; but I retained the flower, and the
expiration of the time found me in California, whence I
returned it with the following lines:—

> Here is thy flower, though rudely pressed
> 'Tis as I clasped it to my breast.
> And, like some sentinel at his post,
> For ten long years I've guarded close
> This little talisman of thine,
> That I would fain have claimed as mine,
> But would not 'vantage by my wrongs—
> To thee and thine the pledge belongs;

And when I raised it from the dust,
I only held the flow'r in trust.

But oh! how faded is the flower,
Compared with what it was that hour
When I received it at thy hand,
And bore it to this distant land.
Yet not more faded than the one
That bore it from its native home;
For each the burning deserts passed,
And each has felt the mountain's blast;
Together bound and ever one,
We both have felt a tropic sun;
Together we have sallied forth
To frozen regions of the North;
Together in the forest wild,
Where civil life had never smiled,
We've rested from our toil and care—
Our sentinel the grizzly bear.

Thus, guarding it as my own life, ·
I've borne it through this world of strife
Until, at last, the hour has come
To send the little traveler home.
And when its pallid form you view,
Remember that my words were true.
Although the pledge in jest was given
Its place of register was Heaven.

And now one boon I ask alone,
That this you'll guard as I have done;
And when you view its petals fair,
For its poor guardian breathe one prayer.
This from your friend and servant true.
So, lady fair, a long adieu.

THE SYLPHIDE.

All hail to thee, sylphide, fair queen of the mountain;
    Let angels thy dew-gleaming footsteps sustain,
Whose impress a shadow ne'er made on the fountain,
    Whose footfall no imprint e'er left on the plain.

Seraphic in form, and surpassing in beauty,
    Her sex are all pigmies in honor and worth,
So constant in love, in affection and duty,
    Earth never before to such graces gave birth.

But why so dejected, my day-star of glory?
    Oh! why art thou doomed thus to sigh when alone,
While pensively gazing on mountain-tops hoary,
    Or lulled to repose by the rill's mellow tone?

Have the hopes of thy youth all like angels departed
    And left thee to mourn the deep blight on thy soul?
Has fortune thy fond expectations deserted,
    O'er which now nor beauty nor charms hold control?

Or by destiny doomed to still deeper dejection,
    By stern, unrelenting fate's crushing decree,
That places a barrier between thy affection
    And the one of all others the dearest to thee?

If so, I can sympathize with thy condition,
    Although my poor heart has long since ceased to love;
To soothe the afflicted of earth is my mission—
    A delegate sent from the high court above.

So look upon me as a friend and a brother;
    Believe me that such I shall ever remain.
In truth, you may say we have not the same mother,
    Yet friendship's kind impulse is warming each vein.

ODE TO THE RT. REV. J. K. BARRY.

WAFT, ye winds, some fitting strain
From mountain crest, from hill or plain,
His praise to sing who here has come,
And left his family and home,
   And crossed the deep where billows roar,
   Then sought the California shore.
   Were it for gold he crossed the main
   I should not write this feeble strain.

But how delightful 'tis to feel
That one from love and Christian zeal
Should cross the deep where billows roll,
His only gain, the immortal soul.
   Now in the halls that long have rung
   To Bacchanalian's thickened tongue,
   By him, that sacred truth is taught,
   That souls by Jesus' blood were bought.

He labors hard, he's labored long,
And in the cause is waxing strong;
But where are Zion's sons to aid?
Have they not down the cold stream strayed?
   Has not that filthy lucre, gold,
   Made many a Christian heart grow cold?
   But bid them listen to thy call,
   And sound the trump from Zion's wall.

And when thy limbs enfeebled grow,
From godly labors here below,
May peace and quiet close thy eyes,
And angels bear thee to the skies,

Where brighter gold than mortals coin
Shall in thy crown of glory shine!
A passport, in the halls above,
To the eternal throne of love.

MONTEGA'S ADIEU TO THE FOX.

ADIEU to this valley—the sweetest on earth,
Adieu to the ashes that first gave me birth,
Adieu to the Fox, with her green shaded shore,
For thy crystal waves I shall visit no more.
Adieu to the islands that dot thy bright strand,
Adieu to thy scenery so varied and grand.
Though the white man may dot the country around,
And cities may rise on my old hunting-ground,
Where the red man sported in innocent glee,
The breeze of the morning ne'er floated more free.
Their day-dreams were happy, their visions were bright,
And in their rude shelter their slumbers were light;
But where's now the odor of wild rose perfume,
That swept o'er the plain in the bright month of June?
Now adieu to that council hearth ruined and cold,
Where burned the war-fire of the Fox chieftain bold.
Adieu to the graves of our fathers who've fled,—
We would not recall them again from the dead,
To witness the sorrows of those that are left;
Our kindred, our country, of all we're bereft.
Who pities the red man?—his rights are unknown,
He wanders dejected—no kindred nor home.
The white man knows naught of his sorrows nor pain,
And the son of the forest scorns to complain;

For soon I will pass o'er that river so bright,
That I have surveyed in the visions of night,
Where pale-faces' knives are no longer than mine.
To fight the great battle all red men combine;
Montega will join them, with quiver and bow,
To the land of the spirits I'm anxious to go.

LINES.

Oh! list, ye nymphs of grace divine
  Not to an idle tale,
But list ye to this lay of mine,
  As borne thee on the gale.

I speak to thee of beauties rare,
  Not faded yet by time,
And beauties that you cannot share,
  Or I'd be claiming mine.

Another claims that lovely cheek,
  Where richest crimsons flow,
And eyes that kindness doth bespeak,
  A bosom white as snow.

Of gentle mien, of graceful form,
  And manners much refined,
To grace the fate for which you're born,
  So, Mary, be resigned.

The day it came, the die was cast,
  Thy fortune it was made;
So, mourn you not for scenes now past,
  Nor fortune yet upbraid.

It was yourself that played the game,
And sealed it with a *smack*,
And, as you did not like your name,
You changed it into *Mack*.

So, Mary, now be kind and true
Unto the choice you've made,
And when these lines you come to view,
Just think on what I've said.

Whilst passing down life's eventide,
We'll see the heads of flax,
And, asking what we have espied,
You'll say, They're little *Macks*.

ON SLANDER.

I'M seated by the babbling brook
To read a page from nature's book,
And trace each evil from its birth,
That can afflict this mortal earth;
And in their various stages trace
Which most affects the human race.
First in my catalogue I'll bring
What mankind deems the greatest sin—
He who has slain his fellow-man—
Inhuman brute! him let us scan.
He's taken that which God has given,
And robb'd earth of a gift from Heav'n.
But one received the fatal thrust;
But one heart mingled with the dust.
This crime is known as *mal in se*,
So *mal in factum* let it be.

Next jealousy, with eye of green,
Within my catalogue is seen;
It binds the sense, makes man a slave,
And is more cruel than the grave.
A family circle feels the sting,
And yields to that despotic king.

But last of all, and worse I claim,
Is slander. Oh, that cruel name;
Its poisonous breath pervades the land.
It chills the heart, benumbs the hand;
Its fatal fang and poisonous breath
Are to be dreaded more than death.
It will its horrid form intrude
'Mid circles gay or solitude.
The maiden's fame lost in a day,
Nor will it spare the matron gray;
For which they must a by-word lay,
From youth till resurrection day.
The hand that would donate most free
Is struck down by this calumny.
I ask you one and all to tell
Which crime is most deserving hell?

LEONATUS.

LINES RESPECTFULLY ADDRESSED TO ——.

I WISH the world to understand
My creed is here laid down,
And they who raise opposing hand
Shall meet my lasting frown.

A friend that is not my friend's friend,
   He scarcely can be mine,
And he who would my friend offend,
   Our friendship can't combine.

Some wish to choose for me my friends,
   Say who are fit and true;
But this will never suit my ends,
   No; this will never do.

Because I will not sell a friend,
   Let him be high or low;
To whom I shall my hand extend,
   I am the one to know.

Perhaps a friend of worth to me
   May be of different grade,
By other friends may seem to be
   A dead weight on me laid,

Although that friend may still be true,
   With heart as pure as snow :
Shall I discard him to please you ?
   I proudly answer, No.

But when I see a want of worth,
   My confidence betrayed,
I then rebuke the erring earth,
   Withdraw all pledges made.

For if my dog should chance to be
   By all my friends despised,
My dog my only friend should be—
   The rest all sacrificed.

THE WILL OF LEONATUS.

I DIP my quill to write my will,
    As slander has me slain.
Let this attest my last bequest
    Is made with feeble frame.
By wish inclined, and strong in mind,
    My will I thus have planned:
Bequeath and give to those that live
    Within this Western land,
Good-will to all, both great and small,
    For this they surely need;
And love I'll add—they want it bad—
    So now let me proceed.
A patent plan I'll give to man
    For saving of his lungs—
When scandal rolls, let honest souls
    Just halter-break their tongues.

And here's a sword that e'er will guard
    All those who choose to wield,—
'Tis for the youth, its name is Truth.
    To fend, you need no shield,
For it will slay or so dismay
    Each falsehood, as it flies,
That ere you know you've dealt a blow—
    The foe before you lies.
A measure small I'll give to all,
    A little balance scale,
Justice its name, from whence it came,
    To tell you I shall fail.

To be sincere, I hold it dear,
  And make a small reserve,
But feel inclined to ease my mind
  By giving who deserve.

There's one gem more I hold in store.
  It is so rich and rare
I do intend to recommend
  That ladies take a share.
You wait to see what it can be—
  Charity is the name.
If each will share the gem to wear,
  You'll save each other's fame.
If this small store is rightly wore
  Within the human breast,
This bitter strife would lose its life,
  And man would find a rest.
In witness here that I'm sincere,
  My name is written thus,
My usual hand I still command,
                    L. A. LEONATUS.

WRITTEN ON THE SUMMIT OF FITCH MOUNTAIN WHILE
SITTING ON AN ANT-HILL.

LITTLE ant, come, tell me why
Thou hast built thy home so high;
These high cliffs why didst thou scale
And leave the warm and pleasant vale?

Has the same God that gave thee breath
Inspired in thee the thoughts of death,

Like man, creation's lord while here,
And fitted for another sphere?

Like his, doth thy ambition rise,
To endless life beyond the skies?
And is this mound, on which I've trod,
A temple of the living God? .

And didst thou choose this mountain high
To bring thy worship near the sky?
And didst thou tread, as Moses trod,
With priestly step, the mount of God?

Methinks I hear the answer, " Yes;
As creatures we could do no less
Than offer from this lofty shrine
To our Creator praise divine."

If so, I'll heed thy warm appeal;
I reverence and respect thy zeal,
And peaceful leave thy busy home
Wiser than ere I hence had come,

In knowing that beneath my feet
Worshiping congregations meet,
Serving with thought sublime, as we,
In their own way, the Deity.

A DREAM.

My drooping lids o'erhung by care,
I fell asleep whilst in my chair.
I dreamed as man has seldom dreamed,
Was omnipresent, as it seemed.

And backward rolled the wheels of time
To early Asia's sunny clime.
I stood by Moses, side by side,
And saw the visions he espied.

In fancy then I saw the stroke
That in his wrath the tablets broke;
Though vexed was he, it made me laugh
To see poor Aaron's golden calf.

I stood upon the Red Sea coast,
There saw the tide sweep Egypt's host.
I saw Alexander's archer train
Take the rock Ardes of the plain.

I next saw the immortal birth
Of the Messiah come to earth;
I saw him, when a babe, indeed,
He seemed the nurse's aid to need.

Whilst in his youth I passed that way,
Saw parchments there before him lay;
I saw China's Confucius' name
Inscribed upon the parchments plain.

I read in those the source and fount
Of Christ's great sermon on the mount;
A doctrine taught in days of yore
By Chinese prince long years before.

I traced him through this lower clay,
And watched each mesmeric display;
I saw him manlike meet his doom,
And godlike rise from Joseph's tomb.

I knew that I was not deceived;
Unlike the Jews, I then believed.
I saw his doctrines then advance
From bloody Rome to skeptic France.

With Bible doctrine it was hurled
To every nation of the world,
Where men prepar'd all to receive,
Need only hear it to believe.

Soon I beheld another scene,
That changed the aspect of my dream;
From Ishmael there sprung a light
That even pierced Arabia's night.

I saw a caravan depart,
Journey'd with it to Smyrna's mart;
I saw one sit beneath a yew
That by the way for ages grew.

But the old tree had quite decayed,
Refused to man or beast its shade;
But when great Allah sat him there,
The tree spread forth with foliage fair.

The prophet then the desert bless'd,
As many Arabs will attest,
And a hardened wretch was I
Not to believe in great Allah.

But when I saw him raise his brand,
Defeat his foes by blowing sand;
As well as illustrations given
Of midnight trips to seventh heaven;
31

And when I saw the murderous snare,
And saw the holy prophet share
The poisoned meat, that harmed him not,
Though others to the grave it brought,

A convert to his faith was I,
And shouted for the great Allah.
I saw him bend each tot'ring shrine,
I saw him march to Palestine.

Against the Turks he took the field,
I saw Constantinople yield,—
Where'er Mahomet stretched his hand,
The nations fell at his command,

And scepters they were worthless then,
For all became good Musselmen,
And when his frame by death was bound,
He could not rest upon the ground.

His coffin sought the ceiling high,
And would have flown into the sky,
But no attraction called it forth
To leave behind its native earth.

Content with man, his power to show,
Mahomet wisely stayed below,
And left with us his mighty shade,
His friends to soothe and doctrines aid.

'Twas then I saw a star arise
Beyond the sea in western skies;
I asked permission then to go
See what that satellite would show.

The land I saw was far away; .
I read its name—AMERICA—
And when I reached the distant ground,
I heard a low, unearthly sound.

~ In accents soft, but very clear,
It came unto my startled ear,
"The book of Mormon has been found,
And excavated from the ground.

"Great Joseph Smith, it is decreed,
The only man the book shall read."
And Joseph to his task then went,
A prophet he, in pity sent.

Joseph the words of Mormon told,
From hieroglyphics wrought in gold;
But, oh! the wicked heart of man,
They scoffed at Mormon and his plan.

Joseph his sword, like Allah, drew,
And mustered all the Mormon crew.
Rushed forth to combat, sword in hand—
Alas, they lacked Arabia's sand.

And these brave, warlike Mormon sons
Were driven out by Missourians;
Then Illinois, that bloody State, .
To Mormon's prophet owed a hate.

And it was in these wicked lands
That Joseph healed with righteous hands,
Or so his twelve apostles said—
I, by their word, was convert made.

But soon these wicked men conspired,
Their minds with indignation fired,
When they in secret laid their plan,
Went forth and slew this holy man.

By his death groans I was awoke;
My very frame in terror shook;
I thought upon the vision past;
I conn'd it o'er from first to last.

I scann'd at length our Christian views,
I turned me back to skeptic Jews,
I traced Mahomet from his birth,
Throughout his wild career on earth.

On Mormon's book I some time thought,
And viewed the changes it had wrought,
And asked myself, as well as you,
Which of these creeds, if any's true.

As they will show to men of sense,
Their proofs internal evidence;
That all are right, these proofs will show.
If all are right, why differ so?

A DIALOGUE BETWEEN THE HEAD AND HEART, AS TO
WHICH HAD THE STRONGER CLAIMS
UPON THE SOUL.

A STRANGE dispute arose one day,
Or so I've heard old people say;
Between the heart and head the strife,
The fount of reason and of life,

As to which had the strongest claim
Upon the soul, the heart or brain.
The heart now vindicates his cause,
By logic backed, and nature's laws.

HEART.

I claim the soul of man is thought,
And that is by pulsation wrought;
The blood is oxidized by me,
And 'genders thought, as you may see.
And in addition to this plea,
All sacred history doth agree;
That the heart is good or evil,
Works for God, or for the devil.

HEAD.

To your first position I'll concede,
In acquiescence to your creed,
That the immortal mind's the soul,
That governs and that guides the whole.
I further grant what you maintain,
To wit, the blood assists the brain;
But when you claim the heart alone
Doth set King Reason on his throne,
I will take issue with you there,
And try to shew by reason fair,
That blood is but a single spring,
That doth the brain to action bring;
And, by its convolutions wrought,
The brain itself engenders thought.
And to maintain the grounds I take,
A small experiment I'll make:

Detach intellect from the brain,
And let the animal remain;
Then let the blood as usual rush,
With warm and animating gush,
Through all the chambers of the brain,
When back it will return again;
And when it has its functions wrought,
I ask, Will it engender thought?
Decide that point before I go.
The answer's now resounding, No!
Then in this argument you'll find
That blood cannot engender mind.
Regarding what the Scriptures state,
Those records of more ancient date,
And also wrote on the best plan
That could reveal the truth to man;
The heart being the seat of life,
Man thought it, too, the seat of strife;
And that mankind might but believe,
Their teachers would not undeceive;
But led them on as linguists would,
By language that they understood.

HEART.

Your reasons are so wisely chose,
I hardly know how to oppose;
And I'll admit what you maintain,
That the blood works upon the brain,
As farmers work the sterile soil,
That yields its fruit but with his toil;
And, as experiments you've brought
To prove that brain produces thought,

I'll offer one that will suffice
To show where that great lever lies.
I'll stay the blood in the left lung,
And let the venous current run,
Unoxidized, upon the brain,
And there behold the creature's pain;
Witness, yourself, his dying groan,
And see Reason's deserted throne!
As in this dying state he lies,
The blood again I'll oxidize;
Now Reason to his seat is brought,
And Reason only lives by thought!

· HEAD.

Indulging in such wanton strife,
I'll own you might destroy life.
By pouring a destructive flood
Of grosser matter with the blood
Upon the unresisting brain,
It must create disorder, pain,
And drive Thought from his dwelling-place,
To seek a rest in open space.
But by your power to inundate,
That will not prove you can create;
For the tornado sweeps the plain
Without power to restore again.
When the infuriated blast
Assails the ship and springs the mast,
It sinks upon the Ocean's breast,
Its fury spent, and it must rest
Without the power or strength to aid
To destined port the wreck it made.

But I'm not competent, I find,
To argue causes for the mind;
I'll own myself a blundering elf,
And leave the cause with Thought himself.

THOUGHT.

I've listened to your pleas at length,
Their ingenuity and strength; .
And I must say I feel some pride
In being called on to decide.
And I shall thus decide the strife,—
The Heart's the sire, the Head's the wife.
For me, 'tis plain you both have toiled;
I own myself to be your child;
And I am much inclined to see
You both unite in harmony.
But you're mistaken in your creed—
A point on which you both agreed—
You grant me superhuman power,
That I can only claim as *dower*.
I feel myself but mortal earth,
And can't inherit by my birth.
I, by your combined power was made,
And can't exist without your aid;
I'm not the soul, as you have said,
Though to the soul, perchance, I'm wed.
This seems to be quite strange to you,
But 'tis no stranger than 'tis true.
Pray do not seem to be thus riled,
For parents oft mistake their child;
So let me introduce my guest,
Judge Reason, for he knows the best.

REASON.

With Thought for many years I've been,
I'll say, e'er since the world began.
Her power the earth will e'er control,
But still I think she's not the soul.
The truth it is quite plain to all,
Souls e'er exist, or not at all;
And if we argue on that plan,
All brutes have souls as well as man;
For where's the brute to action wrought,
Unless it is by force of thought?
Has not the beast that stores his grain,
Some thought of winter's snow or rain ?
Does not the bee that sips his sweet
Lay up in store his winter's meat?
If mind's the soul, the little bee
Has future claims on Deity.
But now all ask me in one breath,
" What is the soul that lives in death,
That flies from earth to hell or Heaven,
To meet its doom in justice given ? "
My answer is, " 'Twill ne'er be known
Whilst earth's encircled by a zone."

LINES.

[Written on seeing Capt. C. L. Wight, of the Second Regiment of Illinois volunteers, sleeping on the brick floor of the Guard House, Tampico, Mexico, after having spent the night with him as officer of the day.]

SLEEP on, youthful hero, in quiet reposing,
Thy sleep it is sweet and refreshing to thee,
Each quick beating pulse to thy watcher disclosing
His heart that's as buoyant—his spirit as free—

As the first morning zephyr that sweeps o'er the main,
Or thy country's flag that is floating on high,
Or the swift bounding deer that skips over the plain
That glides from pursuit when danger is nigh.

Yes, calm thy repose—that heart seems at rest,
With naught but a damp, cold tile for thy pillow;
But the fond tint of hope, it has softly impressed
A glow on that cheek, pale though not sallow.

Yes, he sleeps, and that in an enemy's land,
Where many a hero has slept in his gore;
Gallant young warrior, though born to command,
Thou soon mayst sleep to awaken no more;

Where no ties of affection nor angelic charms
Shall hasten the brave, youthful hero to greet;
No battle's loud roar, nor display of arms,
Shall stay his advance, or shall prompt his retreat.

Their mem'ry alone to his friends could portray
That heart sympathetic, both gen'rous and great,
That by war and disease had sunk to decay,
Where courage and manhood both yielded to fate.

THE RIO GRANDE SHORE.

THE war-cry is sounding once more in our land,
Each brave heart is bounding to make a bold stand;
The youth of our country in armor shine bright,
Determined on victory, they haste to the fight.
The cannons roar louder, each brave heart seems prouder,
And loud shouts of vict'ry burst forth from the plain,

The Mexicans wheeling, their broken ranks reeling,·
Though vain is the effort to rally again.
Now some eyes are weeping, and some hearts are leap-
ing,
Palo Alto's red field is now covered with gore,
Where many brave heroes lie silently sleeping,
To awake to the call of their country no more,
Whilst the foemen now stand on the broad Rio Grande
Their boats not sufficient to ferry them o'er;
Their terror increasing, equipage releasing,
They have plunged and are lost in the torrent's loud roar.
The cry, " They are drowning," through the camp is
now sounding;
But our boats were removed ere the battle was o'er,
And with faces dejected, our heroes collected
To witness the scene from the Rio Grande shore.
TAYLOR victorious, no name more glorious
Could cheer the brave hearts of Columbia's sons.
Our victory complete, to our foes a defeat,
Come, now shout it aloud with a trumpet's strong tones.
Adieu to those heroes who sank to repose,
Who fought their last battle, and conquered their foes,
Who bravely in action, with the saber in hand,
Sank to rest with the foes near the Del Norte strand.
And to you that survive, who fought sword in hand,
Who obeyed the first call of Columbia's land;
Who fought for your country where the cannons loud
roar,
Amid sabers' bright flash on the Rio Grande shore,
Your fame is untarnished, your honor as fair
As the maiden's first blush, or the bright morning-star.
On earth to reward you no power is given,
Immortal of birth, its reward is in Heaven.

THE PATRIOT'S DREAM.

INTRODUCTION.

I

SOULS of the brave, who, passed and gone
Beyond the praise of mortal tongue,
No longer lead your legions on,
Like the immortal WASHINGTON!
No thrilling shout to freedom's son,
To gird his glittering armor on;
No victory now is lost or won,
● Nor battle stayed at setting sun;
Nor no terrific cannons roar,
To rouse the dreadful god of war.

2

But would to God the trump could sound,
For those now in oppression bound,
And let them pass the watchword round,
To *Canada's* remotest bound;   ·
That freedom's sons might catch the tone
All Tory faction to put down;
While rushing on to liberty,
Their only watchword—victory.

3

The patriot then did heave a sigh,
That's wafted by the breeze on high;
Likewise the spirits of the slain,
" Revenge ! " they one and all proclaim.

Arrayed before their God, they stand,
And retribution there.demand.

4

And now, methinks, I do behold
Bright swords of steel, and crowns of gold,
Descending near with a proud crest,
The haughty tyrants to arrest.
I saw them, marshaled one by one,
In single file come marching down;
I saw their gallant leader mount,
And well I knew the murdered LOUNT.
Then next to him, in this bright train,
Behold the bleeding MATHEWS came.

5

The next I saw was freedom's son,
A warlike, bold Kentuckian;
With rifle long and steel all bared,
For deadly conflict then prepared;
And on his breast he wore a star,
That marked him as a man of war;
His step was measured, firm, and slow—
In him I recognized MORROW!

6

And then the next I did descry
Was WILLIAM PUTNAM'S eagle eye.
I saw his form erect and fair,
His dauntless look and manly air;
I saw him marching to the field,
With vengeance written on his shield.

7

VAN SCHOULTS next came to grace the band,—
An exiled son of Poland's land;
Well trained to arms in days of yore—
A military air he bore!
And as I stood there, quite amazed,
Upon the motley crowd I gazed;
But soon I turned my eye again
From the bright legions of the plain—
When at my side and all alone,
In armor bright, stood captain DONE.
He waved a banner in his hand,
An emblem of the *Spartan band*,
Who yielded not to Britain's power—
Who scorned to flee in danger's hour.

8

And then I turned to look again
On the bright legions of the plain;
I heard a bugle's distant peal,
I heard the clang of hoof and steel!
I saw the warlike hosts did kneel;
And their bent forms did then reveal
Fair freedom's noblest, bravest son—
The great, immortal WASHINGTON!
He made a signal with his hand—
Each chief arose at his command;
Loud shouts burst from the sceptered crowd,
The echo came both long and loud;
Again the hero waved his hand,
Again the crowd obeyed command.

9

His dress was as in days of yore;
A uniform of blue he wore,
A plume of white his cap it bore,
That high above the rest did soar.
His face was pale, though calm his eye—
He looked around, then heaved a sigh;
Bowed to the crowd with a caress,
And thus commenced his last address.

10

WASHINGTON.

"Chieftains of war, in battle tried—
Your country's care, your nation's pride!
Who fought not for an empty name,
Nor shed your blood for gold or fame;
But from the rise to set of sun
Stood as your country's champion;
Who deepest hewed where despots stood,
On plains Canadian shed their blood;
Ye noble shades of earthly dust,
Well might your country in ye trust!
And ye have passed death's stormy waves,
Your bodies rest in earthly graves;
But there they will no longer feel
Oppression's hand nor traitor's steel.

11

"Our country's bound in servile chains,
And pampered despots hold the reins;

With bitter cries our country groans—
Her fairest daughters make their moans;
Her noblest sons have exiles fled,
Or rest with the forgotten dead,
Or groan within some prison cell,
Or in some secret cavern dwell,
Or in a menial, servile way,
For clemency to despots pray;
Or start forth with a stalwart hand,
Strike down some leader of their band,
And then, unaided, he must fly,
Or like a felon he must die.

12

"But haste! ye heroes of the past,
At God's command, shout forth the blast;
Call forth the dead, in battle slain,
And let them all return again,
To meet in field their country's foe,
And deal to them a deathly blow,
And hurl Great Britain from the land
Where freedom's flag has made a stand.

13

'But unto me no power is given,
From the great Judge or court of Heaven,
Now to descend to earth again,
On battle-fields to witness pain—
Else with the sword I once did wield,
I'd march with you into the field;
And then in conflict dread to see,
Strike for a nation's *Liberty!*
But at the bar of God I'll stand
And plead for that devoted band."

14

The heavens rang, so loud they cheered;
I looked again, he'd disappeared;
The bugle sounds its lofty strains,
One living sea now spreads the plains;
All in bright armor now arrayed,
. Marshaled for war and on parade.
I saw their glittering armor flash,
I saw their noble chargers dash;
I watched them long with startling eyes,
As fast to earth the legion flies.

15

When I *awoke* I was alone,
My seat was a moss-covered stône;
The leaves in listless silence hung,
The night insects around me sung ;
The sun had sought the western hill,
Throwing its last rays on the rill,
That murmured on in music sweet,
And played in gambols at my feet—
Then hurrying on in swift retreat,
Some other listening ear to greet;
Or the broad *Fox's* stream to meet,
And roll on with that crystal sheet—
But still my mind will oft revert
To scenes the nearest to my heart.

16

Canadian wilds! my early home,
I think of thee whene'er alone;
  32

An exile now compelled to roam
In a strange land, to all unknown;
None to extend a genial hand—
A pilgrim in a stranger land.

17

The lonely crag to me endeared—
Its mossy brown my childhood cheered.
The rising hill, the creek, the dell,
The ancient tree, the pond, and well,
The field my youthful hand did till,
The plowman's song, the clattering mill:
All these endeared this land to me—
Home of my youth and infancy.
Thy stumpy fields I fain would sow,
The growing thistle up I'd hoe;
Protect my corn against the crow,
And in the depths of winter go
To hunt the deer 'mid four feet snow.
With all those hardships I'd comply,
And labor until called to die,
If but one boon could granted be,
My country's rights,—her liberty.

18

But oh! how could I longer stand,
And see a ruthless Tory band,
Without an order or command,
Wide ravaging my native land.

19

Age was then no guard 'gainst wrong,
Weakness protected not the young;
For them did beauty have no charms,

Save while within the ruffian's arms:
To justice blind, in manners base—
A curse unto the human race!
In parlors grand their horses eat;
Behold their inmates in the street;
Behold that mother far and near
Seeks shelter for her offspring dear,
And when successful, she at last
Can shield them from the winter's blast;
But driven from affluency,
To most degrading misery.

20

While the sire, flying from his home,
Now in a foreign land to roam,
With a sad and troubled mind,
To leave his dearest ones behind:
And rude the shelter they would find
'Mid tyrants who, to justice blind,
Had robbed him of that much-loved home,
And then compelled him far to roam.

21

But hark! again they come—they come,
The bugle sounds, the rattling drum—
Now, *Spartans* bold, defend your home!
But ah, behold in prison den,
Where lies her noblest, bravest men.
With galling chains their limbs are bound,
And, closely pinioned to the ground,
In vain for justice there they cry,
Without a trial doomed to die.

22

While you rule with mighty sway,
Now, Britain, list to what I say:
You'll think of it some coming day,
When colonies are swept away;
And when your empire, proud and vast,
Is blotted from the light of day,
Some passing traveler will say,
" Here was an empire of renown,
That ruled and wore Britannia's crown;
But *she*, like other nations past,
Is crushed by her own guilt at last."

23

But she sinks not to oblivion shade,
Where fated Rome and Greece are laid;
But rises from her fallen state,
With sister nations to be great.
With tyranny no longer wed—
No longer bow to crowned head;
But freedom's living light now shed,
Where tyranny in darkness fled.
Now peace and plenty kindly smile
Where want and misery frowned erewhile.
How cheerful is each village clan,
The boon from God bestowed to man;
How happy then old England's shore,
When despots rule her courts no more!